"When you look at me like that, I forget why I'm here," he said hoarsely.

My breasts were about to slip free of the corset—the barest of motions would send it tumbling past my waist.

"And why are you here exactly? Assuming this isn't some sort of prewedding jitter taking place by way of a dream."

"Hush." His mouth compressed at my words and I arched my back in apology. "Don't worry about it yet. I'm going to ask something of you shortly. There isn't any time to explain, but I need your word that you will do it."

"Is it going to hurt?"

"Not exactly. Not you, anyway," he admitted. "Promise me you will do what I ask? I'm not going to get another shot at it if it doesn't work." The intensity of his expression became despairing and I could only nod in answer.

"And until then?" There was nothing glib about my words, but my body continued to thrum with thwarted desire.

He leaned forward to kiss me, even as he gently laid me upon the bed that had mysteriously appeared behind us.

"I'd think that would be obvious," he murmured. "I take what is mine."

Praise for Allison Pang and the world of Abby Sinclair

"Weird, wild, and ~~wonderful . . .~~"
—Seanan ~~selling~~ author
~~ries~~

"Allison Pang is

~~apism~~

A TRACE OF MOONLIGHT

ALLISON PANG

POCKET BOOKS

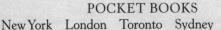

New York   London   Toronto   Sydney   New Delhi

Pocket Books
A Division of Simon & Schuster, Inc.
1230 Avenue of the Americas
New York, NY 10020

This book is a work of fiction. Names, characters, places, and incidents either are products of the author's imagination or are used fictitiously. Any resemblance to actual events or locales or persons, living or dead, is entirely coincidental.

First Pocket Books paperback edition November 2012

POCKET and colophon are registered trademarks of Simon & Schuster, Inc.

For information about special discounts for bulk purchases, please contact Simon & Schuster Special Sales at 1-866-506-1949 or business@simonandschuster.com.

The Simon & Schuster Speakers Bureau can bring authors to your live event. For more information or to book an event, contact the Simon & Schuster Speakers Bureau at 1-866-248-3049 or visit our website at www.simonspeakers.com.

Manufactured in the United States of America

10 9 8 7 6 5 4 3 2 1

ISBN 978-1-4391-9836-0
ISBN 978-1-4391-9843-8 (ebook)

To Dan. Because of reasons. :")

Acknowledgments

Every time I write a book, I always feel so humbled at the people who have supported me during the creative process. (And the lists just seem to get longer as I go.)

To my editor, Adam Wilson, and the fine folks at Pocket—I always roll a 20 to crit. Just saying.

To my agent, Suzie Townsend—As always, thanks for all your support and continuing to believe in me.

To Danielle Poiesz—I count myself blessed for knowing you. And there's no one else I'd rather make unicorn poop cookies with.

To Jess Haines for things better left unsaid. ;-) And mustaches.

To Sarah Cannon—Beta reader and line editor and general commiserator. Also? I rescued her cat from a tree once. Because I am awesome.

To PJ Schnyder—Thanks for all the ballet lessons. ;-)

To Marcus Wolf, guitarist par excellence—Thanks for putting up with musical questions both serious and silly and for answering them all without missing a beat. Rock on, my friend.

To Jeffe Kennedy, who has always been there for me during this incredible journey—and to the rest of my fellow Word Whores for all their continued support.

To the League of Reluctant Adults—Where else can I have snarky conversations about demon peen, honestly?

To the Chatterbox—You ladies constantly amaze me. Thank you.

To Darchala Chaoswind—For all the pretty pictures that somehow always manage to capture my characters so perfectly.

To Irma "Aimo" Ahmed—For secret pictures and private stories that make me smile, and for sad sausage dogs.

Three Paths align
When the Wild Hunt calls
The CrossRoads will crumble
When Eildon Tree falls.

A TRACE OF
MOONLIGHT

One

The fog eddied from the darkness to cocoon me in a soft haze. Something niggled at the back of my mind as I glanced down at my bare feet. They were swallowed below my calves by the mist, but the crunch of sand under my toes felt familiar. The hiss of waves slapped against the edge of a nearby shore.

The rolling scent of brine slipped past on a tattered breeze. Drawn toward the sound of water, I pressed forward, an uneasy chill sending clammy fingers skittering over my skin.

Wrapping my arms around my shoulders, I realized I was naked.

And yet a moment later, a silk dress draped over my limbs, falling to midcalf. It should have felt strange, to know the merest of thoughts took shape here . . . but it didn't. My feet brushed the edges of the wet sand and I paused. I could see nothing beyond the darkness, but the warmth of the water lured me, beckoning with a soft whisper.

Flickers of memory flared up and slid away, the barest hint of scales and a cradle of blue luminescence taking form, but I shook my head and the thought swirled out of reach. Ridiculous idea, anyway. I'd never even seen a mermaid.

Another step and the foam crested past my ankles.

I hesitated.

Abby. A name, whispered upon the breeze. The waves rushed forward, the sudden undertow sucking me into the sand as though it might drag me into its depths. I stumbled, only to be pulled back by a hand upon my wrist.

I glanced over my shoulder, frowning as I made out the features of a man. Ebony hair whipped about his pale face; he gazed down at me, eyes haunted and aching and terrible. I didn't recognize him, and yet his presence radiated like a beacon of comfort in the darkness.

Immediately the waves receded, leaving us in guarded silence. He stared at me a moment longer. When I said nothing, something like grief creased the corners of his mouth.

"If you enter the sea you will be devoured," he said finally.

"Devoured?" I could only watch as the fog lifted at the slight motion of his hand. I saw fins cutting through the surf; the moonlight shattered the darkness to reveal the sharks, shining like living blades in the murk.

I swallowed hard at my own folly. "Thank you," I murmured, my fingers finding his in the shadows to squeeze them. Abruptly he pulled away, his breath hissing as though I'd burned him.

"Who are you? Do you know where we are?"

"You're dreaming, Abby." His lips pursed mockingly. "And I am but a shadow." At my puzzled look, he sighed. "It will be safer for you away from here. Follow me."

Before us lay tall cliffs and a worn path of sand and sea grass, a series of rocky switchbacks leading to somewhere.

"Do you have a name?" The words slipped out before I meant them to, but I dutifully trailed in his wake, bunching the dress at my hips to climb up the bluff.

"If you do not know it, I cannot tell you."

"I don't understand."

"I know," he muttered, a hint of irritation in his voice. "Believe me when I tell you this is not the way things were supposed to have been, but we have no other choice." He glanced over his shoulder at me. "And we have very little time left." As though to emphasize the point, he reached to take my hand, helping me over a piece of driftwood. Now his fingers entwined with mine. A wash of heat swept through me.

"I don't ever remember having such a lucid dream before," I said.

His grip tightened, but he said nothing in return, leading us up the cliff and down a winding path until we came to an iron gate. It was overgrown by high weeds, shut tightly with a lock.

My inner voice was strangely silent. If it knew something, it clearly wasn't planning on saying anything. I frowned at the gate, reaching out to stroke the rusted flakes with a curious finger. The metal chilled my hands to the bone and I got a sense of unhappiness from it.

Which was ridiculous. This was a dream, wasn't it? Inanimate objects didn't have feelings.

"Knock it off," I told it, blinking when the gate

snapped open, letting out a long-suffering creak.

"One problem solved." The man's eyes slid sideways toward me as I gazed up at the dilapidated house.

A once-stately Victorian construct, the place had seen better days. The shutters hung haphazardly and the paint peeled from the siding like strips of tattered paper. The rotting steps made a dubious whimper as we mounted them and headed for the outer porch.

"What a dump," I said.

The stranger flinched, releasing my arm, and an unexplainable sorrow lanced through me.

"I just meant as far as dreams go," I amended hastily, somehow wanting his approval despite myself. "I mean, I live in a friggin' tree palace right now . . . you'd think I'd be dreaming with slightly higher standards."

"You'd think," he retorted. Abruptly he turned toward me. "Who are you?"

"You already know my name. You said it back there. Which reminds me, how *do* you know who I am?" It seemed like a fair enough question for a dream.

"Name tag." He pointed to my chest. Sure enough, I glanced down to see it—a simple little plastic rectangle, the letters spelling out ABBY SINCLAIR in lopsided relief.

I frowned. "That wasn't there before."

He gestured about us. "Dreaming, remember? Shall we go inside?"

I shrugged, intrigued. "I guess." I doubted there would be anything of interest in this run-down piece of crap, but I couldn't remember another dream taking hold of my mind so vividly. Might as well let it play out.

The door opened beneath my touch and I crossed the threshold with a slight twitch of nervousness. For all my brave thoughts, it was still a creepy old house, not counting the stranger, who shadowed my steps with an aura of expectancy.

Inside was nothing special—hardwood floors and dusty shelves, lights flickering as though they might go out at any moment. "I wonder if there's a fuse box somewhere."

"I doubt it." He glanced at me with a ripple of amusement and I flushed.

"Yeah, yeah," I muttered. Ignoring him, I continued walking until I stood in what looked like a family room. The fireplace was choked with old ashes, the dying embers banked into dull sparks. A record player perched on a narrow table in the corner, a stack of records before it. Something about them seemed so familiar, but I dismissed the albums when I read the titles. Who the hell still listened to Tom Jones anyway?

Snorting, I circled the rest of the room, noting the tattered quilt on the faded sofa and the bowl of strawberry potpourri. The man leaned in the doorway, his arms crossed as he watched me.

"This is all very lovely," I said finally. "But there's nothing here for me. It's so . . . empty."

He didn't speak, but his gaze strayed toward the mantel of the fireplace. "Who are you?"

"I thought we already established that."

"I told you what your name was," he countered. "I never heard it from you."

"Abby . . . Abby Sinclair." I tugged on the name tag. "For all that this is apparently some sort of *Alice in Wonderland* moment." A smile drifted over my face. "I'm a princess, you know."

His voice darkened. "A princess? Surely that seems like a lofty achievement."

He brushed past me to the mantel, taking something from the top and tossing it to me. I caught it without a second thought, staring down at the bundled pair of pointe shoes bemusedly.

"Ballet slippers?" My brow furrowed. "What am I supposed to do with these? I've never danced a day in my life. Hell, even my betrothed admits I have two left feet."

He halted as though I'd slapped him. "*Betrothed*, is it?"

"Of course. To be handfasted, anyway." I stroked the satin of the slippers. They were no mere decoration. The well-worn toes were proof enough of that. "I'm not really a princess, though. Not yet. But I will be. A Faery princess, in fact."

"Oh, a fine thing, I'm sure," he said sarcastically. "It seems your fiancé neglected to mention *that* particular detail when he asked me to come here. Typical elf." He fixed me with a thin-lipped smile. "I suppose you truly have forgotten, though the Dreamer in you has not."

"Forgotten *what*? You talk in riddles."

"It doesn't matter." He sighed. "I had hoped things might be different here. This complicates things immensely, but I will make the best of it."

I threw the slippers onto the couch. "You can try, you mean. I don't know what the hell you're talking about, but I think it's time I left or woke up or whatever." I glanced up at the ceiling as though I might will it to happen.

"Stop," he whispered, taking my hand. "Don't leave yet."

Slowly, I turned toward him, a flare of heat sliding up my arm like a welcome friend. I knew this touch. This feeling. His finger brushed my cheek, tipping my chin toward him. A dull thrum beat in my ears, the blood pulsing hot with sudden desire. A hint of gold encircled his pupils, flaring into a brilliant nimbus.

"I . . . know you," I said hoarsely, my knees going weak.

"Yes." And then his mouth was upon mine, and I knew I wanted him. Dream or not, stranger or not, the wanting of him burned the edges of my skin, flooding my limbs like liquid fire.

"What is this?" I gasped, letting him wrap his arms around me, his hand snaking down my hips to cup my ass.

"A gift. The last I can give you." He kissed me again and my eyes shut against the intensity, even as his tongue swept deep. He captured my soft groan. "Look at me, Abby."

I blinked in surprise. We were no longer in a house at all . . . but a ballroom? I gaped as a cluster of masked dancers twirled by us in a rush of spirited laughter and hazy silks. Beneath my feet gleamed a black-and-white marble floor, tiled in a dizzying pattern. Soft light shone above us from a great crystal chandelier.

"I don't understand."

"I owe you a wooing of sorts, I suspect. Consider it a parting memory." He flicked his fingers, and the soft strains of a violin echoed from the far corner of the hall before I could ask him what he meant. I caught a dim glimpse of a cloaked player, but my would-be suitor had other plans than allowing me to discover who it was, for he turned me neatly, his hand upon my waist.

A moment later and I was dressed the same as the other dancers, but in pastel blues and silver threads. "A corset?"

He shrugged. "You might as well get used to it, *Princess*. Besides, I'll enjoy trying to get you out of it."

"Easy for you to say," I grumbled. "You're wearing pants." Which he was. Tight, low-slung leathers and a scarlet lawn shirt. "You look like some sort of ridiculous vampire."

A genuine laugh rolled from his chest. "Can't have that, can we?" He dipped me low and I realized he was now dressed in shimmering blue to match my dress. "Better?"

"Still cliché, but I'll manage."

"That's my girl." He pulled me close again as the music took on a sultry tone, something slower and seductive. "There's only time for one dance, I'm afraid."

"Well, then, I guess we'd better make the most of it." His lips curled into something predatory, but he clung to me harder in a desperate motion that didn't quite touch his eyes. Unaware of anything but the delicious way he swiveled his waist, I let my feet go where they would. Strangely, the steps flowed into each other as though I'd been doing them forever, graceful and unhesitating.

Odd things, dreams.

And my partner was no slouch either.

Our skillful movements soon turned the dance into something else entirely. Fingers stroked over my neck, my shoulders, tracing down my spine. His hips ground into my mine, his mouth upon my jaw. And all of it was subtle enough to seem as though it were part of the dance itself.

We'd done this before.

Halfway through the piece, I realized my stays were coming undone. Struggling to keep the corset from sliding off my chest, I paused, catching a smirk upon his face.

"Charming." I snorted, wondering if he'd been undoing them by hand or by other means. Not that it mattered, really. Dreams were dreams and I was enjoying the hell out of this one. Immediately I stopped squirming and lowered my hands, leaving the corset to slip off as it would.

Spinning away from him, I swayed my hips enticingly. The other dancers faded away, and even the music became nothing more than a distant echo. My bare feet touched the softest of carpets, the lights retreating to only a dim glow.

The dream had changed again.

I glanced demurely over my shoulder at him, one brow arched in challenge. My heart hammered in my chest at the thought of what I was about to do. Whatever was happening here felt terribly right, even if my head couldn't quite wrap itself around the concept.

My dance partner stood several paces behind me, the rise and fall of his chest suggesting a severe lack of oxygen. "When you look at me like that, I forget why I'm here," he said hoarsely.

My breasts were about to slip free of the corset—the barest of motions would send it tumbling past my waist.

"And why are you here exactly? Assuming you aren't a manifestation of prewedding jitters?"

"Hush." His mouth compressed at my words and I arched my back in apology. His hand casually stretched up to push my hair behind my ear. His gaze became half-lidded and hot, drawn to the taut nipple that had escaped its confines.

"Now how did that happen, I wonder?"

"The mind boggles," he purred. "I suppose the only thing to do is to make a matched pair." He found the other breast, his thumb rolling it behind the corset with the faintest of pressure. "It might get lonely."

"Can't have that . . ." I tipped my head as though to expose more of myself to him. Soft heat pooled at the base of my throat and I realized he was kissing me there, his tongue tracing hot circles at the pulse. Something about the gesture niggled at me, its familiarity ringing true, and I said as much.

He grunted in reply, too caught up in my squirming reaction to care, but a moment later he had pulled away. "Change in plans, Abby."

My body shuddered with disappointment. "I wasn't aware there was supposed to be an agenda. This is *my* dream, right?"

He let out a humorless chuckle, shaking his head. "As much as it ever was, I suppose. Don't worry about it yet. I'm going to ask something of you shortly. There isn't any time to explain, but I need your word that you will do it."

"Is it going to hurt?"

"Not exactly. Not you, anyway," he admitted. "Promise me you will do what I ask? I'm not going to get another shot at it if it doesn't work." The intensity of his expression became despairing and I could only nod in answer.

"And until then?" There was nothing glib about my words, but my body continued to thrum with thwarted desire.

He leaned forward to kiss me, even as he gently laid me upon the bed that had mysteriously appeared behind us. "I'd think that would be obvious," he murmured. "I take what is mine."

As though this last interchange had freed him from whatever thoughts had been tormenting him, he tugged at the top of my corset, growling with approval at the newly revealed flesh. "Gods, but I've missed this." He went silent, suckling at the nipples until I jerked toward him, an electric pulse of pleasure shooting to my groin. I rolled my hips at him, but he was already there, one hand rucking the skirt up to my waist.

If I'd been wearing underwear, it was gone a moment later, his hand sliding between my thighs. I scissored them wide and bucked up to meet his fingers, letting out a gasp of relief when he slipped one inside. I tore at his shoulders, pulling the shirt away from him like paper. My palms stroked his naked chest and down the muscled ridge of his abdomen.

With a groan he laid claim to my mouth. The motion of his fingers grew bold. I rocked in time to the movements, feeling them echoed in the way he slid against me. He chuckled at my whimper.

"Too easy." His eyes glowed brighter still. I caught the flicker of what might have been antlers sprouting from his brow, but he turned—and they were gone.

"You talk too much." I brushed my lips over his

jawline, grinding harder against him. Small ripples of pleasure radiated with each clever stroke. "And what's too easy?"

One dark brow arched in amusement, his fingers crooking up as his thumb pressed down. "This."

Rational thought fled as I tumbled over the edge, the orgasm hitting me fast and hard, leaving me almost sobbing with its intensity. A satisfied croon rumbled from his chest. Was he laughing? My body continued to vibrate happily along, not caring.

"Delicious," he sighed, his lips parted as though he was . . . drinking? His face lowered, gaze burning at me. "Whatever happens, Abby, I have no regrets. About any of it." Confused, I frowned at him. "The mechanics are going to be too difficult to explain right now . . . just do as I ask. You have the power, Dreamer. Please."

"What are you going to do?" I shifted as though to roll out from under him, but his hands tightened around me. A tremor ran through him, but it wasn't desire.

It was fear.

Clasping me to him, he pulled me onto his lap. His erection remained beneath me, but it seemed to be an afterthought for him at this point. One hand stroked my cheek, the other cradled my head. "I'm going to kiss you now, Abby."

"All right," I said slowly. He hesitated for the briefest of moments, a bitter smile crossing his face as he lowered his mouth to mine. It was strangely chaste, hovering and light as though he couldn't quite find the right rhythm.

What the hell. I'd make it easy for him.

My fingers twined through the dark locks of his hair.

He stiffened slightly, but I tugged him closer, opening myself to him as well as I could. He nipped at my lower lip, our breath mingling hotly.

"All of me I give to you," he whispered, the words slipping away into the darkness, and his eyes flared painfully bright like golden waves in an infinite sea. He shuddered, his exhalation filling my lungs until they burned. "Now drink *my* dreams."

I struggled, but his hands held me firmly in place. I heard the distant chimes of bells as visions darkened my sight, wrapping me in the memories of an . . .

. . . *Incubus* . . .

. . . *I was crouched in the darkness outside a white picket fence with thorny edges, my hands bleeding from my failed attempts to scale it. Anything to get back to the place of my birth, the warmth of the Dreaming womb, and the inadvertent love of a mother who never knew me . . .*

. . . *I was learning to feed, gleaning off the dreams of others, taking all that I could and leaving only a hollowed longing for an unobtainable sexual perfection . . .*

. . . *I was singing on a stage, holding the attention of everyone. So easy to let my power roll out, lust and desire curling through the room like the flicking tongue of a snake. I could taste the scant edges of their dreams, the weight and the measure as I decided who I would visit tonight, what Contract I would make . . .*

. . . *I was wrapped in her arms and the darkness, her Dreaming Heart welcomes me like a beacon of light in the shadows. I would never belong there, but for a moment I could pretend . . .*

"Ion." The name fell from my tongue with an easy roll. He uttered a low cry, his form seeming to waver, his body vibrating in my arms. A rush of energy pulsed through my limbs once. Twice. And then he faded, a ghostly shadow slipping away.

Remember me . . .

His voice echoed in my mind, even as the white bed seemed to open up, swallowing me into darkness. The scent of rose petals and earth and decaying leaves assaulted my senses. I was falling, my fingers scrabbling at nothing as I hurtled into oblivion.

I'd been crying in my sleep. The damp trace of tears still clung to my lashes. Dimly, I rubbed at them with my hand as I sat up in my bed, trying to remember what had happened. My body thrummed uncomfortably and I knew it had been an arousing dream of sorts, but more than that I couldn't say. I would have to ask Talivar about it in the morning.

The elven prince had a way of being able to see to the heart of my thoughts, even when I couldn't quite understand them myself. Not that he was here now. For propriety's sake we had separate bedrooms. I'd never slept with him before. At least, I didn't think I had.

There'd been some sort of accident in my recent past, one that had apparently taken my long-term memory. No one seemed to want to elaborate on the details. Considering I was supposed to get married to the man, it was a bitch of a thing not to remember the actual proposal.

Perhaps my dream was just a manifestation of wedding jitters like I'd guessed, or even pent-up hormones. But tears? Flopping down in frustration, I stared out the carved window at the moonless night, a rustling of branches the only sound. Usually I found it comforting, but right then it mocked me with its secrets, as though it knew more of me than it cared to tell.

I shifted onto my side in irritation, something hard digging into my hip. Puzzled, I reached beneath me to find several small, round somethings. They jingled, a lost and lonely chime that made my heart ache. I lit the bedside candle and held the objects up to the flickering glow, swallowing hard when I realized I was holding a set of bells, tangled in red thread.

Two

A dream, you say?" Talivar said it lightly, but his good eye looked away from me in a way I didn't like. The Fae couldn't lie directly, but there was something about his expression that indicated he wasn't going to be completely open with his thoughts. Not that I'd told him everything either. Betrothed or not, I would have found it a bit difficult to tell him about being intimate with another man in a dream so real that I'd actually brought a piece of it with me.

I patted the pocket sewn into the inner lining of my skirts, the hard spheres of metal reassuring. Had I betrayed my intended in truth? I shifted in my seat, not sure I was willing to look that deeply at my motivations, and concentrated on spreading a pat of butter on my toast. On the other hand, if Talivar had his own secrets to guard, that was another thing entirely.

Not that it would be entirely unwarranted. He was a prince, after all. If he chose not to let me in on everything, I supposed that was his royal prerogative. I pretended to content myself with the knowledge that maybe things would change once we were wed, but my inner voice mocked the hollowness of that assumption with merciless abandon.

I studied the prince as I nibbled my toast. He was dressed in doeskin trousers and a pleated waistcoat, the ragged cut of his chestnut hair falling rakishly to his scruffy chin. It would have almost seemed respectable if not for the blue tattoos spiraling upon his cheeks and the dark leather eye patch covering the puckered remains of his left eye.

And yet, despite the fierceness that sometimes blazed upon his face, there was a gentle grace in the way he sipped his tea.

An elvish prince to his bones.

A polite cough interrupted my reverie and I realized Talivar had been waiting for my answer. A wan smile crept over my face and I glanced out the window. The early morning sun seemed less bright than it had on other mornings. Less real, maybe. We were sitting in the prince's solar as we were wont to do most days. He tended to eschew the more fashionable crystal and glass rooms his sister favored, and this room was no exception. Carved directly into the tree that housed the palace, the warmly polished wood reminded me of burnished copper. Large rounded windows allowed a glimpse of a sunken garden and provided entry to a wafting breeze carrying a hint of moist earth and wisteria.

Talivar nudged my leg with a questioning foot from under the table. It was something of a secret game between us when we had company, but I wasn't in any mood to play it now. "Abby?"

I shrugged at him. "I'm sorry. I guess I'm not myself today. I feel . . . restless." I stood up as though to emphasize the point, but my thoughts strayed to the dream of the night before.

His face became pensive. "And there's nothing you can remember?"

"Shadows," I muttered. "Shadows and dreams— and why is this so important to you? It was a *dream*. There was a man there, but more than that I don't really remember. He had a name . . . but it escapes me now."

"Perhaps you'll remember it later," he said. "And forgive my concern, my love, but you had been plagued by terrible nightmares . . . before." Again, that hesitation, but he covered it up by pouring me another mug of tea, fixing it with my usual three lumps of sugar. "I've got to meet with Moira to discuss the possible transfer of royal duties from the Queen to her."

A twang of sympathy shot through me. "The Queen still suffers? I thought she was getting better."

His smile wavered. "Aye. Well, the price of the cure was a bit too dear for me, Abby. And it came a little too late. Oh, she'll manage for a while longer, I think, but she continues to fade a little each day. Before long the Council will insist she step down. The poison left her an imperfect vessel." His mouth curved sardonically and he patted his crippled leg. "The gods know we cannot have that."

I reached out to stroke the scarred edge of his face. "Then they are fools. Though I do feel bad for your mother. She has never been anything but kind to me."

And that was true. Since I'd come here, lost memory and all, the Queen had insisted the Court treat me with respect, making sure I had the finest of clothes and the most sumptuous of foods. Every night the Queen held a ball, full of great wonders and magic, endless food and drink, sweeping music and quiet laughter.

It had been fascinating at first, but the days and nights had at some point begun to blur into each other. I could have been here three days or three hundred. For all the Fae's fine words and courtly manners, there was always an aura of strain beneath their polite faces. I rubbed at my temples, the beginnings of a headache threatening to break.

Talivar captured my hands, leaning forward to kiss my brow. "Go and rest in the garden. I'll send Phineas out to keep you company. And then if we have time later, we'll ride out to see the falls. I think you'll like them."

"All right." I gathered my skirts and left, feeling his gaze upon my shoulders. Something was going on here, and even though I couldn't quite put my finger on it, I was not one to believe in coincidences.

The dream.

The bells in my pocket.

Talivar's strange concern.

By themselves I would not think much of them . . . but now? The loss of my memory tugged at me like a tangible thing, tangled in a healthy dose of frustration. Always there was the hint of something looming from the back of my mind. If I could just push through the fog that seemed to wrap up my thoughts, surely I would find the answer. Or maybe it was the question I needed to discover.

I took one last look over my shoulder at the solar, but Talivar was already gone. Fine by me. I knew his garden well enough at this point and I'd never given cause for him to think I would do anything other than what he asked. After all, what else was there to do?

The garden had been allowed to become overgrown and wild, but I suspected Talivar liked it that way . . . or perhaps he didn't care. I was rather enchanted by the curling vines clinging to every wall, each branch nearly as thick as my forearm. Their emerald brilliance twirled and caressed the stone pillars in a dress of sparkling leaves and bulbous blue flowers as large as my head. They only bloomed in moonlight, their tiny stamens glowing with gentle bioluminescence.

There were other flowers, of course—none of which I had names for—and elegant trees with slender branches and leaves of gold. It was not unusual for me to spend my hours here, lounging about in the perfect afternoons. No one would find it amiss if I was not heard from for a while.

My heart beat a sharp staccato, chased by a wave of guilt.

I needed answers.

It seemed wrong to attempt to sneak up on someone I was supposed to love. My own distrust left a bitter taste in my mouth. And yet . . .

"Secrets upon secrets," I sighed. I knew Talivar kept council with Moira in a private wing of the castle, but sometimes they would stroll through the more manicured royal gardens together. With any luck I might catch them there, or perhaps overhear something via the servants' tunnels.

Wrapping my emerald cloak around my shoulders a little tighter, I escaped the far end of the garden through a side door and hastily made my way toward Moira's wing. The few attendants I did see paid me no mind, and it was easy enough to slip into the royal wing proper. No sign of Talivar there, but a passing scullery maid informed me that, indeed, the pair had gone out to the nearby gardens. I thanked her and found another door that led to the hedge maze, keeping a low profile until I spotted them, the sibling elves pacing carefully along the outer edges of the garden, their heads bent low in heated discussion.

". . . and she remembers nothing?" The Faery princess's brow wrinkled. She was clad in an elegant green dress, with jeweled ribbons twined through the chestnut waves of her hair, draping down her back to fasten at her waist. Even if I'd had hair that long, I would never be able to pull off something like that. She shook her head. "So where is he? This wasn't part of the plan."

Talivar shrugged. "I do not know. It is possible the incubus ran into some trouble . . . or maybe Abby couldn't pull him through because of her memory loss." His hand fisted at his side. "Goddess help me but it kills me to see her this way. She's like a shadow, drifting in and out of each day . . . and no closer to knowing herself than she was the day before. And don't even get me started on the TouchStone thing. Do you have any idea how hard it's been to keep her from accidentally touching anyone?"

"What's done is done," Moira snapped. "We cannot change the past and you are wasting time trying to coddle her into remembrance. Whatever possessed you to convince her to wed you?"

He turned away and for a moment I wondered if he'd seen me crouched beneath the hedgerow, but his gaze was distant. "I never asked her," he said finally. "I had but to tell her that we were already lovers and she accepted that well enough."

My mouth dropped as I sank to my knees, confusion and pain shaking my limbs to the bone. *Fool and idiot!* I bit down hard on my fist, trying to keep my breakfast from making a reappearance. If everything I'd been told was a lie, then who the hell was I?

The dream from the night before took on a more sinister tone in my memories. Just what was it that I was supposed to have done?

"I'm surprised Mother even agreed to it," Moira was saying, her fingers gesturing lightly in the breeze.

"Mayhap she took pity on me . . . or Abby, for that matter, given how little time she has left. What is it now, a matter of weeks?" Abruptly he sat down. "I thought if I might get her pregnant, it would nullify the Tithe. After all, the contract stipulates a single soul . . . if there are two in the same vessel, surely that would change things?"

"Perhaps. Perhaps, but delay it a bit," Moira conceded thoughtfully, her gaze suddenly cold as she watched him. "But you would subject her to that? That's more calculating than I would give you credit for, brother."

He shook his head, tugging on his hair in evident frustration. "It was merely a backup plan if Bryston could not break through. To think of lying with her under these pretenses is abhorrent . . . and yet I will do so if it saves her life."

"How noble of you," a small voice piped up from between them, and I realized the tiny unicorn— Phineas—took council with them. He trotted forward, snorting. "Forgive me if I'm not overly impressed with your scheming."

Talivar sank onto a nearby bench. "We're running out of options, Phin. She pledged herself to be the sacrifice . . . and as our mother's subjects, Moira and I cannot go directly against that. To do so would make us oathbreakers."

"And that I will not risk," Moira murmured, her hand up on his shoulder. "The crown is a heavy duty."

"Tight enough to make your head swell," the unicorn grumbled, hopping up onto the bench beside the prince, answering her glare with the snap of his own teeth at her backside.

Delicately, she shifted out of his reach. "I still don't get it. What makes you think having Bryston kidnap her would solve anything?"

"It was a risk he was willing to take," Talivar said. "As a daemon himself, he wasn't bound to the Fae's word. Besides," the prince added wryly, "I suspect he would have tried it with or without our blessing. Why do you think the Queen banished him in the first place?"

Unable to listen to any more of this, I fled. The three of them turned toward me as my shoes scraped the gravel . . . but I could no longer stay here. It was quite obvious that I was only a puppet—my forgetful state being taken advantage of—dancing to whatever sick tune they'd decided to play.

I didn't even begin to want to know what Talivar's thought process was. To think that I'd come to trust the man with my very life . . . my love? And what was a Tithe? Frantically I wiped at my burning eyes, my thoughts racing. Where I was going to go, and how I was going to get there? The beauty of this place suddenly seemed like a Candyland nightmare—as though I'd scraped away the sugar coating only to reveal a rotten core.

"Abby!" Talivar's ragged voice sounded from behind me.

"I don't want to talk to you," I shouted over my shoulder, walking away as swiftly as I dared. "I don't even know who you are!"

"If you would just let me explain," he insisted, his hand closing on my wrist. "Please."

I jerked away and he let me go, even as I whirled to face him. His shifted his weight onto his good leg, but I refused to feel sorry for him. "I don't know what sort of idiot you all take me for, but I'm done. I want . . ."

My voice trailed away. What *did* I want?

After a moment with that question, I proclaimed instinctively, "I want to go home. Wherever that is. Surely I have a family somewhere. A real family," I added darkly. "Not this palace full of liars."

"Abby." He raised a hand as though to stroke my cheek, but I stepped back. He sighed, his gaze troubled. "You *are* home. Please, come with me and we'll explain everything. Or try to."

"Don't trouble yourself on *my* account."

"You don't understand. We *have* tried to discuss these things with you before, but within hours you no longer remember any of it. Some of the small details stick with you, but as to who you are or how you got here?" He snapped his fingers. "Poof. All we're trying to do is keep you safe."

"Oh, sure. By marrying someone you find abhorrent?" My lip curled at him. "Planning on making me some sort of royal brood mare? And what's a Touch-Stone? A Tithe?"

"Abby, it's not like that. Moira is your sister—your half sister . . ."

"How the hell could I be related to Moira?" I snatched at my rounded ears. "In case you haven't noticed, I'm not like you." I paused, something awful taking hold of my thoughts. If Moira was my sister and Talivar was her brother . . . "Wouldn't that make you my brother?"

Recoiling at my words, he let his hand drop. "I know you're confused right now, so I'll forgive that," he said softly. "But I never meant to hurt you."

"I can't . . . be here. This is all terribly wrong."

He nodded, a sad smile touching his mouth. "Even like this, you avoid what causes you pain. Take some time, and when you're ready we'll talk."

I made a helpless gesture at him that could have been a yes or a no, but my body was vibrating with the need to extract myself from this situation. Talking with him should have helped, but all the conversation had done was convince me I didn't belong here. Whatever this Tithe thing was, it didn't sound good. Coldness clenched my heart as the realization slid home.

Sacrifice.

Of course. That's why the Queen had been so generous with me. Why everyone handled me with kid gloves, seeing to my every need. Why they wouldn't look at me directly.

"See if this fatted calf rolls over for you," I muttered. Lost memory or not, things did not add up. I needed to get away and sort out my thoughts. The hedge maze would be as good for that as anything and I immediately retreated into its welcoming puzzle. If nothing else, I could be alone while I figured out what to do next.

I'd always found the maze calming, but today my feet raced along with my thoughts, moving in a singular cadence pounding through my brain with a dull thud. I let my shawl flutter to the ground behind me, my arms pumping as I took turn after turn, doubling back when I hit a dead end.

I turned a corner of the hedge, blinking when I saw the dolphin fountain, its brass fixture spraying a bright mist gaily upon the water. My feet skidded in the gravel, shoes digging in to avoid windmilling headfirst into it. My knee buckled, a sharp pain twisting beneath the kneecap, and I tumbled to the ground.

Gravel stung my palms as I staggered to my feet, fingers clenched around my thigh.

An older man sat on the edge of the fountain wall, his hands and feet clapped in chains, and he watched me slyly as I limped toward the fountain. He was flanked on either side by elvish guards, their faces grim and attentive.

"Stand back, milady," one of them warned. "This man is a dangerous prisoner."

The old man scowled at him before giving me a friendly wink. His eyes were beetle bright, a chitinous shine that was meant to be reassuring, but it cut through me with a calculated edge. "Oh, clearly I'm dangerous, as wrapped up as I am." He rattled his chains in emphasis. "Why, I can barely totter out here for my weekly walk as it is. What harm could I possibly be to anyone now? Be a dear, Reginald, and at least help milady to find her balance?"

I frowned, not liking the twisted pull of his mouth. By the look the guards gave each other, they weren't overly happy either. The dour-faced Reginald sighed and reluctantly stepped forward to lend me an armored arm.

"Are you hurt, milady?" The elf said it by rote, his gaze constantly flicking to the old man.

"I don't know. Something's wrong with my knee, but . . ."

My memory jiggled again as I stared at the old man's face, overwhelmed by visions of scales and a burning fire in my gut. Abruptly, my hands fell to my waist. I had a scar there that Talivar could not explain.

Or *would* not.

"You're trying to place me, aren't you, my dear?" The man snorted. "So noble of you to have drunk that lethe water . . . to forgo your own memories and willingly sacrifice yourself for your friends. Now you don't even know who I am. Does the name Maurice ring a bell?" He let out an aggrieved sigh while I stared blankly at him. "Sort of takes all the fun out of it."

Wordless, I shook my head. There was something about this man that emanated corruption. I didn't need the chains or the guard to tell me that.

"I have no wish to speak to you," I said finally, though that wasn't entirely true. At this point, I couldn't trust my own instincts as to guide me to who was a friend and who was not. "What is lethe water?"

"Water from the River Styx . . . or so the legends have it," the man said mildly, though his tone suggested he didn't actually believe that. "You drank it to seal a deal. With a daemon. You're going to be sacrificed, you know." He smiled.

I sucked in a deep breath, the truth of it ringing through my ears. Impulsively, I fisted the bells in my pocket, clutching hard enough to bruise. "Take me back to my rooms," I mumbled to Reginald. "Please."

Reginald sighed. "I'm sorry, milady. I cannot leave him to escort you. It's against orders. And you should be moving along now."

I released his arm and tested my leg, hissing at the

abrupt flush of heat emanating from the joint. But why? One more mystery of my past I was unlikely to get an answer to. The old man snickered at my grimace.

"Why should I believe anything you say?"

"Because I was there, my dear. Gave me a rather unique opportunity, I must say. You're quite noble in your own way. Stupid, but noble." The man cocked his head at me, gesturing toward my neck with a rattling of chains as I bristled. "The most pathetic thing of all is that you have the ability to leave . . . whenever you want."

Anger snapped through me, a blind rage at the Fae's attempt to keep me in the dark. *Again.*

"*How?* What must I do?"

He answered me with a roll of eyes. "You hold the very key to your freedom right around your neck, woman."

I turned away, my finger sliding up to the amulet at my throat. Yet another riddle, I thought bitterly. Talivar had only said it had been a gift from my mother, and I had found that idea very comforting at one point, but now it was merely a reminder of something I didn't know. I tugged on it experimentally, tracing the heavy stone as it lay in my palm. The well-worn silver filigree caught the sunlight, winking at me.

Perhaps the necklace was symbolic? Maybe the sacrifice wore it so that everyone would recognize him or her. I could take no chances. It would have to come off. I reached behind me, fumbling with the clasp, but again and again the catch eluded me. Maurice chuckled, his voice merry with amusement. Flushing with frustration, I tried again, pulling on it as hard as I could until it cut into my neck, the silver chain burning.

"Why won't it come off?" I snapped, whirling on him.

"My understanding is that it can't come off, my dear. Though I do suspect there may actually be a way . . ." His mouth pursed in a sensual pout. "Would you like me to try?"

Reginald shook his head. "Absolutely not. No one may come within five lengths of the prisoner, under the Queen's orders. And that includes you, milady." He tipped his head. "Begging your pardon."

"I don't care." I drew myself up as regally as I could. Hadn't Talivar said Moira was my sister? "Everyone knows the Queen's stepping down," I bluffed. "When Moira becomes Queen, what do you think that will make me?"

The guard gave me a look filled with pity and I knew that was the wrong tactic. I tried again. "Look, if I'm going to be . . . sacrificed anyway, what difference does it make if I get close to him or not? After all, I'm going to die, aren't I?" The guard's eyes flickered. Answer enough. I let out a barking laugh. "I suppose that's that."

Maurice tsked at me. "A little quick to be giving up, aren't you? The old Abby wouldn't have been nearly so cowed."

I flushed. "I have no memory of who I was," I said coldly.

"For someone who tried to kill you at least once, he's remarkably altruistic with the advice," a small voice retorted from my ankles.

I glanced down at Phineas. "Kill me?" The unicorn shook out his mane, the tiny horn glinting silver in the sun. A scowl crept over my face. "At least he's not lying to me. Hell, for all I know he tried to *free* me and that's why he's been locked up."

"You shouldn't be here, Abby—" Phin began.

"And why shouldn't I try to free her?" Maurice gave me a wan smile. "We mortals need to stick together in this place, don't we? Can't expect a creature like that to understand."

"I want this necklace off, Phin."

"It can't come off." He sighed. "And no one has lied to you. Omitted information, yes—but there were reasons for it. Look, I know you're upset right now, but this is not the way or the place to handle it."

My fingers clenched tight around the bells again. "As opposed to keeping me in the dark?" I inclined my head toward the old man. "*He* says there's a way to get it off. We can 'handle it' however you want, after that."

Maurice glanced toward the tops of the hedges. "I think we're going to need to hurry up this conversation, my dear." His mouth quirked mockingly. "You've got an impeccable sense of timing."

Phineas frowned, his nostrils flaring. I caught the whiff of rotten eggs and smoke on the breeze and exhaled sharply to try to avoid tasting it any more than I had to. Was something burning?

"Daemons," the unicorn hissed. "The castle's been breached!"

Around us the carefully manicured hedges exploded in a great cracking of branches, wood and leaves scattering in all directions. Phineas reared up and shouted something about reinforcements before tearing away into the maze. The elvish guards whirled in unison as the first of the daemons emerged from the broken hedge, his head and body cloaked in black. Swords bristled like quills from his shoulders.

The guard who had spoken to me before snatched me by the arm to press me behind him, my calves scraping against the fountain. Of course, this also put me within reach of Maurice, who studied his fingers. "The sad thing is that a few more minutes with you and I wouldn't have needed this sort of thing. Oh well." He shrugged. "Opportunities never come when you think they should."

The daemon attacked the guards, and I flinched at the sound of screeching metal. "We have to get out of here." I blinked as his previous words sank in. "What are you talking about?"

"Just what I said," he murmured. The clink of the chains rang like a warning in my ear, my brain slowly connecting the sound, even distracted as it was with the fighting guards. Three more daemons had joined the fray, slowly pushing my would-be protectors away from the fountain. Instinctively, my body shifted away from the noise, but Maurice's fingers snatched my hair, yanking me back. He slapped me hard across the jaw when I struggled. My eyes watered with the sting, my own hands coming up to ward him off.

Grunting when my nails scored his cheek, he twisted my hair harder, and slammed my head into the stone wall. I let out a dull groan, my vision going red. Dimly I heard what sounded like Talivar shouting my name, but it came from a great distance, through walls of cotton. The heavy chains rolled thick around my neck, the metal pressing into the soft flesh of my throat.

"And now I'll remove that pretty amulet for you,"

Maurice said pleasantly. I barely registered the words beyond the struggle to breathe, my fingers clawing at the chains. He cupped my jaw, his thumb tenderly stroking my parted lips like a lover. A pause, an anguished cry from someone nearby, and a crack.

Just a little thing, really—a subtle crushing of my windpipe and the twist of vertebrae separating from the base of my skull. The inner part of me gaped with a sort of detached astonishment, Maurice's face the last thing I saw before everything faded into darkness.

And then I died.

Three

I'd like to say that dying was the greatest adventure I've ever had, but honestly? It sucked.

Forget the white clouds and the tunnel with light at the end of it or whatever concept you like, because for me it seemed to involve a shitstack of pain.

And memories. A flood of them, crashing into my mind with all the subtlety of a sledgehammer to the head. They flickered past me as though I was watching a faded movie screen, complete with dramatic slow-motion after school special moments and hyperspeed bursts until I was nearly screaming. And still they poured in, each piece captured and observed like I was catching mental butterflies.

Some I released.

Some I pinned.

Some grew teeth and devoured me.

. . . I pirouetted upon the stage and everything was shadows and light, my limbs moving with the liquid grace of water . . .

. . . Mother, her life shattered in my lap, pain flooding limbs grown cold and broken . . .

. . . me, trapped in a crippled body, trapped in a painting, trapped in my own stagnation . . .

. . . I was signing a TouchStone Contract, the pen scratching into the parchment as I traded seven years of my life to Moira, the Faery Protectorate . . .

. . . I was a KeyStone, the echo of TouchStone bonds vibrating as they snapped into place. I could see each connection like a nick upon my soul, the OtherFolk hooking their essence into mine. I was the anchor, their lives blown over the CrossRoads like falling leaves . . .

. . . Dark skin sliding over my shoulder, clawed and possessive, hot breath in my ear and the promise of an otherworldly pleasure like no other . . .

And then nothing at all.

I jerked into consciousness, a detached calm settling over me. Whatever those memories contained no longer concerned me. My time was done. A thin mist rose up in the darkness that reminded me of the Cross-Roads, though there wasn't a road to be found here. Or much of anything, for that matter. I glanced down to see if I could see my body below me, but there was a big fat nothing anywhere as far as I could tell.

Overall, death was rather boring.

Something jingled in my pocket. I patted down my dress, frowning when I found the bells from my dream. "And here I thought they said you couldn't take it with you," I muttered.

"Sometimes they're wrong," a voice whispered behind me. A frown twisted my mouth as I tried to place it. There was something clinical in the way I accessed the memories, sorting through them until I found what I was looking for.

. . . Painter . . .

. . . Cancer . . .

. . . Betrayer . . .

. . . he was taping my eyes shut, thrusting me into a vat of . . . succubus blood? Painting my essence onto canvas, trapping me a world of nightmares . . .

"Topher?"

"In the flesh, so to speak."

Shuddering, I stepped away from the sound, though I couldn't see him anywhere. "You're hardly one of the five people I thought I'd meet."

"You're not in heaven," he countered. "Yet."

"Neither are you. In fact, you sound pretty good for someone I thought had been turned to dust ages ago."

A ripple in the mist shaped itself into a humanoid form, the shadows darkening into a semblance of . . . something. Topher's voice may have remained the same in the afterlife, but what was left of his body looked like it had been dragged behind a taxi during rush hour. I struggled not to flinch. I'd seen worse, after all. Maybe.

"My punishment," he murmured, motioning at the whole of himself with a severely broken arm. "Sonja has a rather interesting sense of justice. Not that it was undeserved," he admitted with a sad sort of resignation.

The name rolled over my tongue.

Sonja. Succubus. TouchStone.

He had been her TouchStone, bound by Contract, allowing her to feed from him in return for . . . inspiration.

I swallowed hard. The succubus had always been friendly enough to me . . . but then again, I'd helped save her . . . from this asshole, in fact. Who'd murdered at least three of her sisters and helped . . . helped . . . I shook my head as the memories rose up like furious bees.

"*Maurice . . .*" I breathed, suddenly filled with a brilliant fury. "I guess I'm really dead, then?"

"Yes. Maurice broke your neck."

"Seems like a dumb thing to have let him do." I mulled this over for a minute or two, rolling around the scenario in my head. My fingers traced my collarbone and I realized my amulet was gone. I'd waltzed right into the dragon's mouth, oblivious—and he'd killed me for it . . . Apparently my lethe-muddled self was . . .

"Too stupid to live," I sighed. "Obviously. What was I thinking?" Probably an unfair assessment, but in hindsight, it *had* been pretty dumb. "So what now?"

"That's up to you. If you want, I can take you the rest of the way."

"Erm. Last time I trusted you, you, trapped me in one of those paintings." I shook my head. "And what happens if I stay here?"

"You'll fade away, trapped between worlds, but unable to take part in either." He paused. "Like me."

Eww. Not that I trusted his ass to do right by me, but the idea of staying here like some sort of zombie from *An American Werewolf in London* didn't exactly appeal either. Besides, the only person I'd have to talk to was Topher. No thanks.

He stared at me politely as I attempted to make my decision. Not that there was much of one to be made. Ghost or afterlife. "Guess I'll be moving on, then," I said abruptly, though a pang of sadness hung over me. I was leaving people behind, and some things that weren't quite right, but I suspected that would be true no matter when I left. No one ever said that death was convenient.

"Turn that way and follow the road, Abby." He pointed behind me.

Blinking, I gazed down and realized an arching bridge of gold had appeared beneath my feet. It spanned the nothingness with a soft glow, suspended by glittering strings that hung from the mist.

"And here I thought it would be a stairway." I didn't really expect a reply and I didn't get one, but as I shifted to move forward, the bells in my pocket rang out again.

"Something left to do," Topher said, a note of curiosity in his voice. "But you don't have to heed it if you don't want."

"What choice do I have? I'm *dead*. My neck was broken. You think I'll be able to do anything, assuming I could even manage some sort of divine intervention?"

"Always a possibility," he agreed. "But that's a risk no matter what. It won't be like it was before, though. It never is."

"Easy enough for you to say." The fact I was actually arguing the point with a zombie left a bad taste in my mouth. Besides, he'd lost most of his head. Some things you just can't come back from.

The bells jingled again, insistent.

"Time's up," Topher said. "The bridge forward, or the stairs down."

I took out the bells to look at them again, shivering as I saw the red thread.

"Ion," I breathed.

The dream I'd had with him suddenly made a terrible amount of sense and dread pooled in my gut. "Is he dead too?"

The weight of them suddenly seemed to drag my

hand downward. Topher didn't answer and I knew this was my call. I sighed, looping one leg over the rail. "I never was one for stairs."

Topher cocked a rictus of a grin at me, his rotting lips curling in that old familiar way. "Tell Sonja I left something for her in our old place. She'll know what it means." At my frown, he shrugged. "A parting gift."

I squeezed the bells tight. "Seems to be a lot of that going around," I muttered. "Second floor, ladies' lingerie."

I tipped myself forward and plunged into the darkness below.

"Oh, gods above and below, she's breathing!" Fire filled my lungs as I sucked in one gasping breath and another, firmly convinced I had a mountain sitting on my chest. A buzzing of voices surrounded me as I was lifted up. I tried to say something, but the words came out as a muffled grunt, my throat burning with the effort.

"Hush, love," Talivar murmured in my ear. "Your throat was damaged during the attack. I don't want you hurting yourself more." I blinked against the sudden rush of light, my eyes tearing as I tried to open them, but the swirling cacophony around us blinded me. In the haze I caught a mix of courtiers and warriors, silver armor and the distinctive green robes of elvish healers.

Talivar shifted me in his arms before placing me on some sort of litter. I saw a large pillow being carried by one of the healers, something small and white curled on it.

"Phin," I whispered hoarsely, trying to sit up. Pain lanced down my spine and I whimpered.

"He'll be all right, Abby. He gave a lot to save you." The rest of Talivar's words were lost to me when the litter was raised and I spiraled into the darkness.

Unicorn horns are proof against death itself, but not against the hangover that death leaves behind. My head throbbed worse than the time I'd spent an evening drowning my sorrows in a bottle of absinthe with my BFF, Melanie, after a disastrous one-night stand with a vampire.

But I was alive and that was something. I also had my memories back—everything before I'd sipped the lethe and everything after, although some of the later memories were blurry. At least they were there. Apparently Styx water didn't cover the possibility of resurrection. As loopholes went it was a shitty road to take, but I'm not one for looking a gift horse . . . unicorn . . . in the mouth.

What I didn't have was my voice. Oh, the healers had been quick enough to say it would come back. Eventually. For now, though, I'd been left with a set of angry red welts where the chains had strangled me and a throaty whisper that would make a chain-smoking whore blush. For an old fuck, Maurice had a hell of a lot of strength.

With his theft of the Key to the CrossRoads, the entire Fae kingdom was in an uproar. Although I hadn't seen the Queen, I could guess at her mindset. For both her prisoner and the Key to have escaped in one day was sure to stick in her throat.

At least she still had her Tithe, I thought sourly. Traditionally, every seven years a mortal was sacrificed to Hell by the Fae. Hell got a human soul, and in return they'd leave Faerie alone. As situations went, it was win-win for everyone.

Everyone except the mortal, of course.

According to Talivar, Faerie had given up the practice once True Thomas had come along and chosen to align himself with the Fae. He became the first Touch-Stone and tipped the power balance among the Other-Folk, so the Tithes were no longer necessary.

Until I agreed to sacrifice myself by making a bargain with a daemon, offering my own soul as Tithe for a chance to save my friends.

Not one of my wiser moves.

"Guess the road to hell really is paved with good intentions," I rasped, wincing at the way my voice sounded.

My fingers looped through the length of Phin's mane as I stroked the little unicorn's head. Not that he looked like much of a unicorn these days. He had assured me the horn would grow back in time, but given how long unicorns lived there was a pretty good chance I'd never see it restored to its former glory.

For now, the smallest of nubs remained. The rest of it had been used up in the effort to save me. I sighed, but didn't touch it. It looked a bit raw around the edges and I had no wish to cause him more distress than I already had. For now he continued to sleep most of the days away, but this was apparently also normal.

"Battle scars," I murmured, a half smile touching my lips when he nuzzled my hand, his eyes still closed. Inwardly, I worried at the lack of his usual sarcastic response, but maybe we both needed time to recover our sense of humor.

I'd been resting for several days now, and with the worst of the injuries out of the way and the knowledge that I was alive came a certain restlessness. My comfy little nook in the tree palace now felt more like a prison, its golden walls seeming to close in a little more each morning.

And then there was Ion.

The incubus had become the elephant in the room. A big pink one. Juggling pizzas and dildos and wearing a checkered bowling shirt. I still hadn't told Talivar everything about the dream. It wasn't that I didn't trust him so much as that I didn't trust myself. The relationship between the three of us had been complicated before I drank the lethe—the gods only knew where we were going now.

More important, I still wasn't sure where Ion had gone. If he was still alive.

What I did know is I wanted to get the hell out of here and go home. With the way time ran in Faerie, who knew how long it had been?

When Talivar entered the chamber and perched on the bed next to me, I fixed him with as steady a stare as I could. "Where's Ion? I want the entire story this time. You owe me that much."

"We don't know, Abby." His gaze was troubled. Keeping his voice lowered, he bent his head to my ear. "I can't talk too openly about it here, since the Queen had banished him. But he *was* coming for you." He sucked in a breath. "We were trying . . . but weren't sure if you would have your memories or not in the Dreaming. The incubus said he had a hard time finding you there."

I nodded slowly. "To be honest, I don't think I've dreamed much at all. But he was there that night . . ."

"He was going to try to have you pull him from the Dreaming, and help you use the Key to escape."

I mulled that over for a moment. As escape plans went it wasn't too terrible. Brystion and I had always had a special relationship in the Dreaming, and I'd managed to pull him from my dreams before— although we had been TouchStoned at the time and in the throes of a rather intimate moment.

The prince's mouth compressed and I could tell the idea didn't sit completely well with him, but he didn't elaborate and I didn't see the point in rehashing it. "I made sure my movements were known that night, so that I could not be blamed if you were not here in the morning. It wasn't a perfect solution," he admitted. "But if we could get you out of here . . ."

Somehow I doubted the Queen would have stood idle if I managed to get away, but I had to admit my choices were pretty limited at this point. I shifted on the bed, my bad knee aching. "And Melanie?"

"She's . . . gone. The Queen requested her to stay, but she bolted at the first opportunity." He took my hand and squeezed it. "She couldn't bear to see you like you were."

Hurt bloomed in my chest, but I damped it down. "Normal for her," I said brusquely. "She moves on when she doesn't want to deal."

"Not unlike some other people I know," he observed, smiling faintly. "Besides, it's rather difficult to keep the Door Maker within boundaries."

"Yeah, well, there's probably a reason she and I are best friends," I sighed. Hard not to feel disappointed, just the same. Being one of the only mortals who could control the Wild Magic came with its own price, but I still wished she were here.

I tapped my fingers on Phin's flank as my thoughts turned back to Ion. "Where are the bells?"

Talivar stared at me blankly and I realized he had no

idea what I was talking about. I had a moment of panic trying to remember where they'd gone. "Where's my dress? I want to show you something."

"We cut it off of you," he said, finding it lying on the floor next to the door. I eyed the amount of blood on the front of the garment with a grimace of distaste. I hadn't looked at myself in the mirror yet, but judging by the tenderness along my jawline there was a fair amount of bruising. "I was going to have them burn it."

I waved at him to bring it over, my throat starting to hurt. Annoyed at my own weakness, I felt around for the pocket in the inner lining, relief flooding through me when I found the bells. Carefully I pulled them out, holding them in my palm so Talivar could see.

"I brought these across with me. From the Dreaming." I coughed. "They were his."

"So where's the rest of him?"

I flinched, my fingers clutching them against my chest. "I don't know. Jesus, Talivar, I don't *know*. One minute he was there . . . uh . . . drinking my dreams, I guess, and he said something about giving me all that he was . . . and then I woke up." The last of the words became a thick mumble and I dropped my gaze. I didn't know if he knew what the drinking involved or not, but that didn't mean I wanted to talk to him about it. "I don't know what it means," I added bitterly, heartsick. "Did I kill him?"

"If you did, it would not be through any fault of your own." His thumb brushed away the hot sluice of tears that suddenly burned from behind my lashes. "My lioness," he sighed. "We have served you so ill here."

I swallowed hard. Some hero I was, weeping like

some sort of lovesick . . . *princess* . . . waiting for her prince to come rescue her. "What about that shithead Maurice?"

"That is a problem. The Queen has her men scouring the edges of Faerie, but with the Key, he can come and go as he likes. There's no telling where he is."

I scowled at my hands. "I was an idiot. If I hadn't—"

Talivar pressed a finger to my lips. "I share the blame with Moira for not having better measures in place to contain him. Somehow he managed to sneak in the mercenaries. Someone here in the castle is a traitor—of that I have no doubts. An attempt to free him would have happened one way or the other, but the loss of the Key—"

"Your grasp of the obvious is stunning as always, highness," Phineas mumbled, prompting a strangled squeak from me.

"Phin! You're awake!"

He cracked an eye open at me as he raised his head. "You two make a good couple, have I mentioned that? Imagine all those precious little child progenies you'd have."

Talivar snorted, but a flash of good humor played over his face at the pun, his relief evident.

I gave the unicorn a delicate nudge with my thumb, grinning like a madwoman. "That's enough out of you, hornycorn."

"It's never enough, Abby," he sighed, rolling over so I could stroke his tummy. "But I'll take it under consideration."

I obliged for a minute before turning my attention back to Talivar. "So what's to keep Maurice from just 'popping' in and out of the Court with a friggin' army in tow?" I slumped, wincing at the tender slide of skin against the pillow. "Forget the whole Tithe thing. At this point all of Hell could sweep through Faerie."

Talivar's breath slid out of him with a hiss. "There are rules," he said softly. "If we provide the Tithe, then they are forbidden to enter our lands."

"Didn't seem to stop them before." I pointed to my throat.

"Those were mercenaries," the elf snapped. "They hold no allegiance to any but the one who holds the purse strings. Even in Hell there's a sense of honor that must hold true—or the CrossRoads would fall into chaos. And that benefits no one."

"And since when has Maurice ever cared about honor?" Phineas let out a weary sigh. "He's human and not bound by Hell's rules."

"That we know of," Talivar said. "Who knows what sorts of bargains he's made? The best we can do right now is guard any wayward Doors that lead directly into the palace. He may be able to move around at will, but he still needs an existing egress."

I looked away, my gaze drawn to the fading sunlight outside. The words he'd left unspoken lay between us. There was still the matter of the Tithe to address, and unless we could manage to convince the daemons to let it slide, I was still on the hook for that. I wasn't naïve enough to suggest an alternative, but that didn't make the situation any easier to swallow.

The truth of the matter was the OtherFolk needed mortals, even if they didn't want to admit it. The system may not have always worked well, but without it they'd be in trouble. And even if I suspected humans might be better off without it in the long run, I wasn't the one to make that judgment call. Besides, a little magic in the real world was a good thing. In the mean-time . . .

"I want to go home," I said finally. "At least for the time I have left. I need to find out what happened to Brystion, if I can. And Melanie." Talivar's mouth compressed at my words and I shook my head at him. "I had a life once, Talivar. A real life, even if it was shitty, compared to all . . . this. I want it back."

He stood up abruptly, the overcoat snapping to atten-tion as he bowed formally, the motion almost masking the hurt in his gaze. "Of course. I will see to making the arrangements immediately." Before I could say anything else, he turned on his heel and disappeared, the door shutting quietly behind him.

"That's not what I meant," I whispered into the nearly empty room, but I knew the words were hollow even as I said them. I *did* want to go home. The fairy tale was getting old and if I wasn't going to have a hap-pily ever after, that was fine by me, but I wasn't going to sit here for the rest of my life either. What was left of it.

"No words of wisdom from the peanut gallery?" I prodded Phineas with a finger.

"There's nothing to say," he muttered. "I think I've done everything that could be expected of me at this point. I mean, there's a raving lunatic on the loose with the ability to move all around the CrossRoads at will. What's to worry about?"

One blue eye fixed on me as he raised his head. "But don't take your frustrations out on the prince. He was doing the best he could by you, even if it was a silly plan."

I flushed, remembering my bold words to the in-cubus in the dream. I'd nearly forgotten the handfasting thing. "Well, shit. Am I supposed to actually go through with it? I mean, there's not much point now." I squeezed the bells in my hand, ignoring the guilt in my gut. Whatever happened to Ion, I couldn't help but feel responsible, even if I hadn't been aware of what I was doing at the time. If I could find the Dreaming again I would look for him, but otherwise . . .

"Sonja will know how to find him, assuming we can contact her." I glanced down at Phineas. "You in?"

"Do I have a choice? Besides, where you go there's bound to be bacon." He rubbed the stubby horn on my elbow. "I know I'm not exactly the handsome fellow I was before, but I suspect I might come in handy in the long run." He grimaced as something cracked in his joints. "Feeling more of my age these days, I'm afraid."

I scooped him up into my lap. "How old are you?"

"Old enough. Not that I didn't think I would out-live you at some point, but I couldn't bear to have it end like that." He butted his head against my arm, his eyes closing as he snuffled into my chemise.

"I know." We sat for a few more minutes and I wondered at what I'd done to inspire such loyalty among my friends. I didn't voice the question.

The unicorn sniffed. "Jesus, Abby. You stink. When was the last time you had a bath?"

"I love you too, Phin."

"Yeah," he sighed. "I know."

Four

A sharp nip on my backside jerked me from an uneasy and restless sleep. I swatted the unicorn away and sat up, yawning. I'd been unable to reach the Dreaming at all this time, which didn't surprise me much, given how tired I'd been.

"What do you want?" I mumbled.

"Breakfast," Phineas announced primly.

"Gods, what I wouldn't do for a Denny's right about now."

"Moons Over My Hammy." He sighed. My stomach rumbled at the thought, but there wasn't much point in wishing for what couldn't be. Stretching carefully, I patted my neck with an experimental touch. The welts protruded less than they had, but the rawness still lingered. At least they weren't infected. Although it seemed vain to worry about that when I actually had the use of my arms and legs.

And—oh yeah—wasn't actually dead.

I tottered over to the washbasin on top of the dressing table, the intricate carvings on the drawers catching my attention the way they always did. The water in the basin steamed slightly and I knew the serving girl must have brought it up a short while ago. Efficient and quiet was a winning combination, even if I'd probably never get comfortable with having people wait on me.

I made a cursory attempt at splashing the water over my face, though my bones ached for a proper bath. The mere thought of a hot shower made me groan into the hand towel I used to pat my face dry. That done, I finally turned to face the mirror. "Might as well get this out of the way," I muttered, trying not to flinch away from my reflection.

I paused for a few moments, letting the brutal reality of what Maurice had actually done to me sink in. The welts were ugly and expected . . . but my forehead was an aurora borealis of bruising in myriad blues and greens.

"Christ, I'm lucky he didn't bash my skull in too, while he was at it."

Phineas coughed politely. "Who said he didn't?"

I frowned, pressing my temple. "At least my nose isn't broken." On impulse, I braided a narrow band of my hair, tying Ion's bells to it. They chimed in an almost amused way and I flushed despite myself. "I just don't want to lose them," I told my reflection with a prim twist of my lips.

"Keep talking to yourself and people are bound to think you're nuts, you know."

"Get in line," I retorted, moving to find some clothes in the wardrobe. I shuffled through the layers of silk and tulle with a sigh. I needed pants. "Don't I have anything other than dresses in here? I feel like Princess Barbie."

"Well, that would actually make sense, wouldn't it?"

I stiffened, recognizing the clipped tone of the Queen's voice. While my lethe-hazed self had seen the Queen as a friend, I knew better now. Still, best to try not to piss her off more than I was already going to. Regret at not having Talivar here warred with relief that he wouldn't have to see her treat me like dog crap. I hastily threw on a clean chemise.

"Your pardon, Your Majesty, but I'm afraid I'm not decently suited to receive you." I peeked out of the wardrobe, heart sinking as I watched her sit in the large chair next to the window. Unusual for her to take such an interest in me, but given the situation, I suppose it could be expected. However, it did sort of beg the question of why she had come here directly, instead of demanding a more formal audience. Somehow I doubted it was out of concern over my health.

"I will wait," she said as she waved her hand at the wardrobe with the careless arrogance of someone who is used to being obeyed without question. I was gratified to see that the madness that had plagued her before seemed to be absent, but the lack of her use of the royal "we" flared a warning in my gut.

The Queen was not one for informality.

Phin was remaining strangely quiet, an exaggerated snore suddenly vibrating from the bed that sounded an awful lot like AC/DC's "Big Balls." I snorted. Faker. The Queen had no love for the little beast, though, so perhaps it was for the best.

I struggled with the lacings of the light blue overskirt, finally managing to make them look halfway presentable. "Your Majesty?" I attempted the small beginnings of a smile, a tight flush of pain at the creases of my cheeks. Her gaze flicked over me mechanically, assessing the damage on my face and neck. I stood my ground, keeping as calm as I dared. I'd never realized how much Moira was like her mother, but I could see it now in the detached smoothness of the Queen's face.

Royalty had no time for such petty things as feelings.

She motioned for me to sit on the bed and I took the opportunity to play the game of Whose Head Is Higher.

"Does it hurt much?"

"Enough," I said. "But I am very grateful for the help your healers could give me."

She frowned at the harshness of my voice. "It sounds as though they did not do all they should have."

"It's fine. The circumstances were rather *unusual* . . . I'm grateful to be here at all." Her face darkened and I decided reminding her I was the reason Maurice was gone was probably a very stupid thing to do. "I thank you for coming to check on me personally," I added hastily. "Though your son has been doing an admirable job in that respect."

"Has he now? I wonder," she murmured. "Are you still set on being handfasted? Given the change in your . . . situation?" The gleam in her eyes would have had me retreating several steps had I been standing. Mad the Queen may have been, but she hadn't stayed Queen as long as she had without being able to see a very large picture.

She snapped her fingers, impatient at my silence, and a serving maid appeared holding a vessel of wine and two stone goblets. At the Queen's request, the maid poured the wine and set the cups on the small table beside her. "I knew very well what he was planning, but I wanted to see how far he would take it," she said mildly, picking up one of the goblets and holding it out to me. "Come and drink. I would see what it is about you that he finds so fascinating."

I didn't need Phin's warning cough to tell me this was probably some sort of trap, but I also couldn't refuse the woman without fear of setting her off. Cautiously I slid off the bed and knelt at her feet. Galling to think of bowing to anyone, but I'd found that if played the part willingly, she would accept it—even if neither of us was fooled.

A subtle baring of the virtual throat, I supposed.

Her gaze darted over my face and neck, fixating on where the amulet had been. "Careless," she reprimanded me.

"Yes," I agreed, not bothering to point out that I wasn't responsible for Maurice's actions. Or the daemon mercenaries. Not that it mattered. I was already so far down on her shit list, I doubted I could do much else to lower myself further.

Her cool fingers brushed against mine. Did they linger more than they should? I held up the goblet, peering into the depths as though I might pull answers from the liquid. It looked harmless enough—but the last time I'd accepted a mug like this I'd lost my memories. My own choice, but still.

The Queen must have sensed my hesitation and she smiled, taking a sip of her own. "'Tis a healing draught," she murmured, the words tinged with dark amusement.

"What are your plans . . . now that you've been . . . reborn?" Such a casual question, but layers upon layers of meaning were wrapped in that phrase, the crispness of the word "plans." She hadn't forgotten the Tithe in the slightest.

Her mouth curved into something that was probably supposed to be reassuring, but the ruby darkness of her lips hinted at something more sinister. It took every ounce of will to carve my own mouth into a returning grimace. A fleeting glance at the mirror showed the horror of my efforts, but the Queen didn't flinch.

"I would like to go home," I said finally. "There are things I need to take care of there . . ."

A drawn-out sniff was my only answer. "How tiresome. I would have thought you might attempt to get to know your . . . relatives better."

The alarm bells in the back of my head went off with a vengeance. She hated that I was related to Moira, even if it was somewhat convenient to have a mortal KeyStone tied to the family. But then, I imagined having your lover stray every few years would have been bad enough. The fact that said lover had actually dared to procreate during that time surely left a sting. Hell hath no fury and all that.

My thoughts turned to Melanie and Katy and all the rest of my friends. "I have a family there, Your Highness," I said softly. "And I rather think I've given enough of myself to my family here for the time being. Surely you cannot question my loyalty?"

"Clearly not," she retorted dryly. "Drink. You insult me with your hesitation."

I flushed despite myself. "Your pardon, Highness." I paused a moment longer and took a sip. It went down easy enough, whatever it was. Not quite water, not alcoholic, but with a hint of lavender. Perhaps it truly was nothing more than a healing brew.

Her smile disappeared abruptly. "I think . . . that I would very much like you to stay here. In fact, I insist on it, Abby Sinclair. You will not remove yourself past the boundaries of Faerie until I release you."

I blinked, the truth of her words vibrating into my bones, an echoing mockery of a TouchStone Contract. "What have you done?" I whispered, letting the goblet drop to the floor. It shattered into pieces, the carved stonework scattering over the wooden floor.

"It's a geas," Phineas said grimly from the bed. He'd jerked upright at the noise, his nose quivering.

"Why didn't you tell me?" I glared at the unicorn, my arms shaking with the need to lash out. "If you knew it was a geas, why didn't you stop me from drinking?"

He glanced over at me, the nub of his horn barely peeking out from the tangled mess of his forelock. "We're not TouchStoned anymore, Abby. We lost that when you . . . died. I don't sense things about you as well without it." His tail lashed around his hocks like a cat and he let out a weary sigh. "And it wasn't the drink that did it directly. You'll notice she drank it too?"

My brow furrowed. What had Talivar said about enchanted food?

"Intent . . ." I muttered. "It wasn't the drink—it was the intent behind it. I'm a fucking idiot."

"The beast speaks the truth," the Queen said simply, placing her own goblet on the windowsill. "And so do you, it would seem."

"You poisoned me in your own house? Doesn't that smack of some sort of guest-friendship treachery?" My mind continued to whirl. "And what do you mean I can't leave?"

Her upper lip curled in disdain. "Just as I said. You

will not be able to step onto the CrossRoads without my permission. In fact, you will not even be able to attempt it without severe . . . discomfort." Her brows arched as though she was contemplating several possibilities. And enjoying them all.

"As to why?" She shook her head, the blond curls cascading down her neck. "I am not an idiot. I know very well what my children have planned and I will not give up my throne simply because they think I'm ill." She leaned forward so that our noses nearly touched and I could see the madness still lurking deep within her gaze. "I have far too much invested here to throw it all away. You're too rare an asset for me to let you leave, KeyStone," she hissed. "And if you can't leave, then neither will my son. Keep a bitch in the kitchens and the dogs will continue to sniff for her, as they say."

"Not if the dog has any balls," Talivar said mildly from the doorway. A glimpse at his face told a much different story. His good eye burned with fury.

She met his gaze, impassive. "Then I guess I don't have much to worry about."

The prince's head jerked as though he'd been slapped, and for a moment I could see the similarity in the arch of their brows and the set of their jaws.

"Don't you?" He strode past her, his presence filling the room with a regal righteousness to match her own. "You've gone too far," he snapped. "Abby helped save your life! Offered herself up to save mine . . . to save our kingdom, and instead of focusing on the true problems at hand, you settle for a petty game of thrones borne of jealousy." He thrust his hand through his hair. "To keep her here after she has died for our cause is beyond cruelty."

"So says the one who only yesterday conspired with his sister to take my throne from me," the Queen sneered, straightening in her chair. Her hands folded primly in her lap as she regarded me like something she'd found under a microscope. "Abby is no longer your concern."

His mouth pursed. "Fair enough. Then I'll *make* her mine." He pushed past me, and I noted he was dressed for traveling beneath his cloak, a thick leather vest overlaying his tunic suggesting an extended journey might be in order. I couldn't help the small smile from reaching my lips as he looked at me.

"And what do you intend to do? Kidnap her? Spirit her away from the palace? She *cannot* leave." The Queen let out an angry laugh. "I'll have you hunted down for treason, son or not."

He paused, as though weighing his options for a moment. "Witness," he said suddenly.

She stiffened, nostrils flaring. "You can't be serious," she said, her gaze darting to me. "I'll leave."

"*Witness,*" he barked. He held out his hand to mine. "Take it," he said softly.

"What are you doing?" I was all for finding a way of escape, but not under any false pretense. Something in my face must have shown this because his mouth gentled.

"Handfasting. Become my wife, Abby."

"I will not allow this farce to continue!" The Queen rose to her feet. Snapping her fingers, she called for the guard, her face pinched. I hesitated.

"We have no time," Talivar hissed beneath his breath, catching my cheek to turn me toward him. "Please."

Dimly, I heard the clatter and shouts of elves from

the hall. I had no real idea what the repercussions of this act were going to be, but given the choice of staying here trapped with an insane Queen as a possible daemon sacrifice versus a marriage of convenience to a man I cared pretty deeply about seemed like a no-brainer to me.

At least in the heat of the moment.

"This is not how I would have planned it," he told me, echoing my own thoughts as I thrust out my arm. "But I'm not sorry it's happening." Before I could say anything, he pulled a silver blade from his hip belt. "Just a nick." Swiftly, he sliced each of our palms, his fingers entwining with mine as he pressed them together.

A shudder ran through my arm, a ripple of power sluicing over my flesh.

. . . *memories of sunlight and the sweet scents of the forest, the twang of a bow at my ear, the rush of blood from the silver doe as I offered her heart to the old gods . . .*

. . . *I was ensconced in silks and velvets, the ladies of the court twirling about me like a bouquet of living flowers, and I their eager honeybee . . .*

. . . *Ropes bit into my wrists, an iron-tipped quirt rending the flesh from my back. I rolled upon the road, her lifeless face staring as my knee was crushed, the bones twisted. And then the poker was thrust into my eye and I knew only the need for vengeance . . .*

. . . *I was completely and utterly alone, limping through the empty hallways of the palace, my crippled footsteps echoing with all the hollowness of my heart . . .*

Ion's bells chimed plaintively even as the Touch-Stone bond snapped into place, my bones nearly vibrating at the strength of it. "I'd forgotten about that," I said hoarsely, Talivar's gaze showing his own surprise when it found mine. TouchStones were usually bound via written Contract—but I was a KeyStone, which meant I could create a bond via touch, an ability he had chosen not to utilize in the past. I smirked. "People are going to talk, you know."

A smile kicked up at the corners of his mouth. "Sod what anyone else thinks."

"Aren't there supposed to be ribbons or something to bind us together?" I frowned at the crimson trickle between our hands.

"Those trinkets are mostly symbolic," he said. "The blood was the important part."

"Not that it matters," said the Queen, turning her head from the hallway. "Since I didn't see it, it doesn't count." Her smile became triumphant, even as the first guard loomed from the doorway. "A handfasting must be witnessed."

"Witnessed," Phineas sat up abruptly from the bed. He waggled his beard at the Queen. "Witnessed by the 'beast.' It is done."

An ugly laugh escaped her and she gestured at the guards to take us. They hesitated. She was their Queen, of course, but she was also sort of insane. And the prince had their loyalty as a brother-in-arms in a way that couldn't be easily overcome.

Talivar raised his hand, stepping in front of me as though to block their view. "I claim first night, as is my right."

Time slowed for a span of heartbeats, the prince and the Queen staring each other down like leopards over a newly killed gazelle. The Queen's eyes narrowed when he did not back down and I could see her reassessing the situation. No way of retreating without losing face, but nothing good was going to come out of the simmering boil of hostility that hung between them. I tugged on Talivar's sleeve, and the motion attracted her attention long enough to ease the tension a hair.

"One night, I grant you," the Queen said between clenched teeth. "But do not force my hand further. I expect you to present yourselves to the Court tomorrow. And then we shall see what is to be done." Her upper lip curled tight and she gazed down at the unicorn before sweeping from my bedroom in a whirl of skirts. The guards gave Talivar a troubled bow and followed suit. Talivar slumped, exhaling softly.

"Well, at least we didn't have to bolt out the window. Yet," he snorted, giving me a rakish grin. "Though it would probably make for a better story later." Reluctantly he released my hand so I could sit on the bed.

I stared down at the slice in my palm. "What the hell just happened?"

"You traded in a potential Evil Stepmother for an Evil Mother-in-Law," Phin said. "I've never seen anyone quite so talented at digging a hole as deep as you do. It's like you *trained* for it."

"I wasn't asking *you*."

"I bought you some time on a technicality." Talivar sighed, rubbing his thumb against his own cut. "The handfasting will only be for the standard year and a day. Assuming there are no children," he added. "We can cross that bridge if we come to it, but as my wife you'll be able to move about Faerie with a greater level of protection than you would otherwise." He let out an embarrassed cough. "Technically you belong to me now . . . and for tonight, at least, that overrides the claim of the Queen."

"Hooray for women's rights," I retorted. "And

children would only be a worry *if* we were sleeping to-gether . . ." His brow arched and I flushed, heat spark-ing behind my cheeks. *Well done, Abby.* ". . . not that I'm suggesting you did anything dishonorable when I had no memory of you."

"No, I didn't." His jaw tightened. And I believed him. Even if things were still a bit hazy in places, I knew now that he'd had nothing but my welfare on his mind. But it still rankled that I'd had to be protected at all. On the other hand, my first independent act as an amnesiac had been to get myself murdered. Crapshoot, either way.

"Sorry," I murmured, squeezing his hand in apol-ogy. "But time is running away from me and I need to catch myself."

"Consider yourself caught, then," he said wryly. "For all the good it does you."

"We're going to have to talk about some things," I warned him, yanking on Ion's bells.

"Yes. But not here. And not now." Stooping, he snagged a few items of clothing off the floor, eying them critically. "We'll get you something more appro-priate later. Come on. I've got my horse saddled and ready to go."

"Where are we going?" I craned my head toward the door. "Surely they're not going to just let us waltz out of here?"

"Well, we could waste time consummating our union instead, if you like." His brow rose knowingly at me and I flushed despite myself. He shook his head. "You want to hang around long enough to present our marriage to the Court tomorrow? The only reason we got away with this much is because of the guards . . .

and Phin. Even the Queen can't go against elvish protocol on a whim." His expression sobered. "But don't expect any such gifts tomorrow . . . I'd be surprised if she even let us get that far."

"Doubtful," Phineas agreed, giving himself a little shake. "After all, as far as Maurice and the rest of the kingdom are concerned, you're the Tithe. Announcing you as the wife of the prince will open the door to a lot more questions than she's probably willing to answer."

"Right. Whatever Maurice's game is right now, I can't risk him coming to find you here," Talivar said abruptly.

"And where are we supposed to go?" I paced the length of the room, the walls seeming to close in on me like the bars of a tiger's cage. "If I can't travel the CrossRoads, that sort of limits us, doesn't it?" Another thought struck me. "And what if she sends a pursuit?"

"You're talking to someone who spent nearly twenty years outrunning his father's men," Talivar said sadly. "We'll manage." I started for the door but he shook his head. "Through the garden. She'll have put a guard outside my door, and I'd rather spare them any more grief than they're already going to get."

"She won't put anyone outside the gardens?"

"She might," he admitted with a sigh. "In fact, she probably will. Guess it's a good thing I sent Moira on ahead to meet us outside the palace walls with my horse. Of course, that was before all this happened, so it's a rather fortunate run of timing." He pulled at his mouth wryly. "Between that and a certain secret passage, we ought to be gone before they realize it."

"I do so like a man with a plan," I murmured, scooping Phin into my arms. The unicorn let out a snort but wisely said nothing.

Talivar shrugged, cold amusement burning from his good eye. "Well, when you thumb your nose at the Queen, it helps to have options. Including a way to get the hell out of Dodge, as you mortals so quaintly put it."

"Then lead the way . . . husband mine," I said, the word rolling strange and foreign on my tongue. With a self-mocking smile, the prince bowed and took my arm, leading me from the bedroom chambers that had been my home for the last several weeks and into the wildness of his gardens.

I did not look back.

Five

Icy rivulets of rain trickled down the back of my tunic, setting off another round of shivers. I ducked beneath the low-hanging branches of a pine tree, its needles made soft by the downpour. "I'm getting wet," Phineas complained, his muzzle pressing against my neck.

"I'll make sure to punch your membership card when you leave," I muttered, shifting him in my arms. "Or you could go back, if you wanted."

He shuddered. "No thanks. Some of those spiders were almost as big as me."

The "secret" passage through the garden was less an actual doorway than a slim tunnel through a moss-riddled break in the wall. The reason for the garden's lack of upkeep became evident when Talivar had to cut through several feet of brambles just to reach it. The bioluminescence of the flowers seemed dim, but the bluish aura was enough to see by.

"It seems smaller than I remembered," Talivar mused aloud. "Or perhaps I've only grown larger since I last used it. I was only a lad then, after all."

Phineas had gone first, his smaller size ideal for making sure there was nothing waiting for us on the other side. I'd squirmed through afterward, contorting through the rocky passage with only a small amount of difficulty. Good thing I wasn't claustrophobic.

The prince collapsed the tunnel on his exit, a couple of muttered words resulting in a small rumble as the stones clattered into place. "Surprised it lasted this long," he said, giving me a sideways smile from under his hooded cloak. "I bought the charm from a hedge witch as a boy so I could get out to court the village girls. Later on it served me well enough to escape my father's wrath."

"Almost seems a shame to destroy it now," I observed, peering into the darkness around us.

"It served its purpose, Abby. That's all I could have asked . . . and something tells me I won't be returning."

There was a tightness in his tone that warned me not to press the issue, and I slipped my hand under his cloak to squeeze his hand. After a moment he squeezed back, kindly not mentioning the way my fingers trembled. We stole away in silence, finding Moira next to the withered stump of an ancient oak.

The princess sat upon her mare, the reins of her brother's stallion knotted at the pommel of the white leather saddle. She looked at us gravely as Talivar explained what had happened, her face troubled as she dismounted. "You don't have much time," she said finally, gathering the edges of her cloak around her shoulders to ward off the chill. "I shall attempt to stall them in the morning, but I fear the Queen will not be denied this."

She took my hand, staring at the cut with a sigh. "I'd nearly hoped this was merely a trick of some kind."

"Just think," Phineas piped up from my arms. "Now you're sisters twice over." He ignored the sour look the three of us sent his way, giving an equine shrug. His beard waggled at us. "Calling it like I see it—you know what they say, right? If you can't keep it in your pants, keep it in the fam—"

He let out a squeal as I yanked on the offending bit of fluff.

"That's enough."

"Indeed." A faint smile touched Moira's lips, even as her finger reached out to trace my cheek. "I would not have wished this upon you for the world, Abby. Keep her safe, brother," she murmured, giving us both a hasty embrace before remounting; she disappeared into the mist, the harness bells fading into silence.

Talivar stared after her a moment longer before getting me seated in front of him, our thighs pressed tightly together. One arm snagged me hard around the waist, and he clucked the horse forward, his heels pressing quick into the beast's sides.

It should have been romantic—the young newlyweds fleeing the kingdom upon a stolen steed, flanked by birdsong and their own pattering heartbeats. And perhaps it was, for a few hours. And then the rain began, the dampness seeping into my clothing until I shivered nonstop.

Talivar pulled me closer, nipping at my ear. A flush of warmth raced through me. Of course, the effect was ruined by the flatulent unicorn in my arms.

"What the hell have you been eating, Phin?" I coughed as his backside let out another unapologetic squeak.

"The healers have been feeding me a lot of roughage. Supposed to give me strength or something."

"Or something," Talivar muttered. "Maybe we should bottle it up and use it in the upcoming war with the daemons."

"I heard that," Phineas said, blowing out hard. "Maybe I am a little ripe," he admitted.

"Yeah, well, don't think you're sleeping in my bedroll tonight."

"As if I wanted to be anywhere near you two," he retorted. "*Wedding night* and all."

I let out a grunt, not sure I wanted to touch that particular subject. Though he did have a point. I elbowed Talivar in the ribs. "So . . . uh . . . just what *are* our plans for tonight?"

"I'm flattered you think I'm going to be good for anything of that nature," he said dryly. "We've got a long way to go—and we'll be walking as soon as I turn the horse loose." He chuckled at my questioning grunt of incredulity. "We need to disappear, Abby. A horse eats and shits a lot. Where we're going we'll move faster without him."

"Crafty," I said lamely. I didn't know the first real thing about living rough, so I was more than willing to let Talivar play Aragorn if it gave us a real chance of escape. So here we were, several hours later. He'd turned off the road at some indiscriminate location, stripping the horse of what looked to be a bedroll and some odds and ends, his bow slung lightly over his shoulder.

Slapping the stallion on the rump, he sent it galloping down the road and into the mist, sighing as the darkness swallowed it up. "He'll find his own way home. The mud will make it easier for the Queen's men to track us, so we'll take to the water," he said finally, leading me to the shallow banks of a fast-running stream. "This isn't going to be pleasant, but if we can get enough distance between us and the road, we'll have enough breathing room to set up a camp."

"Camping on my honeymoon," I muttered. "Hoorah."

"I'll try to make it better than that," he said slyly. "I know where the best hot springs are, after all."

"I'll bet you do. Not that it matters." I groaned as fire swept up the inside of my thighs, my muscles cramping. "If I ride anything else in the next three weeks it will be too soon."

He let out a noncommittal laugh and took my hand. Mountain streams run deep and cold even in the Faerie world, and this one was no exception. Immediately, water seeped into my boots, flooding through the tops when I stumbled into a deeper eddy, my trembling legs having forgotten the basics of movement.

Time became a blur of damp and cold and darkness as we trudged through the woods. Or, really, I was the one who was trudging. Talivar stepped neatly as though he were dancing, each careful slide of his foot finding a quiet place. I might even have been jealous about it, if I could have stopped shaking long enough to put two coherent thoughts together.

Phineas had passed out ages ago and the little shit was getting heavy. I'd have made him walk, but as deep as the stream was, he would have been swimming before long and I wasn't going to be that cruel.

Around and around, Talivar led us up and down and

out of the stream and across the stream until I couldn't have said which way we were going. For all I knew we'd been walking in circles for miles.

My foot slipped on a pile of slick leaves and I staggered against him. He paused, letting me catch my breath for a moment. "There's a small copse at the top of the ridge," he said. "Just a little farther and we'll get a chance to rest, Abby."

I grunted at him, too tired for words. I understood his methods. If I stopped now I wouldn't start up again, but that last bit seemed to stretch on forever, until I lost myself in a trance of mechanical movement, each leg lurching as though there were anchors hanging from my calves. When he finally motioned that I could stop, I sank where I stood, my entire body quivering.

Phineas slipped from my arms with a little bleat, his mane a drenched mess. "See you've fixed the château up nicely for us, prince."

The prince pulled back his hood with a sour look. "At least it's stopped raining." Which it had, with the exception of the excessive dripping from the trees. Talivar squatted down beside me, cupping my cheek tenderly. "I'm sorry, Abby. I hadn't planned on taking this route, but I had to get us as far from the road as I could."

"Pretty goddamned out of the way, if you ask me." Phineas grunted. "What are the chances of a hot dinner? I'm starving."

"Can't imagine why you wouldn't be," I said. "After all that hard pulling you did to get me up the mountain."

"Yeah, yeah. Everyone's a critic."

"Let me get the shelter set up first, and then we'll

see about something to eat. I can't promise us a fire tonight, but if we manage to elude detection, we may be
able to chance it tomorrow."

I mumbled something that could have been a blessing or a curse, my eyelids drooping with weariness.

Talivar let out a soft chuckle and set about building a primitive lean-to with what looked like a leather
tarp. "Look in the saddlebags . . . I've got some jerky
in there if you're hungry. I'll set up a few snares before we bed down and get us something fresh for
morning."

My stomach rumbled and I rummaged through the
outer pockets, my fingers stiff. Phineas wasn't helping
matters much, thrusting his nose directly under my
hand.

"Dude," I hissed. "You're getting in the way."

"And you're moving too slow. Some of us would like
to eat before we pass out."

"Go nibble some violets or something," I snarled,
swearing as the knots finally untangled enough for me
to get my hand inside. A triumphant sigh escaped me
when I found the jerky and I quickly passed Phineas a
handful before taking a bite of my own.

A little stiff, maybe, but I would have eaten shoe
leather at that point. Another quick investigation into
the bag turned up Talivar's usual flask of whiskey, and
I sent a shot or two of pure elven spirits rolling into my
belly. Immediately, warmth suffused upward, a flush
of heat sparking into my cheeks. "See you packed the
good stuff."

"Well, it is our wedding night," he said dryly,
emerging from the shelter. "Can't disappoint my bride
too much."

"It can only go up from here," I assured him, taking

another swig. "So what now? How much time do we have before they realize we're gone?"

"Midmorning," he said after a pause, sitting down beside me. "Though I'm sure the Queen already knows. She's not stupid . . . just bound by protocol." His mouth crooked up. "If we had done things properly, I would have had you instated in my quarters, so I'm sure my sister will make a big production of getting that done. With any luck, it will be tomorrow afternoon before they come searching for us."

"Small favors," Phineas said with a yawn. "But where the hell are we going? Can't stay up here . . . indefinitely . . . Abby's got things to do . . . plus . . . Maurice is still on the loosssss . . ." His voice drifted away and a moment later the unicorn was snoring.

The prince and I exchanged a glance and he shrugged. "We're pretty far off the beaten path right now. The nearest Door to the CrossRoads is miles away, so there shouldn't be any surprises. Plus," he added casually, "this is troll country. No one comes here to vacation, if you catch my meaning."

"Great," I said, images of bridges and billy goats and being pulled into little bits of Ab-B-Que filling my head.

"We'll be okay. This time of year, they're following their herds. Shouldn't be too hard to avoid them, since they smell like rotting flesh."

"Herds of what? And ewww."

"Goats. Duh," Phineas mumbled crossly, rousing. "Think maybe you two could shut up for a while? Some of us would like to get back to sleep."

I rolled my eyes. "By all means, hornycorn. I need to get out of these clothes anyway. I'm freezing."

"Hubba hubba."

Ignoring him, I let Talivar pull me to my feet. "Don't suppose you've got an extra shirt or something in there?" I glanced toward the saddlebags hopefully. "I think I've got an entire pond in my boots."

"We'll find something, but yes, you should get out of those things." He cast a look to the sky. "The weather has turned. It should be a clear night."

I shivered, giving him a wan smile before heading toward the lean-to. I pried off my boots immediately, my toes pale and numb and wrinkled. Digging through his pack, the prince pulled out one of his extra tunics. It was long enough that I could wear it as a nightshirt, and I shucked off my wet clothes without a second thought. Sighing as the dry cloth hit my shoulders, I sank down to the comparatively luxurious bedroll, tucking my knees up to my chest and wrapping my arms around my legs.

Part of me debated the wisdom of my current state of mostly undress, but my worry was less about wedding night jitters and more about the possibility of having to run bare-assed down the hillside, pursued by a grumpy troll. Besides, at the moment the only smexy time I was going to have was the sort that involved passing out and drooling all over my arm.

The prince shook out my damp things and hung them over a tree branch. "I doubt they'll get particularly dry, but at least you'll sleep better for not being in them." His face sobered as he looked at me regretfully. "I'm sorry," he murmured. "Things shouldn't have happened like this."

"And yet here we are." I shrugged. "It wouldn't be my life if it wasn't messed up."

His hand snarled in my hair, pulling it over my

shoulder with callused fingers. A moment later and his mouth was on mine, soft and tender with a hint of something far stronger. He lingered there, sliding his hand to the back of my neck before pulling away.

"I'm going to set those snares," he said finally, his smile rueful as he tucked the woolen blanket around my shoulders. "As pleasant as this is, there are things that need doing before I settle down for the night."

I made a mild noise of protest, but it was halfhearted at best, exhaustion taking my libido over its knee and spanking it soundly.

"I'll be back soon." If he said anything after that, I didn't remember, and sleep swallowed me into nothing.

Warmth.

Blissful, enchanted warmth suffused my skin, radiating down my spine. Sometime during the night Phineas had crept in beside me as well; a light snoring vibrated low against my hips. I cracked a bleary eye toward the opening of our shelter as false dawn crept over the edges of the treetops.

Talivar's fingers shifted, spreading gently beneath my breast, his mouth brushing my neck. Dimly I wondered if we should have set a watch or something, but undoubtedly the prince knew what he was doing.

"Everything okay?" His voice was a soft murmur in my ear.

"Mmm. Just wondering if we're actually safe."

"Nothing's ever safe, Abby." He shifted so that his head was pillowed on his arm. "But for now we're as safe as we can be. I left a few trip wires to warn of anyone's approach. We'll know someone's coming, anyway."

"Good enough." I nestled against him. "Where will we go?"

"I've been thinking on it," he said, "and we need to aim for the Barras. Kitsune might be willing to hide us for a time, and we'd be able to get access to more information that way."

The Barras was a traveling kingdom composed of the ragtag remains of the Unseelie Court, broken up and banished to wander aimlessly through the realms of Faerie. Although not officially recognized by the Queen, it did still retain a certain level of sovereignty. And we had friends there. Still . . .

"How are we going to find it? And what if it moves too close to the CrossRoads? Won't that trigger the geas?" The idea of traipsing over the verdant mountains of Faerie was a romantic concept, but that didn't mean I wanted to spend the next three months sleeping outdoors either.

"I'll try to scout it out in the morning. If I can get a message or two out, I may be able to discover where it's going to be. And as for moving . . . well, maybe we can talk to Kitsune about that. There may be a way to slip your leash yet."

I made a little grunt of affirmation. The Barras didn't have an official leader, but the fox-woman certainly had no qualms about making her wishes known. She had more resources at her disposal than we did at the moment anyway.

"I'll come with you," I snorted, shifting my legs stiffly. "Assuming I can even walk."

"Ah, not this time," he said sheepishly. "I'll move faster without you, and I'd rather . . ." His voice trailed away awkwardly, and I closed my eyes.

"Yeah, I know. You don't want to waste time trying to make sure I don't break my ankle tripping over a log."

"It's not that, Abby. You're relatively safe up here. If something happens to me . . . If I get caught, then I want you free and clear."

"A hermit in troll country. Free and clear of all but a bevy of billy goats. Maybe I'll take a troll as husband and pop out a few halfling babies?" I elbowed him in the ribs, the jest merely an effort to hold in a sudden wave of despair.

His grip about me tightened, one hand cupping my breast in a move that was more protective than sexual, not that that stopped my body from responding to it. "Never," he murmured, nuzzling my cheek. I turned my head, letting him capture my mouth with his. A half sob caught in my throat. "I thought I'd lost you, Abby."

"I thought I'd lost me too," I whispered, blinking back a hot rush of tears. It was as though the quiet of the almost-dawn finally allowed me to realize how much had happened in the last few weeks. The enormity of my own death lingered like an icy shield around my chest. Had I made the right decision by returning?

"We'll find a way out of this mess. And find your incubus," he added after a moment, his lips curving wryly. "And I'll make this night up to you, I promise."

I could only nod into the darkness, swallowing against the hard lump in my throat. I had the most messed-up relationships of anyone I'd ever known, but untangling them would be the least of my issues. I had to find a way home. Shivering, I snuggled deeper into the curve of his abdomen. For now, I would wait to see what the morning brought.

The next time I woke up, the sun was streaming into the lean-to, the early morning glare a welcome relief to the rainy evening of before. Lonely birdsong swept in with the light breeze, calling in some secret language I didn't know. It was still a comforting sound, reassuring to think that something so normal could be in this place.

I stretched and realized I was alone. A flush of panic rushed down my spine and I snatched the blanket up around my shoulders, leaning out of the shelter. Phineas was curled up on a flat side of a large slab of granite, calmly watching me.

"'Bout time you got up, lazy bones."

"Where's Talivar?" I shook my head, remembering our conversation from a few hours ago, my ears feeling as though they were stuffed with cotton. "He's gone."

The unicorn nodded. "Left a few hours ago . . . as soon as it was light."

"I feel so damned useless." I let the blanket drop from my shoulders as I inspected my still-damp clothes. "Just another goddamned damsel in distress, sitting around waiting for someone to come rescue me." I snagged my chemise and shook it savagely. "Call me Rapunzel."

"Join the club," the unicorn snorted. "I'm nothing more than a P. T. Barnum reject at the moment, so quit feeling sorry for yourself."

I paused at this, eyeing my damp dress with distaste. "You didn't renew our TouchStone bond," I said finally.

"True. But I didn't have much choice, Abby." He waggled his brows toward the remainder of his horn. "It's rather difficult when the seat of power is . . . flaccid."

I blinked. Talivar had said the unicorn had given up much for me, but I'd assumed it to be mostly cosmetic. "You're without magic?"

"Mostly." He lipped at a hock aimlessly, like a cat that has suddenly started grooming itself in an effort to avoid something. "I've still got a trick or two up my sleeve, but for all intents and purposes, I'm without resources."

A twinge of guilt rippled over me. "I'm so sorry. I didn't mean to make you do that."

He shrugged. "It is what I was sent to do. Your father saw rather far into the future once."

"Not far enough, apparently."

"He can't control what's going to happen. It's never been that specific . . . but he knew what was probable."

"I guess I should be grateful, but what's the point?" I sank down next to him, the warmth of the rock expanding into my legs. "He made his choice long ago," I said bitterly, thinking about the Queen. *Your mother-in-law*, my inner voice said snidely, starting up a rousing chorus of "I'm My Own Grandpa."

"And you're making yours," he pointed out. "As it should be. There's no statute of limitations on making mistakes. We make decisions based on the best information we have."

"Maybe," I groused. "But I don't want to talk about it anymore. I think I've done enough wallowing for one day." I slid into the slightly damp chemise, struggling to tie up the sodden lacings of my dress. Chilly for certain, but at least I didn't feel quite so naked. My boots, however, were still fairly squishy and I decided barefoot would suit me for a while longer.

Talivar had left the jerky behind and my stomach rumbled at the idea. "What was that you were saying yesterday about a Denny's?" I sniffed at it, my nose wrinkling as the scent of rotting meat hit me in the face. "I didn't think jerky went bad—"

"It doesn't," Phineas whispered. "Don't move, Abby."

I froze, the hairs on the back of my neck standing on end. The shadow of something loomed beside me and I swallowed against the gag reflex as the rotting smell grew stronger. My eyes watered as though I'd bitten into an onion. Made of ass.

Slowly I turned my head to catch a glimpse of a bulbous, blue-skinned face offset by tiny brows and massive pointed ears. Half-rotted furs hung from the creature's waist, a fact for which I was terribly grateful. I had no desire to see what a troll looked like in the buff.

Of course, the fact that said blue person was only waist high to me did play into my assessment.

"It's an oversized Smurf," I muttered, trying not flinch when it poked an inquiring finger at my thigh.

"That's a youngling," Phineas retorted dryly. "Mommie dearest is behind you."

Whirling as the sun was momentarily blotted out, I craned my head upward.

"Ah," I said cleverly.

The mother troll stood a good eight feet high or so, but unlike her shapeless, flabby offspring, she was built like a weight lifter of Arnold proportions. "Guess goatherding keeps you in better shape than I thought."

The troll woman stared at me impassively while her child poked me again. This time I stood still, unsure of how I was supposed to react. A sudden squalling sound made me duck in spite of myself. Most of the jerky was yanked out of my hands, and the little creature shoveled it into his maw. I caught a glimpse of moss-colored teeth before what was left of my breakfast disappeared.

"Lovely." I sighed when it continued to paw at my skirts. "I thought Talivar said we wouldn't run into these guys."

"*Probably* wouldn't," Phineas pointed out. "And she's got her cub with her . . . and oh, yes, there they are." He sighed as the troll woman yanked on a leather cord and a cluster of little goats appeared. They looked a bit less than thrilled, but I could hardly blame them. They *were* being dragged behind something that smelled like the love child of boiled leather and a corpse.

"Hellloooo, ladies." The unicorn arched his neck at them coyly, making a little humph in the back of his throat when they ignored him. "I used to be a unicorn, but then I took an arrow to the knee." He pouted.

Apparently having decided I wasn't any sort of threat, Big Blue gestured at her son to follow her, her gaze suddenly falling on where Phineas still sat. She pointed at him and jabbered something at me. I frowned at her.

"He's not for sale," I said slowly, unsure of her words.

"She doesn't want to buy me," Phineas said, his

tone frosty. "She wants to . . . breed . . . me. Apparently she lost her billy goat a few days ago and without him, her stock will . . . dwindle."

My mouth pursed despite myself. "So what's the problem? You were just ogling the nannies a second ago, right?"

"What I do on my own time is my own business," he sniffed. "Being sold for my services is demeaning."

"But being a man-whore to goats isn't?" I rolled my eyes at him, but shook my head at the troll. "I'm sorry, but he's not currently up to the task." I held up a stiff finger and let it droop, ignoring the outraged squeal behind me.

The troll woman bared her teeth at me in what I think was a smile, her next pantomime suggestive of eating him. Nothing went to waste in troll country.

"I'm fattening him up first," I assured her, nodding my head and holding my arms out to the side and rubbing my belly. This seemed to please her well enough. She grunted again and started toward the shelter of the trees, the goats ambling behind her in a parade of caprine misery. The troll child gave me a last poke, his mouth curving into a truly dreadful grimace. "Right back at you," I murmured, looking down at the remainder of the jerky for a moment before handing it to him.

He let out a groan of pleasure, stuffed it into his mouth, and stumped off behind the goats, his bare feet leaving behind a trail of broken shrubs. Sinking down next to Phin, I let out a sigh. "Well, that was interesting."

There was no answer from the unicorn, but a second later, burning pain shot through my ass.

"Jesus, what the hell was that for?" I hissed, rubbing the bite vigorously. "I'm only wearing linen skirts, asshole."

"I'll show you a task or two I'm not up for," he snapped, baring his teeth at me again.

"Fine. Whatever." I headed over to the lean-to, glancing up at the sky as I did so. Silly, since I couldn't tell time by the sun, but I supposed it was better than staring at my feet, which was my other option. I eyed Phin, wondering if I shouldn't at least attempt to apologize, but decided against it. He could be a real shit when he wanted to be. "Shouldn't Talivar be back by now?"

The unicorn stared at me for a minute longer, his jaw set firm. "Maybe," he said finally. "Assuming he's not being pursued or something."

"That's reassuring."

"You want me to suck up to you and kiss your ass with false hope or do you want to hear the truth?"

"What choice do I have?" I started to fold up the tarp and blankets, rolling them into something that looked like it could be carried without too much trouble. I was running on the assumption that we'd be moving along as soon as the prince returned, but even if he wasn't being pursued, that didn't mean I wanted to wake up with a troll in my bed later.

Still. The sun climbed higher into the sky with no sign of my would-be husband. I began pacing aimlessly, my legs still aching from the night before.

"How long do we wait here?" I muttered, torn between worry for him and the burning need to find a way free of the geas. Answers weren't forthcoming and finally I made up my mind. "I'm going to go look for him."

"And how will you know where to go?" Phineas watched me from his perch on the stump.

"I don't know! But I can't just sit here." I snatched at the rucksack and tossed the loose odds and ends of the camp into it.

"Don't be stupid," the unicorn snapped. "He knows these woods and you don't. He's a big boy—and he knows better than anyone what the stakes are."

I drew myself up. I knew Phineas was deliberately baiting me to keep me distracted, and my anger gathered, eager to lash out, when suddenly a cry of pain sounded from below us.

I froze. Talivar?

Leaving the bag, I snatched up the dagger Talivar had left behind. Not that I knew dick about fighting with knives, but I'd take it over being unarmed.

"Careful, Abby. We don't know what's down there."

"That was Talivar. There's something wrong. Come on."

Without waiting to see if he would follow, I half slid, half ran down the rocky outcropping. Twigs rolled beneath my feet though I did my best not to sound too much like a bowling elephant as I scrambled through the brush. My own exhaustion long forgotten, my fingers curled around the dagger hilt with a shaky dread. I paused in the shadow of a fallen pine. Phineas slid to a halt beside me, his ears twitching madly.

"This way," he hissed, leaping onto a stump with surprising grace. His tiny hooves dug into the bark as he jumped again. Without hesitation, I followed him, keeping focused on the flashing white tuft of his tail.

And then I saw them, three of the elves tall and glittering in their pale armor as they stood in a semicircle around . . .

"Talivar!" His name flew from me in a hoarse cry, my abused throat unable to pitch my voice into anything louder. The elves heard me anyway, heads turning as I stumbled into the clearing. Talivar slumped against the thick granite of a crumbling boulder, his bad leg twisted beneath him.

He grimaced when he saw me, but I ignored it, my gaze drawn to the crimson stain spreading over his thigh. Whirling to face his attackers, I brandished the dagger, placing myself in front of him. My inner voice snorted with laughter at this. After all, it wasn't like I'd actually be able to keep them from taking him. I certainly wasn't any sort of battle-hardened fighter.

On the other hand, I was also the Tithe at the moment. Expendability issues aside, I would bet I wasn't supposed to be hurt. At least not too badly.

One of the guards turned toward me sympathetically. "I'm sorry, Lady Abby. It's only orders. And we have to take you in."

"Do your orders include *hurting your prince*?" I gripped the blade tighter, sliding into what I figured was a reasonable fighting stance. The fact that the elves didn't react was a pretty good indicator that my definition of reasonable was probably about a one or two on the suck scale.

Behind me I sensed Talivar struggling to get to his feet, one hand leaning hard against the rocks. The hiss of his breath was the only indication of the pain he must have felt. He gripped my shoulder with his other hand, the tremble in his fingers sliding over my skin.

"I would not see them harmed simply for following the Queen's command," Talivar murmured.

"A little late for that." The guard gave me a bitter smile. "The prince has acquitted himself quite well, as you can see."

I blinked at him and stared at the other two, finally noticing that one sported a nasty bruise on his face. Another cradled a newly useless arm, Talivar's arrow protruding from his shoulder.

"Did I say harmed? I meant dead," the prince said pleasantly, but his grip tightened on my shoulder with each word. Bluffing was only going to get us so far, and we'd run out of time.

"So why not call it even?" I gestured toward the woods in a vain attempt to avoid an actual fight. "Go on your way and say we escaped?"

"Abby, they cannot lie," Talivar chided me gently before turning a dark gaze on the guardsmen. "Not that I plan on simply letting them take us."

"The Queen is rather vexed with you," the uninjured guard noted, a grim set to his mouth as he took a step toward me.

Talivar shrugged. "Well, it was my wedding night. I find the hard ground more accommodating than the Queen's hospitality."

"I'm sure we can arrange conjugal visits," the guard sneered, his patience clearly running thin. Snatching at my wrist, he yanked me toward him.

Not really having anything to lose, I slashed wildly, my blade grinding off his armor. I spun away, using my momentum to break his hold on me. My head ached slightly with the movement, reminding me that I wasn't really in top fighting form either. From the corner of my eye, I saw Talivar attempt to stay upright

long enough to nock an arrow to his bow, the scarlet
stain on his thigh spreading wider.

I feinted and scored a slice on the wounded guard's
nose, but a moment later I was knocked to the ground,
my hand jerked up high behind me.

"That's enough. Just come along quietly," the guard
with the arrow wound said softly.

I rolled, trying to throw off his weight with little
success, even as the other guards pinned Talivar to the
rock behind him.

"It's a good thing I don't have your sensibilities,"
Phineas grumbled from somewhere near my feet. Before I could ask him what he meant, the unicorn opened
his mouth and let out a squealing bleat that sounded an
awful lot like a . . . goat.

A goat being sodomized by a rhino, but a goat none-
theless.

"When she shows up, tell her they tried to take me."
He dropped to the ground and rolled onto his side,
squealing.

"She *who*?" Talivar frowned at him, exchanging a
puzzled look with the guards.

I coughed as the rotten-flesh smell filled the air for
the second time that day. The guards released us as
the she-troll clambered over the rocks with surefooted
grace. This time her son was not with her, but she gave
a sorrowful cry when she saw Phin's body lying mo-
tionless.

Who knew they felt so strongly about their breed-
ing stock?

Never one to pass up a possible opportunity, I
rushed to Phin's side. My shoulders shook with a the-
atric sobbing that would have would have won me an

Oscar. Clutching the unicorn to my breast, I let out a wail as I pointed to the guards behind me.

"They killed him!"

The troll squinted with a dull sort of intelligence, rage whirling over her face. With a roar, she charged them. The elves scattered before her fury, melting into the woods. Howling her frustration, she pounded a meaty fist into the side of the mountain before launching herself after them.

"You know what else troll country is famous for, Abby?" An audible click cracked from behind us as Talivar limped beside me.

Inwardly I sighed, knowing I probably wasn't going to like the answer. "Do tell."

"Landslides."

Six

I stared at the prince blankly for a moment. The foundation of the overhang trembled, and I ducked my head against the showering explosion of tiny rocks. Small bits of gravel stung my cheeks.

Another rumble and the rocks began to fall in earnest. A massive boulder thudded toward us and I jerked Talivar away, hard enough to make him trip. I had only a moment to realize my mistake before his body thudded into mine, sending us both off balance. Phineas let out a squeal of panic, his hooves digging into my shoulders as I let him go, my arms windmilling to keep us upright.

I flailed and arched my back to stay on my feet, but the ground shook again and sent me hurtling onto a fallen log, Talivar sprawling on top. The slope bucked and we all began to slide down the hill, sled style.

"Well, this sucks," Phineas snapped, grunting as Talivar shoved him ungraciously out of the way. The unicorn bared his teeth and clambered on top of the elf, the three of us balanced precariously.

I craned my head around Talivar's shoulder, trying

to see where my feet were pointed. "If we hit anything I'm going to break my legs."

"Then don't hit anything," came the helpful reply. Talivar dug into the ground with his bow, trying to halt our descent. I heard a yelp and glanced over to see one of the elves disappear beneath a pile of rubble.

So much for him. Dimly, I wondered if the others would be hurt as well, but decided I didn't much care. Talivar's people or no, I wasn't inclined to look kindly on being captured. I winced as we bounced off a jutting rock, pulling my legs up to wrap them around Talivar's waist.

It would almost have been comical if I hadn't been so busy steering us around a cluster of trees. My teeth clacked together at another jolt, the earth beneath us giving way into a thick mud, the remnants of last night's soaking rain smoothing the way.

I scrabbled at a sapling, letting out a yelp as the friction burned my hands. We swooped off a small divot in the rock, catching air for a few seconds before slamming down on the flattened edge of packed earth beside the riverbank. Dazed, I could only blink at Talivar when he snatched at my arm to drag me up and lead me into the water, his panicked words spurring me to cross the shallows as fast as I could.

I only caught a quick glimpse at the other side of the river before we disappeared into the coolness of the trees, halting a few minutes later.

Breathing hard, I sank to my knees. "Do you think they'll follow us?"

"No." Talivar coughed, his head drooping with weariness. "They caught the brunt of it on the other side. We were lucky." He glanced through the trees. "And we've got the advantage of the rock slide and debris covering our tracks. If they don't find any signs of us nearby, they may assume we were swallowed up by it as well."

"It's the little things. How badly are you injured?" I ripped off a scrap of my chemise to bind it over the wound on his leg. The way his trousers stuck to it I couldn't tell how deep it was, but better to at least stop the bleeding now. I'd worry about cleaning it out later.

"I'll do," he grunted. "We need get out of here. Kitsune has offered you sanctuary if you can get to the Barras."

"I suppose that would work in the short term. But something tells me the Queen isn't going to sit idly by. Besides, what good does that do us if I still can't leave Faerie?"

"We," he said dryly. "*We* can't leave Faerie."

"Huh?" I glanced up, knotting the last of the bandage. Field dressing for the win.

"That's how the guards caught me. Turns out your geas transferred to me when we TouchStoned. Bit of a bitch, honestly, though I don't think my mother knew it would happen." He blanched. "Let's just say we don't want to approach the CrossRoads anywhere near a Door. The aftereffects are very unpleasant."

"She said they would be. How far away is the Barras?"

"Assuming Kitsune still waits for us, at least half a day. Maybe more if my leg doesn't hold out. And we can't use the roads at this point. We'll have to make do cutting across the rough country along the edge of the Borderlands as our straightest course."

He rubbed a weary hand over his forehead as he sat up. "Damn." His bow had snapped in our flight down the hillside. He stroked the cracked edge of the wood sadly. "That's a pity. Better hope we don't run into anything else along the way."

"Dude, you can barely stand up, let alone draw the thing," Phineas snorted, his mane still slick from the water. "And we're wasting time."

"At least let me carry it."

Talivar let it slide to the ground. "There's no point. It's kindling now." He stared at it for a moment and I wondered what memories he was chasing.

I laid my hand on his shoulder. "No more splitting up. We're a team."

I caught a flicker of chagrin in his gaze that made me wonder what his initial plan had been. "No denying you anything, love." He found a narrow tree branch from a nearby deadfall. Testing his weight on it, he sighed. "Not much of a walking stick, but it will do."

"Can Kitsune lift the geas?" The fox-woman was formidable in her own right and a powerful healer. If anyone could undo it, it would most likely be her.

The prince shook his head, grimacing when he attempted to put additional weight on his leg. "I don't know. She seemed to indicate that the Queen must be the one to do it."

"Fat chance of that," I snorted. "At this rate we'll be lucky if your mother doesn't kill us both. She's waiting for us to give up and do what she wants."

His face flattened as I draped his arm around my shoulders. "She'll be waiting a long time, then. I will not be going back."

Phineas and I exchanged a glance. Not that I didn't expect something of the sort. Talivar had been under his mother's thumb for centuries. Why he hadn't given Faerie the collective finger and bailed a long time ago was a thing I'd never been able to fathom. I wondered if his deep-seated sense of honor wouldn't get him killed someday.

"Talivar?" My arm wrapped around his waist to give him a squeeze, but he did not look down at me.

"I only wanted a chance to be happy," he muttered, his mouth a thin line. "Why is that so hard?"

Without waiting for a reply, he leaned heavily against the crude walking stick and the three of us staggered deeper into the woods.

Nightfall found us huddled beneath the shelter of a lichen-coated rock formation. It kept the falling drizzle from the tops of our heads, but the ground beneath us was chillier than I liked.

Talivar tipped his head so it rested on the granite, his shoulder slumping hard. I pushed the damp tendrils of hair from his forehead, frowning at the heated warmth emanating from his skin. "You're burning up."

I shoved Phin from my lap to inspect the elf closer, unwrapping the bandage from the wound on his leg. A dark stain encircled the skin. "What the hell is that?"

He blew out hard, peering at his leg in the darkness. "Their weapons were coated with a light poison. Meant to slow us down." A dry smile flickered over his face. "Just in case."

"How long will it last?" Phineas inspected it, nostrils quivering.

"Depends on how much was on the blade. It's not lethal. Just inconvenient."

"I'll say," I muttered. "How far off are we from the Barras?"

Talivar shifted against the rock. "From here, it could be several more hours. Though with me like this, it might be days."

"We don't have that kind of time." I stood up, brushing the dirt from my knees. "I'm going to see if I can find help. Which way should I go?"

My brave words about the insistence of teamwork a few hours ago came back and mocked me, but to his credit he didn't even mention it. He pointed weakly toward a clearing through the trees. "We've been traveling parallel to the road for a while, but in this case, you'll make better time if you're not getting lost in the woods."

"Thanks for the vote of confidence."

He shrugged. "I know you, love. This isn't your element."

"What about me?" Phin butted my calf, nipping my skirts in irritation.

"Stay here. In case someone . . . finds him." I went silent trying not to think of just what else was out here that might be interested in something sick and bleeding. "Besides, I'll make faster time if I don't have to carry you."

He bristled slightly but nodded. "Don't be too long."

"I won't." The words were hollow, but they were all I had to offer.

I pressed a kiss to Talivar's forehead, his glazed eye spurring me to movement. The woods closed tight around me as I left the clearing.

The last time I'd found myself wandering aimlessly around Faerie alone, I'd been unceremoniously dumped from the back of a puca and into a pond. This wasn't all that much better, though I was certainly drier.

Still sore as hell, though.

I'd stumbled onto the road Talivar had indicated, but I stayed on the edges of it, narrowly avoiding an elvish patrol by taking refuge in a ditch. Judging by their pace, they weren't looking for me anyway; the galloping horse hooves drummed into the distance.

Messengers, perhaps? It gave me hope that I'd nearly found the Barras—though I was beginning to question our quest to seek refuge there. If the Queen was already searching for us, I wasn't sure how much protection Kitsune would be able to afford us. Still, what choice did we have?

The guards came back a short time later, forcing me to hide a second time, but they rode slower now, their helmeted faces turning this way and that. When their heads twisted in my direction, I froze, but they continued on without incident after a few more moments.

I sagged, exhaling softly, my legs no longer wishing to move. "Just a little farther," I promised them, but it wasn't like I really knew. My eyelids fluttered shut despite my best efforts to remain watchful. "Maybe I'll rest here for a few minutes. Only a few . . ."

"*Absinthe?*"

I jerked awake, my head cracking into the bark of the tree behind me. The sting arced across my scalp as I blinked blearily at a familiar wet snout.

"Jimmy?" I struggled to get to my feet, but he laid a comforting hand on my shoulder.

"Nae, lass. Dinna fret. Ye're among friends now, aye?"

I swallowed hard, trying to decide if I was dreaming or not. Jimmy Squarefoot was a Lesser Fae of the Barras with a pig's face and a hunching lope. Despite his odd appearance, he had never been anything but kind to me and I owed him a lot.

"Where's the prince?" he asked gently.

"Shit! Talivar. He's back there"—I pointed into the darkness—"but I don't know exactly where now, and he's hurt. He's been poisoned and he can't walk."

Jimmy snuffled, his tongue curling around one jagged tusk. "Aye, well. I'll finds 'em, belike." He tapped his nose proudly. "Best nose in six counties, ye ken."

"I remember. But be careful, Jimmy. The Queen's men are out looking for us."

"Aye. That's why I'm here. Kitsune sent me to find ye. We expected ye here hours ago."

I pushed up against the tree so I was standing, the pine sap sticky on my palms. "We ran into some trouble. I was trying to find help."

His mouth broadened into a grimacing smile. "And ye've found it, lass. Ye've found it."

The hot water stung the myriad cuts and bruises upon my skin. Gingerly, I sat in the small copper basin, my limbs folded up to maximize the water coverage. The tent I was in was blissfully empty of company, as was my mind, thoughts of the last part of my journey drifting into a blurry haze.

True to his word, Jimmy had indeed found Talivar, sending me on ahead via a turnip cart pulled by a pair of fanged llamas. Our arrival first alerted Kitsune to the elf's weakened condition.

Although the remnants of the traveling kingdom were much as I remembered them, an air of change swept about the mishmash of tents and vendor stands. The folk moved with a sense of purpose, a hint of excitement buzzing through the crowds. Last time they'd been preparing themselves for a possible battle against the same daemons who'd invaded Faerie, but this was different . . .

Perhaps it was only that the Queen had finally re-opened the CrossRoads, but it felt like there was something more to it.

Pride.

Not that I'd had the energy to ask. At the moment, I could barely keep my eyes open long enough to acknowledge Kitsune's presence when she had emerged from her tent to meet me, wrapped in a brilliant sapphire kimono. Her fox ears had swiveled at me curiously as I explained the situation, the fathomless black depths of her gaze resting on me with quiet concern.

She'd clapped her hands in unspoken command and I had let myself be led away, even as Talivar was taken in the other direction. Some part of me should probably have been worried at this, but I'd chosen to throw my lot in here. What else could I do but trust her?

So here I was, attempting to clean myself up—with a modicum of success. As warm as the water was, I had the sudden urge to remove myself from it, the soft robes laid out for me beckoning. Dunking my head beneath the water one last time, I emerged already half-asleep as I slipped into the robe. I barely managed to towel off my hair before I lay down on the stuffed pallet, the robe only partially drawn closed. A moment later, I slithered into welcome oblivion.

The scent of ginger permeated the darkness with a familiar tang and I knew Kitsune was nearby. I cracked an eye to see her shadowed silhouette, golden in the flickering candlelight as she stared unblinking. Muscle cramps seized my leg as I stretched, and I bit down a yelp. Given the last few days, I couldn't really wonder at the charley horse. I slammed my foot down on the ground, the heel pulled back to try to relax it.

Kitsune looked at me curiously as the pain subsided. I drew the robes together about my shoulders.

I sat up straighter on the other side of the low table she knelt behind. "Thank you for taking us in. How is Talivar?"

"Talivar is fine. I have cleansed the poison from his body and he recovers swiftly." She slid a steaming mug over to me. "This time you will drink it," she said firmly.

"Yes." I'd refused to take any form of sustenance from her when we'd met this way before. At the time, I'd no reason to trust her word, though if I had, things might have turned out differently. By accepting a meal from her, I'd be under her protection in an informal sort of guest friendship.

At this point I'd take every bit of protection I could.

I sipped the tea, sighing as a delicate warmth crested over my skin, followed by a twist of irony in my gut. I could only hope Kitsune's intentions were more honorable than the Queen's.

The flavor was light, with a hint of vanilla. "It's good."

"Of course." She sounded mildly offended but I smiled at her in thanks.

"I just wanted to say how grateful I am that—"

One smooth hand rose in warning. "Do not thank me for this, Abby, for I do not do these things for you."

I sat on my heels, stung by her brusque tone.

"I told you once before that a cure for the Faerie Queen would not be welcomed nor sought after, and yet I procured it, upon your request."

"Hardly out of the goodness of your heart," I pointed out dryly. "I seem to recall there was a fair amount of contraband involved as part of the trade on my side."

She nodded. "Yes. And for that I am grateful. Such a gift was beyond measure, but I'm not sure it will be worth it in the end. Better, perhaps, if the Queen had died, or been forced to step down."

I shrugged at her. No matter what I'd tried to do since becoming involved with the OtherFolk it had almost always been wrong—though I could admit I probably wouldn't be in this mess if I'd let things alone.

Or you could be dead, my inner voice reminded me snidely.

I did die, I reminded it, *so shut up.*

"Fine. I fucked up. What is it you expect me to do? I'm under a geas and that limits my options." I set down the mug a little more forcefully than I intended, the tea sloshing over the sides.

"I would not undo it, even if I could." Kitsune dabbed at the spilled tea with a small cloth.

"That's a hell of thing to say," I snapped, my fingers trembling in sudden anger. "And why not?"

"Interfering in another's destiny is never wise," she replied calmly. "This knot you must untangle for yourself." Her golden eyes narrowed and I shivered beneath her scrutiny. "Or not, as the case may be."

"How very Zen of you." Part of me wanted to rage at her about the unfairness of it all, but what was the point? She'd already made her choice. I was on my own.

My hand traced over the bruised ring at my neck. "It seems you were right about me not being the Key's true owner, but I think I've paid the price for that."

She took my hand in hers, rolling it over to expose

the cut on my palm. A hot flush swept over my cheeks as she stared at the crescent-shaped nick. Trust Talivar to have put an artistic flare into it. At least it would be a pretty scar.

"Where is he?" I was tired of playing games.

"Would you truly bind yourself to him? Wed him in truth?" Her ears flattened for a moment. "Would you share his destiny?"

I swallowed. No lying here. But I wasn't sure I knew the truth. "I will do what I must to make things right. *Whatever* that is," I added a moment later before reaching into my hair to find Ion's bells. They jingled as I untied them, cradling them in my palm.

The fox-woman didn't touch them, but her mouth curved into a crooked smile. "The thread of destiny weaves as it wills, I see." She sighed and patted my cheek. "You have a heart big enough for them both, Abby, but sometimes that's not enough."

Before I could ask what she meant, she pulled something out of a loose bag at her waist and slid it across the table.

My enchanted iPod.

I picked it up with a rueful smile. "Got everything you needed, I take it?"

"In a manner of speaking. We weren't able to replicate it exactly, but close enough." A frown played about her lips. "I know you said it had an infinite playlist, but it only ever seemed to play Pink Floyd's 'Wish You Were Here.'"

"Stubborn thing." I pressed shuffle and the little device immediately began to chug along, AC/DC's "Back in Black" popping up on the screen. "Well, I'm glad it was useful."

"Exceptionally." Her face became sly. "We've nearly

managed to get firearms to work. We've even started pairing up with military humans . . . Special Forces? We find they make excellent TouchStones to some of the more . . . martial OtherFolk. We call them Touch-Stone Tactical."

I raised a brow, trying to envision OtherFolk Navy SEALs or Green Berets. "They'll be a nightmare."

"I certainly hope so," the fox-woman agreed. "They aren't ready yet, but with enough time and training, we'll have the most formidable army out there." She stood gracefully. "Get dressed, please. There are things we must attend to this night. Talivar awaits you."

As Kitsune slipped through the tent flap I realized her presence seemed diminished. I couldn't help but think I'd said the wrong thing.

I fisted the bells for a minute. "What am I supposed to do?"

If I was expecting an answer, I didn't get one. In the end I rewove them back into a tiny braid and found a simple gown of soft blue silk that had been laid down beside the table. Thankful for the lack of buttons and findings, I wriggled into it and smoothed the scoop of the neckline.

"Should match the bruises perfectly," I muttered, finger combing the loose strands of my hair. Kitsune's words had worried me and I wished Talivar and I had not been separated, if only to keep me in the loop.

I bound my still-damp hair into a simple bun. I had no pencils for it this time, but I found a strip of silk to tie it all together.

When I emerged from my tent, I realized it was evening; the deep purple of oncoming night streaked into the fading sea of red haze. The energy swirled by me in electric anticipation. I could taste it on the air, and in the way the people moved around me, hurrying with a single-minded purpose I could only guess at.

I caught a few furtive glances here and there, but I was ignored for the most part—a fact I was rather grateful for. I'd been the center of attention enough times to know I didn't particularly like it.

I headed toward the largest source of light, my feet carefully balanced on the wooden boards laid across the deeper ruts. As I rounded the corner, a sharp tug on my skirt stopped me abruptly as I was pulled back a few steps.

"Abby?"

I relaxed at Talivar's voice, turning to see him half-hidden beside an empty apple cart. He was dressed in sable, his vest cut neatly to the frame of his hips, and his hair hung loose and wild about his face. He hadn't shaved, and the scruff on his chin leant him a rakish appearance that I found not at all unpleasant.

"Trying out for *The Pirates of Penzance?*"

His mouth twitched, but there was a tightness about his good eye that belied the humor.

"What's going on?"

"Something that should have happened a long time ago. It will all become clear in a few minutes." He cupped my cheek, one finger brushing my jaw. "I will ask nothing of you that you aren't willing to give."

"Gee, it sounds so reassuring when you say it like that. I'm already technically your wife at the moment. What else could I possibly have to give you?"

"You and I both know the answer to that," he murmured.

I glanced down at his leg. "How's the injury?"

"Better. Kitsune saw to it. I'll be taking it easy for a

few days, but it's much improved." He shook his head. "So much that I owe you. Come on."

I frowned at him. The prince usually wasn't one to drop such cryptic remarks and I didn't like it. But there was no more time to ask questions as he whisked me forward, his hand gripping mine tightly. It was less a possessive motion than a seeking of solace.

A large crowd had gathered in a semicircle around an elegant bamboo table. The people of the Barras stood silent as we approached, strange in their myriad forms and races. They gleamed with a different sort of beauty than the Sidhe, limbs too long, ears too large, eyes too slanted and dark. Delicate wings, insectoid faces, animal ears, and pointed teeth. Row upon row of them stood in a muddle of tattered clothing and ragtag weapons, cloaked in an eerie elegance.

The Unseelie Court had been greatly diminished several hundred years ago. That Talivar had had something to do with it was fairly obvious, although he'd never given me the straight story. I knew it had something to do with his father and his own crippled anatomy, but I'd never learned more than the little bits Talivar had mentioned.

On the other hand, by the time I knew the Barras existed, I'd had far larger things on my mind than dredging up the past.

But here we were.

Kitsune stood formally at the far side of the table, her serene face as unreadable as always. Her ebony hair fell like black silk to her waist, her ears pricked delicately toward us. Phineas sat on the end of the table closest to me, troubled. I hadn't seen where they'd taken him, but he'd gotten the Emerald City treatment as well.

His coat shone like new-fallen snow, the short nub of his horn barely peeking through the fluffy mane.

Jimmy Squarefoot gave me a lopsided grin from where he stood, his snout twitching comically. My hand slipped from Talivar's as I approached the pigman hoping to give him a more proper greeting. Grunting something unintelligible at him before crawling into his wagon fell a little short of manners and I owed him more than that.

"Absinthe." He bowed to me formally, his ears flopping over his brow.

"Just Abby now." I glanced over at where Talivar now held quiet council with Kitsune. Absinthe had been the name I'd given when we first met. Names in Faerie tended to have power, and at the time I'd had no idea if I could trust the odd little figure.

"That's mighty kind of ye, but Absinthe does me fine." He paused, dragging his thick-knuckled fingers over his forehead. "Many things afoot here, ye ken. 'T'will be interesting to see what the prince does."

I frowned at him. "Does?"

He shifted uncomfortably, the cloth strips on his feet scraping against the dirt. "Aye. 'Tis a Faery matter, I suppose."

I sighed. "Isn't it always?"

Kitsune raised her pale white hands in some esoteric sign meant to indicate quiet was required. She had an impeccable sense of dramatic timing anyway. Her tail twitched behind her, showing a flash of soft white fur at the tip. Glancing at Talivar, she inclined her head. "Are you ready?"

He gave a stiff nod of his head, his chest rising sharply.

"As you will. I hereby bequeath the care of the Barras and the remainder of the Unseelie Court to the Crippled Prince, known henceforth as the Crippled King."

An excited murmur swept through the crowd, but I could only stare when he bowed, silent as she laid a small crown upon his brow. The moniker wasn't unfamiliar to me, but it was the first time I'd really seen him embrace it. Before it had always been said with a hint of mockery, the Fae condemning him for being physically flawed.

The crown was more of a circlet really—a delicate filigree of jet-black metal lit with its own fiery essence, and inset with a series of small blue gems. It fit him perfectly, confirming my suspicions that it had been made for him . . . most likely some time ago. Talivar gave a tight smile at my obvious confusion before turning to address the others.

"Two hundred years ago, my father used me as an excuse to decimate the Unseelie Court. You offered me sanctuary when my own people would not." He removed his patch, the puckered scar silvered in the torchlight. "Even now, I am made outcast by my own mother for not having the physical perfection the Sidhe insist upon."

There was the bitterness of truth in his voice and my heart ached to hear it. The Seelie Court was the flip side to the Unseelie—though its insistence on physical perfection in its rulers was only one of the dividing points between the two.

"I was granted rulership by Kitsune many years ago. I chose not to accept—but I see now that I will never be considered anything but imperfect by my

Seelie kin. And so I ask you to exercise your judgment upon me, that I might be found worthy of leading the Unseelie Court into a new time of prosperity."

"The outcast leading the outcasts," Phin said quietly as he hopped off the table to find his way to me. I scooped him up and backed away from the ceremony.

The crowd shuffled past me to circle around, gnarled fingers and elongated limbs reaching out to touch him. He'd closed his good eye, accepting their verdict, whatever it was, without complaint.

"Why do I suddenly feel like I'm on the Island of Misfit Toys?" I couldn't even muster the strength to laugh at my own joke, a sick sense of anticipation rolling through my stomach. There would be no turning back from whatever was happening here and I felt a pang of sorrow at the loss.

Naïve of me to think my life would ever return to normal, but some small part of me had actually enjoyed the idea of being his wife, even for a short while. The side of me that read romance novels, anyway.

I wasn't entirely sure how this was going to help our cause of getting the geas removed, but maybe as ruler of his own kingdom, Talivar would be able to negate it.

Talivar's shirt was removed, exposing the spiderwebbing of scar tissue down his left side. I turned away from this display when he started to slide his trousers away, the crippled leg shrunken and bowed without the external protection of his clothing.

Anger flushed through me, that he was forced to humiliate himself, but it was tempered with sadness. He'd shown me his scars before and they had never bothered me. After all, I had plenty of my own, both inside and out.

But that had been something private, and a selfish

part of me disliked sharing what he'd given me alone.

I understood his reasons, but handfasted to him or not, this was not my place.

I retreated toward the edge of the clearing as someone started a brisk tune on timpani, soon joined by a flute and a guitar.

"Guess it's time for the party?" I said nervously, trying to tamp down my rising panic and sliding sideways to let a gaggle of goblin children run past, giggling.

"They've got a lot to celebrate," Phineas pointed out. "The acceptance of an actual royal leader is a big step toward getting their kingdom back—and Talivar has just upset the political power base that's been in place for a very long time."

"So I gathered," I said dryly. "But I don't think I have it in me to become their Queen . . . assuming that's what he had in mind." And I didn't. While I had a vague understanding of the current circumstances, deep down a part of me resented the hell out of Talivar for putting me in this position. Which was probably unfair, but everything was happening so damned quick.

"It's not," Phineas murmured. "He would have run that by you first—I'm sure of it. Nothing's changed about your current relationship."

"I'm handfasted to a king, Phin. How is that 'unchanged'?"

A loud cheer rose behind us and I stifled a sigh as I headed back to find my tent.

Now that we were relatively safe, the weight of the geas gnawed at me. All well and good to lead the Barras into the civilized world, but I had things to do. The bells in my hair chimed in agreement.

A guilty flush passed over me at the thought of the

incubus. Where had he gone? My fingers drifted over the bells, twining in the thread. And how would he react knowing I'd become Talivar's wife? I wasn't sure if needing to escape the evil mother-in-law would be a good enough excuse.

I gratefully ducked into the relative quiet of my tent when I found it, glad to be out sight. Could I reach him in the Dreaming? Phineas squirmed in my arms and I set him down and lit a new taper; the old candle was sputtering out.

The ground resonated beneath my feet as the celebration hit its stride and I frowned.

E Nomine's "Mitternacht"?

"That sounds awful bassy for Faerie music." Images of a medieval Goth rave filled my head and for a moment I was tempted to take another peek.

The unicorn shrugged. "I suspect the technology you left behind was put to very good use." He flashed me a little grin. "At least it hasn't completely gone to waste on weaponry, anyway."

"Mmm. I'm not sure that was one of my wiser moves."

"It would have happened sooner or later. Better that it was at least offered in peace." He paused, ears swiveling as the beat of the music changed. "You sure you don't want to go back out there? Shake your groove thang?"

"Any other time maybe, but I'm not in the mood to dance tonight." There was too much on my mind to think of really cutting loose. Too many threads hanging without an answer, and I couldn't bring myself to be part of the festivities. I shook my head at the unicorn.

"Suit yourself." He gave a little whinny and ducked

out through the tent flaps, his tail twitching behind him.

I stared at the place where he'd been, feeling strangely empty. My fingers found the bells in my hair again and I stroked them so that they chimed. "What do I do now?"

They didn't answer. In the end, I spread out the blankets on the pallet beside the now cold tub. I realized I didn't know if Talivar would be joining me. Perhaps I should have gone to his tent? His *royal* tent?

Not that I knew where it was. A bitterness swept over me, tinged with horrible loneliness. A few weeks ago I'd made a deal with a daemon to try to save my friends. I'd never thought so much would happen in such a short time.

The hot rush of tears flooded my eyes and this time I didn't try to stop them. What a mess I'd made of my life. Despair crested until I was sobbing, my shoulders shaking in time as the beat changed into the Tom Jones version of "Black Betty."

Quaint. And oddly apropos.

I may have been Talivar's wife in name, but I was still in the dark as much as I'd ever been. That he hadn't trusted me with his plans hurt me far worse than I'd realized.

On the other hand, it was unlikely he'd had much time to think about it on the road. It was entirely possible he had fallen victim to Kitsune's opportunism. I doubted the fox-woman did anything out of an altruistic heart.

Nothing to be done about it now.

But I could still do something about Ion.

I'd told myself I'd been too injured or too tired to try entering the Dreaming the last several nights, but I knew the truth and I was terrified. If Brystion was truly gone? And I'd been the one to kill him, even unknowingly?

Chickenshit, Abby.

I wiped the wetness from my cheeks, feeling like an ass for breaking down. "Only one way to find out," I murmured to the flickering candle. If I could assess what had happened to him, I'd be better able to move forward.

I curled into a ball. Outside, the music continued to thrum away and my heart picked up the beat, vibrating in time until I slipped into sleep.

Seven

Ripples in the darkness.

The pit of my stomach dropped to find myself here again, the waves pinched with a deceptive stillness. A current stirred by my toes, the brush of something large sending chills through my legs. I swallowed hard against a rising panic, and the cotton dryness of my mouth flushed with salt as a whitecap slapped me in the face.

My breathing went shallow, the rise and fall of my chest echoed in the hammering of my heart. Dimly I reached for the training Bryston's sister, Sonja, had started with me, trying to find the last bit of calm to gather my power around me and consciously control the Dreaming.

Shield . . .

I imagined a white light, fitting it to my skin and pushing out. Something scraped my calf and I bit back a whimper, the hot warmth of my blood spilling into the stinging sea.

Don't move . . .

Push. Push. Push.

I got a basic handle on it, finally opening my eyes to find myself glowing, the edges of my shield a few inches away from my body. It was enough.

I stifled a scream as the first shark rolled past me, its tail propelling its massive form with a slow ease. No rushing in for the kill yet.

The bells in my hair chimed mockingly. *What are you afraid of? You* died. *What could possibly frighten you here?*

Get over yourself.

The thought splashed over me even as anger flooded my limbs. It was right.

Was I simply a hapless dreamer?

"No," I whispered. "No." I was a KeyStone. Touch-Stone to the King of the Unseelie Court. Daughter of True Thomas. I'd worn the Key to the CrossRoads. I'd made a deal with the devil and come back from the dead.

I was a motherfucking *Dreamer.*

The power exploded from me in a heated shimmer, white flame pushing away the darkness, the thick sense of nothingness enveloping me against the glare. For a moment I caught the slivered edge of a dorsal fin slicing past me and then it skittered away into the void.

A momentary thrill of victory swelled my chest as I realized I'd actually managed to thrust my nightmares into some far distant corner. Not defeated, of course. I wasn't sure if the darkness that lingered in my psyche would ever truly be lifted . . . but this was a start.

What had Sonja told me that one time?

You limit yourself to your own sense of physics.

The bells sounded a soft ring of agreement and I scowled at them, the shield settling into a slightly less obnoxious glow.

"Float," I commanded, watching as it became more of a sphere. I shrugged at myself. Glinda the Good Witch it would have to be. Abruptly, the water around me receded and the bubble propelled itself upward. My hands stretched out as though to lean against the curved walls, but I hesitated, unsure if it would pop should I touch it.

Which was ridiculous since I was standing on the thing. I let my fingers slide against the surface of the shield, a thrum of power racing up my palms to my elbow.

A tingle pulsed in my chest. *Home.*

The bubble shifted direction, leaving the cold blackness of the sea behind it. I'd traveled this way once before, only Brystion had been the one to create and control it. The memory of it clung to me in an un-subtle reminder of what had happened next, the way our lives had entwined and the betrayal afterward.

And still. Where had he gone?

Beneath me, the sea faded away. The sharks did not make another appearance, but I kept a watchful eye anyway. I had my momentum; I wasn't sure if I'd be able to get it again if I let my defenses drop.

Where was the Heart of my Dreaming? I peered into the darkness, straining to see the shadow of the old Victorian, the iron gate around it, but in the end there was nothing but fog. I hesitated, not wanting to press my luck too far. Sonja had told me I had the power to be a DreamWalker during our training, and Ion had actually shown me the Dreaming Hearts of others, but the last thing I wanted was to stumble into someone else's dreams.

Not like this.

On the other hand, I didn't want to wander around in

this void for too much longer. And if I stumbled across the CrossRoads? An uncomfortable twist roiled in my gut. Would the Queen's geas apply even here? This was not the time to find out. Besides, even if I could make it to the CrossRoads from here, my body would still be in Faerie. Without Ion or Sonja to help me back to the Dreaming, my physical body would die.

I didn't want to do that again either.

"A few more minutes and I'll try to wake up," I told myself. Worry niggled at me. Where the hell was my Heart? I'd always been able to find it before.

The mist began to dissipate as my brow furrowed and I realized I was standing in the burned-out remains of a forest. Charred and blackened bark peeled away from a crumpled willow tree, its leaves nothing more than tattered bits.

I stared at it. I knew this tree. This was *my* tree. From my garden behind my . . . house. I stood up with a jerk, pacing away from the fallen giant. My foot scraped against concrete. I knelt and the shield faded, taking away most of the light. I'd have been more concerned about that, but my attention was on the bricks I'd stumbled upon. The foundation.

My fingers traced a circle in the soot. The house at the center of my Dreaming Heart had burned too. What the hell had happened?

A lump formed in my throat. All those memories . . . but they were *my* memories. I could remake this place.

Assuming there was enough of it left to respond.

"What now?" My voice sounded hollow in my ears. If I was expecting an answer from Ion's bells, it wasn't forthcoming.

"Abby?"

I startled, rising to my feet to see Sonja standing there. Her eyes were wide with confusion, her blood-red wings arching protectively behind her.

"Sonja. What happened here?"

The succubus lowered her wings, still staring. "We thought you were dead. That Maurice had killed you."

I snorted. "He did. I managed to bounce back. I'm lucky like that."

She let out a sob. "Oh gods, Abby. When we heard the news—"

"Where's Ion?" I cut off her rambling. It wasn't like the succubus to be so hesitant. "What the hell happened to my Heart?"

She blinked at me. "You died. When a mortal dies, their Dreaming Heart is extinguished. You were *gone.*"

"Well, I'm here now," I said dryly. "More or less."

She grasped my hands as though she didn't quite believe it. "You have to come to Portsmyth. Right now."

"I can't. The Queen laid a geas on me. I can't leave Faerie at all." I let out a bitter chuckle. "And, of course, it gets even more complicated than that, but I'm working on it. Talivar too." I decided I didn't want to go into the handfasting thing just yet. "What about Ion? Something . . . happened . . . didn't it?" I pulled the bells from my hair. "And I was left with this. I thought I'd killed him somehow."

She shook her head, her gaze drawn to the bells. "No. He's not dead, but he's changed . . . I've been coming here the last few nights to try to find out the truth, but when I saw that your Heart was nothing more than a husk, I feared the worst."

"Changed how? There's something you're not telling me."

A soft sigh escaped the succubus. "It would be better if you could see it for yourself. He is all right for now, but . . ."

"Why can't he come meet me here?" I nodded at the ruined foundation. "Surely that would be easier? I'll wait."

A sad smile flickered over her face. "He's not the same man he was, Abby. He can no longer find his way to your Heart."

"He *what*?" The idea was incomprehensible. "That makes no sense. He's an incubus. He was born of the Dreaming. Hell, he lived here for—what—a year?"

She gave me a wry look. "I'm not entirely sure of the details. You know how stubborn he is—he won't tell me what he tried to do."

I rolled the bells in between my fingers. "He tried to rescue me," I said hoarsely. "I was supposed to bring him back with me to the palace through the Dreaming . . . but something must have gone wrong."

"I'll say," she muttered. "I'm going to find him and let him know you're okay. That should calm him down some and we'll see what we can do about breaking your geas. There's nearly always a loophole to these things."

"Talivar didn't think so."

"I'm a *daemon*, Abby. Believe me, there's *always* a way." Her smile became a bit more feral and predatory than I liked, a subtle reminder that she wasn't always the nicest of creatures. Which reminded me . . .

"Oh. Um. This is going to sound sort of odd, but when I died, I bumped into Topher. He had a message for you."

The blood drained from her face. "What did he say?"

"Well, the long and short of it is that he admits

the punishment you administered was fair." I shuddered, not really wanting to remember it. "But he said he left something for you. He said you would know where."

Her lip curled. "If you were not my friend I would kill you for telling me that." The anger drained from her as she looked about my Dreaming Heart. "But you did die . . . and you couldn't possibly have known."

"Do you know what he meant?"

"Yes. It can rot, along with him." She whirled savagely away from me. "I will meet you in the Barras tomorrow and we'll see what can be done."

Her wings unfolded with a violent crack, propelling her upward and into the darkness. I caught a flicker of silver in the distance that might have been the Cross-Roads, but it was gone before I could really tell.

Still reeling from the news of Brystion's inability to come here, I sank to my knees, my fingers trailing in the dried-out leaves. Pissing off his sister hadn't been high on my to-do list, but at least I was a little closer to answers and a plan. Knowing that the others would be made aware of my plight made me grateful and a little less alone, and that was far more comfort than I'd expected.

As for this place . . .

I glanced about at the ruins. "Might as well get started." My hands dug into the dirt, and I closed my eyes, commanding the Dreaming to bend to my will. Grass . . . trees . . . the moon? The power drifted through me, the bells in my hands seeming to chime in approval. Odd how much easier it seemed this time.

The scent of something green filled my nose and I concentrated harder. When I had first arrived here last year, everything had been in place. The house, the forest, the sea . . . all of it built in my subconscious through all the years of my life. Memories upon memories.

I didn't want to try to re-create that now, but at the very least I could make it more pleasant than the char it currently was.

A cool softness burst beneath my feet and tickled my palms. A cricket chirped beside me, the insectoid violinist making me smile. Silver-bladed glass gleamed in the moonlight, growing over the foundation of the house, cloaking the ugliness in greenery.

Saplings thrust up from the ground, and the air was filled with tiny seedlings, white puffballs of potential, sifting through the night sky. At least I could do this much.

"Good enough," I muttered, rolling onto my back to gaze up at the moon. The little details could come later. "Time to wake up."

"Abby." Talivar's voice murmured to me in the darkness.

"I'm awake. I think." I rolled onto my side to see him sprawled out beside me, the last of the candle guttering on the table. The dull thrum of the music no longer vibrated through the ground so I could only guess that the festivities were over. The noisy part, anyway.

"You disappeared." His words weren't a true accusation as much as a statement of fact, but there was hurt behind it anyway.

"I didn't want to be a distraction." I paused. "Your Majesty."

He grimaced, his head flopping onto his hands. "I've been avoiding that particular title for longer than I care to say."

"So why now? And why didn't you tell me?"

"I hadn't planned on it," he said after a moment. "But it seemed like a good idea at the time." He cupped my cheek. "It doesn't matter. It's all just politics."

I snorted. "Is it?"

"Well, not *all* of it." His mouth met mine for an instant. "Not this part."

He shifted so that he was lying on top of me, the warmth of his body flooding my limbs. I didn't really think about it as I kissed him, a sudden need to be wanted filling me with a terrible desire.

And yet . . .

"Bryston," I whispered. "He's alive. Sonja told me. I met her, in the Dreaming."

He pulled back, his gaze unreadable. "A bit unromantic to bring him into our marital bed, don't you think?"

I turned away from him. "Maybe. But, Talivar . . . I don't think I can be your Queen. I don't know if I'm ready for that."

A low chuckle escaped him. "I know. Which is why I've only declared you my TouchStoned consort at the moment. The handfasting is sufficient. No one would be surprised if I took a while to find a Queen, given the circumstances." His mouth twisted wryly. "And quite frankly, I've other things on my mind at the moment."

He pressed a finger to my lips. "I am more than willing to share you—rather than lose you completely."

But would Bryston agree to that?

My inner voice remained silent. Hell, I didn't even know if *I* could agree to that. Once again, circumstances beyond my control were sweeping past me, and far too quickly than I liked.

I went silent, allowing him to pull me into his arms. His hand stroked my hair.

"Does this concept displease you so? What is it you want, Abby?"

"I wish I knew," I muttered. "I could do the clichéd thing and mention how I want my old life back, but I suspect it's long gone . . ." I shook my head. "I need to know who you are, Talivar. I know the you that I lived with for so long, but this other side of you? The royal side? Ever since we came into Faerie there's been a stranger in your skin."

I let out a breath I hadn't realized I'd been holding as he stiffened. "One minute you're all full of secrets and then I look at your eyes and I'm back teaching you the Hustle on a Saturday night at the Hallows. I can't make the two fit together. I'm letting you manipulate my destiny for a chance at escape, but that's not what I want. For either of us."

The prince sighed and held me a little tighter. For a few minutes I didn't think I was going to get an answer. Finally he shook himself and got to his feet. "Come on. Let's go for a walk."

"It's a little late, isn't it?" I took his proffered hand anyway, my bad knee cracking slightly as he pulled me toward him.

He smirked. "It's good to be the King."

"Someone's been watching too many movies," I said dryly, but I made no protest when he slipped his cloak over my shoulders.

"Ah well. They haven't thought to start posting guards around me yet, so we don't have to do anything drastic for a night out." He took my hand and the two of us emerged from the tent into a quiet row. "Not that sneaking around isn't fun," he murmured, leading me through a winding path between the tents and away from the Barras proper.

Here and there I caught the low sound of music and the muffled clink of glasses, indicating the celebrating was still going on. I felt a guilty twinge. I was taking him away from this. It seemed rather selfish of me.

A high-pitched cry of pleasure rose and fell from a nearby tent. I flushed hotly despite myself when Talivar squeezed my hand, but couldn't bring myself to look at him. We'd made love only once—but even that had been under some rather awkward circumstances.

It had, however, involved a hot spring And I wouldn't have minded revisiting *that* particular scenario.

Beside me, Talivar let out a snort, but he said nothing else until we were past the makeshift paddock filled with drowsing horses. The prince glanced down at me, the remains of the flickering torchlight illuminating part of his face.

"Kitsune and I are cousins, you know. Distant ones, to be sure, but our bloodlines do share a commonality, through my father's family."

"The same father who had you crippled?" I said it bluntly. Hell, there was no point in dancing around the subject at this point. Besides, we were married.

He gave me a strained smile and started walking again and we began to climb the soft grass of the steep hillside beside the encampment. "Aye. My mother couldn't stand it, knowing that Unseelie filth ran through my veins . . . even if it didn't really show, save for the facial hair." His mouth pursed. "But my father's beard never seemed to bother her when he had it, so who knows?"

"She's a woman of . . . peculiar appetites."

Which was putting it mildly. She was batshit crazy. He shrugged, limping slightly as we crested the hill, the two of us sagging to rest on a fallen log. Below us, the lights of the Barras twinkled merrily, shadows dancing around the center with ragged fluidity. Talivar stared down at this, his face lost in thought for a moment.

"I told you I had that tunnel made in my garden so that I could court the village girls." A smile touched his lips. "Partially true. When I was younger, I tended to be more bold about my exploits. The Unseelie Court was different and exciting, compared to my own."

I snorted. "You don't have to explain it to me. I've seen it, remember?" If I'd had to live in the palace on a permanent basis I'd have gnawed my own feet off to get away. I didn't mention this aloud, but he raised his brow at me anyway. I coughed and he chuckled.

"My family's differences aside, I was very fond the Unseelie Court. Kitsune and I became quite close. Not romantically so; she was more like a sister than anything else. It was tolerated on both sides for a while, perhaps simply to foster goodwill between the two kingdoms."

"But . . . ?" I nudged him with a gentle elbow.

The words drummed out in a monotonic flatness. "I was caught courting an Unseelie maiden. That was considered a problem, at least for my mother."

"They asked you to stay away and you didn't?" My heart ached for the boy he had been.

"Why would I? The threats were always hollow . . . and even if I occasionally gave in to them, the night would come when the moon would be out and the summer winds sang a heat into my blood that bade me to creep from my window to see her."

For a moment I was tempted to ask what she looked

like, but what did it matter? It certainly wasn't any business of mine.

I let my head drift to lean against his shoulder, a soft breeze sneaking under my cloak to set a trail of goose bumps over my arms. We sat there for a few minutes and a contented warmth flushed over me.

A soft sigh escaped him. "And one morning as I left our trysting spot I was ambushed by what I assumed were nobles of the Unseelie Court. I thought they were merely unhappy with my liaisons with the girl. I expected they'd rough me up a little and let me go. After all, I was the prince of Faerie. Even if they intended something more, a ransom would not have been out of the question and would have netted them far more than my death."

A bitter chuckle shook him, the muscles of his arms tensing at the memory. "They killed her outright before me, slicing her throat as though she was merely an afterthought." He paused. "Which I suppose she was, to them."

"Jesus, Talivar. I'm so sorry."

His mouth twitched, the stalwart veneer finally starting to crack. He'd been holding back on this for a long time . . . but I could understand why. How do you explain that the last woman you courted ended up being butchered simply for loving you?

His nostrils flared. "I fought, of course, but in the end there were too many of them. They crushed my knee and took my eye and left me to lie in her blood upon the road."

I frowned at him, my hand lightly brushing his bad leg. "But I thought your father did this to you. Isn't that what you told me?"

"Oh, my father's men were quick enough to demand recompense from the Unseelie Court for the injury caused to me. The Court, of course, refused, claiming they had nothing to do with it."

An uncomfortable thought wended its way through my mind. "It was a setup, wasn't it?"

He glanced down at me with an inscrutable gaze. "Aye," he murmured. "My father's own machinations gave me these injuries. His people carried it out . . . all for an excuse to crush the Unseelie Court beneath his boot once and for all. I was to make sure I accused the right people, of course."

"But the Fae can't lie," I pointed out. "So that makes no sense."

"Lying is not the same as omitting information. The fact that my father neglected to mention his part in the ruse means nothing. And no one would think of questioning the king directly. At the time, I myself had assumed it was the Unseelie Court that had attacked me—my father saw no reason to dissuade me from that opinion. Kitsune begged me to give her time to find out who my true attackers had been. At the very least, she could help turn them over to my father, instead of having the two Courts at war over me." He sighed. "When I refused to testify in the interim, my father was so furious he forbade the healers from seeing to me." A grim smile crossed his face. "And you've seen the outcome of that."

"I can't believe Moira would have stood by and let that happen. Your mother?"

"Ah, but Moira was only a little thing then. She had no real power. No way of influencing the Court." His head tipped downward. "And my mother's motivations have always been nebulous. I suspect there was a part of her just as happy to see me taken down a peg. I was already damaged goods by that point."

"Making room for her daughter." I scowled. "Moira told me as much. But your own family, Talivar? Those are the people who are supposed to be looking out for you."

He gave me a wry smile. "You said it yourself. Sometimes family isn't about what you're born into, so much as the family you make." His forehead dropped to rest on mine and my arms curled around his neck as he pulled me onto his lap. He buried his face in my hair, clinging to me tightly. So much pain and he'd borne it for so very long.

"When Kitsune found me again, bearing evidence of my father's betrayal, I confronted him. He had me whipped before the court as a traitor. It was the only excuse he needed to invade the Unseelie Court. The Barras arose from the ashes of the aftermath of that battle, and I . . . I killed my father for it."

His fingers curled, biting into my shoulder. "I tore out his throat with my bare hands, Abby . . . and spent the next twenty years running from the justice of the Court. Eventually I claimed sanctuary at the Barras and Kitsune took me in, giving me a chance to negotiate the terms of my surrender." He waved his hand off in the direction of the tents with a weary snarl. "The rest of it can wait for another night. And so now you know what sort of man your husband is."

I tightened my grip, all the pieces sliding into place. "For a prince, your life sure as hell hasn't been very charming," I murmured, pushing the hair away from his forehead. His blue eye glittered in the fading starlight and I kissed him.

"Not until now." His mouth brushed mine, gently

sliding over my cheeks and my chin, breath puffing against my face. "And if I have cause to love you for accepting me as I am, then so be it. There are worse reasons to love someone."

I made a muffled sound of agreement at him as he kissed me again. This time his tongue darted out to skim the inside of my lips. Unusual for him to be so aggressive, but given what he'd just told me, I could understand his sudden need to assert himself.

I nipped him hard, pulling back to hold his face in my hands. "I do love you, Talivar. I do. But where can this go? You're going to live a very long time, and I'm not. You're going to have responsibilities that I can't help you with."

And it was true. I did love him. I could even run with the "friends with benefits" concept for a while if it wasn't going to be long term—but I couldn't give him my heart blindly. Maybe that made me more pragmatic than romantic, but I didn't have time for romance.

Not until I got my own life straightened out, anyway.

On the other hand, who knew when *that* would happen? Dying had shown me that I couldn't take my time for granted. Here and now was what it was, and there was something sacred about that too.

The elf hummed against my throat, punctuated by a series of tiny kisses. "The future holds what it holds," he said finally, echoing my thoughts. "We cannot predict it. I have sat by the wayside of my own life for far too long, waiting for the right thing to happen at the right time. Trying to be the good man. The faithful son. The supportive brother. The cast-aside prince."

He paused, one hand hovering over the expanse of

thigh exposed by the riding-up edge of my dress. "Tell me to stop, and I will."

"You *are* a good man, Talivar. Don't stop."

The ambiguous nature of my answer wasn't lost on either of us. He didn't stop to question it and I didn't try to clarify. For the moment, I didn't want to think of anything at all. I knew any chance of us ever being a normal couple was pretty much nil, and tomorrow those chances would be narrower still.

But tonight was still tonight. I pulled him down so that we tipped into the grass. A moment later and my breasts were freed, the neckline of the dress shredded. My nipples perked in the chilly night air; he let out a groan and fell upon them in a frenzy of gentle teeth and hard tongue, suckling one while his fingers paid court to the other.

My back arched and he moved over me, one arm wrapping beneath my waist to pull me closer. My fingers drifted into his hair, sliding over his pointed ears. His breath hitched at the attention, halting the rhythm of his mouth, and he broke off long enough to give me a hot, sloe-eyed glance.

I couldn't quite keep the teasing smile from crossing my face, and tweaked the point of his ear. He bared his teeth in a snarl before returning to my breasts, the tips already aching at his momentary abandonment.

"I thought you said next time we'd be doing this in your bed." I wiggled my hips at him in jest, my knees parting to let him sprawl between them. One hand slid up my thigh to give my ass a pinch.

"I can stop," he said mildly, but his face told a different story. "Of course, then I'd have to stop doing this . . . and this . . . and *this*." Each word was punctuated by a knuckle brushing over my sex, spreading me farther apart to dip into the wetness there.

"Uh. No." I fisted my hand in his hair, shuddering as a wash of pleasure swept through me.

"Thought not." He smiled at my whimper even as he fumbled with the belt at his waist, undoing the laces of his trews with quick fingers. I reached down to guide him toward me, his erection butting into my palm.

He let out a strained hiss as I stroked him, shuddering when I slid the edge of his pants down over the curve of his ass. Mouth tracing a heated trail between my breasts to my neck, he rolled on top of me, silencing my panting groans with a kiss. A moment later and he was inside me, hips shifting in a slow and easy rhythm. The frantic flutter in my belly quieted with each thrust.

Odd to be rutting on a hillside above the tattered remains of a kingdom, but here I was.

I said as much and he smiled against my mouth, capturing my soft cry when he angled me upward and sped up the pace. My hand roamed over the still-clothed shoulders and over the bare patch of skin at his waist, curling into the curve of his ass to spur him along.

He growled softly, nipping at my lower lip. "Wife."

The sound of the word vibrated through me, driving home the reality of my situation. Also? I suddenly realized we weren't using any protection. I opened my mouth to make this point, but he cut me off with another kiss, even as he reached between us to stroke my clit.

And then I was coming, a slow, rolling orgasm that left me gasping, my head tilting back in the grass. My nails bit into his flesh as his teeth grazed my ear, his own breath coming in hoarse groans. He stiffened, mumbling my name into my neck, sprawling on top of me with a last exhalation.

We lay there, entwined and silent except for the hurried huff of our breathing and the muted chirps of nearby crickets. Talivar's fingers feathered through the tangle of my hair, the bun long since come undone.

My questioning brain had fallen silent, sated by answers and the soft thrum of pleasure that continued to ripple over my skin. He rolled over and tucked me in beside him, wrapping the cloak over both of us.

For a moment I debated bringing up the lack-of-protection thing, but what would be the point? What was done was done.

And I still needed to find a way to get home.

"Love you," he murmured, shifting me in his arms so that his body curled tightly around me.

My eyes drifted shut at this admission, but somehow I couldn't quite manage to say it back. If he noticed, he said nothing, and a moment later, I slid away into the darkness of sleep, his breath light against my neck.

Eight

Morning came in a fog of warmth. I was no longer outside, wrapped in the dew and my lover's cloak like some sort of vagabond romance heroine. I was disappointed by this, although the feather-stuffed bedding beneath me was probably a hell of a lot more comfortable than wet grass.

Judging by Talivar's pile of belongings in one corner I was probably in his tent. It certainly wasn't mine, though how I got here I couldn't remember. The elf in question was nowhere to be seen.

I rolled over with a sigh, tension knotting my stomach. Even though we'd only been traveling for a few days, I had the sick sense that my life was slipping away. How much time had passed in the mortal world? Would I arrive home only to find my mortal friends were now far older than me?

Sonja's words pattered through my brain. If they all thought I'd died . . .

My nostrils flared as I bit back a rush of panic. Sonja would tell them. She had to. Visions of being trapped on the wrong side of some invisible wall, shouting at people to hear me, filled my head.

Oh, but I had been there too, hadn't I? Maurice had trapped me in a painting . . . and Ion had been the one to find me. The others had helped set me free. The thought of waiting for them to do it again was irritating in the extreme.

I traced my fingers around my neck. The abrasions were slowly fading, but some part of me knew I would never really be whole again. The bells in my hair chimed, but there was something mocking about the sound. The weight of it pressed heavy on my chest.

Abruptly, I threw off the cloak. I was still dressed in the shredded remains of the blue silk thing from the night before, but I was done with looking prim and proper.

I wanted some pants, goddammit.

"You decent?"

Before I could even answer, a white muzzle slipped through the tent flap.

Phineas blinked owlishly at me. "You're awake?"

"Obviously. And nice of you to knock."

"Not like I haven't seen it all before."

I scowled at him. "Don't remind me. Be useful for once and help me find something to wear." I looked around the tent. "That's not a skirt," I added.

"Not planning on being barefoot and pregnant in the kitchen for the next few years?" He arched a brow, narrowly dodging out of the way of my swiftly following foot. "Joking."

"Fine. Whatever." I waved him away, fighting between the urge to pace around the room or simply sink to my knees in despair. What the hell was wrong with me? "Where's Talivar?"

Phineas shrugged. "He was called away to do something kingly, no doubt. A liaison from the Faery Court arrived this morning, demanding your return."

"Word gets around fast." I frowned at the inside of the tent, finally snatching up Talivar's cloak to throw it over my shoulders. "Don't suppose they've got anything to eat out there."

"Mmmph." He paused, his ears twitching. "Nobu is here too."

A chill ran through me at the mention of the daemon's name. "Shit. I was sorta hoping the Tithe thing would go away."

I stared at Phin, panic lurching in my heart. "You don't think he's here to try to . . . uh . . . collect me?"

"I suspect your husband would have something to say about that. Besides, the time limit's not up yet. He'd have no cause."

"Wonderful." I poked my head outside the tent flap, relieved to see the usual hustle had apparently slowed down some. Phineas brushed up against my leg and I glanced down at him. "Why are we still here, anyway? I thought the Barras was required to be on the move every twenty-four hours."

"There's a lot that's changed," he said quietly. "The rules of the game reset when Talivar took the crown."

"I'm not even remotely interested in playing. I just want to get out of here." I slipped out of the tent and struck out into the now somewhat familiar mishmash of awnings and encampments. "But first, I'm going to get some new rags if it kills me."

Not that I had anything to pay for it with—but hell, I was the King's TouchStone and consort. That ought to be enough to get me something on credit.

I trotted down the makeshift rows for a while, vaguely aware that I was in the Lower Crescent. "Now, where the hell is the Hive . . ."

"Perhaps I might be able to help with that?" Nobu's smooth voice purred from the shadows. He moved beside me with all the grace the bulk of his dark wings would allow, which was considerable. He was dressed far more conservatively than I'd seen him before, his spiky hair dyed a muted dark blue at the tips. "You're a rather hard person to get ahold of, Abby Sinclair."

I tried not to flinch and kept on walking. "Death will do that to a person."

"Clever girl." His voice held smug amusement.

"There was nothing clever about it," I snapped, whirling on him. "If you think I did it simply to get out of our deal, then you're mistaken. Believe it or not, I actually do honor my word. And if I was going to try to escape I sure as hell wouldn't have chosen to get my head half bashed in to do it!"

His face sobered. "For what it's worth, I actually believe you."

"Serves you right anyway." I turned away and kept walking.

"You've grown a stiffer spine since I last saw you. Interesting."

I waved him off, marching toward the first storefront that appeared to sell clothing. "I don't think we actually have any business, Nobu. So if you're here to chat, you can be on your way."

He eyed my neck. "I can no longer sense the Key's presence. It's true, then? That Maurice escaped with it?"

I stiffened, not needing Phin's warning cough at my ankle to keep my mouth shut. "Does it matter?"

"It might." He tugged on my hair, pausing when the bells chimed. "Faery owes us the Tithe, true . . ."

"You tricked me with the lethe bullshit, so don't come crying to me because I inadvertently spoiled your plans."

"You haven't technically spoiled anything," he said mildly. "One way or the other the Tithe must be filled."

"My wife will not be filling it," Talivar said coolly, shoving his way between us and removing Nobu's hand from my arm. The prince was an imposing figure in his own right. "And unless you have any further business here, you are no longer welcome in my kingdom."

The daemon blinked, his dark eyes darting between me and Talivar. "How very interesting, indeed." He bowed formally. "Another time, perhaps, Your Highness."

"I doubt that." Talivar's gaze held steady as the winged daemon strode off.

The prince finally tore himself away as Nobu disappeared into the crowd. "What did he want from you?"

"The Key. He wanted to know if I still had it."

Talivar glanced in the direction Nobu had gone. "He's up to something."

I snorted. "Who isn't? I didn't give him an answer, but he probably figured it out anyway. What can I do about it? Maybe if he knows I don't have it, he can go bother Maurice." Which would be a total disaster. The thought of Hell holding that sort of power was mind-numbing.

I pointed at a pair of leather trousers hanging from one of the nearby stalls. "What I really want right now is those."

The prince's mouth twitched. "Anything for milady."

Ten minutes later found me finally clothed in the low-slung pants, a loose top, and a bodice that was a tad tight for my liking, but it would do well enough. At least I didn't have to deal with skirts; that was a small miracle in itself.

"You're tense," Talivar observed.

I bit my lip. "What happens if I don't fill the Tithe? Does that mean someone else has to go in my place? Some random mortal the Queen accidentally picks up?" I supposed there were people I wouldn't mind being sacrificed too much, but I couldn't make that judgment call.

His mouth became grim. "If we cannot find a mortal, then we must sacrifice seven of our own people. Faery souls are apparently not as valuable."

I shook my head. "I don't know if I can do this. I've been so focused on getting myself out of this mess that I didn't even think about what would happen if I actually succeeded."

He grabbed me by the shoulders. "This isn't for you to decide, Abby. I will not lose you again . . . not even to your own sense of nobility."

"But I made the deal with Nobu. I offered myself up—should someone else pay for that?"

"You made the bargain with Nobu, true—but the Queen is the one who agreed to the Tithe to begin with. It was her . . . weakness that allowed the daemons to get as much of a foothold as they did. It is on her head to find a solution to this."

I let out a humorless chuckle. "Because *that's* worked out so damn well thus far. Besides, you and I both know her solution is to find me and force me into the being the Tithe anyway, so where does that get us?"

"Touché," Phineas murmured at our feet. "Speaking of which, I'm assuming that's what the liaison wanted to talk to you about?"

"Something like that," the prince said dryly. "The Seelie Court isn't willing to recognize my claim yet, but they don't actually have much choice in the matter, and Kitsune refused to have anything to do with their envoy without me there. I was actually on my way to meet with him—and I thought Abby should come. After all, it concerns her too." He squeezed my hand gently, slipping his fingers between mine. "I would not deliberately keep such secrets from you."

The thought warmed me despite the way my heart beat faster. Such a coward, I chided myself.

The three of us wended through the Barras. Things had picked up and the usual crowds were building in a brilliant cacophony of sound. Polite nods were offered to Phin and me as we walked past, but it seemed less than I would have expected, considering Talivar was their new liege.

"Under new management," I muttered.

Talivar shot me an amused glance. "It may take a while for people to get used to the idea. I'm not in a particular rush to formalize things."

"Do we know who the liaison is?" Not that I had influence with any of them, but if I knew who it was, I could at least attempt to tailor my response accordingly. With all the time I'd spent in the Court, I knew a few individuals who weren't too bad, even if the rest were stuffy-assed prigs.

Talivar let out a grunt. "It's the Steward."

I frowned, my footsteps slowing. "My father is here?"

I'd barely seen him since I drank the lethe—and

certainly not in any official capacity, though I began to wonder if that was more the Queen's doing or if he'd avoided me to spare me her wrath.

I stifled a snort. If so, that hadn't worked out too well.

"It makes sense." Talivar gave my hand a squeeze. "My ascent to the 'throne' is going to be troublesome for any number of factions . . . as is the fact that you're with me. Breaking protocol is all well and good, but eventually it catches up with you."

"I'm surprised Moira didn't come, honestly."

He shrugged. "She may have tried. More likely she declined, in order to assure people that she has no plans to defect to this Court."

"Shit makes my head spin," I muttered, rubbing my temples. I couldn't keep half this stuff straight on a good day, but every time I turned around now it seemed as though there was a new law or rule or something just waiting to be broken. I was a little tired of dealing with consequences I had no control over.

Kitsune's tent loomed over the next row, the familiar scent of ginger wafting on the air. I let go of Talivar's hand. I wanted to face my father under my own power here, even if it was in this small way.

Two elvish guards of the Sidhe Court flanked the tent. Talivar inclined his head to them as he pulled back the tent flap, but they stared straight ahead.

I didn't know how things were supposed to work between Courts as far as respect went, but the way things were shaking out I wasn't sure if Talivar had gotten quite as good a deal as he thought. He ducked inside and I followed, blinking as I adjusted to the shadowed interior.

Kitsune knelt before her usual table, her hands

folded primly before her. The fox-woman was nothing if not a master at masking her emotions. I'd hardly ever seen her appear anything other than serene.

Her tail flicked when she saw us, an unreadable warning flashing on her face. "The Steward of Elfland has some rather interesting news to share." She gestured to him with an elegant hand.

My father sat cross-legged on the other side of the table, his expression nearly as emotionless, but I could see the strain in the pinch of his cheeks. He tugged the edges of his waistcoat. "The Queen has been removed from the throne," he said without preamble, but I thought I detected a shiver in the tone of his voice.

And with good reason, really. As nuts as she was, she had still been his lover for hundreds of years. She was the mother of at least one of his children. He'd been with her in one capacity or another for longer than I could comprehend any rational relationship lasting. But somehow it had.

Talivar stilled at his words. "And Moira?"

"Soon to be crowned the new Queen." My father exhaled heavily. "She would have your council."

The alarm bells rang in the back of my head, echoed by the sound of the bells in my hair. As estranged as we were, my father hadn't even acknowledged my presence. Rude in the extreme, but now that I thought about it, he hadn't even come by to see me after I'd died. The thought hurt more than I liked to admit, but I shook it off.

"What about me? My geas? Will she be lifting that? Getting rid of the Tithe?" I pushed past Talivar to kneel at Thomas's side, my tone brusque. My father's eyes barely flickered, never leaving Kitsune's face.

"I don't know, Abby."

I rolled back on my heels. "I suppose I shouldn't be surprised. You can't even look at me to tell me the truth of it. Why are you even here?"

Now he *did* turn toward me and it took all I had not to retreat beneath the coldness that lay within his gaze. Ageless or not, my father looked . . . old. Weary. He was still handsome, certainly, but there was a tiredness about him that I didn't remember from before. "I volunteered."

"As what? A messenger boy?"

"As a hostage, Abby." Talivar's hand lowered to my shoulder. "Isn't that right, Thomas?"

The bard nodded. "Both to alleviate any suspicion on the part of the Courts, and also as a guarantee that the Queen will not attempt anything untoward." His mouth twitched. "Any more than she usually might."

"Because *that's* so reassuring." I rubbed at my forehead. "So now what?"

Kitsune poured me a cup of tea, indicating I should drink it. "Now you see why I wanted you here."

"Yeah. But can we really trust this? The Queen would never give up her power willingly—and sure as hell not under these circumstances." I exhaled slowly. "You've met the woman. I doubt she does anything for anyone but herself."

The fox-woman shrugged. "It was not always that way, though I have felt the brunt of her wrath more than once."

An understatement if I'd ever heard it, but most of the denizens of the Barras had felt the Faery Queen's high-handedness in one form or another. Two hundred years was a long time to live in exile.

My father said nothing, which wasn't particularly reassuring, but Talivar nodded. "I will go. To alert them of the changes here, if nothing else. Family not-withstanding, I suspect Moira's request for council may alter somewhat once she discovers the situation."

Thomas's expression became wistful. "For what it's worth, lad, you have my support." His attention fell on me. "You both do."

There might have been a hidden meaning behind those words, but it was too little and far too late. I chewed on my lip. No real help for it. Talivar was going to need his freedom more than he needed to be Touch-Stoned to me . . . until my geas was lifted, anyway.

"I release you," I murmured, feeling the bond be-tween us snap with a surprised twang. The elf jerked back, startled.

"What did you do that for?" Hurt flashed in his gaze.

"You need to be a king, Talivar. You can't do that if you're chained here with me. At least this way you can travel the CrossRoads without being subjected to my issues."

His mouth compressed into a thin line but he nod-ded sharply. I had the feeling we'd be discussing it later, but at the moment, even he had to agree it made the most sense.

Kitsune watched the entire exchange with a curious expression. "And what would you have us do with the Steward, my King? Should he become a guest of the Unseelie Court after all this time?"

Talivar grunted an assent. "Let him stay here. He's served Faerie long and loyally these many years—I would not see that wisdom go unused." The elf king bowed elegantly to us. "I've some preparations to make, if you will excuse me?" Without another word he ducked out of the tent. I stared at the spot where he'd been, unsure if I was hurt or relieved he was gone.

"Awkward . . ." Phineas muttered. "Well played, Abby."

"What choice did I have?" I avoided looking at Kitsune. I was in no mood for discussions about destiny or red thread or any of it.

"There's always a choice," Kitsune murmured. "He needs to make these first few decisions on his own—or he'll spend the rest of his reign questioning everything he does."

An odd smile crossed her face as she turned to Thomas. "I'll admit the irony of hosting you here is somewhat disturbing, but I'll have a tent set up."

"No stranger than for me," he admitted wryly. "And I'm grateful for your hospitality, circumstances being what they are."

An uncomfortable silence hung in the air, thick with unspoken history. I wanted no part of it.

A hint of my uneasiness must have shown on my face. Phineas shook out his mane. "I'll get him settled, Abby," he said softly. "We'll play chess or something."

"All right." I gathered myself to my feet, uncertain of where I was supposed to go next. "Guess I'll leave you guys to it." I left the tent without looking back. Which was probably fairly rude, given what had just transpired, but what else was there to say?

"Jesus, I'm so tired of this."

Simple.

I wanted things to be simple again. I wanted to go home and hang with my friends. I wasn't one for shirking my responsibilities, but it felt as though I was hurtling off the cliff so fast I'd end up road pizza in a hot second if I didn't learn to grow wings.

I ducked down two different rows of tents, catching a few stray glances from a gaggle of goblin women, but I was too caught up in my own inner wallowing to pay much attention. I didn't want to head to my own tent, and certainly not to Talivar's. He had enough on his plate without suffering through another bout of my whining. Besides, he had bigger things to worry about.

Restless, I had the sudden urge to test the boundaries of my geas. I knew the Queen's warning should have been enough . . . but not even Talivar had really told me what the effect would be. Only that it should be avoided.

Fuck it. Maybe it wouldn't be as bad as he said? Kitsune always traveled with a portable Door of sorts. Last time it had been on the outskirts of the Lower Crescent.

The bells in my hair mocked me with a solitary chime but I told them to shush. Stubborn thing that I was.

I crisscrossed my way through the Hive, heading for of the Lower Crescent. My shoulders crawled with the feeling that someone was watching me. Not that I could really tell. The Barras was in full swing—a brass band could have swept through and attracted no more notice than a fly at the rate things were going.

"Abby?" I whipped around to see Sonja beckoning me from between a set of tents, her scarlet wings shifting nervously.

Relief shot through me. To see a familiar face was beyond welcome. Even if I'd spoken to her the night before in the Dreaming, flesh and blood was an entirely different thing. She was the first outside friend I'd seen since all this other crap began.

I hugged her hard, falling into her arms as she

embraced me, a question burning on my tongue. "Where's Ion?"

She exhaled sharply and pulled back, her expression troubled. "He doesn't want you to see him yet."

"See him? I don't understand." I cocked a brow at her, my arms crossing. "You know, I'm really getting tired of people leaving me out of the loop."

"It's complicated." The bells in my hair jingled mockingly. Her eyes narrowed. "I didn't realize those were anything more than a dream."

"Yeah, well, life is odd that way." I reached up and touched them. "So why are you here, then?"

"I wanted to make sure you were truly alive . . . Ion insisted."

"You'd think he might check on me directly." I swallowed the hurt, trying not to be too disappointed. My mouth quirked. "Did I mention I was sort of married now?"

The color drained from her face. "You're *what*?"

"Handfasted, I guess. To Talivar. Seemed like a good idea at the time." I rubbed the sudden rush of goose bumps rippling over my arm. "He's King here now, by the way."

"You don't say," she muttered. "Just how powerful is that geas you're under?"

"I don't know . . . Talivar got a taste of it because we were TouchStoned. Although we're not anymore," I amended. "He said it was pretty bad, but I was going to test it out myself. Right now, in fact."

"Think I'll tag along. The only way we'll be able to figure out how to break it is to get an idea of how it's put together."

She fell into step behind me, lost in her own thoughts as we meandered through the Lower Crescent. Her wings attracted little attention, but there did arise a few suspicious murmurs from the occasional cluster of Fae. I suppose it might look bad for me to be consorting with daemons given the current political situation, but I wasn't going to turn down help from a friend, regardless of her Path.

Besides, she was my only real link with Brystion. And I could trust her.

My nostrils flared as I approached the bamboo frame of the Door, my stomach fluttering. My inner voice questioned my sanity for attempting this, but I couldn't see letting it go without knowing for sure what would happen. I stared at the frame for a few moments. Based on Talivar's explanation, I half expected to be rolling on the ground by now, but other than the tingle of anticipation beneath my skin, I couldn't detect any difference.

"Going somewhere?" Nobu stepped around the far side of the Door. His own wings ruffled in the breeze as he cocked his head at me, his gaze lingering on Sonja.

The succubus held her ground. "You keep rather interesting company, Abby."

"You know me. I'm a magnet for assholes." My eyes narrowed at Nobu. "And it's none of your business as to where I'm going. I don't belong to you."

He shrugged. "As you say. I no longer have a vested interest in anything you do."

"Really? None at all? Not even for the sake of the Tithe?"

"None whatsoever," he said pleasantly. "My curiosity in that department has been well sated. Leave or stay, it's all the same to me."

"I don't understand. What about our bargain?" His tone was fairly convincing, but there was something he wasn't telling me. As much as I didn't want to be the Tithe anymore, there was *no* way he would ever let me out of it so easily.

His wings flared out in a menacing fashion, a hint of displeasure snapping through his dark eyes. "Our bargain, as you so quaintly put it, indicated you would be the Tithe, true enough . . . but more specifically it was under the assumption that you had the Key. Without it, any old mortal would do."

I blinked beneath the coldness of his tone. "So why not take me anyway?"

"Because I need the Keybearer to—" He shook his head. "It doesn't matter now. What matters is that the Key is now in the possession of Maurice and I don't need you anymore."

Sonja crossed her arms. "The way I heard it, he's been a shill for Hell the whole time . . . so what's your problem? If the Devil wants the Key, it seems like a shoo-in at this point."

"Who said anything about Hell?" Nobu's upper lip curled. "And being passed over is not something Maurice took well. To toss him aside publicly? Whatever our previous relationship was, it's now long gone. He holds no allegiance to any but himself."

I could buy that. I'd seen the man's face when he realized Nobu and I had outmaneuvered him at the last moment to keep him from being released. That it was a bargain to my detriment would have made very little difference to him.

I should have felt at least somewhat relieved at this revelation. To no longer have the weight of the Tithe hanging over me. But there was only a sick realization that someone else would most likely have to take my place . . . and things were never this easy.

Nobu gestured at the Door. "I'll be taking my leave now—but rest assured I'll be back to collect the Tithe. One way or the other, Faerie still owes us. If I were you, I wouldn't stick around too long."

I backed away from the Door. "I can't."

"What are your choices?" Sonja pointed out. "Wait here and hope the Devil likes to play cards?"

"He does, you know," Nobu added. "He's a wicked cheat, though."

"Not that helpful, thanks."

"Such loyalty. Suit yourself, Abby." Nobu touched the Door and I tried not to flinch as it lit up, an electric hum vibrating over my skin in answer.

"That's not so bad." I exhaled softly.

"Famous last words," Sonja muttered, as Nobu disappeared through the doorway with a flash of silver.

A lance of fire cut through my gut, my stomach roiling as though I'd swallowed a tub of Atomic Fireballs and washed them down with a chaser of lighter fluid. Gagging, I sank to my knees with a gasp. I caught Sonja's eye for half a second before vomiting noisily at her feet.

Which would have been fine the first time, but the moment I stopped long enough to wipe my mouth on my sleeve, another cramp tore through me, sparking off a second blast of nausea. The Door was still activated, its silver sparkles falling upon me like glittering snowflakes.

Knives prickled over my palms where one of the sparkles touched it, branding me to the bone. Every instinct urged me to run from the Door, my mind gibbering madly, somehow knowing that even if I crawled until my feet were bloody stumps I would *never* be far enough away.

I whimpered, my limbs shivering as Sonja dragged me away from the Door, neatly skirting the puddle of puke. Immediately the burning nausea receded. The Door shuddered and winked out, and relief flooded my veins. I lifted a shaking hand to push back my now-sweaty hair, the gritty sweet taste of bile lingering on my tongue.

Staggering to my feet, I only managed a few steps before I sank to the ground, my head on my knees. "I never thought I'd actually wish to die again, but that just came pretty damn close."

Sonja stared at the still fading Door. "This geas is linked to proximity. You didn't react until Nobu went through it, so it's the activation that's the key. I wonder . . ."

"You have an idea?"

"Just that there are other ways to get to the Cross-Roads than Doors. Certain times of the year where the veil between Paths and worlds is very thin. Sometimes you can cross right over without using a Door at all. Like during Samhain, for example."

I ignored the quailing part of me that wanted to know which year it was back home—time traveled oddly between worlds, and I'd long since given up trying to figure out how it worked. Something to do with the sun and the moon and a bunch of other metaphysical crap I'd never actually had explained.

I rubbed at my chin with my wrist. "So what now? I don't think I can sit around and wait for Samhain or whatever to roll around. And I should probably let Talivar in on this too, you know, seeing as we're married and all."

Sonja's lip curled. "I'll talk to Bryston. He's always been better at thinking outside the box—now that we know what the trigger is, he may know of a way to counteract it."

"Short of trying to escape through the Dreaming, I honestly don't know. And that wouldn't help me in the long run anyway."

"No." She hesitated. "Will you be okay?"

"As okay as I can be." I snorted. "Make sure you bring the barf bags with you next time. Think I'm going to go get cleaned up."

"All right. Come to the Dreaming later and I'll let you know how things went. Nice touch with the new grass, by the way." Her face crinkled into a sad smile. "You're learning."

"I can be taught. Sometimes I actually listen."

"And you only had to die once." She smirked. "At least now I know how to get you to pay attention."

I bit my lower lip. "Could you tell Ion I want to see him? Please? I know you said he's doing okay, but . . ."

"I'll tell him."

Before I could answer she hugged me again, pressing a gentle kiss on my forehead. And then she was gone, wending through the crowded paths of the Barras without looking back.

Nine

Talivar was not overly thrilled to hear about my little rendezvous with the daemons: "You're playing straight into their hands and I didn't leave my kingdom and my kin to save you, simply to see you throw everything away."

"Sonja wouldn't betray me. Not like that. And Nobu . . . probably would," I admitted. "But I think there's something else going on. He's playing his own game—I just don't know what it is. But I don't think we'll get any answers soon. What did you think about Sonja's suggestion? The Samhain thing?" I was far more interested in ways to help me break the geas than guessing at whatever Nobu was doing.

He scowled. "It's an old story. Hell, the writer of it is sitting two tents down. You should ask *him* about how relevant all this is to getting rescued."

His mouth pursed at my nonplussed expression. "My father, you mean?"

"Aye. Thomas played the same trick on my mother years ago . . . or his lover did, anyway. Vexed the Queen something fierce, but she never tried to bind him to her like that again. Ask him about 'Tam Lin' and see what he has to say about it."

I let his words sink in for a moment. "Tam Lin" was a ballad of a man who had been held captive by the Queen of Faerie, only to be rescued by his mortal lover. A mortal lover who had pulled him off his horse as he rode upon the CrossRoads with the Queen . . . breaking the spell.

"And you think something like that might work?" I shook my head, easing onto the pallet on the floor. I would definitely have to ask Thomas—ballad or not, details could so easily be changed over the years, and who knew if he'd changed any of it to protect the Fae?

I removed the shirt I had on and wiped my face with a clean cloth. "Did you find out what's going on with Moira? I'm assuming you were able to travel the CrossRoads without incident this time."

"They wouldn't let me into the castle," he said dryly. "Apparently I've been branded a traitor and I have to go through the 'proper' channels now."

I frowned. "Moira wouldn't do that."

"You know what a stickler for protocol she is, and things are so volatile right now she may have to do things she doesn't agree with, purely to keep the peace. At least until she becomes Queen in truth." He waved me off. "I have no fear of my sister's betrayal on that account. I'll simply need to play the game according to the rules."

"And what does that entail? Enlighten me, oh husband mine," I drawled.

"We'll meet at Eildon Tree at midnight, of course, with our respective households. It's partially to display our power and partially to put us on equal footing." He looked at me ruefully. "You'll be required to attend,

I'm afraid. Even if you're no longer technically my TouchStone, you're *mine*."

I bristled and his face softened. "Plus, I want you there, Abby. No secrets, remember? You need to see how all of this works if you're going to be a part of the family . . . for however long that is." He left the rest of it unsaid, but I knew what he meant.

On impulse I reached up to stroke his cheek and pulled him down beside me. Not that there was time for anything, but he sank into the mattress, wrapping his arms about me so my cheek was resting in the crook of his arm. His fingers found the back of my head and stroked it gently, twining the loose strands of my hair.

"Sonja still wants to try to free me, Talivar . . . and I think she has the right idea. Even with all the rest of this political bullshit, you have to admit if I can get myself away from Faerie, that will be one less thing they can hold against you. At least it will be a reprieve of sorts—and I may be able to help you more from the mortal world." My mouth tightened. "If you had the Wild Magic on your side . . ."

"Assuming you can even find Melanie, I would never use her like that. Not unless she volunteered." His fingers tightened in my hair.

I stifled a snort. He wasn't lying . . . but circumstances changed everything. And I had no doubt that if the shit really hit the fan, there wouldn't be much he wouldn't try to help save his kingdom.

And even if he wouldn't, there were plenty of others who would.

"I'm going to go check on my father. Maybe he can give me some . . . insight," I told him, a wan smile curving my lips as the elf kissed me.

*   *   *

Thomas was but a few tents away, as Kitsune had promised. Phineas had scrounged up a lute and the two of them sat there singing sea chanteys of all things. Phineas shot me a warning look as I entered the tent. My father had his eyes closed, lost in the music.

I'd never actually seen him play before. At Court, the Queen was too jealous to let anyone else hear, and if he had played music when I was a child I didn't remember. In an effort to keep my existence under the radar, some of my memories had been stripped so I wouldn't be forced to ask my mother any awkward questions.

I understood the reasoning behind it, but it still pissed me off to no end that I'd been kept in deliberate ignorance.

But that could be dealt with later. Or not at all. I knelt to listen, the rise and fall of his voice almost tangible. It spun around the tent with a simple power, the notes spilling from his lips with ease.

For a few brief moments I let myself be transported, the singular quality of his voice bringing the story in the song to life:

> I was on board a ship, the waves rocking beneath my feet, the splash of the sea spray spattering the deck, the distant clarion calls of the sirens from the rocky isles enticing me closer . . .

I blinked. I'd been turned into a mermaid while trapped in Topher's painting, so the irony wasn't lost on me, but it was still a tad unnerving for all that. Shaking myself out of my stupor as the last of the music faded, I coughed politely to let him know I was present.

His eyes fluttered open and he favored me with a small smile. "Any news, lass?"

"Not really. Talivar said we have to go to Eildon Tree to meet the other members of the Seelie Court. Something about a Mexican standoff, I guess." I blew my bangs from my eyes. "Sounds like more bullshit grandstanding, you ask me."

"Politics usually is," Phineas pointed out. "That doesn't mean it doesn't serve a purpose."

I flopped onto my elbows. "Whatever. I just wanted to let you know that I was tagging along." I looked at my father. "I suppose you probably should as well?"

"As the hostage, it might make things go smoother," he agreed. He set the lute down, but his empty hands appeared awkward in his lap, the left pinky tapping upon his thigh.

"Do you miss her? The Queen?" I blurted the words before I realized what I was saying, the heat of a flush rolling over my cheeks.

"My relationship with her isn't really your concern, Abby," he chastised me gently. "Not that part of it. And I am here by her request as much as I am for Moira."

"I wish you'd been that loyal to me," I muttered, ignoring the way he flinched. "Did you even visit me after I died?" Silence was my only answer. I snorted. "I don't even know why I bothered asking."

Something inside me clenched down, my emotions frozen. As much as I needed the information, I couldn't quite bring myself to question him any further. Not about that, anyway. Abruptly, I got to my feet.

"What do you know about the ballad of 'Tam Lin'?"

His brow furrowed. "I wrote it, if that's what you're asking . . . though it was under a different name. The

Queen wasn't particularly pleased, as you can well imagine." A pained smile crossed his face. "I could play it for you, if you like."

A subtle peace offering, but not one I had time for. "I just want to know how it works. How was your . . . lover . . . able to free you?"

"Janet," he corrected me. "She was more than just my lover, at the time. It was during one of the solstices. Everything is thinned then. The Queen was parading us about as she was wont to do in those days . . . see the lay of her lands, that sort of thing. But I'd told Janet where to find me upon the path, and she did, the delightful woman. She found me, saw right through the Glamour, and yanked me straight from the saddle."

His mouth flattened. "The oddness of it all—the stories say I shifted my shape until I became a lump of coal and she tossed me down a well, but that last part never happened. The shapeshifting was the worst part of it. It wasn't a Glamour, but it felt like I was being turned inside out, and I lashed out at her. By the time we were done she had a black eye and some cracked ribs, but somehow she managed to keep hold of me."

He paused. "It's more than the holding on. It requires that a mortal do it . . . can't just be some random OtherFolk." The blue eyes blinked painfully, tearing beneath the memory. "It's almost as if they become *your* TouchStone. Like your time in Faerie changes you enough to make you nearly part OtherFolk yourself. Their soul anchors yours, pulls you back to the Fourth Path, but the force of will that it requires is fierce . . ."

An odd chill wriggled down my spine at his words. If I stayed here long enough would I lose my humanity? It only strengthened my resolution to get the hell out of here. Somehow.

"It changes you," he added softly. "The both of you . . . because the trust it requires is beyond that of mere friendship." He exhaled sharply as he leaned his head against his seat. "I did not return to the Queen until Janet died, you know. I owed her and her child that much. I'm not sure the Queen ever really forgave me that transgression, but what else could I do?"

"Nothing," Phineas said softly, blowing the forelock from his brow. I wiped away the hot rush of tears from my cheeks. So much that Faerie had taken away from us . . . it had stripped us of our pasts and our futures. It was too easy to blame the Queen, though. After all, some of us gave ourselves over willingly.

"And yet you repeated it again, didn't you?"

"I have a weakness for mortal women," Thomas admitted. "Your mother looked very much like Janet. And she had much the same sort of strength."

I digested this statement with equal parts sorrow and anger, wondering what sort of life this other half sibling might have had . . . and if he or she might still be alive, here somewhere in Faerie, another mortal victim seduced by the twisted denizens here.

Heartsick, I turned away, not wanting to head down that path.

I had my own plans to make, and even though I didn't know how things were going to go down tonight, I'd be damned if I wasn't armed in some fashion before I got there.

I rode pillion behind Talivar, one of Kitsune's coal black mares prancing beneath us. Puca, I corrected myself. Not the same one that'd dumped me in the pond during my first visit to Faerie, but the golden glow from its eyes gave it away. It wasn't like I normally cared much about the color of horse eyes, but one wild ride on a Faery steed tends to make a body wary forever. I checked out of habit now, even if the chances were high that it was Glamoured.

This one didn't seem inclined to gallop away with me, but I suspected that was more Talivar's doing than anything else. It was probably bad form to dunk your king on the way to a formal meeting.

My father rode behind us, led by Kitsune on another pair of horses and the rest of the royal entourage accompanying us on foot. Great balls of witchlight swept past, pulsing in wild colors, illuminating the darkness until I felt as though we were in the funeral procession of an Oompa Loompa.

On any other occasion I would have found it charmingly creepy, but there was too much at stake for me to really relax about it. Talivar's hand tightened on mine, but my tension didn't ease up.

An honor guard of sorts flanked us—Unseelie goblins and wights of a particularly violent nature. Redcaps. Nucklavee. Boggarts. An odd mix of elongated limbs and fanged teeth, scales and prickly spines. The stuff of nightmares at the best of times, now they had something to fight for—and that lent them an even more sinister air.

I shook my head against that image, not liking the connotation of that at *all*.

Eildon Tree itself was off-limits to any sort of weapons—on this, each Path was in agreement. It was far too precious a resource—the thought of accidentally setting it on fire, for example, was enough to cause Talivar to blanch openly.

"There," he murmured, his head inclining toward

the pale branches of the tree. I could see the dim out-
lines of the others waiting for us. We'd had to take the
long way since I couldn't travel the CrossRoads, but
Talivar refused to go ahead without me, and his Court
wouldn't let him travel alone.

And so here we were, our entourage approaching
the Tree with cautious optimism.

The Tree hadn't changed much since I last saw it,
but it had only been about a month or so, after all—
even if it felt like a lifetime. A hawthorn, ancient and
gnarled and covered in small white blossoms. Strips of
cloth and shiny baubles hung from its branches—the
wishes of innumerable pilgrims, searching for answers.

Above us, a trace of moonlight gleamed through
the clouds, the edges of the Tree illuminated like glass.
Just beyond us, the CrossRoads shone in a crystalline
ribbon. A twinge of anxiety rippled through me. I was
still technically in Faerie and I hadn't stepped on the
CrossRoads . . . but this was getting awfully close to
skirting the boundaries of my geas.

The last thing I wanted was to trigger it again.

On the far side of the Tree I could see the silhouettes of other riders, the pale banners of the Queen
held aloft. Moira was beneath the Tree itself, mounted
upon her white mare, her face unreadable.

Carefully, Talivar dismounted, helping me down.
As soon as I touched the ground, the urgent thrum of
the Tree's EarthSong rumbled through my feet, beckoning me to come and sit beneath its branches. He
linked his arm through mine and we headed to where
Moira was, Thomas and Kitsune trailing behind us,
Phineas at my heels.

A blissful look flickered over my father's face. This

had been the very spot where he'd first met the Queen, after all. It appeared the years didn't diminish the magic of it for him.

Moira dismounted, clad in a dress of glittering silk. I stifled a smile. I could always count on my sister to put everyone else to shame in the fashion department. Her dress wasn't the only thing glittering, though. I could see the shine of tears when her gaze fell upon Thomas.

She knew something.

"Brother," she said thickly, moving to take Talivar's hands in hers. He kissed her knuckles, and I caught the slightest tremble in her fingers as she withdrew before she turned to me. "Sister."

Kitsune approached us, serene. "Will you acknowledge us, Princess? Does the Seelie Court now choose to recognize her shadowed brothers and sisters?"

The words hovered upon the fox-woman's breath, hope and longing and a tinge of resignation all wrapped up in a sad tone. This wasn't the first time this question had been asked.

Moira bowed her head, the moonlight catching on the slanted edges of her ears. "We cannot."

Her words were met with complete and utter silence. The Tree's branches rustled in the darkness, the soft wish-knots fluttering in the breeze. I had one on there, I realized, though I hadn't wished for anything.

Maybe I should have.

The tension between the four of us tightened as Talivar and Moira stared at each other, locked in silent communication. I pressed past them so I could touch the Tree. The vibration of its song grew stronger and I laid my hand on one of the branches, the bark thick against my palm.

Immediately the music filled my ears, driving me to

my knees like it had the first time I'd been here. My vision wavered as once again I was plunged into an odd vision, the spiraling of futures unweaving before me. I'd never be able to follow them or figure out which path to take, but that didn't matter. The Tree wasn't about that anyway.

. . . *the CrossRoads spanned the earth, silver ley lines of magic, crisscrossed in a tangled web of destinations and Doors, and for a moment I could see the way the four Paths unfolded across it, Eildon Tree the linchpin in the center to hold it all together* . . .

Behind me I could hear the others arguing, but it was the dim buzzing of bees, easy to ignore—until Moira began to lose her composure.

"You know why I can't do this," Moira snapped, her voice brittle. "I'm not Queen yet, and to attempt to overrule Mother's wishes would be a disaster."

Talivar's reply was muffled and I turned, pulling away reluctantly.

"What is she talking about?"

Whatever he was about to say was drowned in a sudden explosion and the rattling whizz of some sort of projectile.

"Oh, fuck." I turned around wildly, trying to figure out where it was coming from.

Talivar shoved me down into the grass as the rush of booted heels clattered past. The stench of sulfur flooded my nose. Daemons. "'Ware the Tree!"

Tree, hell. I struggled to look behind me. "Get my dad!"

"Stay down," the prince hissed, rolling off me to slip into the darkness. Hooves pounded the dirt, and I covered my head with my hands, the breeze of the panicked horses whisking over my head.

I elbowed my way closer to the Tree. Being trampled would suck just as badly as being shot and I had no intentions of catching a stray anything, thank you very much.

Besides, the Tree was sacred to the OtherFolk in a way I couldn't really comprehend. It was bound to be the safest place to find shelter.

Above me the witchlights flickered, sending out purple shadows. I caught a glimpse of Kitsune wielding a wickedly sharp katana. Her body slid through small openings amid the swirling haze of bodies and horses, the tip of the blade flicking out here and there. All the while her face remained as calm as though she were cutting a bouquet of daisies.

Moira had disappeared, swallowed up in the center of her own guardsmen, and I . . . was fending for myself.

A sharp pain dug into my side and I smacked at it, freezing at the answering grunt and the soft slide of fur against my hand. "It's me, Abby."

"Phin? Jesus, what's going on?"

"Mercenaries," he grunted. "Borderland mercs . . . guess whose calling card they've got?"

"Fucking Maurice."

Something let out a guttural snarl from the shadows and I froze. I'd been here before. Wriggling on my elbows, I slithered farther away. A silver flash lit up the night.

The CrossRoads . . . There was a Door nearby. Not that that helped me any. The real question was who was leaving . . . or coming here. There was a twang as arrows were loosed, followed by pained cries in the dark.

The rotting edge of sulfur stung my nose and I

clenched my teeth against the roiling wave of nausea knotting my gut. Wherever the Door was, I was getting too close to it, the geas kicking in with a vengeance.

Crap.

"Where's Talivar?"

"Cutting a rug in a daemon tango," Phineas snorted, squinting over my shoulder. "Someone's gonna need a dry-cleaning service."

"I hear blood's a bitch to get out of leather." I gritted my teeth as another wave of queasiness swept through me. "Where the fuck is that Door? I'm too close to it." Something soft and wet burbled nearby. I shuddered, peering through the branches.

"Do you see Thomas anywhere?"

"Moira took him with her group." Phineas slunk lower into the grass. "Think we need to stay out of it until the two Courts chase these assholes off."

"Well, well—what a surprise to see you here . . . alive."

I whirled to see a leather-clad daemon leaning against the Tree, flicking ash from a cigarette with a neat snap of his wrist. As daemons went, he was the dapper sort—neatly dressed, slicked-back scales, and a tidy row of horns upon his brow. It might have looked reassuring, but it was the ones who appeared most civilized who were usually the biggest bastards.

And I'd had dealings with this particular daemon before. *Cigarette*, my mind named him, pulling the moniker from a past memory.

"I could say the same," I drawled. "Nice to see you're still flaunting the Versace."

He shrugged. "It's nothing personal."

"It never is." I backed up a step as he approached, dropping his cigarette butt into the grass. It smoldered in a reddish haze, a curl of smoke rising from the silver blades.

"I do believe Maurice would be rather pleased to see you."

"No doubt." A flash of white at my feet told me Phineas had bailed. Given my commitment to our friendship, I was just going to assume he was mustering up someone with a weapon. Meaning, I needed to keep this asshole talking. "Think I'll take a rain check."

"How disappointing." His smile widened to reveal a set of prickly looking teeth. Inwardly I sighed. One of these days I was going to have to get my Buffy the Vampire Slayer action on and learn how to fight. I ducked beneath the lowest branch, the song of the Tree pulsing up my arm as I leaned on the it for balance.

"You're not going to be able to take me anyway," I muttered, almost hoping the geas would flare up the way it had earlier. The thought of vomiting all over this fucker cheered me up immensely.

"Says you."

I wondered what would happen if I were knocked unconscious. Would the geas kick into effect if I wasn't willfully attempting to break it?

I swallowed the taste of bile and ducked behind another limb. Cigarette wasn't really trying to pursue me yet and the longer I kept him talking, the better off I'd be. He smirked, blue scales gleaming, and then lunged, twisting his body around the trunk to snatch at my hair.

The Tree let out a shudder when he touched it, scraps of linen fluttering to the ground.

"Don't do that," I hissed at him. "Those prayers belong to other people."

"Casualties of war."

I stared at him. "What are you talking about? We're not at war."

"Not yet."

He bared his teeth in a snarl. I retreated another step, my back scraping into the bark. The EarthSong hummed stronger and a soft twang of warning vibrated through my spine. I blinked, the glow of fire lighting up the night air.

Fire.

"Oh, shit!" Cigarette whipped around, his own eyes widening. Snatching my hand, he yanked me backward, our bodies tumbling into the thick grass as a high-pitched whistling scream tore past us. The field lit up like the crispy edges of a burning snowflake, silver and gold and bloodred streaming behind the tail of the fireball.

Heat flushed over me and the Tree let out a groaning pop as it was hit, the cloth wishes igniting in a multicolored breeze. A gasp escaped me, even as another wave of cramps swept through my gut. Cigarette blinked dumbly at the smoldering ruin of the Tree, as a low wail rippled up from those who still stood.

"Fuck this." The daemon rolled off me.

"Maybe you ought to consider working for someone other than a psychopath," I snapped.

He let out a brittle laugh. "You think I've got any choice in the matter?"

Talivar staggered toward me, anguish written on his face. Before I could say anything, Cigarette hoisted me over his shoulder.

I kicked at the mercenary, my ears still ringing from the explosion, but he ignored me. "I'm out of here."

"Let me go! I can't. I have a geas—" My words were drowned as the Tree gave another shudder, the bark splitting with a massive roar. Cigarette didn't bother slowing down, his arm clinging tight around my waist.

Abruptly we were standing in front the silvered edges of the Door I had sensed, and I began to dry heave in anticipation. Smoke guttered, hiding us in a thick cloud. The Door arced in a silver flame before us and I squinted through tearing eyes.

"Can't . . ." I mumbled thickly.

"Watch us," Cigarette snorted. And then something steamrolled into us, our limbs tangling in a heap as we hurtled through the Door and onto the Cross-Roads.

I slammed into silver cobblestones, my breath rushing out of me in a whoosh. Beside me Cigarette grunted, muttering something profane, but I hardly noticed as I crawled to my knees, vomiting profusely.

"What the hell—" Cigarette's voice cut off with a yelp as he was barreled over by another figure. I caught a dim image of fists and some sort of blade, the stench of sulfur and a guttural moan, but I had no time to thank my would-be rescuer.

Fire ripped through my veins, burning liquid licking along my skin. Blisters bubbled on my flesh, my mouth hung open in a silent scream. Flames coated my tongue, scorching down my throat and into my gullet.

This was not the gentle shape-changing of the Dreaming, steered by me—this was the uncontrolled snapping of a curse set free without limitations.

My bones melted and forged into something new, crushed and reset. Dimly I heard someone calling my name, but I couldn't see anything beyond my own pain. I broke out in scales, my legs and arms absorbing into my rib cage, my spine lengthening, my teeth growing pointed.

I twisted around someone, coiling, coiling, squeezing.

Fingers bit tighter, arms trembling, but they didn't let go of me. A span of heartbeats and I shifted again, into something large and furry, with biting fangs and tearing claws. I want to shred flesh, fill my mouth with blood . . .

"—an illusion," someone gasped. "You have to fight it."

The voice. A man's. Did I know it?

Not Cigarette, surely.

I vomited bile upon him, belching smoke in his face. I couldn't seem to focus on it, my whole being needing to move, to get away. To be *free*.

My organs rearranged again and I was some great monstrosity plucked from the sea, a living death of fins and teeth and an insatiable hunger that could never be filled. I would consume this fleshly annoyance that bound me here against my will.

His hands slid over my face to cup my chin, forcing me by inches to look at him. Somehow he captured me with his gaze and I stilled, my sides heaving. We were in blackness, the CrossRoads stretching out beyond us in silver sparkles. I began to shiver, the fire morphing into a bitter cold, turning my limbs to ice.

He shuddered and I realized he was succumbing to it too. The bells in my hair chimed discordantly, and the sound cut through my own internal screaming. Somehow I opened the inner channels as though I might TouchStone him, but there was nothing there, save a shadowed emptiness I could not seem to fill.

His mouth pressed on mine and it was all sweat and

skin and tongue. I trembled with it, his hands roaming through my hair. I'd become myself again, but the chill continued to burn, my heart fizzling like a lump of coal extinguished in a bucket of water.

"Ion?" The name filled my mouth.

"Hush now," he whispered and held me tighter. "It's over."

Ten

I stretched out in a familiar warmth, surrounded by my own sheets. My own scent, wrapped in flannel. I jerked awake, struggling to sit up as I stared into the darkness.

My mouth tasted of ashes, my body ached as though I'd been turned inside out and back again, my limbs swollen and heavy.

I was home. In my apartment?

But I'd been on the CrossRoads . . . and there had been fire . . . daemons . . . the Tree . . . Ion . . .

"Brystion?" I whispered it, afraid I might spoil the dream if I said it too loud.

"I'm here." His voice sounded rough and raspy, and I tracked its location to finally make out his silhouette in the rocking chair in the corner. I turned on the light, trying to comprehend what I was seeing.

My heart pulsed into my throat as though it meant to take flight, relief and a silent shudder of hysterical laughter thickening my tongue into cotton.

"Ion," I said hoarsely. "What's going on?"

"We broke your geas. You're free." He didn't move

from the chair and I stared at him. He was in his mortal form, pale and beautiful, but his eyes were sunken, without their usual arrogance. The chiseled cheekbones were still there, but hollowed, and several days' worth of stubble crested the rise of his jawline.

Something wasn't right here.

"Where are the others?"

He shrugged. "At Eildon Tree, I suspect. To be honest, I don't care."

"But Talivar? Phineas?" I slid off the bed, wrapping the blankets around my shoulders as I walked toward him. I was naked beneath them, which was for the best, given that my clothes were probably not worth saving.

I stroked the roughness on his face with a curious finger. "That's a new look for you, isn't it?"

He said nothing, but his lips compressed.

I turned his chin so he was forced to look at me. "What's going on, Ion? What the hell happened to us in the Dreaming? Why didn't you come see me before?"

"Does it matter?"

"Of course it matters! Christ, Ion, I thought I'd killed you!" I slid a tendril of damp hair from my face, surprised to notice I'd been cleaned up. I must have been pretty far out of it if I didn't even remember being bathed. "How long have I been gone?"

"Several months . . . I guess. I lost track of time . . . after you died." He snorted. "I've been crashing here; I hope you don't mind."

"Just like old times," I murmured, earning me a mouth twitch. "But I still don't understand what's going on."

He captured my hand and pressed it to his cheek, his lips brushing over the palm. "I never thought I'd see you again," he whispered. "That I'd given it up for you . . . only to have you disappear . . ."

He kissed my hand again and a flutter raced up my arm.

But it was different somehow. In the past, Bryston had never hesitated to use at least a bit of his formidable sexual power to invoke a response I usually had to struggle to resist. This time, there was something off . . .

"Well, I'm here now. For whatever that's worth." I leaned down and kissed his forehead. "It's good to be home, such as it is." I glanced around my room, basking in the worn furniture, the Celtic wall tapestries, the glow of the lamp on the bedside table. *Home.*

The digital clock dutifully displayed the time. It was nearly noon, and I almost laughed at how normal it was to have a clock to look at. "It's not much, but it's mine. I don't think I ever quite appreciated that before. Elves have perfectly lovely decor, but sometimes it's nice to have things be normal . . ."

My words trailed away and I had the feeling he wasn't really listening. And then his eyes popped open, dark and anguished. Without a word, he hoisted me into his arms, launching us toward my bed, his mouth nipping at mine.

"What are you doing?"

"Think that's rather obvious, Abby."

I placed my hand on his chest and shook my head. "Are you serious?"

"I have to make this right. "Somehow."

"I hardly think this is the time for a bedtime romp." I hesitated. Had Sonja told him about my handfasting?

"No. Just . . . let me hold you. Please." His voice

took on a desperate edge, and I allowed him to place me on the blankets. He made no move to search out my naked form beneath.

"Are you all right?" I asked.

He buried his face in the nape of my neck, his fingers curling into my hair tight enough to make me cry out. "You were dead, Abby. You were dead and I was here and I couldn't get to you in time. I couldn't find you. I looked and I looked and you were gone and you left me here . . ."

I'd never seen him like this. "How long has it been . . . since I died?"

"Six months after you drank the lethe. Three weeks since I was told you died."

My brain tried to wrap itself around loss of time. The loss of my memories. The loss of my *life*. The rational part of me attempted to figure out the date. I'd last been here in late July, so that meant it was now . . . nearly February?

On instinct, I wrapped my arms about his shoulders, both of us beginning to shake with the reality of our situation. And even if I continually felt as though I was being buffeted by forces I could never quite escape, this moment held a particular tenderness that belonged solely to me.

And him.

"I'm here now," I repeated.

He kissed me hard then, but it wasn't a sexual thing as much as a reassurance that I was actually here. I returned it, tentatively, my mouth upon his. We clung to each other until he let out a shuddering breath, his body slumping so that he sprawled out beside me. One hand stroked my forehead, brushing over my mouth again and again, every nerve shivering with potential.

My lips parted to capture his finger, halting his incessant movement. His breath hitched, as an incoherent sound escaped him.

"Gods, this is real," he said hoarsely. "You're real. You're fucking real."

"Yes?"

He stared at me, but his eyes were dark, without a hint of gold.

"I'm sorry, Abby. I'm so sorry." He rolled away, draping his feet over the edge of the bed before moving to the window. I broke out in goose bumps as the warmth of his body disappeared and I draped the blanket around me in a shield of cotton.

"What just happened here?"

"I thought you were a dream. I have this dream . . . every night."

I cocked my head at him. "A dream? But I thought incubi didn't dream."

Before he could answer, the bedroom door burst open and Talivar strode in, his face blackened with soot, Phineas trotting at his heels. The elf barely acknowledged Bryston, wrapping me in his arms.

"Oh, Abby," he murmured, with barely a tremor in his voice. But it was all there in his gaze, fear and relief and a terrible sorrow. "You're alive, love. You disappeared through the Door and I thought . . ." He pushed the hair away from my forehead and planted a kiss there before capturing my mouth.

"Helloooo awkward," Phineas muttered from the doorway.

I fidgeted under Talivar's sudden scrutiny, his gaze darting between me and Bryston with a grim understanding. "So that's how it is."

Phineas made a little "O" with his mouth, his gaze

darting between the three of us. "Exit, stage right." His hooves rapped on the floor as he bolted for the kitchen, leaving me to face my tangled responsibilities alone.

I winced, trying not to glance at Brystion, who was carelessly throwing on his shirt. "A daemon pulled me through. One of the ones from before . . ."

"I knew him," the incubus said shortly. "When I worked for Maurice."

Of course. I tried not to flinch. When Sonja had gone missing, Brystion had agreed to work for Maurice to try to find where she'd gone. The price for that information had been me, even if Maurice had been pulling the strings all along.

"Did you know he would be at the Tree?"

Ion shook his head. "I just wanted to see you for myself. Sonja said you were at the Barras, so that's where I went. But I got there too late. By the time I tracked you down to Eildon Tree, things were in chaos. When I saw him drag you off through the Door, I followed." His upper lip curled, an echo of his normal confidence sparking over his face. "Of course, I also killed the fucker."

"You'll forgive me if I don't remember that part," I said dryly. "Shapeshifting into a snake and puking my guts out sorta took most of my attention."

Talivar frowned. "How did you break the geas?"

I gave the king a wry smile. "We pulled a 'Tam Lin,' I guess, though I'm not entirely sure how. I thought it had to be done during a solstice or something."

The elf's frown deepened as he looked at Brystion. "That's a rather interesting ability . . . for a daemon."

"The CrossRoads run thin at Eildon Tree," was

all Bryston said, and the following silence stretched out into something far more uncomfortable than I liked.

I fidgeted with the blanket and turned toward Talivar. "The Tree? What happened to it? Where are the others?"

A note of grief tinged his voice. "It's damaged, almost beyond saving. Your father was injured, but he'll survive."

"And what happens if the Tree dies?" I didn't want to ask, but I had to.

"I don't know." His nostrils flared wide. "The Tree is everything. Without it the CrossRoads will most likely collapse . . . I don't know if the Paths will even be able to survive without it."

"I don't understand. Why would anyone try to destroy it? And why now?"

Talivar gave me a helpless shrug. "I wish I knew."

"So what do we do?"

A hand dropped onto my shoulder. The bells in my hair chimed as Bryston tipped my chin toward him. "*You* don't do anything."

"What are your intentions here, daemon?" Talivar edged beside me, the two men facing off with grim determination. "This doesn't concern you."

"No," Ion agreed, glancing down at me. "I told you before that I'd take you from Faerie to save your life. I failed you once and I will not do so again."

"Abby belongs with me, with her family." Talivar's upper lip curled in a snarl.

The incubus snorted. "Does she? Have you asked her what she wants—would you even listen to her if she told you?" He shook his head. "I've tasted her dreams, elf . . . I know her far better than the rest of you."

"Nobu put you up to this, didn't he?" Talivar growled. "What little balance we had with the daemons is gone now."

"Nobu had nothing to do with this." Bryston arched a brow at him. "And I don't recall you being quite that concerned about that possibility before. A little bit more distasteful now that you wear the crown, isn't it?" he drawled.

Talivar stiffened. "That was different."

"Different because you could blame it on *me*." Ion's mouth kicked up into a crooked half smile. "I wouldn't worry about the blame. After all, I claim the Fourth Path now."

The blood drained from my face. "But that would mean you're . . ."

"Human. Mortal." He nodded, raising his head at Talivar. "And therefore not under the jurisdiction of your claims. Not at Eildon Tree. Not here."

"But—"

Talivar's eye narrowed. "Human?"

Bryston's mouth twitched as he lifted my hand to place a gentle kiss upon the palm. "Our Abby has talents she hasn't even begun to tap yet. She's a Dreamer. I am a creature of the Dreaming. Even without her memories, she was somehow able to Dream me into mortality . . . and that's no small feat." His fingers twined in my hair to find his bells. "Not that this was my original intention."

"Do you want them back?" I still hadn't quite grasped the implication of whatever he thought I'd done . . . but the pieces fell into place rather quickly.

If he was no longer an incubus, then he couldn't reach the Dreaming the way he had before.

He shook his head, withdrawing his hand regretfully. "They belong to you . . . That part of my life is over."

"Why would you do this? That wasn't even remotely close to the plan." Talivar's brow drew down, the soot making him appear even more disturbed.

"It wasn't my first choice," Ion admitted. "But when I finally managed to break through Abby's memory issues in the Dreaming, I realized I would not be able to pull her out of Faerie." His gaze shifted toward me. "The mechanics . . . are rather specific and would have required us to be TouchStoned on top of everything else. And I would not force that upon her."

"I dislike what you're insinuating, dream-eater," Talivar said darkly. "I assure you, all I have done is for Abby's sake."

"As have I," Ion murmured.

I moved away from both of them. "What difference does it make? We're here now and this is what we're stuck with, so maybe we could wait for the man-pain explanations until later?"

Sucking in a deep breath, I sank onto the bed. "I know I've fucked up here on so many levels . . . and we're going to need to work this out. I know this. But there are bigger things at stake here than us. I love you both . . . in different ways. And that's a cop-out—and I realize it—but I don't know what to do about it. So until we can sit down and have a powwow to discuss our feelings, I think we need to accept it and move forward."

Was there such a thing as Faerie marriage counseling? I suspected not, given the way so many of the stories went. I rewarded them with a wan smile. "Considering I've lost my memory and my life and my freedom in a matter of weeks, I'd like to think I've earned a temporary pass on my romantic entanglements."

Talivar exchanged a look with Brystion and rubbed a soot-smeared hand through the bramble of his hair. "Obviously we know Maurice was behind the attack, though beyond that? I cannot imagine why he would have chosen to attack the Tree directly. He's always wanted power, but without the Tree, there won't be anything left to rule."

"Maybe it was a mistake? What if he didn't know we were going to be there? Maybe things just got out of hand." I chewed on a thumbnail.

"Who can say why he does anything?" Brystion paced around the room like a caged thing. "For all we know he just did it to knock us all off balance so he can sneak in and do whatever he had planned to begin with."

"That Key around his neck isn't going to help matters much," I pointed out. "He could show up anywhere . . . at any time."

Talivar exhaled slowly, musing over my words. "True enough, though all of the Paths are involved now . . . not even the powers that be can ignore what he's done this time. Stirring up mischief between the Paths is one thing, but to obliterate that which is most sacred? Even Hell will be howling for his blood."

"You can't possibly think of putting Abby into the middle of this," Brystion snapped.

"No. Not this time." Talivar pressed a finger to my lips. "He's right. The Courts are in chaos. We still have the Tithe to think of—at least if you're here, you can't be considered for that. And I need . . . time to regroup without—"

I snorted. "Distraction, I get it. I'm a liability now." I couldn't stop the bitterness from slipping into my words. If I'd actually become his Queen instead of merely a consort, would things be any different?

And would I want that sort of responsibility anyway?

"You will be safer here, Abby." Talivar cupped my cheek. The warmth of his hand seeped into my flesh, but coldness gripped my gut. A flicker of emotion danced over his features, but neither of us gave voice to it. "I would have you stay here and out of the worst of it for now. If we have need of your . . . services, then I will call upon you. But here . . . you could be my liaison to the OtherFolk in this realm. Help me retain order here."

The prince paused, "Eildon Tree is dying. We're going to need someone who can tap into the Wild Magic."

Melanie. Her unspoken name vibrated silently among the three of us, along with the implications of who would most likely be tasked with finding her.

"Unbelievable." Brystion turned away, his hands clenching into fists. "You fuckers continue to use her until the end."

"Ion—"

"And *you*—you let them!" He whirled on me. "Time and again, you give and you give and you give. What happens when you have nothing left?" There was a mad sort of anguish in his face and I knew the words were half directed at himself.

I really looked at him then, seeing what I hadn't before.

However easily he claimed I'd removed his daemonic nature, it was clear the effort hadn't been kind to him . . . with the light flickering over his face, I could see the stress lines on his brow and dark circles beneath his eyes. Even his physique seemed lessened, the cheeks gaunt and a wired tension flexing beneath his shirt.

"I don't know," I said finally. "I don't *know*. But I know I'm here and I'm alive and the people I care for are all okay and I'll take it." I grabbed his hand, ignoring the way he flinched. "For now, I'll take it."

"Not that you have any choice," he muttered, but his fingers twined with mine, knuckles clamping hard enough to bruise, the slightest of tremors running through him. The incubus—*former* incubus—was barely holding on.

I tugged on Talivar's sleeve. "I'll do what I can. Are you still Protectorate here? I've been out of the loop."

He gave me a pained look. "Yes, but I'll need to find a replacement."

I didn't really want to do deal with any of the Protectorate bullshit at this point, but I would worry about that later. "I'll see what I can do."

The elf hesitated, kissing me briefly before pushing something into my hand. I glanced down at it, though its familiar beveled edges made it easy to tell what it was.

"My iPod?"

"You left it behind in . . . our . . . tent. I thought you might like to have it." He gave Brystion a faint smile. "Take care of my wife. I'll be coming back for her."

Brystion's fingers pinched tight enough that my knuckles popped, but he made a noncommittal grunt that I could only take to mean yes.

And then Talivar was gone, the door shutting behind him with a click of finality that felt like the shattering of everything I knew.

Eleven

Ion and I sat on opposite sides of the room, looking everywhere but directly at each other. Each time I glanced up, his eyes darted away. When I could no longer stand it, I slid off the bed and into the bathroom, the blanket still around my shoulders.

After spending so much time in Faerie, where everything was done for me, it was a relief to do things at my own pace—and that included taking a piss in my own toilet. I'd take running water over the rustic charms of a chamber pot any day of the week.

I shut my eyes for a moment and breathed in the still-damp scent of lavender shampoo.

Home.

I was home.

A thick lump had worked its way into my throat and I swiftly shut the door. I wanted privacy for this. The lock had barely turned before the first tears spilled forth. I wiped them away and let the blanket drop to the floor.

I moved toward the sink, forcing myself to look at my reflection. I don't know why it was suddenly so important but I needed to make sure I was still myself.

I looked like a ghost, my face paler among the freckles than I remembered. My auburn hair hung limp past my shoulders; my usual pink and blue streaked bangs were washed out. On instinct, I found the bare patch from my accident, the place where the hair never grew quite right. Beneath that scar lay a metal plate and the seat of my seizures, the reason why I was here.

I let my hair fall back over it, my fingers drifting over my forehead to the yellowing bruises at my temple and jaw, the faded marks around my throat. I hesitated when I reached the empty place at my neck, somehow still expecting to find the amulet there.

Guilt washed over me. If only I'd been faster. Or smarter. Or stronger.

A shuddering sigh escaped me as I swallowed past the ache and the little voice in my head insisting that all of this was my fault.

"No, it's not," I told the mirror before giving a cursory examination of the rest of my body. The silver scar at my belly where Maurice had stabbed me was still there, and my knee still bent too far. Otherwise, I was just a mix of scrapes and bruises from the last several days . . . and time would heal those.

As for the rest of it? I stared at my hair for about twenty seconds, chewing on the inside of my cheek. So many things I needed to do. So many people depending on me again.

And yet . . .

"Fuck it."

I opened the cabinet beneath my sink and pulled out the familiar brushes and the jars of Manic Panic hair dye. Like a warrior girding herself for battle, there were things I needed to do. Armor wasn't always made of metal—and I'd be damned if I met my destiny with my roots showing.

Phineas eyed me critically when I emerged a few hours later, freshly showered, newly dyed, and slightly made-up, my eyes smudged with kohl. I'd put my hair up in its usual bun, twisting a set of pencils through it. Ion's bells hung loose from a lone braid over my right shoulder.

"Not exactly Joan of Arc, but it'll do."

"Always appreciate your vote of confidence, Phin. Stay out of my underwear."

"I would *never*."

I breezed past him to my dresser, searching for something to wear. "That would be more convincing if there weren't already hoof prints up here."

He *hmmmphed* at me, but I only spared him a quick glance before searching out Brystion. He was still slouched in the chair where I'd left him, his legs sprawled out in haphazard fashion. Something like a smile flickered over his face when he saw my hair.

"I wondered what was taking you so long."

"We mortals don't have Glamours to change our appearance." I tugged on a strand of brilliant pink. "And sometimes doing things the old-fashioned way works best."

His lips pursed, a humorous gleam lighting up his eyes. "So I've noticed."

"Well, hopefully you've noticed that I'd like to get dressed too?" I arched a brow at him, wrapping the towel tighter around my chest. "Not that you haven't seen me naked before or anything, but a little privacy would be nice. And that goes for you too, Phin."

"Spoilsport."

"Out." I pointed toward the kitchen and gave Brystion a hopeful look as my stomach rumbled aloud. "I know we have a lot to do, but I think some food might be in order?"

One corner of his mouth kicked up in amusement. "Some things never change."

"No," I said ruefully. "They don't."

I scraped the last few bites of the omelet into my mouth, savoring the melted cheese with a sigh. "You have no idea how I've missed this."

He smirked, shoveling down his own forkful. "At least I didn't lose this ability."

"Mmmph. How exactly does that work, anyway? You're human . . . but . . ."

"But nothing. I'm fully mortal, from what I can tell. I have to sleep. To eat. I've got more limitations than I've ever had before."

Phin snorted, lapping up his own plate of eggs. "Little harder to get into the ladies' pants these days?"

Brystion gave the unicorn a sour look. "Nice horn. And no. Not that I've exactly been trying," he said dryly. "Funny thing about being human? It puts a damper on the whole dream-eating gig." His gaze became intense as he looked at me. "I don't have to do it anymore, Abby. I can be . . . me."

I swallowed a sip of tea. The rawness of his expression twisted my heart. He'd always hated that part of himself, that innermost loathing at what he needed to do to survive, even as he'd accepted it as what he was.

For all that incubi were oversexed and oversexualized, when it came down to what he looked like, he was often changed by the thoughts and desires of those around him . . . to become that which they most wanted.

Nothing of me is mine . . .

The words echoed through my memory, a mix of old hurt and a displacement of self I knew all too well. I took a closer look at his face, but he seemed much as I remembered him.

"Are you stuck looking like that now?"

"Does it displease you so much? Even when I gave you my essence, your dream self appears to have shaped me to that which you like best." He cocked a brow. "I suppose I should be grateful I didn't end up with pointed ears."

I scowled at him. "Low, Ion."

His shoulders rippled, a touch of his old arrogance lighting up his face. "You'll forgive me for being a tad pissed off that you ran off and wed him after I went through all of this?"

"It wasn't as though I had much choice in the matter," I snapped. "Time was running out. And that stupid—"

"Geas. Yes, I know." He laid the fork down, thrusting his fingers through his tousled ebony locks. "I just wish we'd been able to figure out some other way to get you out of there. This wasn't exactly what I'd intended."

"And here I thought you were trying to become mortal to free me."

A scowl crept over his face. "Don't be stupid. You didn't have the geas when I found you in the Dreaming that night. It's like I told the elf . . . we would have to be TouchStoned for you to pull me through, and I wasn't sure you would be able to manage it."

He paused. "I thought by having you absorb my essence I could pull you into the Dreaming. For real."

In the past, I'd inadvertently pulled him from the Dreaming into the mortal realm without the use of the CrossRoads . . . but we'd been TouchStoned and making love at the time.

I cocked my head. "And yet you still took the time to get me off," I noted.

His eyes darted away. "Yeah, well," he muttered. "If it was the last time I was going to do it, why not at least enjoy, eh? Besides, I needed the extra power boost."

"So, I guess that begs the question. How do we reverse your transformation?" I stared down at the dregs of my teacup, unsure of my own motives. In some ways, his newfound mortality changed the game completely. And I wasn't sure what to make of it. I'd always told him I never wanted to him change . . . not for me, not for anyone. He was what he was, and as much as it hurt sometimes, I'd come to accept that as part of the deal. But now?

His fingers walked across the table to swirl over my wrist, brushing over my palm to linger between my knuckles. "Are you sure you'd want that?" Shadows upon shadows. "I don't even know *if* it can be reversed, Abby. I can't get to the Dreaming like I used to."

"But Sonja said you couldn't . . ." I bit my lower lip as I realized what he meant. "No. She said you couldn't get to *my* Dreaming Heart. But when you sleep you're like everyone else?"

"Yes," he said hoarsely. "I have my own Dreaming Heart now." The longing in his gaze shattered me to the core. Incubi had no Dreaming Hearts. They were born of it, spun from the stuff of dreams and nightmares by inadvertent Dreamers . . . but once born, they could never return.

Which had led me to lending him mine. But having a metaphysical boarder in one's dreams could be a bit odd, particularly when we split up. Although he had continued to protect me from my nightmares, even so.

"And I'm not sure I want to give it up." He let out a humorless chuckle. "It's what I've always wanted, after all."

"Well, I suspect we'll have some time to figure it out . . . assuming it even is a possibility. In the meantime, we might want to get you established as a 'person.' If you're in this for the long haul, not being one would make things tough when it's time to collect social security anyway."

He rolled his eyes at me and I laughed. "Just saying."

"Social security? Please. Tough is not being able to walk into the Spank Bank and pick out my own movies. At least *you* look human." Phineas clambered onto one of the extra chairs, his nose quivering. "Think maybe you could 'just say' some more bacon my way?"

I shoved the remaining slices in his direction, slumping against my own chair. "Why don't you just use the Internet for your porn like everyone else?"

The unicorn fixed me with a cool stare. "You really want to see my browser history pop up every time you go to check your e-mail?"

Bryston and I both shuddered. "No! But that doesn't mean I want to be tripping over loose copies of *Donkey Dongs 2* whenever I'm trying to use the DVD player."

"Duly noted. And for the record, I had *no* idea what that was when I rented it." Phineas flashed his still-chewing teeth at me in a grotesque leer. "I thought it was a documentary."

"Mmm."

We fell silent then, and I pushed the last few bits of my toast around my plate, trying to think of what else to say. *Best to leave that one alone,* my inner voice noted.

Which left the other topics I'd been avoiding.

If I'd thought things couldn't get any more messed up after the events of last year, I'd sorely underestimated the fickleness of the gods. I coughed awkwardly and turned toward Brystion. "So how have things been since I . . . left?"

"About the same. Once the Queen reopened the CrossRoads, most of the remaining OtherFolk bolted back to their respective realms, at least for a while. I don't think any of them wanted to take the chance they might get trapped again." His mouth tightened. "We had a lot of funerals for those who didn't make it." A guilty wave flushed through me. In an effort to protect Moira, the Queen had shut down the CrossRoads, cutting the OtherFolk off from the magic they needed to survive. One more thing I was indirectly responsible for.

I winced. "I have the feeling I need to call a whole bunch of people." I'd left without saying good-bye, except for a handwritten note detailing my plans. As farewells went, it probably sucked, but I didn't have much time, and I couldn't risk my friends talking me out of what needed to be done.

"Probably would be a good idea. Without an actual Protectorate here, you're about the next best thing."

"Why do I get the feeling you'd like to see that change?" I nudged him under the table with my foot.

"It doesn't really matter what I'd like. You will do what you will do. It's part of your nature, apparently. Not that it's a bad thing," he admitted. "But yes, I would have you give all this up."

"And where would I go, Ion? I can't leave my family in the lurch. Not with the Tree and the Tithe bullshit."

"I know." A smile of wry resignation crossed his face. "Just don't leave me behind."

"Is that what this is about? Me leaving you behind?"

He waved me away as he stood up and gathered the dishes to put them into the sink.

I decided to let it go for now. I knew him well enough by this point to realize he wasn't going to answer until he was ready . . . if then. The incubus had a tendency to play his cards so close to his vest that half the time I didn't think even he knew what he was about.

"I stood up, brushing the crumbs off my lap. "So. Game plan?"

"Go ahead and get your things together. I'll call the others and tell them to meet us at the Hallows." He didn't turn around, his shoulders rigid as he scrubbed at one of the plates.

Inwardly I sighed, but I left him to it. We had bigger things to worry about, as usual.

"Meet me at the CrossRoads," I intoned softly at the door to the Hallows.

The pass phrase did absolutely nothing.

"I forgot. Brandon changed the code a little while ago. Things got hairy during the funeral wakes—we had several groups stopping by to take out their anger here." He grimaced. "He got tired of cleaning up the mess."

It wasn't surprising to hear. The alley leading to the

OtherFolk bar was hidden by a Glamour that did a lot to prevent hapless humans from wandering within range, but even magic wouldn't be able to hide a protracted mob of angry Fae or Daemons forever.

"So what's the new pass code?"

"Speak, friend, and enter," he muttered, not blinking as the door lit up in a haze of silver.

"Because *that's* original."

"I hear the classics are best." He gave me a gentle shove through the door. I blinked as we entered the dimly lit bar, the familiar scent of stale beer lingering in my nose.

As bars went, it was typical in most ways—dance floor, stage, barmaids and drinks and big-screen TVs—but it was the patrons who normally made it stand out. Each night was a mishmash of pointed ears, feathered wings, sharp fangs, and the Glamoured beauty of the OtherFolk nightlife.

But at three in the afternoon, it was a tad early in the day for much of a crowd. The bar was empty except for the subdued gathering before me.

Brandon. Roweena. Robert. Charlie. Benjamin.

Werewolf bartender. Faery liaison. Angel bodyguard. Human ghost whisperer. Kid Icarus.

You must gather your party before venturing forth.

My brain superimposed their images as though I were in some sort of computer game—like I might be able add up their stats and come away with a rowdy band of adventurers, off to seek fame and glory.

But not this time.

Of Melanie there was no sign, and her absence made the room seem that much more stark to me.

I had only a moment to realize Katy wasn't there either before Brandon launched himself at me with a whoop, his furry arms snatching me up and spinning me around.

"Don't ever do that to us again!" he snarled, the tone made all the odder by the dancing delight flickering in his golden eyes.

I couldn't stop the pathetic grin from spreading across my face in return, my breath coming in a laughing sob. "Put me down, you sad excuse for a carpet. You're making me dizzy."

His muzzle leaned in close to my ear, a pink swipe of tongue darting over the lobe as he growled something profane.

"I missed you too," I said and hugged him tight against a sudden rush of tears. He dropped me gently to my feet, one clawed hand ruffling through my hair. "If you ever pull a stunt like that again, I'll—"

"—be getting in line behind me," Robert said dryly, his wings flaring out with an audible crack for emphasis. "Of all the stupid, pigheaded things to do . . ."

"Yeah, well, I died for it, so let's call it even, okay?" Not that I didn't deserve to be called out, but I didn't have to like it.

Robert cocked a brow at me. "Aw, Sparky."

The angel was built like Superman on steroids with a jaw so square it could have been used to lay tile, complete with dark hair and laser blue eyes. He used to intimidate the hell out of me, but he'd mellowed out considerably since becoming a father.

I glanced over at Brandon, trying to change the subject. "Where's Katy?"

The werewolf shrugged. "College. We're doing the long-distance thing at the moment, but I've been toying around with maybe moving out West to be with her."

I did a double take. "You'd shut this place down?"

He grinned wolfishly. "Oh, I'm sure I could find someone to take it over, but . . . yeah. I miss her," he said, his tone suddenly mournful. For a moment I thought he might actually start howling, but he flicked his ears. "Though she says it's 'good for us' and she wants her 'independence,' or something like that."

"Well, she is still awfully young. Maybe she just needs some time to figure out who she is?" My gaze darted to where Bryston stood, still lingering in the doorway as though he wasn't entirely sure of his welcome.

The others saw where I was looking, and Robert coughed uncomfortably. Before anyone could say anything, Phin trotted forward from where he stood at Ion's feet, shaking his mane. "I know you're all speechless at my beauty, but let's not be rude, children."

"Your . . . horn . . ." Brandon said weakly.

"Alas, given up in noble self-sacrifice to save the woman of the hour." The unicorn waggled his beard hopefully. "Think that deserves at least a bowl of rum, don't you?"

"Indeed." The werewolf and I exchanged a look and I shrugged, walking to where Bryston stood before taking his hand firmly into mine and pulling him back to the others.

It was unlike him to be so cautious and I wondered how much of that was because he was human now. I was used to the OtherFolk perception that mortality was weak—most of them tended to treat me like crap. It didn't take much to understand their discomfort to see one of their own changed so severely, regardless of the Path he walked. I hadn't been around to see how the dynamic had changed, but it was obvious Ion disturbed the others terribly.

Charlie was the first to step forward, her mouth twisted in a tight smile. "Thank you for bringing her home," she said softly.

Ion nodded, but bitterness lurked behind his eyes.

Charlie was one of my oldest friends, but our relationship had been strained the last year or so. In part because she'd been kidnapped by Maurice in an effort to get at me . . . and in part because of . . .

. . . a high-pitched giggle echoed from behind Robert's massive wings, a toddling Benjamin shuffling his way over to us. The result of an illicit love affair between Moira and Robert, Benjamin was a perfect tiny replica of his father, all stubborn mouth and stubby limbs.

"Who's my little man?" I crouched to my knees, my arms open, wondering if he would even remember me. "Auntie's missed you, you know." He stared at me for a moment longer and then a smile broke out on his chubby face. I scooped him up and he clung to me, his fingers twiddling in my hair for a few minutes before he began to squirm in that way that babies and cats do when they didn't want to be touched anymore.

His little wings beat frantically and I let Charlie take him, pleased to see how well they were bonding. I suspected things would get messy once Moira came back into the picture, but no sense in courting trouble about it now. Beside, I had enough crap on my plate.

"Well, this has been . . . heartwarming," Roweena said dryly from her perch on the barstool. The elven liaison hadn't bothered trying to insert herself into my personal space yet, but I detected a faint hint of amusement about her slanted eyes, even so. The elderly Fae resembled a kindly grandmother—but the sharpness of her tongue could have doubled as battery acid.

"We could practically write Hallmark cards about it," I agreed. "Seeing as there aren't many ways to say 'Happy you're not dead' nicely."

"Indeed. But somehow it's never that simple with you."

"No. And as much as I'd love to continue with the greetings, we've got bigger issues. Again." I paused for a moment, making sure I had everyone's attention for the announcement. "Eildon Tree was attacked, by Maurice."

My mouth went dry as Roweena's face paled. "I don't know what the full extent of the damage was, but Talivar says it's possible the Tree won't survive." My gaze swept the tiny group of people, trying not to waver beneath the widened eyes and disbelieving stares.

"Also . . . Talivar is king now. Of the Unseelie Court."

"Impossible!" Roweena whispered. "The Queen would never allow it . . ."

"The Queen no longer rules; Moira does—or she will soon enough."

The elf sank into her seat with a look of dread.

"I'm guessing that news hasn't been made public yet," I said.

"No," she snapped. "Nor should it until the monarchy has had a chance to make things official. Of all the times to see a change in command . . . ."

I put my hand on her arm. "I know your loyalty is to the former Queen . . . but she was completely deranged while I was there—you read my letter."

"I know. I just can't believe she would do such a thing."

"Believe it. She's the one who prevented me from leaving once I . . . stopped being dead. And . . . uh . . . I'm sorta handfasted. To Talivar."

Robert's head snapped toward me. "But that would mean you're—"

"No . . . I'm not his Queen. Not yet." I interjected quickly. "It means nothing at the moment, except that I've got a few more responsibilities than I had before."

He snorted. "If that's what you believe, then you're more naïve than I thought."

"Abby's always good for that," Ion muttered, his hand squeezing mine. "But I admit I always found that rather charming. And irritating," he added a moment later.

"Yeah, well, we can't all be perfect."

"So what do you intend to do?" Roweena gazed at me as though she expected me to disappear in a puff of smoke.

"Talivar asked me hold down the fort here while he assesses the damage to the Tree, and the two Courts decide if they're going to work together." The elf twitched at this statement and I stifled a sigh. Hundreds of years of prejudice weren't going to be undone overnight, but at least she wasn't openly rebelling at the thought.

"I'm going to need help." I gave the braid with Ion's bells a nervous yank. "Portsmyth needs a proper Protectorate to start with."

Roweena nodded, her usual businesslike efficiency popping into place like a mask upon her face. "Yes. If both Talivar and Moira are headed for rulership, they cannot fulfill their duties here." Her expression became troubled. "However, we need the backing of the Faery Council to appoint a new one, so in the interim you are still on the hook. Death or not, you are the TouchStone bound to the current Protectorate—at least on paper."

"Figures." Ion let my hand slip from his and I began to pace around the bar, my mind whirling as I tried to decide our best course of action. "I'm not sure Maurice realizes I'm still alive, but I would bet even money he'll know soon enough."

Robert nodded. "We'll want to get you some protection for sure . . . at least around your apartment. Will you be reopening the bookstore or the Midnight Marketplace?"

Part of my previous duties for Moira had been to run the storefronts that she owned: a used bookstore she had made her mundane center of business—and a magical one, intended to be available only for Other-Folk travelers who might need to find more esoteric goods.

I bit down on my lower lip. I'd ransacked the magical shop trying to find something to trade with Kitsune for her help to find a cure for the Queen's madness. If Moira knew about it, she hadn't mentioned to me, but I owed it to her to at least clean up my mess. Slowly I nodded. "Yeah, but . . . I think I want to change the format of it. There's going to be a lot change coming down the pipeline . . . not to mention the Tree issue. It wouldn't be a bad idea to keep it open as a gathering place to share information. A safe haven for anyone unsure of what they're supposed to do."

Roweena nodded at this, satisfaction crossing over her face. "About time," she murmured cryptically. "You'll have my backing on this. I'll make sure the Council is informed."

Brandon disappeared behind the bar for a moment,

sliding a glass of Diet Coke my way a few minutes later. "You look like you could use it."

"Mmmph." I took a sip and sighed. "So . . . this leads me to the question of the day. Does anyone know where Melanie is or how we can get ahold of her?"

There was a moment of uncomfortable silence that stretched into something ridiculous and I finally set the now-empty glass onto the bar. "I know she left. But surely she still has her cell phone? Something?"

Charlie shook her head. "As far as we know, she just got on a bus one morning and disappeared."

I raised a brow at them. "And not a single one of you thought to follow? To ask her what was wrong?" My gaze darted to Brystion and he flinched. That wasn't really fair of me, and I knew it, but I also couldn't believe she wouldn't at least have left him some way of contacting her. They'd been through an awful lot in the past.

On the other hand, I knew damn well what it was like to be so wrapped up in despair it was easier to run away than face the reality of it all.

"She went to New York," Brystion said abruptly.

The others stared at him. "Well, it might have been helpful to have known that at the beginning of this conversation," Robert snarled.

The incubus didn't look at me. "She was there looking for an alternate way to free Abby. She has a lot of connections, being what she is, and New York has a more . . . diverse population of OtherFolk."

"OtherFolk more willing to do things they probably shouldn't, you mean." Charlie's mouth compressed into a tight line. "Didn't she know you and Talivar were working on a way to free Abby?"

Brystion snorted. "Of course she did. But that

didn't mean she agreed with what we were doing—"

"But you know where she is, right?" I interrupted, trying to keep us on track. "Some way to leave her a message?"

He hesitated. "The last time I talked to her was to tell her you were dead, Abby. I haven't heard from her since."

I exhaled slowly. "I can't believe there isn't at least some record of a virtuoso street busker somewhere? She's the goddamned Door Maker."

"Most of us only know her when her power manifests itself . . . it's the Wild Magic that draws us to her," Brystion said. "Or used to, in my case."

Robert nodded. "Call it an echo, maybe. The Cross-Roads respond to it and we can feel it too." His look became grim. "Her music has gone silent."

"I don't understand. I've never seen her go for more than a day without playing."

I paused, something cold gripping my gut. "You think she's dead?" My voice was small against the possibility, but even I had to admit something didn't make sense here. "Or what if . . . what if she tried to make a deal with the . . . with someone?" I didn't want to mention the Devil's name aloud. I hadn't had any dealings with him personally, but Melanie got skittish every time it had come up. No sense in attracting undue attention.

I stared down at my empty glass, the beads of sweat trickling down the sides. I didn't want to even consider the possibility that my best friend might be gone.

"There's always Nobu," I pointed out. "They were TouchStoned once . . . and they've got a bond of some sort . . ." I hesitated, not sure if "bond" was the word

I was looking for. Close enough. "He obviously still cares for her."

I knew the daemon still loved her—they'd been TouchStoned traveling musicians and lovers . . . until Melanie had attempted to outplay the Devil's TouchStone and lost. She gained her violin, but only at the cost of Nobu, who'd given himself over to Hell to save her.

And Nobu was the daemon who'd given me the lethe water, twisting my words after I attempted to make a bargain with him to free her. On one hand, I totally sympathized with his position . . . but on the other? I couldn't trust him at all. He'd already shown a rather key ruthlessness when it came to protecting Melanie and I couldn't knowingly expose the OtherFolk in my charge to that sort of potential two-facedness.

Talivar's charges, I corrected myself. Though I might as well have been the Protectorate in truth.

The others looked at me curiously, but I was unsure of what to tell them. After all, this was really Melanie's story to tell. If she hadn't shared the details of how she'd gotten her violin with them, it probably wasn't my place to reveal it either.

On the other hand, the shit was pretty much hitting the fan at this point, and the more people knew, the better off we'd probably be in the long run.

"What is it with you two and the bad boys?" Robert rolled his shoulders.

"You're one to talk," Ion snapped, bristling.

"That's enough of that," Roweena said mildly, weary resignation in her face. "We're not going to get anything done here if you can't manage to work together for at least five minutes."

Robert scowled, but withdrew, hoisting Benjamin into his arms. "You do what you want, Abby—you're going to anyway. I'll support you, but promise me you won't do anything as reckless as before."

"I understand. We'll leave Nobu out of this unless we don't have any other choice. In the meantime, I'm going to start making phone calls. Someone has to have known where she went. Even if I have to start calling hospitals." I shuddered at the thought. "I'll be in the Marketplace if you need to find me. Don't worry—I know what I'm doing."

"Famous last words." Our eyes met, the angel's mouth twitching. And then he smiled.

Twelve

What hell happened to this place?" Brystion let out a low whistle as he strode around the aisles of the Midnight Marketplace, avoiding the shattered crockery and scattered books strewn over the hardwood floor.

A thin layer of dust lingered on the shelves, illuminated by the fading balls of multihued witchlight faintly pulsing above us.

"*I* happened to it," I muttered, shaking out a pile of stuck-together parchment. "Jesus, what a mess."

"Nepotism works wonders, you know," Phineas observed over a slanting pile of books. "But even so, you'll be lucky Moira doesn't fire your ass."

I shrugged. "I'll take being fired over watching my friends get traded to daemons any day."

"Point taken. Though I'm not sure who got the better deal," he muttered.

"Yeah, well." I glanced around at the shambles and sighed. If Katy were here, I knew she'd be more than willing to pitch in . . . and Melanie too. But then, she was sort of the reason I was here, wasn't she?

"It's too quiet in here," I mumbled, digging the iPod from my back pocket. The dock and speakers on the counter were still in good shape and a moment later OneRepublic's "Secrets" blared forth, filling the broken shadows with bittersweet memories.

I debated trying to shuffle it, but the device had a mind of its own. Undoubtedly I was in for a few hours of angst-ridden lyrics and emo melodies.

I eyed the fallen bookshelves in irritation. "I wonder if Moira would care if I turned this place into a café of some sort."

"Progressive of you," Ion said dryly. "Maybe you can give me a job as a barista."

"Well, you *can* cook," I said. "So we can serve coffee and bacon sandwiches. And shelve oodles of pervy romance. Which you can read aloud to the customers while wearing nothing but an apron."

Phineas rolled his eyes, trotting to the rear of the store. "Well, you have to have goals."

Ion scowled at him. "I probably *will* need a job if I'm stuck in this form."

"You can still sing, can't you?" I blew the dust off the cash register, wiping the glass counter with a rag. "I mean, I'd think you would have the same talents as before."

"I suppose. It's just . . . different."

"Little harder to throw yourself out there without that smexy magic to back you up?"

"Could be." He paused. "Have you given any more thought to what you'll do if you can't find Melanie?"

"I've been trying not to, honestly. I can't bear to really imagine her as gone . . . and if we don't find her, I think we're all pretty fucked. If the Tree dies completely, I don't think we're going to *want* to know what happens next." I stared blankly at the door. "I suppose the mortal world will still exist, but we'll have lost something," I said softly. "As much of a pain in the ass as you OtherFolk have been, I still have to admit my life is richer for knowing you all."

I glanced down at my crippled knee. "I don't know where I'd be right now if I hadn't stumbled my way into town. Probably dead."

Melanie had invited me to Portsmyth after the accident that had destroyed my previous existence, introducing me to a world far larger than I knew existed. It may not have replaced my old life . . . but it sure as hell had given me a new one.

"You're stronger than that."

"Maybe now. Not so much then." Everything had been so raw in the beginning. I came out of my coma to discover my mother was dead and I was nothing more than a cripple with a seizure disorder. I could barely stand to be touched or talked to. I'd withdrawn from all of my dancer friends, bitter and jealous they retained the capabilities I no longer possessed. I waved him off since this wasn't really a road I wanted to head down. The point was that I had come here and I had made a Contract with Moira. The rest was history, I supposed.

My mouth made a line that was supposed to be a smile. "At least I know what awaits me on the other side."

He stiffened. "Don't even go there, Abby. It's not remotely funny."

I flushed. "I know. The most I can do right now is help out here as best I can." I shrugged at him. "I'm fairly useless at the moment otherwise. No special powers, anyway." I waggled my dust rag at him. "Except maybe cleaning. And even that's pretty suspect."

I glanced down at the cell phone in my pocket. "Cleaning poorly, and making phone calls."

Which led to the next thing I had to do. I'd already tried every phone number I had for Melanie—all were now listed as disconnected or unavailable—which left her parents. I'd only met them once, during Melanie's short stint at school. It hadn't been long enough to get much more than a perception of serial stage-mommy syndrome.

Well, that and the few minutes I'd had with her mother after Melanie had left the school altogether. I'd known she was having issues, but I hadn't realized how deep or involved they'd been, particularly with her family life. Her mother had grilled me for ten straight minutes as to the whereabouts of her daughter, but as distraught as she was, I had gotten the feeling it was less over the fact that Melanie was missing than the fact they'd lost a commodity.

And possibly tuition money they'd already paid.

But in the end, I had no answers to give them. Melanie had met me for coffee and a bagel one morning, said good-bye . . . and that was it.

Or was it? I frowned, searching my memories. Had there been a guy involved? She could have been with Nobu at the time, but I honestly couldn't recall seeing him. On the other hand, OtherFolk had Glamours up the ass, so he could have damn well looked like anyone.

But still. Nobu might have better insight into where she might have gone, but I'd promised he would be a last resort, so it was back to phone sleuthing.

With glass clinking as Ion swept up broken bottles, it took me only a few minutes to dig up Melanie's parents' listing. I knew vaguely where they lived based on comments from Melanie about her hometown, so I ran through the online white pages until I found the most promising number, and started with that one.

It picked up after two rings.

"Hello?" The voice was smooth, with a brittle sophistication that could only be her mother's. Would she remember who I was?

"Uh . . . hi. I'm looking for Melanie. Melanie St. James? I'm a friend of hers." I paused. "This is Abby Sinclair. We went to Juilliard together."

My words were met with silence but I thought I detected the briefest flare of breath, as though the woman were trying not to sniff at me.

"I'm sorry, but there is no one here by that name."

Well, shit. "Okay, but do you have any idea where she might be? She's been gone for a few weeks at least and her friends are very worried about her."

Another long pause. "I remember asking you the same question, a long time ago, Abby Sinclair. I do not know where she is. And I do not care."

Dangerous ground here . . .

"But she's your daughter. Don't you want to know she's safe?"

"I'm sorry, there's no one here by that name." The connection cut off abruptly and I was left to stare at my phone with a frown.

"Well, now I know why she didn't go home," I muttered, something uneasy taking root in my gut. I couldn't quite put my finger on it, but . . .

"She never talked about them much on the road, but they sounded like gits of the highest order." Ion shoved another set of books onto the shelves without bothering to look at the titles.

"I get the feeling there's a lot Melanie doesn't really

talk about." I sighed. "Well, unless we drive to their house, we may be out of options." I tapped the counter in irritation. "Although, there's nothing that says we can't send a . . . messenger of sorts, right?"

"Like a pixie or something? They're flighty. But might not be a bad idea."

"Of course, that begs the question of how to get ahold of one," I said sourly. "My connections are somewhat limited at the moment."

He grimaced. "I'll try to work on that."

"That's not what I meant."

"Oh, children, shush the hell up," Phineas snorted from my feet, the nubbed horn poking through the top of his forelock in an obscene gesture. "You're mortal. He's mortal. Get over it and use your damned cell phone to call in a few favors. There's not an OtherFolk being this side of the CrossRoads that wouldn't bend over backward to help Melanie in some fashion . . . if only to put her in their debt."

Ion and I shared a chastened smile. "Aye, aye," I murmured, pulling the phone out again.

A few hours and a pizza delivery later, Didi the PETA pixie strolled through the door. The little blonde was dressed in baby blue instead of her usual Barbie pink, but otherwise, she was unchanged from the last time I'd seen her.

She eyed the carnage with a raised brow before trotting over to me, gossamer wings fluttering. "I'd say I like what you've done to the place, but . . . uh . . ."

"It's not intentional, I assure you. Once we get things back in order, I'll be reopening for business. But in the meantime, I could use your help."

"Lame." She wrinkled her nose. "I'm not much good at cleaning."

"That's not what I meant." I shook my head. "I need you to go to New York."

She blinked. "What?"

"New York. Melanie is . . . missing. I want you to see if you can find a hint as to where she might have gone."

A scowl fluttered over her face. "Anyone ever tell you it sucks being your friend? Everyone seems to die or disappear around you."

"I take no credit for this one. I was dead at the time." I snagged another slice of pizza.

Brystion scratched out something on a piece of paper and handed it to her. "There's a werewolf there you should look up. Marcus. He's a guitar player— Melanie used to travel with him back in the day. It might not be a bad idea to check in with him."

"You're assuming I'll even agree to this." Didi pouted at me. "Every time I try to help you, something wonky happens."

"You know what kind of wonky shit is going to happen if you don't help me this time? Eildon Tree is going to *die*, and then what will you do?"

Her face bled white. "Well, when you put it that way. What do you want me to do, exactly?"

"Check out the music clubs, the OtherFolk hot spots. It doesn't make any sense to me that she'd completely disappear . . . not for this long and definitely not without music of some form."

"Why do I get the feeling I'm going to be stuck looking at every street busker in the subway?"

"You know her . . . just look for the redhead with the purple sunglasses. Probably playing death metal Mozart in Times Square."

Didi gave me a dubious look and then nodded. "I'll see what I can find out." She waved and flitted out the door. Convenient, anyway. I realized I hadn't asked her if she'd needed a TouchStone, but if she'd had issues, she hadn't seen fit to bring them up.

"Well, that's that, I suppose." I brushed my hands on the pockets my jeans, still marveling at the fact I wasn't wearing a gown. And that I had real underwear on. It was the small things.

As I stood there musing over another shelf of dried herbs, the iPod switched songs into Eric Hutchinson's "You Don't Have to Believe Me." I found myself tapping my foot, and when I felt the smooth glide of a hand upon my shoulder, I smiled.

"Care to dance?" Ion asked it mildly, and if there was no flash of gold lingering in the dark of his eyes, I recognized that inner hunger quite well.

I pursed my lips at him. "Lead on."

Something satisfied flickered over his face as he pulled me into his arms. There wasn't enough room to really get going, but we swayed up and down the aisles, narrowly avoiding the shelves and the other debris. Phin stoutly ignored us, which was fine with me, although I caught his tail sweeping gently to the rhythm anyway.

Once again, I felt a pang for Melanie's absence. With her here, it would have been a proper moment between friends, but I'd take what I could get. Bryston wasn't doing anything fancy as far as footwork went. Just an arm around my waist and our hands clasped and his not-so-subtle way of steering us toward the rear of the store.

"Any particular reason for this impromptu bout of two-step?" I murmured.

"Overtaken by your shy beauty. Plus I wanted to touch you."

"Honest, anyway."

"Have I ever been anything but?" He tipped my head up and we both snorted at the lie, but didn't pause in our movements. "Besides, I've missed this." He spun me out. "I've missed *you*."

Even though it had only seemed like a few days or weeks to me, for my friends it had been so much longer. Months. I'd gone through my own "there and back again," though, so it wasn't like any of us had gotten out of the deal unscathed.

He pulled me closer and I dropped my head to rest on his shoulder. Strange to feel the absence of burning heat when I touched him, but it wasn't a bad thing. The soft exhalation of his breath ruffled over my hair, his chin resting on top of my head, and I couldn't help the shiver from sliding down my spine.

For all that he'd been inside my dreams for so long, for all that we'd already done so much together, this quiet dance was the most intimate moment we'd ever had. Simply because it was so . . . simple. No magical powers to draw us together. No required sexual feedings. No . . . nothing.

We'd talked about it before. Wondering if our attraction to each other simply stemmed from his being an incubus and my possessing Dreaming powers. It's a hard thing to have to question, particularly when it feels so goddamned good to give in.

And yet here he was. And here I was. Dancing in the tattered remains of the Midnight Marketplace with only our own skins to shield us.

When he kissed me, I let my eyes drift shut, losing myself in the feel of him. The taste of him. No hidden tricks of emotional lust or my own mind turning him into something else based on my desires. And then I stopped thinking altogether, as his hands cupped my face, holding us in that moment until we trembled with it.

I looked up at him finally, still surprised to see the dark of his pupils without the typical flicker of gold. He cocked a brow at me, his mouth kicking into a crooked smile as though he knew what I was thinking.

"I begin to understand now," he said, wrapping me into his arms to finish the dance.

"I suppose I could tell you it's about time."

"You could. But I'd ignore you." He nipped my ear gently. "Besides, I'm not one for sleeping with married ladies."

I rolled my eyes at him. "Not even in their dreams?"

"That's different. I'm merely giving them 'inspiration' for later moments with their husbands." His mouth quirked. "Sometimes."

"Indeed. How noble of you."

He shrugged. "It does put us in a predicament, Abby."

"I know. And I suppose I ought to figure that out soon." Talivar had told me before that Faery wives weren't actually expected to remain faithful . . . and neither were Faery husbands. That should have been reassuring, but it really wasn't. And I was treading on dangerous emotional ground. Regardless of what the elf thought he believed in, I knew he would be terribly hurt at any betrayal by me.

And honestly, wouldn't *I* be if he were to do the same?

I sighed. "Nothing ever gets to be easy, does it?"

"No. But life isn't supposed to be easy. If it were, what would be the point?"

"I guess. So what now?"

"We keep dancing. And figure things out later."

"Assuming there will be a later," I muttered darkly. "If the Tree dies, we're probably pretty screwed."

"Probably," he agreed. "In which case we can fuck like rabbits until the CrossRoads collapse."

"What happened to being honorable?" I laughed.

"Under those circumstances, honor can go take a flying leap." His face became sly. "If I'm going to die, might as well be while I'm between your thighs."

"You stay classy."

"It's what I'm good at."

I shook my head at him and he kissed me again, shoving me hard against the counter. "Just something to think about," he murmured, his hand sliding over the inside of my arm.

I opened my mouth to reply and realized the store had gone completely silent. Even the iPod stopped playing. "This can't be good." I slipped out of Brystion's embrace, making my way up to the front.

"Abby," Phineas said sharply, his blue eyes filled with an odd sort of anguish.

My heart dropped.

Something bad had happened.

"What—what is it? Talivar?" I asked, stepping over a box of crystal flagons.

Nobu loomed in the doorway. His ebony wings mantled like a thick cloak behind him, his face a thundercloud.

"What are you doing here?" I frowned. Not that

I would object to any additional help at this point, but . . .

I glanced down, Brystion catching my arms as I sank to my knees. In Nobu's hands lay the familiar curve of Melanie's violin.

Thirteen

"What the hell—?" I carefully took the violin from the daemon. The weight of the wood pressed heavy in my fingers, the usual silver shimmer absent from the surface. I bit down on my lower lip. Melanie would never part from her beloved instrument, even in the direst of circumstances. I could buy that maybe she wasn't playing it—but to leave it behind?

Given how ballistic she'd gone when it was stolen before, there wasn't a chance in hell she'd voluntarily give it up. It was part of her soul, after all. I cradled it in my arms, staring at it as though it might somehow provide me with answers.

"Where did you find this?" I asked.

Phineas reared up on his hind legs to sniff the instrument.

"Not where I should have." Nobu brushed into the store, booted heels whip-crack sharp upon the wooden floor.

My face grew grim as I looked at Ion. "Do we need to start looking at obituaries?"

The daemon shook his head, his words cutting. "I

would know if she had passed on. That doesn't mean she's not in danger." He glanced over at the violin. "If she is parted from it for too long . . ."

"So what do we do? I've already called everyone I know . . . I've got Didi scouting the streets of New York . . ." My voice trailed away, my fingers tracing the curved side of the violin. "The Dreaming. What if we tried to find her there?"

Brystion snorted. "The irony being that if I were still myself, I might be able to do it."

"What about Sonja?"

"She never had the same sort of friendship with Melanie that I did. Without having the 'signature,' we can't just arbitrarily find someone . . . and Mel wasn't TouchStoned to anyone at the time either, so we don't even have that."

I eyed Brystion. "What about me?"

"What about you? You don't have the Key anymore . . . even if you wanted to try the trick you used to before, you couldn't."

Which was true. When I'd worn the Key, I'd been able to tap into its potential for opening Doors nearest the thing I most wanted to find. It had been handy . . . until I inadvertently started a war between Hell and Faerie with it.

"No. Not that." Irritated, I flicked my thigh with my fingers. "I meant me, in the Dreaming."

He blinked. "DreamWalking? I don't know if you'd be strong enough for that. It takes so much control, Abby, and that's something you've been lacking. Would you be able to push your way past those nightmares?"

"I don't know." Months ago, Sonja had shown me the way the Dreaming was connected . . . how people in the real world often had tenuous bonds within their dreams . . . and how such bonds could be traversed by Dreamers.

I was mostly untrained, but I'd be more than willing to give it a shot if it meant getting my best friend back. To keep her from doing something stupid, if nothing else. On the other hand . . .

Nobu's mouth pursed. "And what happens if it doesn't work? What happens if you fuck something up in her head?"

"Back off, Peacock." Ion bristled beside me. "We're doing the best we can."

Phineas nipped my ankle. "Don't be such dumbasses. Take Sonja with you. I'm sure she won't lead you astray."

I glanced at Ion. "That should work, right? She was teaching me before."

"She was teaching you theory," he corrected. "It's not really the same thing."

Nobu threw up his hands. "I have no time for this. If you find her, let me know—otherwise I'll be out searching for her myself. Guard that violin with your life." He whooshed out the door, a few stray feathers floating in his wake like tiny black snowflakes.

"He's worried," I observed.

"Nice to see you've retained your penchant for stating the obvious," Phin said, snorting. "I was afraid you lost that when you died."

"Shut up." I nudged him away and snagged my iPod before damping the witchlights. "Come on. Let's close up here and call Sonja . . . and then we'll see what I can do." We trudged outside and I tapped a combination into the wall. The Door to the Marketplace flared once and then faded away in a shower of silver.

Ion slipped his hand into mine and led me up the stairs to my apartment, Phin trotting behind us. "I wish I could help you with this," he muttered, his voice suddenly agitated. "Messing around in the Dreaming is so dangerous for the untrained, Abby. If I was still an incubus, I could lead you there, possibly ride the link myself."

I rewarded him with a tight smile, touching the bells in my hair. "Somehow I think you will be."

The Dreaming was silent when I arrived after a fitful attempt to sleep. The grass had grown in my absence, tall and wild. Vines of swiftly twining greenery trailed over the iron bars of the gate, but no crickets chirped, no fireflies flew.

It was just me and the breeze and the tumbledown foundations of my old house. A part of me wanted to start creating again, forming the Dreaming into the shape that I willed, but I would need all my strength to concentrate on finding Melanie. Redecorating could come later.

I caught the faint brush of an amber shadow lurking outside, a hint of red feathers.

Sonja.

I opened the gate to let her in, giving her a tight smile.

"Are you sure you want to do this, Abby?"

I nodded. "What else can I do? I have to at least try."

She paused, her dark eyes weighing me for a moment. "All right, then. Let's get started. You remember the basics? How to shield?"

"Yeah." I imagined the white light, the bubble surrounding me and pushed outward. Light as a feather and stronger than steel, a guardian of myself, made to protect me from the shadows of my night-mares.

It was something I'd never really managed to do be-fore . . . at least, not very well. I'd always had to strug-gle with it, trying to wrap my mind around the odd physics of the Dreaming. Even when I'd finally gotten around to creating a tiny shield, it paled in comparison to what Ion could do . . . the way he manipulated the Dreaming to his will.

He might not have previously had a Dreaming Heart of his own, but his very essence had been of the Dreaming itself. He could bend it, warp it, wend it, draw strength from it . . . As could Sonja.

I glanced up as I realized Sonja had gone quiet, star-ing at me. "Where the hell did you manage to learn that?"

I was glowing with silver light. I blinked and the halo damped down. "I don't know. When I came here last time, I had to fight through the sharks. This is what I made."

She shook her head. "You've got a shitload more power now than you did before. I don't know if dying opened up your inner channels or what, but if you're able to produce a shield like that, you'll have little trouble trying finding your way through the rest of the Dreaming."

An uneasy thought twisted through my gut. "What if it's what Ion did to me?"

"Did you manage to pry that out of him?"

"Sort of. He . . . uh . . . made me drink his dreams. It wasn't supposed to turn him human . . . he was trying to reverse what we did before. He was trying to pull me into the Dreaming and out of Faerie."

The succubus swore under her breath. "Idiot. You

can't do shit like that." She swept up to me as I let the shield fall away, her fingers digging into my hair for the bells. "I knew there was more to these than a souvenir . . ." Her dark eyes bore into mine. "Whatever you do, do not lose them. You hold his life in your hair here . . . and quite possibly the only way to turn him back."

"Balls on a string," I muttered, and she snorted.

"To put it bluntly, yes. It's like the essence of who he really is was trapped in them." A sigh escaped her. "Do you remember anything of what I taught you before?"

"Yeah. Ion showed me what the whole Dreaming looked like the last time I saw him here." And he had. The incubus had stripped away he illusory safety of my Dreaming Heart, revealing it as a single point in what I could only describe as some sort of metaphysical universe . . . each Dreaming Heart a sparkling solitary star in the darkness of the unconscious mind.

Sonja had told me that a DreamWalker could move between them. Not everyone's, of course—but between those to whom the Dreamer had a connection. Friends. Family. TouchStones. And quite possibly enemies. What mattered was the strength of the emotional connection between them.

And Melanie was the sister of my heart.

"All right, then. You're going to need to feel this out a bit, but once we step outside the gate, I want you to put your shields back. I'm going to lead you to the very edges of your Heart. I want you to concentrate on your feelings for Melanie. Your best memories. That sort of thing. If I can get you turned in the right direction, you'll vibrate like a string. We get that, we can follow the path to where she is."

"And if there's nothing?" I hated to ask it.

"We'll cross that bridge when we come to it." Her mouth twitched into a soft smile. "Let's keep that upper lip stiff, shall we?" She linked her arm through mine and together we slipped past the gate.

I shut it carefully. No sense in letting something else inside while I was gone. Sucking in a deep breath, I pushed out again, the light of my shield illuminating the cobblestoned path before us.

Sonja made a curt nod and abruptly the gate faded away, along with the remains of my Dreaming Heart. Once again, I was plunged into darkness and shadow. In the distance I glimpsed the silhouettes of my sharks, but there was something far less sinister about them.

Maybe if I believed they had no real power over me it would be true. I ignored them and they seemed to do the same. Maybe it was a subconscious truce. Whatever it was, I'd take it.

We were rising, or the path was falling away. I couldn't quite figure it out. Tiny pinpricks of light beamed, but they were so very far away. Sonja's wings were outstretched and there was a feral gleam in her eyes as the light from my shield played over her skin.

I wondered if she'd fed.

She turned toward me and nodded. Trusting her to know what she was doing, I let the memories of Melanie sweep by like a river of . . . music.

Of course, what else would it be?

Notes and half-forgotten chords swirled about me . . . the piece she'd played during one of my recitals so long ago . . . the first time I'd seen her play at the Hallows, her solo slipping off into a wild cadence, dancers spinning and spinning and spinning on the dance floor. The night she took me out when I first arrived in Portsmyth . . . the way the Doors flared to life when she played, opening the CrossRoads.

Door Maker, the OtherFolk named her. Player of the Wild Music. Violin virtuoso. Street busker par excellence. Traveler of the roads. Juilliard dropout.

The names were many, but just facets. Bits and pieces of how others saw her, but none of it really came close to all that she was. For a moment I imagined how Nobu fit into the equation, if she had loved him . . . what her true ties to him had been.

But above all, she was still my friend. Red-haired. Green-eyed. A cliché of beauty and soft curves and violet tea-shades, leather corsets and combat boots. The flash of her teeth when she smiled. That odd little quirk of her brow when she found something amusing. The crooked knuckle on her left pinky. The spiral tattoo on her shoulder. The silver scar at her jawline . . . the Devil's kiss, marking her as His.

Where are you?

I cast the thought into the Dreaming.

What did she dream of? What nightmares did she face?

But I knew the answer, didn't I? I imagined her violin, shining silver beneath the light of the CrossRoads. I didn't have the full details of how she'd received it, but I knew her reaction when it had been lost before.

A vibration thrummed through me, faint. The merest tickle at first, becoming sharp and frantic. The image of the violin grew stronger and more vibrant. A wave of despair washed over me, nearly driving me to my knees. My shield wavered and I lost the vibration as I tried to keep it from collapsing.

Sonja's head jerked toward me. "There," she murmured, her hand pointing into the darkness. "It's coming from that direction . . . assuming what you've found is actually her." The succubus's mouth compressed. "There are mimics out there."

"It felt like her. I think."

"Try it again. We need to be absolutely sure before I lead us there."

I nodded, my eyes drifting shut again. This time I immediately brought up the violin and the reaction was a tangible. Pain. Panic. Fear.

Abby?

"It's her," I gasped.

"Hold on to it." Sonja snatched my hand, her power lifting us and hurtling us forward. "Whatever happens, don't drop the connection."

We plunged into the darkness, my stomach rolling as I held on to that tenuous bond, feeling it slide from my mind like rainwater through a sieve.

Hold on, Mel . . .

Abruptly Sonja stopped, but I hurtled forward like a slingshot, her hand slipping from my grasp, my shield flickering as I realized I was on a path. Not the CrossRoads—no silver here—but dark cobblestones of sable with a pale flicker of light bursting over them like the electrical impulses of a neuron.

Everything went black, and then . . .

. . . *I was on a stage, playing and playing and playing. My fingers bled with music and my neck burned with the knowledge of who I was really playing for and I could only close my eyes against it because Abby was gone and it was for nothing . . .*

. . . *I was in the back of the battered van, lying in his arms. A soft grunt in the front passenger seat told me the incubus was getting his usual blow job from that Elizabeth girl, and Nobu snorted at me. Quietly, we snuck out*

*and wandered beneath the night sky, his wings trailing
behind him like a shadow . . .*

*. . . I was playing for an audience of paper dolls. I
longed to set them free, burn them with my music the way
it burned within me. Would they burst into flame and
ash? But I was only a little bird in a gilded cage. I sang
for my owners upon their command . . .*

*. . . I am dying. My soul has been stripped away, and
there is nothing left for me but to fade away, the Wild
Magic muffled and quiet . . .*

"Melanie!" I shouted into the void, unsurprised
when the darkness swallowed up my voice. I pushed
out on the shield, illuminating as far as I could go. My
mind was whirling with her memories and her inner
anguish and for a moment it threatened to pull me
under. I took another step closer, trying not to drown
in them.

What would happen if I was absorbed into her
dreams? Strands of darkness tangled around my legs,
my arms, pulling me down and down and down.

I struggled with my shield, swallowing a cry as my
mouth was covered, my vision going red. In panic, I
lashed out, the shield fading away.

No!

"No," I mumbled. I would *not* go down this way.
Abruptly, I stumbled forward as something slammed
into me from behind, scraping the top of my head like
a torpedo of sandpaper and teeth.

What the hell?

My own nightmares loomed out of the shadows, the
sharks' teeth gleaming in the electric violence as they
surged forward to rend and tear at the inky tentacles
that gripped me.

I had only a minute to wonder before my mouth was freed. My mind pulled away from what it was seeing, my shield falling back into place, and I concentrated on making it stronger.

The oddness of having my own nightmares fight Melanie's was completely fucking with my head. And still the sharks tore into the darkness until I could see what appeared to be the glowing glass edge of . . . something.

Her own inner shield, perhaps? Sonja had told me normal dreamers had their own inborn defense. Melanie's had taken the shape of a metallic dome.

My sharks began to circle closer and closer, their bodies skimming over the thick crystal. They were searching for a weakness, I realized. One retreated into the darkness, whirling around midway and slamming itself into the wall.

"Stop!" Instinct told me that breaking into her Dreaming Heart like that was going to cause more harm than good. If her inner psyche saw me as a potential enemy, I'd never get in to see her. Plus, the thought of unleashing my nightmares upon another soul was repugnant in the extreme.

She had her own demons to fight. She damn well didn't need mine.

The sharks continued to circle and I forced my shield to flare out even farther, the light spreading like a halo to bathe hers. "Enough." I commanded. "You are no longer needed."

Those dead eyes rolled white as they passed, but amazingly enough they undulated away through the Dreaming.

I suppressed a shudder. For all that they were obeying my commands, I was always going to be a short step away from being consumed myself. Dangerous things to let in, nightmares.

I paced around the outer edge of her Dreaming Heart, my feet treading in what felt like a deep groove.

"Melanie?" I said it softly this time, sending my mind out in a quiet probe, testing for any weaknesses I could find in the structure. Somehow I would find a way inside, but it had to be of her own volition, or it would be for nothing.

There . . . I caught the flicker of silver in a faint etching over the nearest point to where I was. The dome itself remained dark, but there was an almost friendly wink to the light. It looked like a door. Encouraging.

"It's Abby . . . would you let me in?"

The light of the door paused and began to melt away. I placed a tentative palm on it, a rush of warmth shunting up to my elbow. Melanie . . . or something akin to her inner essence, anyway.

There were shadows here, but I caught a familiar hint of laughter as well, the music in my ears suddenly soaring into a crescendo.

I was beginning to understand the level of intimacy Bryston had had with me. There was a sacredness to it and that required a certain amount of respect. But she still needed to let me in.

I pressed harder upon the doorway.

"'If music be the food of love,'" I quoted at it. An inside joke between us, but as far as passwords went, it wasn't bad.

"Please."

The door wavered, abruptly disappearing. Off balance, I tumbled in, unsurprised to feel the breeze of it closing behind me. Trapped then, though I wasn't worried about it at the moment.

I found myself standing in front of a stage. A quick glance about revealed I was in an auditorium, but not one I recognized. It was empty. Hollow. Quiet except for the warped hum coming from center stage.

Melanie stood there, playing stiffly, as though she were merely a rag doll or a puppet, her limbs clearly controlled by some other force. It didn't even look like her . . . instead of her usual bohemian chic, she was dressed in a long-sleeved silk button-down, a wool pencil skirt, and sensible shoes. Her normal unruly red riot of curls was pulled austerely away from her face.

And the music was . . . wrong. A deranged version of "Twinkle, Twinkle Little Star," out of tune and weak.

Her eyes cracked open at me as I approached the stage, but with a glazed focus. "I'm broken." She laughed harshly. "The music's broken in me and I can't ever fix it."

"Well, you're going to have to. We need your help, but you're going to have to tell us where to find you first."

"You're dead. What right do you have to tell me anything?"

I hesitated. *Fuck it.*

"I'm your goddamned best friend, Mel. That's who I am." I climbed the steps, unsure of where this newfound cockiness had come from, but I wasn't going to question it. "And the rumors of my death have been greatly exaggerated."

She stared at me, the tattered violin lowering as she turned to really look at me. "Prove it."

I cocked a brow at her. "Shall I dance *Swan Lake* for you? Or do I lay it all out and do 'Thriller'?"

Her mouth twisted. "You're just a projection of my imagination."

"No. I'm DreamWalking . . . and let me tell you, it's not exactly pleasant. I could have done without ever knowing Ion got a blow job from Elizabeth in the front seat of your van, you know. Assuming that was actually her," I amended.

I gently stroked her arm, frowning when I saw the bloodstains on her wrist. "What the hell is this?"

Buttons popped off the hems as I shoved her sleeves up to her elbow, my mouth dropping when I saw the crisscrossed marks decorating the pale flesh of her inner arm. "Did you fucking try to kill yourself? Did someone do this to you?"

A humorless laugh escaped her. "I used to cut myself a lot. When I was younger. A child prodigy, taught to perform on the stage at her mother's command for the amusement of others. Never allowed to play with other children. Never allowed public school. Or TV. Or the radio." Her emerald eyes met mine, their emptiness chilling as she thrust her wrist at me. "This . . . this I could control."

"Jesus, Mel. I had no idea."

"No one did. That was the point." She snorted, an inelegant, hateful sound. "I always wore long sleeves to all my concerts. My secret revenge against all of them."

Her chin trembled and she pushed it out at me in defiance, a tendril of her hair escaping the tightly wrapped bun. The seconds ticked by until I lost track. We could have been standing there for a few moments—or forever.

"You were lucky," she sobbed suddenly. "Your mother never forced you into dancing . . . it was something you loved. I never had a choice."

I cupped her cheek and pulled her into my arms. "You have a choice now," I murmured.

"Do I?" She dropped the violin so that it shattered at our feet, the wood splintering in a horrendous caterwaul. "I've trapped myself, it seems." She hugged me tightly, her whole body shaking with great, wracking waves of grief.

So much sadness that I'd never known about. Melanie had always seemed to have it all . . . but this secret pain was unlike anything I'd ever seen in her before.

Caged bird, indeed.

Nobu had had the truth of it and my respect for the sin-eater went up several notches.

She pulled away from me, her mouth a tight line. "If you're not dead, what happened to you?"

"Well . . . I did die, Mel," I said softly. "Maurice killed me, but . . . I got lucky, I guess. Phin brought me back. But the time difference . . ."

She nodded, biting hard on the inside of her cheek.

"Mel . . . where are you? Eildon Tree is dying and we need you. We need the Wild Magic to save it."

Her face paled. "I don't know," she whispered. "I've been asleep for so long."

"A spell?"

"No. I went . . . home after you died. I don't know why. Maybe I just wanted to try to make peace with my family."

I decided not to tell her the way her mother had reacted on the phone when I'd called. Judging by the way her upper lip curled, she obviously had a pretty good suspicion. "I had some kind of breakdown. They hospitalized me. I assume that's where I am now . . . but I can't wake up."

I frowned, something dawning on me. "Your violin."

"They took it from me . . . I guess. Or didn't bring it to the hospital with me." She stared down at the broken bow.

"We have it, Mel." I gripped her hand. "Nobu found it. Tell us where you are and I'll bring it to you. I'll haul ass via car or CrossRoads to find you."

She shook her head. "I don't know. I know I was at the local hospital, but I think they moved me to some sort of psych ward." She flushed. "I went a little crazy at one point, but I just wanted my violin. Think they were too afraid to give it to me. Thought I might break it or hurt myself with it."

"Then you're going to have to wake up, Mel. You're going to have to find a way to get a phone call out to us. Or hell, if you can figure out where you are, I can meet you here tomorrow night. Something. Anything." My voice took on a twinge of desperation.

She blinked at me. "Your eyes are glowing, Abby." She took a step back. "I don't think you're who you say you are—Ion?" Panic crossed over her face. "But he isn't . . . get out! Get away!"

My eyes?

I barely had time to process this bit of information before the auditorium began to collapse. Plaster sifted down like hail. A chunk of the ceiling shattered inches away from my feet and I ducked, scrambling for the door.

"Mel!" She wheeled on her heel, bolting off the stage and disappearing into the dust kicked up by the debris. I tripped on the broken violin, the wood melting into a sticky puddle as the floor dissolved.

I sank into the stage and into the darkness.

"Shit." I pulled my own shield tightly around me, just in case. Melanie wasn't a Dreamer, but I was in her head and there was no telling what she might do

I pressed my way through the darkness, my shields glowing dimly. It was enough light to see that there was nothing here at all.

No hope for it, then . . . I'd scared her off and I didn't have it in me to chase her down like a frightened rabbit. Although it also begged the question: How was I going to get out of here?

"Melanie! You have to wake up! We need you! We're coming for you, Mel. You have to let me out!"

My only answer was silence. And then a soft beam of light appeared below me. My exit? Abruptly I sank, as though some great force was shunting me down and out. I didn't fight it, unsurprised when I was deposited neatly outside Melanie's Dreaming Heart, the hole shutting behind me with a despondent clank.

Fourteen

How can you have been so goddamned stupid?"
Sonja paced around my kitchen, her wings flared out
in irritation. "You can't go slamming into someone's
Heart like that! And those freaking sharks . . . attack-
ing it?"

Bryston ran a thumb over my wrist. "Well, maybe
if you'd trained her better . . ."

"Fuck you!" His sister whirled on him. "All of it. I
never asked to try to train her . . . and even aside from
that, *you* gave her your power. Bad enough she barely
knows what she's doing, but now she's got abilities *no*
mortal DreamWalker should have. This is *your* goddamned mess."

He drew himself up, his mouth opening in anger
before abruptly shutting. "You're right. It is." A slow
sigh escaped him. "But Abby's paying the price for
that, not you, so let's not be pulling any martyr cards
today, shall we?"

The succubus snarled beneath her breath before
turning to me. "You're going to have to fix him somehow. Give it back."

He raised a brow at us. "And what if I don't want it?" Ion's hand crept into mine, fingers entwining tightly. "I have no regrets." His eyes darted away as he said it, giving lie to the words, but there was no doubt in my mind that he wanted to believe them.

"I never wanted you to do this, Ion." I shook my head. "But we'll figure it out somehow." A wry smile crossed my face. "Maybe I'll visit your dreams next time . . . a little quid pro quo, perhaps?"

An odd look flickered over his face, but he said nothing.

"You may have to," Sonja said bluntly. "Chances are that's the only way this is going to be reversed. Not to mention we have no idea what the long-term effects will be on Abby."

He waved her off. "Let's focus on trying to find Melanie. My problems can wait."

"Christ—why do you think I'm talking about this? I need *you*, Bryston, not some half-trained Dream-Walker. We're lucky she didn't burn out the poor woman's mind the way she went stomping around there."

"Well it's not like you gave me any direction," I retorted, my own ire starting to creep to the forefront. Tensions were high and I could let some of the attitude slide, but I wasn't going to just sit here and take it either. "You told me to follow the path, and I did. And then you were gone."

Ion's eyes narrowed. "You let her go by herself?"

"I wasn't expecting her to take off like that. She shouldn't have been able to."

Phineas looked up from my laptop, blinking rapidly. Unable to be much help during the DreamWalking, the unicorn had lost himself in a series of RPG games. I'd found him passed out on the keyboard this morning—he'd simply played himself into oblivion. It couldn't be healthy, but depression took multiple forms, and if he needed a little self-wallowing to get over the loss of his horn, then that was fine with me.

"Please shush, children. Some of us have Reapers to fight."

I went over and shut the laptop, ignoring his squeal of dismay.

"And some of us have more to worry about than blowing up pixel baddies."

"Whatever. Every ending was the same anyway." He snarled at me, teeth bared. "Marauder Shields, my rainbow-farting ass."

"Focus, dude."

"Fine. Then maybe the three of you should stop re-iterating the obvious and go find Mel. You know she's in a hospital, probably in New York, right? Freaking start calling them."

"If you'd been paying attention, you'd have realized we've already done that." And I had. As soon as I'd been bounced out of Melanie's dreams, I'd called every hospital in NYC, but not a one had a patient by Mel's name. I stroked my hand down the little unicorn's spine, trying to soothe him.

Bryston tapped his fingers on the table, pounding out a rhythm I didn't recognize. "I've had enough of this." I turned to Sonja. "We're going to need more help than us to get her out and we're wasting time. Find Nobu and tell him to get his ass over this way. Tithe bullshit or no, he wouldn't let *her* die." I twisted the ring on my middle finger. "It's time to bring out the big guns."

"I was bringing out the big guns—until *somebody*

turned off my game," Phineas muttered, stalking into the other room. The TV switched on a second later, the *SpongeBob SquarePants* theme drifting back into the kitchen.

I stared at my feet, trying not to sigh. My husband might be out chasing Maurice, but capturing him would be moot if we didn't get Melanie back in action. I had a moment of reflection, wondering at my own calculating coolness, but if it served me better for it, then I would take it.

"What if I can't find Nobu?" Sonja paused as she headed toward the door.

"Use your daemonly wiles." I fluttered my fingers at her. "Isn't there like a Diner's Club for Daemons or something? Little black books?"

She glared at me, the door slamming behind her as she left.

"You might want to tone down that sarcasm, Abby. After all, she *is* trying to help." Ion pulled me into his lap so his chin could rest on my shoulder. "This isn't like you. I think Sonja may be right."

I nipped at his lip, sucking it hard. "Watch me care."

He pulled away. "I'm serious. You're different. Coming back from the Dreaming this time? You're like . . ."

"I'm acting like you, you mean?"

I eyed the set of his jaw and wondered what it would be like to kiss it, a dark hunger filling my belly with a burning roil. I straddled him, pushing his shoulders so the chair tipped to the floor.

The breath rushed out of him with a whoosh. Not that he was protesting, exactly, but I'd taken him by surprise. Still, a moment later and my shirt was stripped from my body as my tongue plunged deep into the velvet contours of his mouth.

He let out a grunt, his fingers biting into my shoulders as he nipped my breasts through my bra. The electric tingle shot through the tips of my nipples and planted firmly in my groin. I arched against him, his hands fumbling with the clasp.

A moment later and I was free, grinding into him with a fierceness that surprised even me. I sucked in a deep breath, but I was helpless to stop it. Somehow I staggered to my feet, tugging at his arms until he stood.

I wasn't quite ready to take him right on the kitchen floor. Not when there was a perfectly serviceable bed in the other room.

A flicker of masculine desire shone on his face, and if there was anything hesitant about it, he hid it well.

We stared at each other, the scenario playing out between us. Stupid to do it. Stupid to even think on it. But here we were.

Abruptly he scooped me up, my legs locking behind him as he launched us toward my bedroom, his mouth firmly on mine. At least we'd be stupid together. For some reason the thought was strangely comforting.

He didn't bother asking me if I was sure, shucking off the remainder of his clothes with a quick twist before tumbling me backward into the bed. A moment later and he'd yanked off my jeans, hesitating for the briefest of moments before burying his face in my neck. The awkwardness of earlier fled, and it was just the two of us, stretched out and wonderfully naked.

There were no words between us. Time was slipping away by the second, and even if we both knew this wasn't the wisest course, we were committed to it. When he sprawled on top of me, my legs parted to receive him without hesitation. He placed his hand over my eyes to shut them.

"Breathe," he murmured.

My head tipped back as I did what he asked, my body thrumming with need. The bells in my hair chimed enthusiastically and I chuckled. "Is this the part where you say, 'You complete me'?"

"Mmmph. Closer to say I complete you, I think." He found the sweet spot at the base of my throat and I hummed my approval. "But really, at this point we're kind of stuck with each other, wouldn't you say? It's not a TouchStone bond, but you're obviously carrying some part of me in you, anyway."

"Not as much as I could be. You still talk too damn much, Ion." He smiled against my mouth and let me roll him over, content to have me take the lead.

"Only when it comes to you."

And then there was no more time for words. Everything was soft touches and warmth as our fingers found each other with bold strokes. *This is mine . . . and this . . . and this.* My body knew it to be true and opened beneath it.

"Missed this," he sighed.

"It hasn't been that long, has it?"

He pressed a finger to my lips. "Now who's talking too much?" His mouth curved up with a hint of his old arrogance. "Guess I'm not working hard enough."

Before I could respond, he pulled me down, capturing the sound as his hand wandered between my thighs, chuckling when he found me wet.

"Exactly as I remember."

He nipped me hard, tilting my hips up to play there.

I writhed on top of him, crying out as his mouth found a nipple, working in tandem to the rhythmic stroking of my clit until my arms could barely hold me up from trembling.

"That's more like it." His smile grew wider.

With a grunt, I lifted onto my knees, squirming when his cock brushed over my sex. I hung there for a moment, rocking my hips until his eyes narrowed.

"Tease," he growled, snatching me down and thrusting his way deep.

There was nothing left except the blood pounding in my ears as we moved together. He was surprisingly vocal. More so than I remembered, but maybe that was his newfound mortality coming through.

"Deliciously noisy thing," I purred at him. He rumbled his agreement, twisting so that I was now beneath him, my legs wrapped around him as he thrust in earnest. My hands fisted in his hair as the headboard slammed into the wall again and again.

He stiffened, shouting out his pleasure, and I reveled in it, the sound tipping me over the heady wall of my own release. I pulsed around him, the bells in my hair chiming wildly as my thighs clamped his hips.

"Fuck, Abby," he sighed, sliding off to curl around me. I shivered beneath the damp of my sweat and he tucked the scattered blanket around us. "My first time as a mortal."

"Gee, if I'd known I'd be popping your cherry I would have attempted to make it more memorable."

He gave me a dry smile. "I think you did well enough." His mouth found mine for a long, drawn-out kiss. "We'll have to do it again sometime."

"Indeed," Talivar said coolly from the doorway. "Maybe next time you'll invite me to the party." The King strode in wearing dark jeans and a plaid button-down, his hair hanging loose. His gaze hardened as it fell on me and a hot flush rushed over my face.

"I'd say I'm sorry," Bryston drawled, his hand running over my shoulder possessively. "But I'm not."

I pulled away from him, shame biting at my belly. "You're not helping," I snapped, pressing my palm to my forehead. "I'm sorry, Talivar. I didn't mean for this to happen."

"Right." Pain flashed in Talivar's face. "Get dressed and meet me out there. We have news to discuss."

He whirled out of the bedroom, anger clinging to him like a shadow.

"Fuck." I punched my pillow. "Fuck!"

"He doesn't get to be upset, Abby. Your marriage is a sham, and he knows it." Ion slid off the other side of the bed.

"That doesn't mean what we did was right," I said bitterly. "Your essence inside me or not . . . it was a dick move."

"Oh, so now it's my fault. Me and my daemonic essence." He bristled, throwing on his shirt with a savage tug.

"That's not what I said . . ."

"But it's what you meant." He shuffled into his pants. "Maybe instead of blaming everyone else for your issues you should look at yourself." He thrust a finger at me. "I know damn well what it's like to feel that hunger, but there's an element of responsibility that rests on your shoulders." His dark eyes fixed on me, something sad flashing in their depths. "You were looking for an excuse. Glad I could provide you with that."

I drew myself up, finding my own jeans with whatever bit of dignity I had left. "That's not fair, and you know it."

He snorted and headed for the door. "Life's not fair, *princess*. I would have thought you knew that by now." Without waiting for a response, he turned on his heel and slipped into the hallway.

I scowled at the door as it clicked shut behind him, shame and anger at war within me, before digging through my dresser for new underwear. I was done with bouts of self-wallowing pity, however. What else could I really say to either of them? Bryston was right. I had no excuse.

Sighing, I did a quick brush of my hair and hit the bathroom to wash up. Staring at my face in the mirror, I studied my blue eyes. Not a hint of gold anywhere, but I still couldn't shake the feeling that something was wrong. Even now, something inside me ached to be set free.

Something that wasn't mine.

I threw on a sweatshirt and some boots and headed out into the kitchen. The two men were seated on the couch, their gazes stony. Phineas sat between them, all three heads turning in my direction as I strode past.

I took the wooden rocking chair beside the TV, trying not to flinch away from their stares. "Are we having an intervention?" I tapped the edge of the chair.

"Do we need to?" Talivar cocked a brow at me. "I only came to give you an update and to find out how you were doing here. Should I not have bothered?"

"What do you want me to say? Weren't you the one who once said you couldn't trust your wife to be faithful?" The words were brittle in my mouth.

But he had. Something about how the family structure in Faerie families meant that he technically was closer to his nephew than to his own potential children . . . simply because they couldn't trust that their own children really belonged to them.

Given that, I would have thought the Fae could have figured out the equivalent of DNA testing by now. On the other hand, the system had worked for thousands of years. What would be the point of gorking it up? And given what I'd seen of how the monarchy and succession worked, maybe it was better this way.

"Is this really how you want to have this happen?" His nostrils flared. "I would grant you an annulment upon your request—rather than see your contempt for this obviously loathsome situation you find yourself in."

"No," I said finally, my voice small. "I just thought we were going to wait until all this was over to figure it out."

"*You* made that stipulation, Abby." He crossed the room to tip my chin up, forcing me to look at him. "And as much sense as that suggestion seems to make . . . I cannot help but wonder if it's merely your way of putting off that which you don't want to decide."

A snort of agreement echoed from Bryston's side of the couch and I flinched. The urge to crawl out of my own skin and flee shivered within me, but Talivar refused to glance away.

"What if I don't?" I pulled away from him, focusing on the floor. "What if I don't want to decide? What if I want you both?"

"But you don't." Talivar retreated to look out the bay window. "You never did."

"And you're assuming we can actually share that long," Bryston rumbled. "Waiting until things are normal will most likely never happen." His mouth curved up in a self-mocking smile. "Not with you, anyway."

"You sure you even want to stick around?" I mumbled. "There's a refrigerator in the kitchen I can be conveniently stuffed into if you need some motivational angst."

Phineas trotted over to me, his nubbed horn looking even smaller than before. "Maybe you two shouldn't tag-team her into making a decision right this moment." His blue eyes stared us down. "That goes for all of you. However fucked up your relationships are? That's your business. When it starts affecting the things that need to get done? That's mine."

He stomped a cloven hoof. "And right now, deciding who's knocking boots with who needs to get back-burnered."

"Easy for you to say," Brystion retorted.

"I don't want to die," the unicorn said softly. "And without the Tree to keep us safe, we all will. We'll fade at the least, and KeyStone or no, there won't be any stopping it." His upper lips curled. "Maybe not *you*— now that you're pretending to be mortal—but the rest of us?"

He shivered. "So what's your news? We've got some of our own."

"Maurice, of course. Seems he's been stirring up trouble all over the CrossRoads. So many of us have been in shock with the decimation of the Tree, he's been able to come and go as he pleases." Talivar shook his head. "He uses that damned necklace to pop in, steal supplies, move his mercenaries, and then he's gone again before any of us can manage to react."

"And there's no way of following him, I assume?" I tried to keep the despair from my voice.

"Even when we do manage to scout him out on the CrossRoads, he disappears pretty quick somewhere else." The elf frowned, shifting away to pace toward the door, his boots clicking on the hardwood. "If I had to guess, he's got some sort of spot hidden away, only accessible by the Key."

Brystion and I exchanged a look. "Shadow Realm?" I asked.

"It's possible," Ion agreed. "Though it shows a lack of imagination on his part if that's the case."

Talivar's gaze blanked for a moment. "Ah, you mean that disgusting little trick he played on my sister before. And you. Our trackers have indicated his 'signature' cannot be found after he disappears. I supposed it is possible."

"All well and good," I muttered. "But we need to find Melanie." I glanced up at the two of them. "She's dying. We know is she's in the hospital . . . but not which one." I retrieved the violin from the bedroom. "Nobu found this."

The elf frowned at the mention of Nobu. He ran his finger over the chin rest. "She would not have left it willingly."

"No. And I don't think her family understands its importance." I waved my hand at them. "I was about to start calling hospitals again. Hell, for all I know her family put her under something else . . . or moved her out of New York or . . . who knows."

Talivar's jaw tightened. "There may be another way."

"Do tell," Brystion drawled. "Swooping in to be the noble prince after all?"

"It's *King*," Talivar said shortly. "And I meant the Wild Hunt."

Phineas snorted. "Been a while since that's been used."

"Not since the Unseelie Court was in full swing," Talivar agreed. "And I'll admit it's risky to consider it . . . but if not now, when?"

Bryston nodded, his mouth pursing. "If the world is going to end anyway? I suppose it doesn't make much difference."

My gazed darted between the two of them. "Anyone care to clue me in here? We talking horses and dogs and running around the CrossRoads?"

"Calling the Hunt mere horses and dogs is like comparing a chicken to a harpy," Phineas interjected. "Both have feathers, but one is going to disembowel you and eat your liver."

I stared at him blankly and he sighed. "It's one of the most powerful weapons the Fae possess—a host of lost souls and damned Fae, traveling the CrossRoads until they find their quarry."

"Not just the CrossRoads," Talivar corrected him. "The Hunt has its own pathways that override the need for TouchStones or Doors, though it can certainly use them." His gaze became distant. "I only ever remember seeing it once, as a child. To hunt a hapless mortal. I don't even remember what offense he'd given, but I remember the horses. Black ones, made of smoke and fire." He gave me a wry smile. "Or so it seemed through the filter of a child's vision."

My eyes narrowed. "And he was captured."

"Torn to pieces, actually." He shook his head. "The Hunt isn't always about finding things so much as retribution."

"And if you don't find what you're looking for?"

"Then the Hunt rides on." He shrugged. "It's a

death sentence for the Huntsman, really. An endless search, night upon night of riding and hunting without cease."

"And there's nothing that can undo it?"

"Only the capture of what is sought. But Abby . . . being a Hunter changes you forever. Even after a successful hunt, there is always a part of the Riders that crave it. It translates into restlessness at first, perhaps, but . . ."

"Eventually they go mad," Phineas pointed out helpfully. "All of them."

"Well, that sounds lovely." I slumped. "So you're basically talking about unleashing the Nazgûl to what? Find Melanie? Or Maurice?" I blinked up at him. "Because I think we ought to continue to try via mortal means for a while longer. Perhaps Nobu will have a way . . ." I glanced at Bryston. "When we were TouchStoned, you claimed to always know where I was. Melanie has—"

"The mark, yes." Bryston frowned. "But that's more of a direct connection to . . . Him."

"I know. Surely we could at least ask."

"All options must be explored," Talivar agreed with a sigh. "But we're running out of time."

"How long before—" My words cut off as a hissing rumble slammed into the window, sending shattered glass across the room. "What the hell?"

Immediately the edge of the sofa began to smolder.

"Get down!" Bryston hurled himself at me, rolling us onto the floor so the breath rushed out of my chest. I lay there gasping like a half-dead fish, his body covering mine as an eruption of heat exploded past us.

Fifteen

My apartment was on fire.

"The violin!" I scrabbled out from underneath Bryston, a tremor running through me when I realized he wasn't moving.

The elf was already on it, snatching up Melanie's violin. Above me, flame licked the ceiling, the heat burning my face. Talivar thrust the instrument into my hands. He coughed. "It's a trap."

Behind me, Bryston moaned, getting to his feet. The back of his shirt was spattered with blood from the glass explosion. "I'll go with you," he muttered. "Fight them off."

Talivar gave him a look of pity. "No." He drew his blade and slipped out the front door.

"Never mind all that." I clutched the violin. If it got burned . . . hell, my goddamned living room was on fire. Bryston snatched up an old quilt from the couch, attempting to suffocate the flames. Smoke billowed from beneath it, scorching the cloth, but for the moment it looked as though the immediate danger of having the place burn down around my ears was gone.

Which left what, exactly? Waiting for Talivar to play the gallant hero? For someone to toss me another Molotov cocktail?

Hell with that. "Phin?"

"Here." The unicorn crawled out from underneath the chair. "This sucks."

From outside the clash of steel rang up the stairwell.

"No help for it." Bryston scooped up Phin and pulled me out the door, keeping his body flat against the wall as we slipped down the stairs to the courtyard. My hand braced on his shoulder, and the hot sting of blood wept through the holes in his shirt.

"How bad is it?" I whispered, my ears pricked for the sound of police. My neighbors tended to turn a blind eye to the odd goings-on around this place, but I wasn't sure an explosion was going to go unnoticed unless someone had oh-so-politely Glamoured the living hell out of the area before firebombing it.

"I'll live," he said shortly, craning his head around the edge of the awning. Immediately, he jerked away as the swipe of a blade slammed inches away from where his head had been, Phin slipping from his arms. "Fuck."

Ion gave me a shove backward as he ran into the fray, ignoring my swearing. The scent of sulfur stung my nose. Glamour or no, we were fighting daemons.

"You're notoriously hard to kill, girl." Maurice's voice rippled from behind me, his mouth nearly at my ear. "It's becoming vexing."

I spun away from him. If anything happened to Mel's violin, we were totally fucked. He had tried to take it from her before, but I'd always assumed that was to prevent her from rescuing me and Moira from the paintings.

But now I wasn't so sure.

"And you're looking old," I snarled, pointing to the amulet at his neck. "I think you've got something of mine."

"Finders keepers, dear. You didn't really need it anymore, being dead and all."

"You ever do your own dirty work or do you always rely on hirelings?" Behind me I heard a soft grunt and a thud. A body hitting the wall. Somehow I managed to disconnect myself from it, the knowledge that I could stop this thing right now reverberating through my entire being.

Subdue him. Or failing that, keep him here long enough for the cavalry to show up. Maurice cocked a brow at me. "I'm an old man, remember? Think I've earned that right."

"You've earned nothing," Phineas snorted from my ankles. "Except a quick death."

"Why did you destroy the Tree?" I snapped.

His lip curled in a snarl but he didn't answer, lunging for the hand that still held the violin.

I twisted away. "Not this time."

"Odd to see the violin without the player. I do hope nothing's happened to her."

I didn't bother to reward him with a reaction, retreating slightly. His gnarled hand snagged my shirt sleeve, the cloth tearing when I elbowed him in the gut. Not that I knew the first thing about fighting, but I wasn't going to go down like a sheep this time. Maurice never played fair. He rushed me, kicking at my feet. Pain jogged through my bad knee when he grazed the kneecap.

"Shit." My leg buckled and I tucked, rolling myself around the instrument. I felt it scrape along the brick-work. "Phin!"

The unicorn squealed with rage and dashed between Maurice's legs, jumping up to bite the fucker on the ass. The old man's eyes widened as he wheeled to bat Phineas away, but it was enough time for me to regain my footing . . . until my ankle rolled on a loose cobblestone. This time the violin slipped from my hand, flying through the air with a lamenting hum, straight into the outstretched arms of . . .

Nobu?

The daemon's wings snapped open dramatically as he knelt on the ground to catch the violin in its descent.

Maurice had won his way free from Phineas, his jaw tightening when he saw the fallen angel. "Come to collect, have you?"

"Our master has lost patience. I've come here to settle the debt." Nobu's hair stuck out like a porcupine's, all vibrant reds and blues, but a tight weariness etched the slanted edges of his eyes. Our gazes met, the anger in his voice tempered by a haunting sadness in his face. Whatever he knew about Melanie, it wasn't good.

"You can try, you mean." Maurice sneered, and snapped his fingers. I caught the movements of additional mercenaries, even as the necklace at his throat began to glow.

He was going to go through a Door. I didn't have time to think, because at this moment, nothing else mattered except stopping him. He ducked beneath Nobu's wing as the daemon rolled it around the violin protectively.

"Oh no you don't." I barreled toward him, knocking Maurice to the ground. My knee made a popping sound as it hit the dirt, but I was beyond caring. Somehow a piece of glass ended up in my hands, the edge slicing my palm. Hissing past the sting, I slashed down at him, something feral taking over my brain—the knowledge that this man was the source of all the pain my friends and I had suffered. I opened my mouth to scream at him, but the words died, lost in a guttural cry as blood spattered against my face.

I fell to my side, something hard slamming into my head. Dimly, I was aware of Maurice scrambling to his feet, the last flare of blue illuminating my retinas as he disappeared, my vision fading with it.

My eyes burned as I sat up, the sting in my hand throbbing up my wrist. My face prickled with gravel. Apparently I'd been left where I'd fallen, but I didn't think I'd been out long. Phineas limped over to me to nuzzle my hand.

"Get up, Abby. We need you to pull it together."

The seriousness of his tone slid through my consciousness, despite the ache in my skull. It was dimly reminiscent of a seizure, without the low thrum pulsing in my ears to indicate it as such.

An eerie silence filled my ears. "What's going on, Phin?"

"We've got company."

"More? The police?"

"Not yet. Talivar placed a Glamour over the courtyard, though, so we should be okay when they do show up."

He disappeared around the corner, indicating I should follow with a nod of his head. Rolling to my feet, I staggered after him, the world freezing up as I took in the scene before me.

Blood and glass sprinkled over the ground like crimson flowers, the scent of smoke still wafting on the air from my apartment. Bodies of daemon mercenaries lay in a heap in one corner, Talivar cleaning the blood from his sword with a vicious efficiency. Beside him, Nobu stared across the courtyard at the Door, increasingly agitated. I recognized the look all too well. He had a decision to make and I could probably guess what it was, but undoubtedly my opinion wouldn't be welcome.

Some things you just have to come to by yourself.

A deeper hue of red moved beside the door where the Marketplace usually opened up and my heart stopped.

Moira knelt there, Brystion's head in her lap, his dark hair sticky and matted, the flesh on one side of his face scraped raw. Uttering a low cry, I rushed to his side, my hands trembling as I grabbed the incubus's wrist to check for a pulse.

Moira shook her head. "He'll be okay. It's mostly superficial—he's been knocked unconscious, but he's otherwise unharmed." My sister gave me a wan smile. "Apparently he attempted a bit more than his mortal form allowed."

I frowned at her, my worry for Ion warring with curiosity at her rather convenient appearance.

Talivar crouched beside us, one hand on my shoulder. "We need to get moving—we nearly had Maurice."

"This is beyond Maurice," Moira said quietly. "We must find the Door Maker—the Wild Music is our only chance now."

"And there's no one else who can tap into that? In all of CrossRoads?" I found it rather difficult to believe with all the magic the OtherFolk possessed, none of them could tap the Wild Magic directly.

"The magic that keeps the CrossRoads alive is dying with the Tree," Moira said. "The CrossRoads are getting harder to travel . . . parts of it are disappearing."

"I don't understand."

"The Tree is the heart of the CrossRoads, Abby." Phin sighed. "It's protecting itself as long as it can—sort of like a human body. All the blood rushes to the heart and brain—the limbs are considered unnecessary for survival."

"And what happens when it can't even do that much?" My mouth went dry at the thought.

"Let's hope we never find out." The unicorn shuddered.

"Our father is currently attempting to sustain the Tree as best he might," Moira said. "But he cannot play forever. At this point it's like using a cotton ball to plug a hole in the bottom of a ship." She glanced at the violin. "And he does not have the tools required to fix it."

And that was the rub, wasn't it? Melanie's ability to play the Wild Music was amplified by the violin . . . which Maurice had attempted to take. Again.

"Maurice's destruction of the Tree was no accident," I said. "It can't be. If the violin . . . if *Melanie* is needed to heal it, why else would he be going after it like this? He's already got the Key to the CrossRoads—he doesn't need her as a method of travel. And the violin is useless for anyone else but her."

"He doesn't want the Tree to be healed," Moira said, her face full of sad confusion.

Nobu's nostrils flared. "If he cannot get the violin,

what will stop him from trying to take care of things on the . . . other side?"

"So what do we do?" Ion winced as he rubbed the side of his head, shifting to sit up. He waved us off, his jaw cracking as he popped it back into place.

Talivar stared down at him. "Nothing." His gaze flicked to my cut palm. "Abby struck Maurice hard enough to make him bleed. It's enough."

"Enough?"

"For the Wild Hunt," he told me gently. "Scents can be hidden behind Glamours, as can appearance, but blood will tell." His fingers crept down to stroke a curved horn at his belt. It was black and twisted, shimmering with the same black light as the crown Kitsune had given him. "Blood always tells, and we will have our vengeance in the end, if nothing else." He nodded toward Nobu. "Can you find her?"

The daemon shifted the violin in his arms. "Forsworn or not, I have no choice, it would seem. It's the lesser of two evils, even for the Master."

I suppressed a shiver. The casual way he spoke of the Devil was a tad unnerving. I was pretty damn sure I didn't want to be anywhere close to meeting the fucker. "Do you know where she is?" My voice came out in a raspy croak. "Even if we find her, what if she's too weak . . ."

The daemon's mouth sneered. "Oh, I know. It was the last thing her mother told me before I swallowed the sin of her envy."

I blinked. "Envy?"

"Of course. The woman never could stand that her daughter shone so bright." His eyes slid sideways at me. "Why do you think she tried so damn hard to snuff it out?"

"She . . . never told me."

"She *should* have told those fuckers off years ago, not run home to them over . . . you." One brow cocked up at me.

"Oh, sure, blame me," I snapped. "You were the one who had to get all tricksy with the lethe."

Beside me, Ion let out a rattling cough. "Uh, Abby? Maybe we can get a move on here."

A hot flush of guilt rushed over my face as I turned toward him, an idea clicking in my head. "You know," I said casually, "if Mel's in the hospital, you might be our ticket there. ERs suck, but I think you're gonna come up short in the healing-via-dream department."

His lips curved into a self-deprecating smirk, wincing as his face tightened. "That's me. I'm a helper."

"Out of the question." Nobu's nostrils flared. "I don't need you."

"Then why come here at all? Why not just go get her first?" My eyes narrowed.

"For the violin, you half-wit." The fallen angel's wings cracked open as he paced away, the violin still in his hands.

Bryston pushed off the ground with a wince. "We're coming too. You owe me, Peacock."

I raised a brow at the nickname. It fit him well enough. I'd forgotten the two daemons had known each other . . . before.

"It's our right," Ion said savagely, one hand resting heavy on my shoulder. A tremor ran through his wrist and I had to admit Nobu was probably right. But agreeing to that made it more real than I wanted to admit, so I clamped my hand over his, glaring at the winged daemon.

"We've earned it. And Melanie trusts *us*." I left the insinuation hanging there and he scowled.

"So be it. But I will not slow down. For either of you." Nobu clutched the violin tighter, his gaze meeting mine. "We'll have to be as quick as we can. There aren't any Doors directly into the hospital where she's being kept, so we'll have to be cautious."

I caught Talivar staring at us with an odd smile and I reached forward to take his hand, my heart breaking for what he was about to do. There was no time for this. No time at all.

"Are you sure you want to do this? Isn't there another way?"

"We don't always get what we want, Abby. I thought you would have figured that out by now." He bent to lay a soft kiss upon my lips, and another on my palm, something sad passing over his mien, but he said nothing. A moment later, he had picked up the piece of glass I'd stabbed Maurice with.

Moira's face had gone very pale, but she remained as steadfast as ever. Always with her it was duty before all else. I admired her for it, but it made for an extremely lonely life.

"Be thou safe, brother," she said formally. "Hunt the CrossRoads and may your quarry be found."

He raised the ebony horn to his lips, a single pealing note escaping from the funnel. It was harmonious for the briefest of moments before spiraling down into a discordant murmur. My ears vibrated and I had to shut my eyes as the Door flared to life before us, and what appeared to be a herd of coal black horses emerged, each with its own rider.

"One ring to rule them all," Phin muttered, "and in the darkness bind them."

Shadows clung to the horses, their flanks gleaming with sweat. Smoke steamed from flared nostrils, and a flicker of flame sparked with each prancing hoof upon the cobblestones. One of them whinnied and the sound nearly dropped me to my knees. I could hear it then, the whispered promise of an eternity of terror; the riders' myriad voices echoed about us, wrapping me in a singsong plea to . . .

. . . *Run, little rabbit. Run and run and run and bleed and run some more* . . .

"Snap out of it, Abby." Talivar's hand on my shoulder brought me back to myself. I choked on a nervous laugh.

"You're going to ride with *them*?"

"*With* them? No." Talivar gave me a pained smile as he took the bridle of the one riderless horse. Besides him, a cluster of hounds wove about his legs, bone pale and red eared, long tongues lolling mockingly.

"Lead them to save my people? Yes." He held out the bloodied piece of glass to the hounds, standing still as they swarmed over him, noses picking up the scent.

Immediately they began to bay, hurtling through the Door. Tipping his head to us, Talivar mounted quickly and pointed at the other riders, taking the lead as the last dog disappeared, the horses' hooves clattering on the cobblestones.

A moment later they were gone, and the air hung with an odd stillness. Moira stared after the place where her brother had been, anguish on her face. She dropped her head as she turned to me.

"This is not how things should be," she murmured. "He takes on too much . . . and yes, it is the only thing to be done now."

"What will you do?" The words came out more challenging than I'd wanted, but I couldn't help the bitterness from sweeping through the tone. I pushed it away. What was the point? The princess would do as she would. As she always did.

She embraced me suddenly, the slimness of her form feeling alien against me. I hadn't quite realized how damn tiny she actually was.

"This is such a mess. But somehow, with you at our side, I feel as though we might see it through. And if not . . . well, it has been my honor to claim kinship to you."

Nobu rolled his eyes. "You know what the problem with the Fae is? You're all a bunch of fucking drama llamas." He touched his palm to his forehead. "Oh, la, I might actually have to do something instead of just sitting around looking pretty."

Ion made a strangled noise, but I couldn't decide if he was laughing or not. Hurt flashed over Moira's face.

"That's enough," I said, pushing between them. "If we're going to work together, then let's do it. Enough with the posturing." I looked up at my apartment. "Give me a sec."

I retreated up the stairs and stared at the shattered window pane. No time to clean it up, but I couldn't leave it like this either. I snagged my cell phone and my backpack. No telling what we might need, but the staples always seemed to work best.

A quick phone call to Robert to give him a rundown on what happened. Knowing is half the battle and all that.

Plus, we really needed someone to dispose of the daemon bodies before they began to stink any more than they already did. They tended to be flammable at the best of times, and as Moira's former bodyguard, Robert would have an excellent handle on that sort of thing—not to mention running interference with any potential law enforcement that might show up.

On impulse I grabbed a towel and filled it with ice, tossing it to Brystion when I rejoined the others. "Can't let that pretty face mar too much."

"I hear the ladies like the scars."

Nobu snapped his fingers, impatience rolling out of him. Without another word, he strode toward the Door, beckoning at the rest of us to follow.

Washed out and faded, the hospital looked as though it had long ago given up whatever ghost it had. If it had ever truly been a place of healing, there was no sign of it now. It made me tired simply to walk through it.

We'd emerged from the CrossRoads a few blocks away and immediately made a beeline for the ER, but one look at the hungry, desperate eyes of those in the waiting room changed my mind about trying *that* particular route. Bad enough to take the time away from someone who actually needed help, let alone subject Ion to it.

"Christ, I wouldn't want to wake up if this was where I'd end up either," I muttered. Nobu's Glamour shielded us in the meantime but it felt weak, as though he was too distracted to set it properly. Ion limped beside me, scanning the hallways.

"What are we looking for?"

Nobu frowned, cradling the violin in his arms. "One of those wards . . . the ones they put you in when they're afraid you'll hurt yourself."

"She said she had a breakdown, but a ward seems so . . . extreme." I frowned, trying to place the time frame. "I don't know how long she's been here."

"It was a cover for her mother," Nobu said. "For her own good, of course. A chance to stop talking about Faerie and music and things that 'aren't real.'" A shadow crossed his face. "I think she found *me* real enough, though."

We ducked down another hallway, flattening against the wall as an orderly swept by, eyes dull and bloodshot.

"And just . . . uh . . . what is involved with eating a sin?" I asked, not really sure I wanted to know. My gaze slid sideways to Ion. "Is it anything like eating a soul?"

As far as I knew the incubus had never actually done it, but he'd nearly tried it on Maurice once, back when I was trapped in that awful Shadow Realm of a painting. Sometimes I felt as though Brystion had been treading a fine line along his daemonic heritage. Being born of the stuff of dreams and the Dark Path put him closer to Hell than the rest of us, but as he'd pointed out before, actions did make a difference. So what would happen if he did venture down that way?

Nobu cocked a brow at me. "I hardly think now is the time for such a discussion." His face became sly. "If you like, perhaps I can eat one of your sins when we're done."

Ion tensed, his hand locking onto mine. "Careful, Peacock."

The sin-eater snorted, but turned away, gesturing at us to follow. The maze of hallways continued until Nobu sighed. "My powers are fading. It's too much to hide all of you and my movements from . . . Him." he said finally. "We may have to try something else."

I cocked a brow at him. This was something I could do. "Give me your hand."

"You can't be serious," Brystion rumbled, his upper lip curling into a sneer.

Nobu blinked, realization dawning. "KeyStone. I had forgotten."

"Yeah, well, don't get too comfortable with it. It's only until we get out of here."

"Drain her, Peacock, and I'll kill you."

"My, my, jealous you'll never know what this feels like again?"

I jabbed the daemon in the chest with my index finger. "Knock the shit off and give me your goddamned hand so we can do this and get the hell out of here."

Nobu exchanged a nonplussed look with Ion. "Bossy thing," he murmured, but he held out his free hand to me.

I slipped my fingers into his, opening up the things that made me a KeyStone, my inner self resonating at its own frequency, attempting to find a match in Nobu. The fallen angel's eyes closed, his body twitching.

"Don't fight me," I murmured. "You have to want to let me in."

He relaxed, the breath rushing out of him in a whoosh, and I seized the opportunity. For a moment we hovered there, his essence coyly rolling away from me, but I clamped down on it. There was always a chance this wouldn't actually work, but as long as both of us were willing . . . Abruptly the visions assaulted my mind, like they always did.

. . . I told her. I told her this would only end in disaster. If I had been stronger, I could have eaten her sin and none of this would have happened . . .

. . . dark feathers, all around me, propelling me up and up and up, but it isn't high enough. Below me, the CrossRoads streak into the darkness like the sil-

ver strands of a spider's web. I will never be able to fly away . . .

. . . she's in my arms, the caged bird is nearly free, and her skin is alabaster pale, but it's her music that compels me and draws me in. It flutters out of reach like a delicate songbird and as much as I want to capture that part of her, if I try too hard, I'll merely crush the life from her . . .

. . . oh gods . . . I have to let her go . . .

The bond snapped into place and we stared at each other. His chest rose and fell with an odd rhythm; he was clearly shaken. I could only wonder what he'd seen on my end, but whatever it was, it had startled him. The fact that I'd only really seen bits and pieces of his feelings for Melanie was not lost on me, and I wondered at his ability to hide away the rest of himself.

Some part of this must have shown in my expression, because a grim smile flickered over his face. "Much of who I am is owned by Him. I gave you the part that is not." His bowed slightly. "Such as it is."

"You really do care for her, don't you?"

A sharp bark of laughter escaped him and he gestured at me with the violin. "Whatever gave you that idea?" He pursed his mouth and glanced over at Ion. "Interesting taste you have, dream-eater. This one might even be worth it."

Ion scowled but didn't bother to reply.

With the Glamour renewed, we made a hasty retreat down the next set of hallways. Phineas let out a chuffing noise in my backpack, but I merely shifted him somewhat. He thrust his nose through the opening, his nostrils quivering. "Are we there yet?"

Nobu raised a hand, pointing to another set of double doors, controlled by a badge swipe against the keypad. "Think that's it."

Brystion paused, shoving his hand through his hair. Dark circles purpled beneath his eyes, and I wondered again at how much strain his mortality was causing him.

"Hold up."

I caught the scent of sulfur. "We aren't alone."

Phin's nose quivered. "I thought I smelled something rotten."

Nobu frowned. "If He has found her, my Master might be attempting His own rescue. After all," he added bitterly, "she's no good to Him dead."

An orderly strolled past, humming a deranged version of David Bowie's "Golden Years," the vibrato rippling eerily down the hall. I flattened against the wall, the breeze of his passing lifting the bangs from my forehead.

I nudged Brystion. "There's our stinky man."

"Glamoured," Phineas snorted.

"We'll have to take him out quietly." Nobu's mouth twisted grimly as he glanced down at us. "And one of you will have to do it. My presence here will not be appreciated by Him and may lead to questions and . . . unpleasant things."

"Now who's a coward?" Brystion scowled, but gave a grudging nod. "I'll handle it."

The doors slid open with a chime and the four of us snuck through, trailing in the Glamoured daemon's wake like shadows. He paused, head cocked as though he were listening, but he never stopped that awful humming, the sound of it grating against my ears.

He whisked down the linoleum hallways, shoes

squeaking cheerfully, slowing down to read the numbers on each door. When he got to 807, he stopped and glanced inside, a dark smile on his face. Swiping his badge on the door, he entered the room—

—and was planted on the floor a moment later, Bryston's knee on his back and one arm popping as he rucked it up, dislocating the shoulder.

"Don't move," the incubus snarled.

I barely spared a glance at them, my focus drawn to the skeletal figure in the bed.

Letting out a sharp cry, I rushed to her side. Melanie had always been pale, but her skin was now translucent, as though she were made up of bird bones and leaves. Her once-vibrant red curls lay matted and bedraggled. If I picked her up, her body would scatter to pieces.

A lone IV tube hung limp from her arm. "This isn't a hospital," I choked out. "They left her here to die. They don't even have a monitor on her."

Behind me, I heard a crack and a sigh. The rotten egg smell grew stronger and I knew Bryston had snapped the daemon's neck. I couldn't even be moved to shock over the death, as frozen as I was.

Then Melanie's chest moved shallow and slow.

"Phin!" I yelled.

The unicorn looked up at her gravely. "I'm sorry, Abby. I have nothing left to give her."

"That's not good enough," I sobbed, stroking her face, her lips desiccated against my thumb. I glanced up at Nobu, my jaw trembling. "The violin. Give it to her."

He handed it to me and I thrust the neck into her palm.

Her hand jerked, fingers snapping shut, but it

seemed more instinctual than cognizant. Her mouth twitched, her eyes darting back and forth beneath the yellowed lids.

Nobu's face had grown hard as he stared down at her, one hand outstretched as though he would touch her, and wherever his thoughts were, it wasn't good. Abruptly his fingers fisted and he turned away.

"I cannot touch her," he said harshly. "Or He will know I seek to circumvent His will."

"Well ain't that a bitch, Peacock?" Bryston staggered to his feet. "What the hell do we do with the body?"

Nobu exhaled. "I've got enough power left to Glamour it to look like her. It will buy us enough time should anyone check on our friend here. Someone take that IV out."

With shaking fingers, I pulled back the tape, wincing at the bruises. Memories of my own extended time in the hospital loomed to the forefront of my mind but I shoved them away. That was the past.

I cocked a brow at him. "And whose side are you on, really?"

"Mine," he said shortly, gesturing to Bryston with an odd little bow. "Please."

"The things I do, Peacock." With a grunt, Ion carefully slid his arms around Mel's prone form, cradling her against his chest. Pushing the oily hair away from her forehead, he laid a kiss on her brow. "Hang in there."

I glanced up to catch a look of pure envy flick over Nobu's face, but he swallowed it down quickly.

"Sacrifices," he murmured, hauling up the body of the daemon like a sack of garbage, dumping it onto the bed with a sneer. "This one will be expected to report soon. We should move."

I snatched the badge from his waist. "Here's our way out."

Nobu nodded. A moment later and the body took on the semblance of Melanie, all the more creepy for its lack of movement. The fallen angel gave me a weary smile, and I felt the resulting pull of power on my end.

I gathered Phin into my bag, and cautiously peered down the hallway. Waving the others out of the room, I shut the door quietly behind me, sparing one last glance at the body in the bed.

Bad omens, indeed.

Sixteen

Melanie lay stiff and unmoving in her own bed, her face waxen and pale. The violin remained clutched in her skeletal fingers. Any effort at removing the instrument was met with steel-rod resistance. Slightly reassuring, though the lack of any movement was not. I pressed a damp cloth to her forehead.

She needed a bath something fierce, but she needed to wake up more. Bryston sat beside me, his hand on my leg. Through the doorway, Nobu paced like a caged thing, his usual smugness gone in the wake of the situation. His wings flared out and back and then disappeared altogether. Beyond him, Robert and Charlie sat on the sofa, Benjamin's babbling filling the silence with much-needed levity. Phineas perched at the end of Melanie's bed like a miniature equine gargoyle, his blue eyes staring at her intently.

The clink of dishes from the kitchen indicated Brandon was fixing up something. From the way my stomach was growling, I really hoped it wouldn't be a liquid lunch.

We were gathered in Mel's apartment, filled with its

odd assortment of Celtic ornaments and instruments, amps and sheet music. Controlled chaos is what I'd always called it, with Melanie at the center of it all.

With her so quiet now, the clutter was overwhelming. Sonja brushed past Nobu, her own wings Glamoured away. She laid a hand on Bryston's shoulder, leaning down to whisper something in his ear. He nodded once and followed her out of the room.

I found Melanie's hand and squeezed it. "Please," I murmured. "Please wake up."

Nobu loomed over me, staring at her. "No change?"

Phineas shook his head. "None. I don't know if it's that she's too weak at this point, or if she's just unwilling to wake up."

"We need a healer. I'll TouchStone as many of them as we can find if it will help." I slumped in the chair, my head feeling like it was stuffed with cotton. "In the meantime . . ." I closed my eyes. "I release you."

The TouchStone bond between Nobu and me snapped with a metaphysical vibration, resulting in a startled grunt from him.

Nobu rubbed his jawline ruefully. "New experience for me."

"Yeah, well, we're past the danger point right now and I can't afford to have you draining me. I've got too much riding on my ability to walk." My stomach rumbled. "And it makes me hungry."

"Well, then, I guess it's good Brandon fixed lunch." Bryston approached with a plate heaped with burgers. My belly roiled, but the protein was definitely needed, so I snagged the one on top and ate it, sucking a stray dollop of ketchup from my thumb.

"So what's the plan? Can she be brought out of it?"

"I'm not sure it's going to be as simple as all that,

Abby. It's not a natural coma—her body needs time to adjust to the proximity of the violin," Phineas said, rubbing the nub of his horn on the lump of Melanie's foot beneath the blankets. "And give me some of that. I'm hungry."

Bryston sighed as Sonja stepped in behind him. I took another burger, broke off a piece, and fed it to Phineas.

"You need to tell her," she said, her voice low.

"Tell me what?" I steeled myself against whatever new catastrophe was going to come hurtling itself at me. "I already know things are a little screwed up with whatever happened between me and Ion. Not sure what that has to do with Melanie, though."

Sonja shifted uneasily. "It's not about Melanie."

I set down the last of my burger on the plate. "Enough with the bullshit. Spit it out."

She shook her head. "Better if I show you." Her gaze darted to Bryston and he nodded. "We can do it now. In fact, the sooner the better, I think."

He gave me a wan smile. "I'll have to see if I can meet you there. I don't think I've ever really tried to fall asleep on purpose."

I raised a brow. "Are we meeting in the Dreaming?"

Sonja nodded. "Yes. I think it's time you saw my brother's Dreaming Heart."

"All right," I said finally. "Let's see what damage we can cause." Both brother and sister winced at my choice of words and I sighed. "Once more into the breach, dear friends."

My Dreaming Heart remained silent, the gate unlocking as I approached it to allow Sonja in. Behind me the outer scaffolding of my old Victorian was slowly being pieced together. A small thing, plain and simple, but it felt more like home now.

Perhaps it was only that I was no longer hiding behind my past to avoid thinking about my future, although why my inner brain had decided to go with a more rustic design, I wasn't quite sure. I hadn't had time to take a look inside, but the curling wisteria vines that crawled up the chimney let out a heavenly scent, the green all the more brilliant against the silvery stone.

A willow sapling sprouted behind the house, the wispy branches starting to unfurl tiny leaves, and a miniature brook trickled merrily into a deep black pool, the fireflies playing above it.

Sonja shook her head when she saw it. "You've changed it again."

I shrugged. "Not on purpose. It seems to be manifesting as it will." I waved her off. "Just show me what's going on with Brystion."

She stiffened. "Okay. Then let's go."

We walked out of the gate to the edge of the path like before, staring out at the darkness. "This shouldn't be as hard. After all, the two of you have shared a rather intimate bond via your TouchStoning . . . not to mention he made his home here."

I threw out my thoughts to the pinpricks of light dotting the sky before us. The bells in my hair chimed immediately, ringing with a laughing enthusiasm. *Home . . . home . . . home . . .*

In the distance came a faint echo in response. "There." I pointed as the crystalline road, watching as it shivered.

"Yes," she agreed, taking me by the hand.

I glanced up as we traversed the pathway, but if my

sharks were around, they did not make themselves known. An uneasy flutter took root in my belly, but perhaps they didn't think they would be needed?

"So what is this all about?" I tried to squash the flush of nervousness in my belly. The Dreaming had always been such an intimate place for me and Ion, but always on his terms . . . and in my Heart. The idea of visiting him in his was disconcerting.

If I admitted the truth to myself, I was a little afraid of what I might see. If he had naked statues of me dotting the place, he and I would have to have words.

I said as much to Sonja and she snorted.

"Please. Do you think Ion would stoop to that level of cheese factor, even in his dreams?"

"Not on purpose," I muttered. "Though it might just manifest." And then there was only silence as we faded into the darkness. The bells rang out in small intervals, the responding sound coming louder and louder until we stood outside a gate very like my own.

A deep burnished gold, it was the same color Ion's eyes turned when his incubus form was excited. Beyond the gate was a dark forest, trees clustered so thickly that no light seemed to pass through it.

"So how do we get in? Or will he meet us here?"

Sonja frowned. "It should be open. He knows we're coming. I suspect you've got the key right there." She pointed to the bells. "They certainly seem to be responding to this place."

I hesitated, not sure I wanted to try to force myself in. If Ion had something he needed to show me, then it really should be on his terms.

"Brystion?" I called his name in a hoarse whisper, somewhat unsurprised when there was no response.

With a sigh, I shook the bells in my hair. Not much of a doorbell, but it might be enough to at least let him know it was us.

The gate shuddered at the sound, creaking open with a great whine. I winced at it, but didn't resist when Sonja pulled me inside. The gate slammed shut behind us, the lock turning with a click.

We were engulfed in the woods, the trees pressing thick and suffocating around us. The hiss of pine needles was the only thing I could hear as they sifted off the branches. I blinked. For all that the trees seemed so robust from a distance, they were . . . dying.

"What's going on here?" I already knew the answer, but I needed to hear it from her directly.

"He's not meant to be human, Abby. Whatever you did to him, he can't sustain it." Grief flickered at the corners of her mouth. "He's spent his entire life searching for a way to have his own Dreaming Heart . . . and now he's got one. He's going to burn himself out trying to keep it."

"And what happens when . . . when he can't keep it anymore?"

She shrugged, looking away. "What do you think? His mortal form grows weaker by the day. We weren't meant for this sort of life. *He* isn't." She grabbed my arm, her fingers pressing into my wrist. "You have to give it back. Find him and fucking give it back."

"I don't know how."

"Please." Her eyes filled with tears. "Please. You have to."

I sucked in a deep breath, the weight of everything happening crashing down about me. Melanie. Maurice. Talivar. Bryston. How the hell was one person supposed to handle it all?

One step at a time, my inner voice reminded me. *Or by drinking heavily.*

"Because that's helpful . . ." I muttered at it. "Is he in there?"

Sonja hesitated, her brows drawn tightly. "He's rather . . . territorial about this place."

I nodded. "All right. Let's see what I can do." Some part of me quailed at facing him here, but I also knew the succubus was right. The extra power her brother had granted me wasn't mine to keep . . . and even if it was, I'd be damned if I'd just hold on to it. He'd given so much for me . . . could I do any less for him?

She let me walk away from her and I slipped through the trees, sparing a glance behind me. The succubus seemed so small, her wings hunched and sad.

The trees whispered something to me, but I couldn't quite make out the words. The bells chimed eagerly, though, the pulse of longing sweeping through me, pushing me forward. The branches parted as I walked, letting me into tiny spaces I couldn't have imagined getting through.

I hoped like hell I'd manage to get out if things didn't go well. I wasn't sure if the sharks would subconsciously manage their way in through here.

"Ion?" His name drifted into the darkness, swallowed up between the trees. A faint gold swell of color spilled from some place in the distance, edging the bark with its own halo.

Abby . . .

My name carried on the breeze, swirling around me like a nearly tangible force, beckoning and seductive. A deep pull pulsed through me, taking root in my groin, a flush of lust rippling over my skin and burning my limbs.

The Dreaming Heart of an incubus. I suppose I shouldn't have been surprised at my reaction, given our particular relationship.

Still.

The golden glow grew brighter and I shivered, drawn to it. The trees faded away and I was running, pushing through, and my feet were bare and the pine needles stuck between my toes, but maybe they were hooves, and a set of antlers burst from my brow, a long tail flicking behind me . . .

I blinked. A stone cottage stood there . . . and I was myself. Dressed in my usual jeans and T-shirt.

In front of the cottage stood Bryston . . . or something like him. His figure shifted in and out from his mortal form to his daemonic form and back again, the edges of him blurry, as though his own subconscious couldn't quite figure out what he should be.

"Abby?"

I approached him cautiously, ready to shield myself if necessary. I trusted him, but traversing Melanie's dreams had shown me how easily I could be attacked. His gaze became confused and I stopped. "Are you okay?"

"I don't know." He glanced down, as though trying to figure out what to say. "I can't seem to hold on to the Dreaming." He held out his hand, waggling his fingers. "It's slipping away from me." He lurched forward and grabbed my arm. "Can you help me?"

Heat prickled up my wrist, arousal and lust mixing in a hazy rush. My mouth dropped open despite myself. If he was surprised at my reaction, he didn't show it. His own eyes lit up with a familiar glow and I nearly sobbed to see it, his form becoming dark and antlered.

"Ion," I murmured, stroking the top of his head, the hair trailing through my fingers like wet silk.

"Something's missing," he muttered.

"I know. You gave me your power. Don't you remember?"

His daemon form scoffed at me. "Why would I do that?"

"To save me, Ion. You did it to save me . . . and it worked."

Confusion warred on his face with something far more sly and he leaned forward to kiss me—

Desire exploded as his lips met mine and an instant later we were on the ground, my clothes gone, his clawed fingers pricking my shoulders. He nipped me hard, his cock brushing my belly. I kissed him, pulling back a moment later.

"We don't have time for this right now."

"There's always time for this. For us. Don't you see, Abby? This is how it should be. Every night. Every moment. This."

I shook my head and pushed him off, my shields snapping into place. "This isn't us, Ion. It's whatever you put inside me, trying to get back to you . . . and I can't."

Hurt flashed deep in his eyes, but I pushed away the quell of my own emotions.

"I think," I said softly. "I think this is a defense mechanism of your Dreaming Heart." And why wouldn't it be? After all, I was coming to potentially take it away from him. Surely he'd try to defend it on at least a subconscious level?

"Or maybe this is just the true me," he retorted, rolling away from me. His tail twitched like an irritated cat's.

I raised a brow. "What's inside the cottage?"

"Nothing. Never you mind." He scowled.

"Really? Because you've been all over the place in my Dreaming Heart. I think you ought to let me get a look at yours. It's only fair," I said dryly. Realizing I was still naked, I gathered some of the Dreaming around me and re-created my clothes. All well and good to stand my ground, but I wasn't going to do it in the buff if I didn't have to.

The apparition of Brystion lowered his head, the crystalline antlers growing dull. "Enter, then, if you must."

I cupped his chin, my fingers lingering over his mouth. "I told you once that I never wanted you to become something you weren't . . . not to please me. I meant it. If you truly want a Dreaming Heart, then so be it, but I don't know if I can let you die for it."

"It would be my *choice* to do so," he said, hooves digging into the soft ground. The scent of crushed grass hit my nose and I stifled a sneeze.

"Yes. But at least let me inside." I gave him a wan smile. "I'm selfish that way."

He snorted and shook out his head so his hair rippled over his shoulders, the cupped ears trembling. "We both are."

He moved aside and shoved the door open, gesturing me in. I glanced back but he didn't choose to follow. I let out a breath I didn't realize I was holding and slipped inside, the door shutting tightly behind me.

I blinked, adjusting to the flicker of candlelight. The inside of the cottage was sparse, but cozy. A crackling fire and a battered quilt, an overstuffed couch and a small table with a steaming cup of tea upon it. I hadn't been quite sure what to expect. After all, he had been an incubus. Part of me thought I'd be walking into some sort of bordello. But this . . . seemed rather hollow for all that.

I frowned. Bryston had never been human before, had never had a childhood or a life as anything other than an incubus. He'd complained that he was only the sum of what he'd gleaned off of other people's dreams—his skills, his knowledge. Why wouldn't his dreams be the same?

A thick sadness strangled my throat and I struggled to push it away.

"Ion?" The house creaked in response, but the bells in my hair were silent. Inwardly I wondered if I'd be stuck searching every room for him. I sat down on the couch and picked up the cup of tea, the heat warming my palm.

The door on the opposite side of the room swung open invitingly.

Come in and see. Come look. Look at who I am . . . what I've done.

I sipped the tea instead, staring at the way the steam rippled around the edges. "It's very good," I murmured, and it was. Sweetened exactly how I liked it.

The scent of jasmine surrounded me, heady and nearly overwhelming for a moment, before dissipating. "I would do more if I knew how," Bryston said from behind me.

He was in his mortal form, the daemon doppelgänger nowhere to be seen. "I think it's lovely." I took another sip and set the mug down.

He knelt beside me, something desperate in his face. "I could make you breakfast, if you like? An omelet, perhaps?"

I reached up into my hair and pulled out the bells,

an odd chill lancing through my fingers. "These belong to you, Ion." I thrust them into his palm, closing his hand into a fist, and kissed him.

He closed his eyes. "All I ever wanted was to have my own life . . . be what *I* wanted to be."

"I know. But this . . ." I sighed. "I don't know what to do, Ion. Your transformation—our transference—it wasn't supposed to happen, and you can't sustain it." I shifted over, tugging on his arm so he sat beside me. "Unless this is what you want?" I winced at the sound of my own voice, the way the words broke.

"No. I'm not so despairing as all that." His mouth kicked up wryly. "If it's all the same to you, though, I'd like to keep it this way for a little while longer. If this is the only chance I get at having something of my own . . ."

I rested my head on his shoulder, the last of the fire flickering down to ashes. "I understand. I love you, you know."

The words hovered between us like the soft notes of birdsong or the crackling of falling leaves, the sound of snow as it hits the windowpane. He stilled, and the tension stretched between us, wire tight, as though he were a star about to collapse upon itself. It was the first time I'd ever said that to him. The potential of his power flared to life within him, but he didn't take it, though the answering flutter of it writhed madly in my belly.

He kissed me hard and I let him push me down into the couch. It was as though the words had unleashed something within him, but he didn't go any further than that.

"Later," he murmured. "When this is over, I'm going to show you something . . . just for us."

"Are you sure there will be a later?" I said it coyly, but only to cover up the lance of fear that followed along behind it.

His arms wrapped tightly around me, but he didn't answer. I buried my face in his neck, his pulse fluttering beneath my lips.

"Wake up," he whispered.

Seventeen

I awoke, slumped in the chair beside Melanie's bed. I caught the whispered hiss of low words from the other room, but I couldn't tell what was being said. Somehow I managed enough of a conscious effort to raise my head, wiping the sand from the corners of my eyes.

And blinked.

Melanie was awake. A brittle exhalation escaped her as her head turned toward me. "Abby?"

I bit down on my lower lip at the frailty of her voice. Her trembling hand found mine and squeezed it tight as the first wash of tears welled up.

"I thought you were a just a dream," she said finally, struggling to sit up. "Ion told me you were dead . . ."

"I know." I let her lean on me, propping her up with a few extra pillows. She still clung to the violin with her other hand, but she put her arm around me despite it. For a few minutes we sat there, our bodies shaking with quiet sobs as our minds finally came to grips that we were, in fact, both alive . . . and together.

I broke away first, and laid a hand upon her forehead. She felt cool, but not overly so.

"The others will want to see you. I should tell them you're awake." I hesitated. "Nobu's here . . . and . . . uh . . . I think he did something to your mother. To make her tell him where you were."

Her face paled but she merely nodded. "I'm sure he did," she said finally, her knuckles whitening around the neck of the violin. "I'll talk to him. But first I think I'd really like a shower."

"Yeah. You kinda smell."

She snorted, her mouth twitching, both of us understanding the need to not be bathed in one's filth while standing before one's destiny. "Jesus, I hope I can stand."

"Well your gown's so ripe it could damn near walk you over there by itself, so I think you'll be fine."

Our smiles covered up the worry behind the words and I went into the bathroom to start the water for her—partially to help out and partially to give her the privacy she needed to make sure everything still moved all right.

A knock at the door snagged my attention. "I'll get it!" I bolted to the front of her room, catching her hastily wrapping the blanket around her now mostly undressed form.

I cracked the door to see Brystion and Nobu standing there. Ion had a tray of something that smelled baconlike and my stomach growled in appreciation.

Nobu craned his head around the crack. "I heard the shower."

"Yeah. She's awake." I held my hand up, my foot shoved neatly behind the door before he could force his way through. "But she needs some alone time. You know, girl stuff."

"Move or I'll break down the damned door," Nobu snarled.

"It's all right," Melanie said softly from the edge of the bed. A quick glance behind me indicated she was bedraggled but presentable, a deep sadness still wavering in her eyes. She nodded once at me and I stepped back, tripping over my own feet at the speed in which the daemon thrust his way into the room.

"Seriously?" I turned to snap at him, my jaw dropping as my gaze met Mel's. Nobu knelt on the floor at her feet, his head leaning against the bed, but not quite touching her. When her fingers laced through the spill of his liquid dark hair, the barest of tremors rolled through his shoulders.

She bit her lip. As the first tears streaked down her face, I slipped out the door and quietly shut it behind me. Snagging the tray from a bemused Bryston, I found an empty seat on the couch.

"I suppose someone has figured out which side he's on after all," I murmured, wondering what it meant for them now that he'd touched her. And then decided it wasn't my problem.

Sighing, I proceeded to stuff my face, glancing up between bites to assess who else was still here.

Robert and Charlie were whispering in the corner, Benjamin playing at Charlie's feet. Brandon was gone, but judging by the time he had probably needed to go open the Hallows. And there was Phin, chatting with Didi . . .

"Oh, shit. I totally forgot to call you."

The pixie gave me a sour look. "Do you have *any*

idea how many piss-scented subway cars I rode? I had a stoner chase me up two flights of stairs clapping his hands and screaming about how he was going to take me home and smoke my sparkles." Her face squinched up. "Clap if you believe! Clap if you believe!"

I sniggered into my bowl of mac-n-cheese (with bacon!), smooshing it around with my fork until I regained my composure. "I'm sorry. I am."

She scowled. "Whatever. I'm glad she was found, but next time—"

"Hopefully there won't be a next time," Ion interjected, nudging my arm. "Eat."

"Yes, sir."

"So how is she?" Phineas finally asked, his tail twitching.

"Awake," I said helpfully. "She's very weak, but the close proximity to the violin seems to have helped a lot. Hopefully with some solid food and a bit of real rest, she'll be up to the task."

"We may not have much time to wait," Robert said, tapping his fingers on the table. "Each second is a second wasted."

"And what good would it do for her to go off half-cocked and so sick she can barely play?" I retorted. "You know her. She'll play herself to death if she thinks she has to."

He said nothing, his eyes dropping to where Benjamin rolled aimlessly about on the floor. "For someone who seems to have so easily thrown herself upon the mercy of the enemy, you're hardly one to talk, Abby."

"I was trying to fix things," I snapped, the fork slamming into the bowl with a clank.

"Would you deny your friend any less?" Brystion said softly. "She'll know the risks involved."

I stood up swiftly and hurried into the kitchen without looking at them, rinsing the bowl out with a savage swipe of sponge. The kitchen held so many familiar memories. Me and Melanie at the table with Brandon, sipping absinthe. Me dancing a halfhearted jig as she played on the fly. An all-night movie session of *Sixteen Candles* and *The Breakfast Club* and *Fiddler on the Roof,* curled up on that ragged little sofa.

I shook my head against them. No, I couldn't deny her the right to try to help, but it still hurt like hell to think I might lose her.

And now maybe you understand why she was upset enough to leave?

My inner voice pointed it out calmly, but I had no answer for it. Double standards were a bitch.

I set the dishes in the drain, staring absently at a glassy water droplet sliding over the edge to puddle on the counter. Behind me, a murmur of voices stirred up and I sighed. What new crisis could possibly have been created in the last two minutes?

Tossing the dish towel onto the counter, I thrust my hands into my pockets and leaned against the doorjamb, my mouth pursing as I saw Moira standing there, wrapped in her supreme regal coolness.

Not that she was looking at me at all.

Or anyone, for that matter, other than Benjamin. The elf stared at her child, her face paling, and I realized she hadn't actually seen him since before I died. When she left him with me and her brother.

Months.

I wasn't sure I understood how she managed to keep her composure, but an odd flash of regret twisted her mouth as she sank to her knees. Charlie let out a strangled sound and stalked away and past me into the kitchen, her eyes not meeting mine. And Robert . . .

Robert picked up Benjamin and held him out to his mother without a word. Benjamin's wings spread out and he uttered a soft cry and turned away from the elf. Moira froze, her face ashen.

"I didn't realize he would forget me so quickly," she whispered.

"He just doesn't know you anymore." Robert's voice hitched as he approached her and I slipped into the kitchen to see how Charlie was doing. My friend stood with her back to me, staring down at the sink.

"Funny thing about Faerie babies," Charlie said bitterly. "Apparently they take on the appearance and nature of what and who they're raised with. It's why the Fae are so keen to keep their children in Faerie . . . and why Changelings are so rare these days."

"But Benjamin is half angel," I reminded her. "Maybe he's not subject to the same rules?"

"What difference does it make?" A scowl darkened her face. "His proper mother's here now. Come to take him home."

I put a sympathetic arm around her shoulder. "Maybe you should talk to Robert about it. Some sort of joint custody arrangement?"

She wiped at her eyes. "It's not fair. She just left him with you . . . and didn't come back. What kind of mother does that?" A soft scuff sounded behind us and I glanced over my shoulder to see Moira standing there, Benjamin in her arms. The toddler squirmed when he saw Charlie, a grin spreading over his face.

"The kind of mother I am," Moira said regretfully.

Charlie covered her mouth with her hands. "You weren't supposed to hear that."

The Fae pointed at her ears. "There's not much that slips past these, I'm afraid. But no, I didn't know you were here." She glanced at me. "I only came to assess the health of the Door Maker. I hear she is doing . . . well?"

"She's getting cleaned up," I said cautiously. "We'll have a better idea after that."

"Indeed." Moira shifted the wriggly little boy in her arms. "When this is over, I will be reclaiming my son."

I caught a warning in the tone of her words, even as I stepped forward to put myself between the two women, but Charlie thrust by her, her own arms outstretched. "Fine words from a woman who's done nothing but foist her child off on others," she snapped. Hurt leaked out everywhere. "It's not fair. You have an affair with *my* man and then when your baby becomes an inconvenience you leave him behind . . . and now that I've . . . that *we've* become attached to him, you're taking him away. Benjamin's a person, not a thing."

Moira drew herself up, but whatever she was about to say was drowned out in Benjamin's sudden wail. His face turned between the two women, mouth trembling in confusion. Both women gave him nearly identical stricken looks. I took that as my sign to retreat.

Robert shook his head and sat down as I emerged into the sitting area. "I think I fucked up."

"Well, yeah . . . but I think they need to work it out between them."

"No matter what I say here, I'm going to be in the wrong, aren't I, Sparky?" He gave the kitchen a rueful smile. "I love them both. Not in the same way, but still."

"A regular metaphysical Brady Bunch, that's us." I

shrugged at him. "Odd thing to be arguing about now, though."

"It's been brewing for a while," he admitted. "Charlie's really attached to him, and he's completely bonded with her. It seems cruel to take him away from her now."

I nodded. I knew a little about their infertility issues, but I didn't know if it was because they were different races or if the problem was more of the mundane sort; it wasn't really any of my business, anyway.

Benjamin's wails shut off abruptly, echoed by feminine cooing. I sighed inwardly. At least they weren't fighting over him.

"It's been really tough for Moira too," I murmured. "Sort of the ultimate in career versus family . . . only most of us don't have to deal with an insane mother determined to bring down her kingdom with her madness."

"Or the end of the world . . ." he mused.

"That too."

We shared a glance and a soft chuckle. How things had changed since a few scant months ago.

Phin jumped off the couch. "Speaking of which, we should probably work on a way to get us out of this situation. Babies are nice and all, but unless the little booger has Magic-Tree-Crap-n-Gro fertilizer in his diaper, we've got other things to focus on, yes?"

"Yeah. Has anyone heard from Talivar?" I craned my head into the kitchen, reluctant to have to break up Charlie and Moira's one chance to hash things out. "Moira? Any word from your brother?"

She peered around the corner, her green eyes gleaming with good humor. "The Wild Hunt is still led by him . . . and still fruitless. But there are OtherFolk forces on the move now, and not ones I can control. The plight of the Tree has attracted those who might attempt to take advantage of the situation."

"Jesus Christ. Because my life isn't fucking complicated enough. Is there anything being royalty *does* allow you to control? Because to be honest, it sure as hell doesn't seem like it."

Moira gave me a wry smile. "There's a reason for those tales of debauched younger brothers, you know. Wishful thinking on both sides, I think."

"It's a fucking crock of shit is what it is."

"There are times when I've thought so." She strode out of the kitchen, Charlie at her side with Benjamin on her hip. Charlie's nose was red but she looked cheerful enough.

"I take it you've reached an accord," I said dryly.

Moira gave a cautious nod. "In light of these events, I shall allow Benjamin to stay here for now . . . on the condition he is fostered within Talivar's Court when he comes of age." Her mouth twitched. "And summer holidays belong to me."

I glanced at Charlie and she nodded, Benjamin's arms clutched tightly around her neck. "We both agreed. It would be the best thing for him." Her eyes darted to Robert, something hollow written in their depths. "And for us, long term."

The unwritten message was clear. Charlie was mortal and already close to forty. Her lifespan would be gone and over soon enough, and for a moment I wondered if that was the only reason Moira had really agreed to it.

I didn't know the aging process of mixed Path babies . . . or even how old angels or Fae really lived, given enough time, but there was a damned good chance Benjamin would barely remember the woman holding him right now.

I glanced up as I realized the room had grown quiet. Melanie stood at the door of her bedroom, soft and clean, her damp hair curling into ringlets. Her face had all the color of a bedsheet, but her eyes held a tired gleam of amusement. And triumph.

Behind her, Nobu loomed like a multihued shadow, his hair also tousled and dripping. I cocked a brow at him and the barest hint of a smile cracked the corner of his mouth.

I immediately made a beeline for the kitchen to pour Mel some orange juice and a made her a few slices of toast. Light stuff, given how far out of it she'd been.

When I returned, she was holding court from a seat on the couch, Nobu beside her. She accepted the food gratefully and proceeded to nibble at it as she absorbed the story of what had been happening in her absence. She was remarkably calm, especially given the news about her mother, but that was between her and Nobu.

"So what do you think I can do?" she asked finally.

"The Wild Magic," Moira said immediately. "We need you to try to keep the Tree alive, to help it sprout new branches. We have no other options at this point . . . and things—"

Her words cut off at the sudden knock at the door. We all froze. Robert had indicated this place was guarded tighter than a nest of hornets with machine guns, but we'd underestimated Maurice several times over by now.

Nodding at Nobu, the angel silently slid over to the door, as Charlie quickly retreated into the kitchen, Benjamin tight in her arms.

"Who is it?" Robert demanded, one hand lightly resting on the doorknob.

"Kitsune," came the answer. "And I suggest you open this fucking door before the world ends."

Whoa. The fox-woman rarely raised her voice about anything. Quickly, I waved at them to open the door, revealing a terrifyingly blood-covered visage. Her ears flattened when she saw me, striding into the room without a thought for the gore-smeared footprints she left behind.

Robert stared at her. "What the hell is going on?"

"A gods-bedamned war," she snapped, her lip curling when she saw Moira. "And while you're all in here playing touchy-feely with everyone's wanking feelings, the rest of us are being slaughtered."

Eighteen

We made a solemn and ragtag procession along the CrossRoads.

Melanie had wanted to make us a Door all the way to the Tree, but Nobu wouldn't hear of it. She needed to save her strength for what was to come, and time issues or not, I agreed.

Kitsune paced beside me and Moira, Robert and Nobu flanking us on either side. I held Phin in my arms so he could get a better view of things, but behind us trailed Melanie and Brandon, Charlie and Benjamin, Didi, and everyone else who had been holding vigil inside Melanie's apartment. Mixes of Paths and alignments, but it was a silent crowd overall.

Brystion was directly behind me. I had expected him to attempt to reabsorb his power when Kitsune spelled everything out for us, but he stubbornly clung to his humanity, even though he was clearly weakening with every passing hour.

The CrossRoads stretched out before us, the cobblestones seeming less glittery than before, the edges soft and blurry.

Like they were fading.

The clash of swords sounded from over the hill as we marched into Faerie proper. We crested the ridge to the valley where Eildon Tree stood, its blackened branches sticking out like brittle bones.

My father sat at the base of the Tree, the sound of his harp echoing over the cries of battle. I exchanged a glance with Mel. Wild Magic, but he was clearly struggling to keep the Tree from slagging into dust.

Moira's nostrils flared as she saw the carnage, her warriors encircling the bedraggled group from the Barras. And on the outskirts, a familiar row of daemons was readying for another attack. "Things were in a steady state when I left. I don't understand."

The fox-woman let out a bark of laughter and pointed at the scene unfolding before us. "Not anymore. Three Paths converge upon the remains of the One Tree in bloody battle," she intoned formally.

"That's ridiculous. What could they possibly think this would accomplish?" I whirled on Nobu. "You have to stop this. Get out there and at least try to stall them!"

"I've chosen my side," he said dryly. "They won't listen to me, but I shall see if I can at least discover something useful." His dark wings unfurled, launching him skyward.

Robert's face darkened. I followed his gaze and realized dozens of winged shadows sailed overhead.

"Angels," Charlie murmured, holding an increasingly squirmy Benjamin.

"If Heaven has chosen to involve itself in this . . ." Robert's eyes sparked an eerie blue. He placed a soft kiss upon Charlie's brow. "Wait here." He disappeared in a flurry of pale feathers, streaking toward his fellows.

I looked down at Phin, who had gone strangely silent. "We're pretty fucked, aren't we?"

"Yup." He sounded weary, as though his usual sarcastic nature couldn't be bothered to manifest. "Let's see how Thomas is managing. The sooner we get Melanie installed with the Tree, the better off we'll be."

Kitsune led us toward the ranks of elves. Moira made a quick wave of her hand, and the warriors parted around us, closing ranks as soon as we passed.

A familiar snout greeted us once we hit the inner circle. Jimmy Squarefoot's broad mouth split into a sagging grin when he saw us. "Absinthe. We was afraid ye would not come."

I hugged him tight with one arm, ignoring his surprised grunt. "If I had known, I would have been here sooner." Not that I had any idea of what the hell I was supposed to do, but it sounded like the right thing to say.

Kitsune laid a hand on my shoulder. "Take the Door Maker to your father. Let them sort out what is to be done."

I nodded, my arm slipping through Mel's. A frail trembling shook her wrist as we approached Thomas. The Harper's head drooped with exhaustion, but his fingers stubbornly continued to ply the strings. Blood dripped upon the ground with the steady beat of crimson rain.

I knelt beside him and laid a hand on his brow.

Phineas shook his head in a warning, one hoof digging into my thigh. "He's tranced himself out. He'll have to be brought out of it gracefully."

Behind me, the sound of the violin case creaked and I knew Melanie was getting ready. She hadn't had much time to tune her instrument before we left, but a moment later the hum of her own brand of Wild Music soared around us thick and strong.

A rushing sigh washed over the battlefield, the very air seeming to still as the power of her music rolled over the Tree. I glanced up to see her chin thrust out with its usual arrogance and knew then that I was right.

Melanie would burn herself out to save us . . . and gladly so.

Our eyes met for the briefest of moments and then she closed them, the sad swell of "Nearer My God to Thee" breathing its way from the silver-hued violin.

My father's fingers stilled.

"Now, Abby," Phineas murmured. "Talk to him now."

"Dad?" My fingers curved over his wrist, the heat from his skin like fire. His blue eyes flickered open at me, but they weren't seeing anything in this realm, surely. They were feverish and hot and I knew once he came to himself, the pain would be exquisite.

"He needs a Healer. Find one, Phin."

"Watering the Tree," Thomas murmured, his voice a husky whisper. "The music wasn't strong enough. Tell her that."

"She'll know." Brystion laid a hand on his shoulder.

I startled, having half forgotten he was there. But then my attention was drawn to the Tree. It was . . . whispering. I played my hands upon the remaining bark, but I could detect nothing more than a desiccated pulse. I wasn't thrown into the depths of its EarthSong like before. It sang a song of mourning, a parting dirge to its own existence.

"What can we do to save you?" I didn't know if I

thought or spoke the words, but the faintest of echoes tinkled back at me. I got the impression of a connection to a greater sense of self. Talivar had once told me Eildon Tree was most likely an offshoot of the World Tree, though I don't think even he really knew for sure.

But if that was the case . . . perhaps another offshoot could be convinced to grow here? It wouldn't be the same, of course, but if it would keep the CrossRoads as a whole together?

There was a pause, an odd hesitation as though the Tree weighed my thoughts. I caught a vague sort of approving hum, tinged with a warning. The first Tree was an equal combining of Paths . . . to attempt to force the growth of another in the midst of all this chaos would be an extraordinarily dangerous thing. It would absorb the influence of those around it, which would in turn shape what it would become, and not even Mel's ability with the Wild Magic would be enough to keep it growing to follow its own path.

The idea of having a CrossRoads completely in control by daemons, or all angels, for that matter, didn't bode particularly well, but it would be a chance I'd need to take, as the current alternative would be much worse . . .

Actually, fuck that; if I didn't at least attempt to balance things out, there wasn't going to be much of a future to worry about.

"What do I need to do?" I asked the Tree.

Again, that ambiguity, but what stood out strongest was a vision of my mother's amulet. The Key to the CrossRoads.

Which Maurice currently wore.

I suppressed a shudder.

We wouldn't be able to convince Maurice to come here to fix it of his own volition . . . Besides, did we really want a new Tree created by his warped sense of reality?

No. And the Key stayed on as long as the wearer was alive . . . which really left us with one choice. And not one I was particularly heartbroken about.

Maurice was going to have to die.

"Guess that's that," I muttered.

After a few moments listening to the Tree's song, I emerged from its hazy headiness, blinking rapidly to clear my head. Grimly I noticed the elvish healers had surrounded my father, working their fading magics to heal his worn fingers. Somehow I knew we'd need his talent again soon. Perhaps he and Melanie could trade off for a while, anyway.

Shaking my head, I stiffly got to my feet, my bad knee cracking loudly. Above us the angels swarmed and the daemons continued their raucous shouts of taunting laughter, the sound pressing in upon us with malevolent force.

To their credit, the Fae didn't flinch before it, their calm faces stalwart and smooth, but I wondered how long they'd be able to keep that up. Kitsune tapped me on the shoulder.

"We've established a cease-fire for now. Representatives from all sides will meet in the clearing shortly. You should be there, as ours."

I blinked at her. "Are you sure you want me? I mean, I would think you'd be a better choice."

Her teeth bared in a feral grin. "Of course I would. But Talivar chose you. Therefore, I must obey. Not that I won't be there to nip at your ankles."

I craned my head over the crowd, an uneasy roil in my belly as I was escorted to a silver gilt pavilion, Moira and Kitsune flanking me, Brystion and Phineas behind. We were met at the tent by Nobu and Robert, each with their own contingent of followers.

I sighed. "Now doesn't this look familiar?"

Nobu rolled his eyes at me, but I caught the tail end of a smile flickering against his lips. In the distance Melanie's music continued to waft over the assembly. The daemons and angels turned to stare at her for a moment before focusing their attention on us.

Moira finally spoke up, her voice as ice-cold and collected as always. "We would have all parties quit the field this day and allow us to seek out a peaceable solution." She ignored the mocking chuckles of the daemons, even as one of the angels stepped up, his hair golden in the light.

He jabbed at the Tree with a meaty finger. "This happened on your watch. Faerie is responsible and must therefore pay the price."

Kitsune lowered her head and stepped forward. "And so we shall. We only ask that we be allowed to do so in our own way. Allow us to seek justice against the one who did this."

"And since when have the Fae been aught but duplicitous? When do they do anything save for themselves?" The angel blew out sharply. "It is no wonder you were cast out of Heaven, you feckless bastards."

"That's enough of that," I said finally, unable to remain silent any longer. The sooner we got this over with, the sooner I could turn my attention to trying to find Maurice again. "This may have happened on the Fae's watch . . . but it was a mortal who did it." My eyes flicked over to the daemons. "One I believe that was acting partially with your . . . master's approval at one point?"

"And who are you?" one of the daemons leered at me. "Tasty mortal wench."

Brystion bristled, but I waved him down. No time for that either.

"King Talivar's wife . . . and Her Highness's sister— so I'd say that gives me a fairly high stake in what's going on here." I felt a guilty twinge at my words, but technically Talivar and I hadn't annulled the handfasting. The words were true, even though the sentiment wasn't.

"Another Faerie ally," the daemon sniffed.

"Not quite," I murmured. "I'm also a KeyStone. I can TouchStone any of you, right now, if that would help plead my case here. I won't play favorites—and as a member of the Fourth Path, I have as much a right to speak as any of you."

"Mortals are what got us into this whole mess."

"We're an easy target," I retorted. "And if you'd just listen, I'm trying to tell you I might have a way to fix it."

The daemon shook his head, but Nobu shoved him back. "You will listen."

"Says who?" the daemon spat. "Last I heard, you'd gone rogue." Its smile became toothy. "Freelance, as it were."

Nobu's wings snapped out and the angels tensed, but before I could get a word in, a Door cracked open at the edge of the field, ebony black horses pouring through it with a wave of yelping hounds. Talivar rode at the head of the line, his clothes travel stained and muddy.

"Nine for the race of man," I muttered, ignoring Moira's sharp look. "At least he's not wearing black."

The elf scanned the field, his eye grim and cold until he finally spotted our pavilion. Kicking his heels lightly, he guided the black stallion over to us. Its sides blew hard as he dismounted, handing the reins to what I could only assume was an elvish squire. Talivar pressed past the entire group to find me, his hands clasping mine, lifting them to his mouth so he could kiss them tenderly.

His face had a wan and faded look to it, the edges weary and . . . older than I remembered. "Abby," he murmured, pulling me against him to bury his face in my neck. It was less romantic and more as though he simply needed the touch of another person.

I tentatively stroked his hair, his skin cool beneath my touch. "Are you all right?"

He blinked rapidly and pulled away, his hands trembling. "You have no idea what it's like . . . it's all-consuming." His gaze darted blankly around me. "When I'm riding, there's no room for any other thought."

He coughed, his lungs rattling. "I found him, though. I found the bastard."

Everyone went still at this, their attention riveted on the elf.

"Did you kill him?" Moira's nostrils flared but he shook his head.

"No. He's holed himself up in a Shadow Realm and we cannot reach him." He held up a weary hand. "The Door to the realm cannot be breached directly . . . without the Key," he said wryly, looking down at my bare neck.

"And Melanie couldn't open it? I mean, she can open just about anything, right?"

"Mel needs a Contract," Bryston reminded me. "And the knowledge of where that Door ends up." His gaze darted to where her silhouette stood against the witchlight. "Besides, if she goes to open the Door, who will keep the Tree alive?" He touched my arm, his expression resigned. "There's another way," he said softly.

"How?" Nobu demanded, anger rippling through his voice. "What other choice do we have?"

"The Dreaming."

My legs went shaky as I realized what he meant. "You want me to DreamWalk? Into *his* dreams? Are you out of your goddamned mind?" I shuddered. "It would be like walking through slime. Hell, I barely managed it with Mel and I probably damn near killed her as a result. You heard what Sonja said . . . even with the extra boost I got from you, I can barely manage it."

"That's why you won't be alone," he said dryly. "You'll be the anchor that connects us to him . . . and I'll make sure we walk the tightrope without issue."

"But how? I thought you were going to remain mortal."

He shrugged, a rueful sadness curving his lips in a lopsided smile. "We don't always get everything we want." He untied the bells out of my hair and they jingled with an odd sense of familiarity. "It's time," he agreed, weaving them into his. They rang out in a quiet way, Ion's eyes sparking in a soft gold.

Behind me, Talivar let out a startled grunt, even as Bryston shivered. A moment later his mouth pursed into a familiar smirk, one brow cocked at me. "We'll have to do the rest in the Dreaming, I'm afraid. I gave you my power there, and that's where I'll have to take it back."

He turned to Talivar, his face sobering. "Can you take us to the Door? Assuming Abby and I can manage something on our end, it's very likely he'll bolt."

"Seeing as all he probably has to do is wake up," Talivar said sourly. "As a plan, I don't like it much."

Ion's voice grew cold. "All mortals have to sleep sometime."

I rolled my eyes, and pulled both the elf and the almost-incubus aside. "Let's get out of here. The sooner we figure this out, the better off we'll be. As long as we can get the Key. That's what's needed to heal the Tree. The rest of it doesn't matter at all."

"Are you sure?"

I shrugged. "Sure enough. For whatever that's worth." I glanced back at Kitsune. "And you might want to leave her in charge. There seems to be some confusion as to what role I'm supposed to be playing here in the Court." I bumped Talivar gently. "I'm not cut out for being a Queen."

He gave me a wan smile. "I would argue that point with you, had we the time. Give me a moment to talk things over with her and you can ride with me."

Bryston shook his head. "I'm not risking her getting involved with the Hunt. We'll ride with you, but Abby's not riding 'with' you."

The two men shared a moment of silence, the way they so often did. Talivar's gaze darted toward me. "As you will," he sighed, stalking off to where Kitsune continued to argue with a blue-horned daemon.

"Marking your territory?" I raised an eyebrow at Bryston.

"Still throwing yourself directly into traffic?" he retorted pleasantly. "We're about to confront one of the biggest *douche bags* on the CrossRoads. I'd rather not come out of it only to find out you're damned for the next hundred years or so." He shrugged. "Besides, neither of us is really required to be there physically."

"We're not going to do that to him," I said, my tone grim as I looked at the elf. "Whatever our issues, we all need to work together on this. Besides, if this *doesn't* work? What do you think Maurice's first line of action is going to be? Somehow I doubt he'll wait around for us to try it a second time and I have no desire to wake up to a knife at my throat."

Bryston frowned, touching the bells in his hair. "I'm going to need Sonja's help to reach the Dreaming. I'm a bit trapped at the moment—not really an incubus and not really mortal. Normally I'd just take the CrossRoads there, but I don't know if I'll be able to do it alone this time."

"What happens if you fall asleep?"

"I don't know if I'll still have a Dreaming Heart after this." He turned away, his voice thick with regret. "Dreaming Hearts are only for mortals. Perhaps it will just fade away."

I took his hand. "We'll figure it out."

His mouth pursed ruefully as Talivar approached us. "Guess we'll have to."

The elf eyed us with a slightly sour face, but gestured at us to follow him. "There are a few extra horses with Moira's group. She's agreed to let us use them. I'll send the Hunt on without me and lead you there myself."

Behind us Melanie continued playing. Her music remained strong—the dulcet tones of "Adagio for

Strings" swirling around us now—but I wondered at her fragility. Would she would fly apart into a thousand pieces if I touched her?

Phin pawed at my calf, his ears flattening. "I'll stay here with her. I can't help where you're going anyway, and she needs someone she can trust."

I caught an approving look from Nobu and he bowed to the unicorn in an oddly elegant fashion.

Funny how the world ending leads to strange bedfellows.

The squire I'd seen before led a set of matching white horses toward us. Talivar mounted first, raising a brow as he indicated I should ride in front of him.

Ion boosted me up and into Talivar's arms before mounting his own mare. "Watch over her while she sleeps, elf. What we attempt is extraordinarily dangerous—her body must be guarded at all costs."

"Understood." Talivar blew once on the horn, and the Hunt whirled away and disappeared through the Door they had come. The elf's arms curled tightly around me as he kicked his own horse forward. "I love you, Abby," he murmured in my ear. "Whatever happens . . . remember that."

I tucked the words into my mind, folding up the memory of the sound of his voice at that moment. We stood on the edge of a precipice—like so many times before. Except this time the world really would end if we didn't get things figured out . . . or at least be changed beyond anything I wanted to live in.

I kissed him, my lips brushing his cheek. "I love you too."

He said nothing to this, but nudged the horse on beneath us. I caught Bryston's eye as we approached the Door where the Hunt had gone and the incubus waved before loping off in a different direction. Part of me shivered at the thought of leaving him behind, but he had to work this part out on his own. He certainly didn't need an audience.

But what if he can't reach the Dreaming at all? My inner voice was less snide than usual, but it was a fair enough question. And not one that I had an answer for.

And then it didn't matter because the Door shimmered before us. Taliver didn't hesitate, plunging us through onto the CrossRoads. Melanie's music faded away, along with the hum and buzz of so many Other-Folk in close quarters.

The silence and silver welcomed us, the horse's hooves thudding upon the cobblestones and stirring up the dust.

"Just like old times," Talivar murmured sadly.

A lump rose in my throat. It had only been a few weeks, but so much had happened. There wasn't much else to be said and we rode in relative quiet after that. There was a rattle in his breath I didn't care for and I made a mental note to make sure a healer looked at his lungs once we got out of this whole mess.

We approached the site carefully, though there wasn't anything particularly interesting about it. A small grassy knoll with a rounded door carved into a thick boulder was the only thing of any great import. "That's it?"

Talivar shook his head and dismounted, holding out a hand to help me down. "No. You'd think so, but the clever bastard Glamoured the real Door. It's actually between those two trees. This seemed like a good place to set up a camp to wait for him to come out. This other door appears to be someone's idea of a joke," he said dryly. "I suspect someone nipped if off a certain movie set."

"But Talivar . . . you know the Key doesn't have to work that way. He could use it to open the Door to any-where, not just here."

He exhaled sharply. "I know, but at least we'd still see that there would be some sort of activity . . . I don't know. It's the best I could come up with, Abby." There was an exhaustion in his voice that spoke of not want-ing to admit certain things, and there was no point in belaboring what couldn't be controlled.

"All right." I found a quiet spot beside the hill, and the elf laid his cloak upon it for me to sit on. The rest of the Hunt nosed around the tree line, living shad-ows drifting in and out like a restless tide of horses and hounds. I wondered aloud at their apparent lack of in-terest in the Door.

"The Hunt hunts. The prey has gone to ground and until the hounds pick up the scent, they will wait." Talivar sat down and pulled me into his lap, tipping my head so it rested on his chest. He felt . . . hollow beneath me, but he planted a soft kiss upon my brow, his fingers stroking my cheek. "I will watch over you as you sleep. Whatever happens, you will be safe."

I smiled wryly at him. "I know. I'll see you on the other side. And maybe when we're all done here, we can have a movie night? I've missed that."

He chuckled. "As have I."

I spared a last glance at the Hunt. I couldn't quite keep a tremor of fear from rippling down my spine, but the elf kept up the rhythmic stroke of his hands in my hair, humming beneath his breath.

And then I slipped away.

Nineteen

The Heart of my Dreaming was eerily still, the crickets quiet. A slight rustle crept through the silver grass, and the wind had a salty tang to it. The sea rode upon my dreams, as though my nightmare sharks were rallying themselves to the cause.

I frowned. Perhaps they could be used in some fashion to break down Maurice's inner barriers. I certainly didn't give two shits if he was injured in the process.

Assuming we could find the fucker at all.

Melanie's Heart had been hard enough to breach— and I *knew* her. We were friends. Something told me Maurice wouldn't be quite so willing to let me inside and, given what a complete asshat he'd been this whole time, the gods only knew what he'd manage to do inside his own head.

First things first, though. I approached the gate, my gaze darting about. No sign of Brystion.

What if the incubus couldn't come back this way? I would have to seek him out . . . assuming his own Heart still remained.

A sudden grating crash at the front gate startled me and I saw Sonja there, her eyes panicked. "Abby!"

I ran to the gate, throwing it open. "What's going on?"

"I need you to come with me, right now." She snatched at my hand, yanking me onto the path and in the direction of Ion's Heart. "Whatever you've got inside of you, you have to give it back, right now. He's dying."

A lance of pain tore through my chest and I followed her without a word, skirting over the dimly lit path. Behind me, I caught the shadowed silver edge of fins sliding through the darkness, but I shoved them away.

Not now.

Defense or not, I wouldn't use them against the incubus. I'd inadvertently done it once before and it had driven a wedge between us. I couldn't bear it if it happened again. And I had the distinct feeling that whatever was going to happen now, it would make my previous Dreaming encounters look like a cakewalk.

"What happened?"

"He managed to make it to the Dreaming via the CrossRoads, but instead of the route we normally take here, he ended up in that odd little Heart of his. He's stuck there and it's draining him." She shook her head, moving even faster. "He's not letting me in. You need a mortal soul to sustain a Heart. I don't know what's going on inside."

Another burst of speed and her wings spread wide. "Come on," she snapped. "Use your power. You're not helpless."

I shook myself, realizing she was right, and pulled the Dreaming about me in my usual silver bubble of light. Floating along, I was able to increase the pace until we arrived at Bryston's Dreaming Heart.

Which was almost completely engulfed in fire.

"Jesus, we have to get him out of there!"

She whirled on me in frustration. "I know!"

"Ion!" I screamed his name, the flames leaping higher as I approached. "I'm coming in now, Ion. I'm giving it back to you." I didn't even know what *it* was, but clearly there wasn't going to be any other way.

Trusting him not to fry me senseless, I hurtled my little bubble into the rising wall of searing heat, burning me through my shield. All around me, the forest crackled, pine trees disintegrating like blackened paper. I hurried on. He'd be in the center.

But when I got there, the cottage lay in a smoking ruin, the thatched roof nearly gone, and my heart broke to see his careful work destroyed so quickly.

Where was he? There was no sign of Ion's daemon side like before, but that didn't mean it wasn't there.

Looking at how the fire encircled the cottage, I realized that it was burning *outward*, rather than closing in on the little house.

The door to the cottage creaked open, a puff of soot billowing out. Coughing, I stepped inside, uttering a cry when I saw him curled into a ball in front of the fireplace. Trapped in some oddly fashioned half-form, he was neither human or daemon, both gray-skinned and hairy with eyes the glazed gold of fading embers.

"Shit." I knelt beside him, heedless of anything else, and grabbed a clawed hand. "Ion! Ion, wake up. It's me. Wake up!"

He let out a hesitant groan. "Can't seem to hold on to this place," he muttered. "Can't control it."

"Take it," I begged him. "Take the power back."

"Don't know how. Not sure I can . . . like this."

"Bullshit." I opened the KeyStone channel between us, searching for a way to TouchStone him. If he was partially human, then he was partially OtherFolk. If there was something there, I could feed myself into him.

Emptiness answered my metaphysical probing, like I was shouting in an empty room. *Please, please, please . . .* I shoved in deeper, even as I realized what little contact we had would not be enough.

"Thirsty," he mumbled. "So thirsty."

Not for water, I realized. Dream-eater, he was named. But he couldn't drink my dreams while we remained here in his . . .

"Come on." I tugged on him, staggering to my feet. "We have to go."

He blinked up at me blearily. "Go where?"

"Someplace you can eat. You can't sustain yourself on your own dreams . . . you'll just be devouring yourself."

A frown crossed his face as he worked it through. He gave me a weary smile, his golden eyes taking on an odd humor. "That actually makes too much sense."

"It explains a lot," I agreed. I held myself steady as he pulled himself up, his arm thrown loosely across my shoulder. "You're going to have to stop the fire in the trees, though. I'm not sure I can carry you and shield us both at the same time."

"Amateur," he snorted.

"Look who's talking." I pulled my shields around us as tight as they would go, trying to reduce their circumference.

"Anyone ever tell you how beautiful you are?"

"It's been mentioned a time or two."

We limped out of the cottage, his face squeezed in concentration. The flames wavered and then damped down.

"Won't be able to hold it for long," he said hoarsely. His feet were bent at an odd angle, as though he'd tried to transform into his daemon form and failed. I shifted beneath him to try for a stronger grip around his waist.

"Sonja is waiting for us outside the gate."

He nodded, hissing as his naked foot crunched on an ember. "Feels so real."

"Well, it's not. Remember, you control this place."

"Mmmph."

"Yeah. Now you know how I feel, every time you guys spout off about relying on physics too much."

"Everyone's a critic," he muttered, but the flames died down a little more as we retreated from the cottage. He spared a single glance back at it and sighed. "It was nice while I had it."

"I know." I squeezed his hand and tugged him forward. Time enough later to figure out what to do about it . . . if there even was a later.

Which led to another interesting thought.

The previous times he'd drunk my dreams had always required some form of sex . . . or at least my orgasm. I was hardly in the mood for that sort of thing at the moment. Not that it would have mattered, before. Being an incubus had its perks, and one of them was to emanate a sort of sexual desire that could override most sensibilities.

He no longer had that . . . but maybe I did.

"What's so funny?"

"I'll tell you later." We were at the gate of his Dreaming Heart. Sonja paced outside of it with a restless flap of scarlet wings.

"There you are." She yanked on the gate until her brother stroked it and it rolled open. The succubus snatched at him, pulling him into her arms. "You asshole."

"Nice to see you too," he coughed.

"You look like shit."

"Surprise," he retorted dryly. "I feel like shit."

I snorted. "Come on. Family reunion later."

The three of us carefully walked the threaded path back to my Heart, Brystion leading the way. His legs continued to bend at an odd angle, not quite in full daemon mode, and a stubby tail twitched as we approached the rocky road that led to the sea.

He paused, raising his head as though to sniff the wind, an eerie light emanating from his gaze. Immediately I felt an answering thrum within me. Whatever he'd put inside me before wanted out.

Now.

Sonja glanced at me, her mouth compressed as though she were trying not to chuckle. "I think I'll leave you two alone for a bit, shall I?"

I let out a shaky laugh. "I don't think this will take long. Why don't you see about scouting the edges of my Heart. We've still got to find Maurice."

She rolled her eyes at me, but there was good humor lighting up her face and for the first time in a while I felt as though we might actually have a chance.

Brystion turned toward me, his hand upon the gate. A fierce desire burned within his gaze that had very little to do with civility. "Hungry."

"This is going to hurt, isn't it?" I'd already resigned myself to the fact that having his essence ripped out of me wasn't going to be overly pleasant, but hopefully . . .

His face gentled. "I'll try not to . . ."

The gate tipped open and he pulled me through, cheek pressed against my ear. "Run," he whispered.

I ran.

I pulled the Dreaming around me, my form shifting even as his own form changed, an incubus in his natural habitat. I became a deer, bounding away on cloven hooves. I half expected him to turn into a tiger, but he wasn't interested in the hunting games Sonja and I had played in the past.

At least not in that respect. He shimmered into a stag with a roughness that belied his past grace and bolted after me. I lingered at the edge of the tree line until he caught up and then tore off again, but never too far.

This would have to culminate in the inevitable, but the chase seemed to revitalize him. His nose brushed my hindquarters, teeth nipping at my hocks, and I darted away, kicking up a clod of earth.

For a moment, he ran beside me and I could see the future stretch out before us . . . if we'd had the time to play . . . fox and hound, rabbit and wolf . . . and I finally understood what Sonja had been trying to teach me. What it meant to be a Dreamer in love with an incubus. The infinite playground at our disposal could lend itself to a lifetime and beyond.

But time was the one thing we no longer had . . . and I couldn't pretend to be something I wasn't. I slowed down as we crested a hill, the shadowed silhouette of my house down below, looming in a welcoming sort of way.

I didn't want to go there just yet. This next part was for the wildness of the Dreaming, not the safety at the center of my Heart. The grass swished behind me and

I shivered, throwing off the Dreaming so that I was human again. And naked.

I didn't turn around as he approached, but a pulse of power skittered over my skin when he shifted—though what form he took I didn't know.

And it didn't really matter. The soft chiming of the bells in his hair called me home . . . *called his power home* . . .

I turned, melting into the warmth of his arms. His mouth met mine in a soft flurry of kisses and the swelling roll of need rippled in my belly. My chest ached with it. He let out a grunt as I pulled him down on top of me, my legs already wrapping around his naked back.

"This is not how it should be," he said, shifting so we were forced to look at each other. His gaze was half-feral and gold, the pale markings on his skin faded and worn.

I arched a brow at him. "I'll put it on your tab," I murmured, kissing him again. This time he made no effort to pull away, stretching my arms above my head to brush his lips over the ticklish spot at the inside of my wrist.

And then there was no time left. He slid into me, his tongue probing my mouth. I squirmed at the sudden intrusion, but spurred him on with a nod and a sigh, tugging at his hair to pull him closer.

Heat bubbled beneath the surface of my flesh, skittering back and forth as it looked for a way out. I finally bit his shoulder, hard enough to break the skin. And still it wasn't enough; some inner part of me wanted to rend him to his bones.

"Ion—" I gasped.

"I know." He panted with an oddly inelegant sound,

his usual suaveness shattered like the rest of him. "Give it to me. All that I am . . . that *we* are."

The words took a moment to register. Perhaps in his effort to remove his own essence . . . he'd actually TouchStoned *me*. I didn't ponder it for more than a few seconds, the orgasm rising to life within my belly. It rippled out in the arch of my back and the clamp of my thighs, the scrape of my nails down his shoulders, but he didn't let go.

He swallowed it all. It poured out of me, wave after wave.

How the hell had I managed to take any of it from him?

His jaw dropped, his mouth half-open as he drank and drank. We were wrapped in golden light and the chiming of bells, the answering pulse of sex and something far deeper.

Yours . . . and yours . . . and mine.

I silently cried out as he continued to move, and his eyes flared with a halo of gold as he stared down at me.

"Mine," he snarled. The Dreaming faded away until there was only the black of night left and the soft sounds I made each time he slid home again and again. Antlers sprouted from his forehead, catching my hands where they'd been snarled in his tangled hair.

"Dream-eater," I murmured, laughing when he bit me, his teeth bared in a feral smile. The liquid skin became ebony and rich, the silver tattoos sparking to life with their own inner light.

"Abby." He buried his face in my neck, his whole body shivering as he came. The snap of the Touch-Stone bond slid into place with an audible vibration, the twang of it almost painful. He blinked, stroking the hair from my forehead.

What is this? I didn't think I'd said it aloud, but his eyes answered me, the edges crinkling in a wondering amusement. He disengaged from me carefully, his gaze roaming over my naked form with a supreme male satisfaction. Inwardly I sighed with relief. He'd been transformed into his full daemon form, the lion tail twitching languidly by the sharpened hooves.

He wrapped the Dreaming about us like a cloak, the heat of his skin a beacon in the darkness. "Can you break it?"

"The bond?"

He nodded, a questioning hum in the back of his throat. I shrugged.

"I release you." We paused as absolutely nothing happened. "Uh . . ."

"Uh, indeed," he said dryly. "I think we just made that TouchStone bond permanent."

"Well, that wasn't what was supposed to happen. Is everything else the way it should be?" I waggled my fingers at him.

"You make it sound like it's a bad thing," he retorted, exhaling sharply. "But yes. There's a difference. I feel . . . full." His form blurred into his mortal semblance and back again. "That part's in working order, anyway."

His brilliant eyes narrowed as he captured my chin. Immediately heat swept into my limbs, lust rolling through them to leave me raw and aching. "Good to know that part works too."

I pulled away from him, ignoring the flush crawling over my cheeks. "Yeah, yeah. Great. Are we ready to do this yet?"

He let me stand, turning around to observe his hindquarters with a nod of contentment. I pulled the

Dreaming around me to fashion jeans and tank top. It was harder this time than it had been before and I sighed inwardly.

"What is it?" His ears cupped the night, rotating toward me.

I gave him a sad smile. "I kind of liked the extra power. Being able to do all . . . this without having to work at it. Makes the rest of it seem hopeless, I guess." I scowled at my feet. "Stupid, maybe, but I guess I'm afraid I won't be able to handle things like I did before."

"It wasn't honest, Abby."

I glared at him. "You were the one who gave it to me—without my knowledge, let me add, so don't go acting like I freaking stole it."

"I'm sorry," the incubus murmured behind me, one clawed hand drifting over my neck to rest on my shoulder.

I reached up to grasp it, my mouth going dry as I realized what we were about to do. "I know. I just don't want to fuck it up."

He let out a humorless chuckle. "Me neither."

The admission didn't make me feel any better, but there was something about his sudden rash of bashfulness that made up for his earlier arrogance.

When it came down to it, I didn't want to die again.

"Are we ready?" I glanced over at silhouette of my house, suddenly wishing all I had to do was to find comfort in its inner sanctum. "Your sister is waiting for us."

"Yes."

The two of us strode in silence, making our way to the gate. The earlier fire of passion cooled and there was nothing left for me to hold on to except the awful bit of courage that swirled in my stomach like a wave of butterflies.

Sonja waved at us impatiently when we reached the top of the hill, but the relief in her face shone out at us like a beacon. In a moment, she'd vaulted over the gate, half gliding to her brother and into his arms. They stood there, yin and yang in their gleaming skins, her soft sigh muffled in his neck.

"Are you whole? Are you hurt?" She patted down his shoulders clinically, searching his face as though she might discern some hidden flaw.

"As whole as I can be." His eyes slid sideways to me, but if there was some message written therein, it wasn't for me to decipher.

Sonja looked at me then, her face unreadable. Hesitating, she reached into a pouch at her side. "I don't know if I'll be able to follow you where you're going, though I'll try the best I can." She pulled forth a small vial and thrust it into my hand.

I held it up, frowning at the colorless liquid inside. "What is this?"

Her nostrils flared. "Succubus blood. The last of it."

Realization snapped through me. "*This* is what Topher left you?" I blinked at her, trying to figure out what the hell had ever attracted her to the man, a slow anger erupting in my chest. I bit down savagely on my lower lip.

The succubus let out a shaky laugh. "Abby, in a strange way, I think he was trying to help us."

"How?"

Bryston's mouth opened in a snarl. "Maurice is holed up in a Shadow Realm . . . like the one you were in."

I snapped my fingers. "The paintings . . . it was the

succubus blood that allowed the nightmares to happen there. So you think . . . what? We could use this somehow to bring his nightmares to him?"

"What better way to force him out?" The incubus eyed the bottle grimly. "And it's a rather ironic bit of justice, don't you think?"

"Full circle, anyway," I muttered, and gave him a wan smile. "Have I ever mentioned how much I wish you'd sucked out the bastard's soul when you had a chance?"

"Not half as much as *I* wish I had."

Our gazes met, that moment of shared history stretching out like a road made of regret and lost chances. The irony of it all was that if he had done it, none of this would be happening right now. It struck me as amusing, but in a sick, hysterical way.

"Spilled milk," he said finally, taking my hand in his. "Let's do this."

We all nodded and silently left the inner sanctum of my Heart. I locked the gate tightly. I didn't know if there would be any sort of backlash or not, but the thought of Maurice possibly tracking his way here was enough to give me the shakes.

I created as tight a shield as I could. It was easier now that I'd done it so many times before, but I definitely noticed less power at my disposal.

"So what now?" I swallowed against a suddenly dry mouth.

"This show belongs to you, I'm afraid," Sonja said. "You've got the strongest connection to him at this point, so you'll need to find him . . . like you did with Melanie before. We'll shield you as best we can."

Ion's face sobered. "You'll have to go in alone, but if you can break through to the ShadowRealm . . ."

He tipped my chin up to kiss me. "I *will* find you," he whispered fiercely.

"Okay." I took a deep breath and cast out with my mind, calling up every bit of ugly and foul memory I had of Maurice. The beetle-bright eyes and the charismatic smile. The way he'd gloated over my naked body before Topher shoved me into the painting. Him stabbing me. How he'd finally broken my neck and killed me.

Fury erupted at the thoughts, lighting up the tenuous connections as they spiderwebbed through my mind. For a moment I saw all of it, the strands of everyone I knew, pulsing with small beads of light. The beams were uneven, stronger on some and much weaker on others, and I could only assume the brightness represented the people I was closest to.

A few were nearly dark, surrounded with their own odd energy. Sonja had told me it would be possible to find my enemies and DreamWalk my way to them . . . and it only made sense these threads were my enemies. It wasn't so much that they were weak as that they felt different.

Wrong.

"Beware the dark side of the force," I muttered, giving a metaphysical tug on the largest. The echoing pulse swept over me with an ugly ripple. "That's the one."

Immediately, Brystion and Sonja stepped beside me, their shields locking into place. The tang of the sea rolled in on an acrid breeze and I tasted bile. The sharks were restless, the nightmares gathering their own power.

Somehow I took comfort in that. If they were truly my protectors, at least I wouldn't be completely helpless.

"This way." I stepped on a dark thread. It spiked when I touched it, vibrating like a fly in a spider's web, and I had the feeling we'd just alerted Maurice to our presence.

No going back now.

We slid forward, the tightrope of the strand beneath us swaying oddly, but Bryston made a little shrug and the shield around us steadied. My Dreaming Heart faded away as we moved forward. In the distance I saw little pinpricks of light winking in and out, each one a Dreamer.

It irritated me that Maurice would be one of those lovely little things. The thought was irrational—after all, he was still technically a man and all men sleep sometimes. But the fucker didn't deserve it, and climbing through a sociopath's idea of the land of Nod wasn't anything I really wanted to do.

I kept tensing, waiting for the line to snap, for us to go hurtling into the darkness, where I'd never wake up— but nothing happened. In fact, the journey was completely uneventful, which had me even more uneasy.

If Bryston noticed my discomfort, he didn't say anything, but the long sweep of his tail curved around my calf, the furred tuft giving me a playful swipe as his hand slipped into mine. His face brushed my ear. "No regrets," he whispered, and the sound of it carried into the void and disappeared.

And then we were there.

The Heart of Maurice's Dreaming loomed before us. Honestly, I didn't know what I was expecting. A midnight dark castle with evil spires, perhaps? A gloomy basement filled with butcher knives? At least something straight out of a horror movie, or Stepford-wife perfect.

But I sure as hell wasn't prepared for an obsidian wall of glass and rock, beaming with tiny green thorns made of colored jewels. Eerie and beautiful all at once. And wickedly sharp.

And I certainly wasn't expecting our host to greet us out in the open, calm and relaxed.

"Hello, Abby," Maurice purred from where he stood, leaning against the wall as though he had nothing to fear from it. The Key to the Crossroads gleamed from where it mockingly hung around his neck. "Fancy meeting you here . . ."

Twenty

I froze, his words cutting through me with an electric jolt. The weight of the world dropped away, my vision narrowing until it was just the two of us.

Me and my murderer.

Fear gave way to anger and my fists trembled with the need to beat his face into the floor, to make him admit he was a royal *douche bag* of epic proportions . . . to do *something*.

"I believe you have something that belongs to me," I said coldly, trying to keep my voice from shaking. My nails bit into my palms and I took a step toward him, ignoring Bryston's cough of warning. This was a trap. It had to be.

And yet, I couldn't seem to stop.

"I might," he said mildly, touching the Key. "But it's not like I can give it back, now is it?"

His face barely flickered as I approached him, but his eyes narrowed, the reaction gone so quickly I couldn't have said if it really happened.

"You seem awfully fond of those pet daemons of yours," he observed. Maurice had a habit of talking too much. It was his way of disabling his foes. I got that now. And there was no point in allowing it to happen again.

"Go," Brystion murmured to me. "Keep him from reentering his Heart."

The two of them slid away, their forms shimmering into something else entirely. I didn't spare a glance at either, locked on Maurice. Like a swaying cobra, I had to keep his attention on me.

"You know, I never quite understood why you hated me so much," I said. "Sure, I took your place, but why everything else? What did I ever do to you? Or maybe that's it—all these connections that I have just by accident of birth."

My upper lips curled at him even as I pointed to the amulet. "Everything you've ever had . . . any power you've managed to acquire . . . all of it's stolen." I let the power of my shield drop slightly. "Even here . . . I have more than you."

"How are you doing that?" he snapped. "I'm dreaming. I control what happens here."

I chuckled. "I'm a DreamWalker. Dreams are my specialty."

Okay, I was completely talking out of my ass, and I suspected he knew that, but this was going to play out one way or another.

"You're bluffing. You're a goddamned figment of my imagination."

I blinked and realized that for all his charisma, the man looked like shit. The dark circles under his eyes spoke of personal demons that probably weren't anything I wanted to investigate. Odd, though. And easy enough to press upon.

I took another step closer. I had no idea where Sonja

or Ion had gone, but I had to trust they knew what they were doing.

"I think you've been cornered, Maurice," I said softly. "And you know it. How's life in the Shadow Realm treating you?"

He scowled at me. "I don't have time for this." Abruptly the wall of obsidian broke apart to reveal a small passage.

"Ion!" I shouted the name before I could stop myself. Maurice sneered at me and melted into the metallic shield of his Heart.

"Shit." Bryston materialized beside Maurice and snatched at his arm as Sonja attempted to keep the door from shutting. A flood of dark power erupted from the obsidian shield. Unconscious defenses, I realized. I doubted if Maurice really understood this part of himself, but I hoped that would be to my advantage.

Maurice disappeared through the door. I barely managed to get a sideways glance at Bryston before he jerked his head at me, his dark face contorted with the strain of keeping the passage open.

Neither incubus nor succubus made a move to follow me and I realized they couldn't. OtherFolk would need an invitation or a TouchStone bond for that level of intimacy . . . but I was mortal.

Loophole, my inner voice crowed as a plan started to form. I had the succubus blood, and though I didn't know if I actually had the power to kill Maurice in the Dreaming, I *had* broken through the Dreaming once and onto the CrossRoads. It *could* be done.

And if I ended up in the Shadow Realm with him?

I could maybe get him to leave . . . and go straight into Talivar's hands.

"Find me," I murmured to Bryston. Without hesitation, I slipped in after Maurice.

Black. All of it was black. Not the comforting black of night, but the dark, rotting underbelly of a fetid pumpkin. Behind me, the door to the Dreaming disappeared, leaving me completely enclosed, surrounded by whatever demons Maurice housed in his psyche.

I smiled grimly. If it was a battle of nightmares he wanted, I had more than enough to work with. Would my sharks be able to find their way in here?

I patted the vial of succubus blood in my pocket, its weight solid. One of these days I'd have to ask Sonja how physical objects could make their way in and out of the Dreaming, but I supposed it was a form of magic unique to her kind.

"Woolgathering," I chastised myself, glancing up to see . . . nothing.

The blackness spun out in an infinite plane, without even the silver glow of the CrossRoads to relieve it. What sort of monster was he that he didn't even have dreams?

A hollow wind blew around me and I instinctively tightened my shields before pushing them out to give me a little space between me and the darkness. It was like being in a tomb, and even though the distance didn't really have an effect on me, there was something about the way it pressed down.

Getting the fuck out of here was a tremendously appealing idea.

"I suppose I shouldn't be surprised to see you here," Maurice said, his voice oddly accentuated to seem deeper.

I steeled myself and turned around, but there was

nothing there except . . . Maurice himself. Nothing bowed or broken about his stance, but the gleam of madness roved thick in his eyes . . . matched by the shining blue of the amulet around his neck.

"And here I half expected to see just a giant head," I murmured. "'Pay no attention to that man behind the curtain'?"

"I remember that movie. Saw it when it first came out—took Moira to see it. She couldn't stop laughing at the fairy in the bubble thing. Glinda."

I blinked, unsure of where this conversation was about to go. I'd nearly forgotten he'd been Moira's TouchStone for at least seventy years or so. "She must remember it fondly, because she certainly seems to be rather keen on dressing like her sometimes," was all I could think to add.

"Fae arrogance, to mimic what they cannot create." He shook his head, his hair paling as though the color were draining out of him. "I would assume you've seen that by now. For all their arrogance, the OtherFolk are helpless without us."

I had nothing to say to this. On a number of levels, he was correct. Our souls were the anchor to the mortal realm. But still.

"So why this destruction? I understand you had your beef with Moira . . . with me, even. But why the hell would you break the Tree?" I didn't expect him to answer, and he didn't. I was sure the CliffsNotes version would indicate he only did it so no one else could have it, but in the end it didn't really matter.

"I didn't destroy it all. There's a branch or two still around." He gave me a wan smile. "I keep one in a little pot. Doesn't seem to be doing particularly well, though."

The realization of what he meant snapped through me. *That* was what Eildon Tree had been trying to tell me. Not the Key at all, but that Maurice had a part of her . . .

"A Tree like that needs tending outside any mortal hands. Does she sing to you?" The thought sickened me, though it made a fair amount of sense.

"It hasn't, not for a very long time now."

If there was sadness in his tone, I couldn't hear it, and I had the distinct feeling his indifference wasn't feigned. He genuinely didn't care anymore.

We stood there, staring at each other for another few minutes. He sighed. "Well, I suppose we should get this started." He winked, a malicious twinkle shining from beneath his brows. "I've never fought a Dreamer directly. I imagine it ought to be rather . . . enlightening. Besides, I know what you're afraid of."

Before I could comment, Maurice disappeared, the flickering of the Key swallowed up into the darkness.

He might not have been a Dreamer or had a Dreamer's powers, but I was in his Heart, and he would definitely have the high ground. It had been hard enough for me to manage in Melanie's Heart—and I was her friend and buoyed by Ion's incubus power.

But here?

The ground opened up beneath me, sweeping me away so that I fell. I let out an involuntary cry, but I was done being a victim.

"Oh no you don't." I pulled the Dreaming around me and shifted. Feathers and pinions, tail and talons, I shimmered into the silent shape of a great horned owl.

Gravity wasn't quite what I had expected here, but I could still manage to arc my way so I wasn't simply plummeting downward. I glided forward as best as I could, and my owlish vision scanned the mist.

My beak clicked in frustration. Why was I even playing this game? I just needed to break through to the other side, right?

I hit the wall. A transparent wall, in fact, but I slammed into whatever it was hard enough to break my neck, and the irony of that made me want to laugh. Pain lanced through my skull, and I dropped the owl form, my concentration broken. I slid down the force field, my ears ringing as I tried to retain my equilibrium . . .

. . . and straight into a deep pool of water.

I had to hand it to the fucker. He certainly did his homework concerning the nightmarish aspects of my dreams. When he'd had me painted into an oceanic Shadow Realm before, he'd undoubtedly watched as I'd fled from my sharks.

On the other hand, he didn't really know me. He only knew what he'd seen. And afraid of the things or not, I now had a modicum of control over them. Still . . . could my sharks find their way here?

The waves slid over my head, saltwater pouring into my mouth, my lungs, compressing and compressing until I was silently screaming. I closed my eyes and forced myself to calm.

Shift. Shift. Fins, scales . . . gills. If we were going to play this out, I was gonna do it right. A moment later and I was breathing normally, the water filtering through the gill slits at my neck. Surely Sonja would scoff at me if she saw this—after all, she'd gotten on my case more than once for my limiting adherence to physics while inside the Dreaming, but no point in fighting what my instincts told me to do.

I slipped off into the inky depths, my hair streaming behind me. But I was still going to need light. I concentrated again, conjuring a tiny iridescent ball. Nothing too bright. No sense in blinding myself when all I wanted was my bearings.

My head rushed with the power, making me dizzy. I had to pace myself. Last time I'd tried to break through the Dreaming to the CrossRoads, I swam through it, trying to escape my nightmares.

Which were strangely absent. I didn't get it. What the hell was he trying to do?

Oh.

Teeth emerged out of the darkness with a monstrous alacrity and I skimmed out of their way, the skin of a shark grazing my tail with a sharpness that cut to the bone.

Blood in the water.

But the animal lacked something vital. Without the driving force of my own mental issues behind it . . . it was only a shark, in the end.

Which meant Maurice was slipping.

Enough of this. I pushed down and down and down. The shark followed me, making halfhearted attempts at bites, but I found the more I ignored it, the less it made itself known. The wrongness of this inability grew stronger, but I focused on the task at hand. If I could make it to the Shadow Realm . . .

Deeper and deeper. Down and down and down . . . and there was no end to it. Pity filled me. How empty and awful his life must be to have a Dreaming Heart so empty.

And then I heard it. A ripple in the Dreaming. A song in the darkness.

EarthSong . . .

. . . but so very faint.

I blinked. Maurice's dreams weren't empty because he was dying. They were empty because he'd been feeding them to that offshoot of Eildon Tree. My brain recoiled at the thought. He'd been purposefully distracting me, buying himself time. It all snapped into place—by destroying Eildon Tree and saving a small bit of it, he'd been hoping to create one of his own . . . fueled by his own personal dreams and corruption.

The CrossRoads would be at his mercy, skewed beyond measure. Even if he died, his legacy would live on . . . as the very foundation of the CrossRoads itself.

Fury flitted through me and I stopped short, the shark almost slamming into me.

"Bullshit," I hissed at it, shunting out a white-hot line of anger. It exploded into pieces, shattering in a pink mist of teeth and bits of skin.

I sent out my shield as far as it would go, shoving the water back and lighting up the whole damn place, even as I shifted into my normal form. My teeth cracked together audibly. I'd been in one small room the entire time.

I laid my hands on the obsidian walls, my fingers digging into the glassy rock. "Open."

Open! my inner voice snarled at it.

"You will fucking open to me. You will open." I said it again and again, like an odd little mantra. My fingers sliced open on the rock, the blood billowing around the pale skin of my wrists.

An odd little tweak shunted through me like the chiming of bells.

The TouchStone bond. Where was Brystion? I couldn't bring him here . . . but could I tap into his power? I tried to send some sort of reassurance down the line, but I couldn't tell if he got it. And there was no time to really experiment.

I tried again, pouring every last bit of anger I had into it, the rock cracking open with a last creak before exploding before me. There! I jumped into the hole, the familiar webbing of the Dreaming wrapping around me as I pushed and pushed, the hollow remains of his Heart leaking like water running down a drain.

Another shark wriggled by me, a mere figment. I grabbed the dorsal fin, punching it in the nose. "Your maker—take me there."

It wriggled away, but I didn't let go, and we hurtled downward. In the distance I caught the hazy, fuzzy cobblestones of the CrossRoads far below us, stretched out like spiderwebs. If I let go and headed toward them I could escape the Dreaming . . . but I needed to find that Shadow Realm.

The shark slowed. My limbs moved as though they were encapsulated in Jell-O, the Dreaming growing thick around us. The shark shivered, its body slipping from my fingers as it faded away.

On my own, then.

I wriggled forward, a tiny opening emerging beneath me. I dug my hands into it, scrabbling at to make it larger. And then I fell, floating down and down and down, the last of the shadows parting as I sank . . .

Putrid flesh and rotten eggs. The stench filled my mouth and I gagged. The hum of the EarthSong thrummed in my head, its tone seductive, but with an underlying sadness, as though it were resigned to its fate.

I rolled over, blinking in the dimness of the candlelight. A body lay on its side nearby and I recoiled, recognizing the half-eaten form of a daemon, blood and ashes all around.

"Should I offer you some? I could maybe even heat it up for you," Maurice coughed. My stomach roiled and I dry heaved against my palm.

I staggered away from the body, gingerly avoiding a still-damp puddle of . . . something. Maurice crouched around a small flowerpot that contained a sickly sprout poking through the dry soil. He sneered at me, moving his hand from his side.

"Little bitch, you gave me a mortal wound."

"I stabbed you . . . but not hard enough to kill you."

"Well, it got infected. And so here I am."

The death odor grew stronger. Necrotic tissue. Corpse flesh. Something wriggled through his fingers and dropped onto the floor, pale and white. This time I did vomit, though how the hell a Shadow Self had anything in its stomach was beyond me.

He let out an amused chuckle. "You are so pathetic, Abby. All this power at your fingertips and you waste your time coming after me."

"I need that plant," I said, gritting my teeth.

"Take it," he retorted. "But you won't be getting through the Door anytime soon. It only works for the bearer of the Key."

"You're going to die anyway. Why do you care?"

"That's not what I meant." He snorted. "Even if you get the Key . . . you're not really here. You're a shadow. A piece of a dream. And a fool . . . in a place where your DreamWalker powers don't work. How could you possibly take it? Wear it? And when I die . . . the way to the Dreaming will be shut as well."

Technically he was right. I wasn't an incubus who could just pop in and out of the Dreaming at will. But I wasn't alone.

"I've never been one to let technicalities stop me," I said dryly, pulling the vial of succubus blood from my pocket and rolling it around in my hands. "As you ought to know by now. And quite frankly, I'm tired of your bullshit."

He cocked his head at me, his eyes narrowing dangerously. "What are you up to?"

"You really ought to tie your threads up better than this." I hurled the vial at the floor, the glass shattering, the blood spilling out . . . and time slowed down.

This Shadow Realm wasn't quite like the ones that had comprised the paintings before. Those had been contrived and planned out, each work of art specific to each of its captured souls, but the power of the blood filled me with a heady rush. Maurice's face paled and he hunched over the dimly singing plant. The blood kept coming and coming, spreading to fill every dark corner with its shimmer.

And yet there was something seductive about the blood as it slipped past my feet. Hungry. Angry. The succubus it had belonged to was no longer alive, but her sorrow and regret and brilliant fury were seeping all around us.

And I could tap into it. "Let's see what you're afraid of, shall we?"

I called the Dreaming power to me. While it wasn't quite the same as actually being in the Dreaming itself, I had a hell of a lot more control this time around.

I felt a tug on that little bond with Ion. *Now,* I thought back at it.

But Maurice wasn't going to let us walk over him

quite yet. He stood up to face me, the tattered remains of his shirt black and sticky against the slash in his abdomen.

"I killed your mother, you know. Watched her shatter on the windshield. Heard you whimpering inside." His mouth twisted mockingly, ugly and hard. "I didn't know who she was at the time . . . or who you were, for that matter. But I knew what she had."

The words cut, but like everything else about him, it was an illusion, meant to disarm. To knock me off balance. And I'd already made peace with my mother. I wasn't going to drag her memory in here.

"Too easy. If so, why not take it from her when she died?" I took a step toward him. "For someone who makes such a big stink about power, you seem to have so very little."

Manipulation was his talent, but in a direct confrontation, it wasn't going to help.

Blood trickled from his mouth when he coughed. A momentary sense of panic ran through me. Bad enough if I became stuck in this heinous place without an immediate way out, but I also had to keep Maurice alive long enough for Nobu to collect him as the Tithe.

"I think you're afraid of death. But most of all, I think you're afraid of being forgotten." I gestured toward the plant at his feet. "Trying to remake the essence of the CrossRoads so nobody will ever forget you? Pathetic." Then I spoke softy, "You want to see what I'm afraid of? You're welcome to it. All of it . . ."

My sharks exploded into being, shoving their way from the Dreaming into this Shadow Realm, buoyed by the succubus blood that allowed them to manifest. They circled us, and I reached out, my fingers casually sliding over a dorsal fin.

There was no water here, and yet they glided easily, dark eyes rolling as they passed by. "It took me a while to figure it out. But there's something rather freeing about accepting your fears. They're not always helpful, but fear can also keep us whole."

"Spare me your platitudes, girl." Maurice's eyes became dull. "You're stalling."

"No." I snapped my fingers and the sharks shot toward him, mouths open and eager. One actually managed to snag him on the shoulder, yanking him back several steps. He cried out, a crimson spatter crossing the floor.

Another one, a hammerhead, darted forward to circle him, its belly scraping over his head. A rivulet of Maurice's blood mingled into that of the succubus and I was plunged into visions not my own . . .

. . . *Bryston whimpering beneath my foot as I sliced through his antlers and cut out his eyes* . . .

. . . *Moira on her knees before me, weeping and naked.*

. . . *Benjamin hanging from the ceiling, screaming as I pulled out his feathers* . . .

Fury erupted within me, overtaking all my senses. My sharks reacting by converging upon Maurice in a frenzy of flesh and teeth and the need to slaughter. Detached, I barely reacted when the shredded remains of his hands bounced past my feet.

"Abby." Ion's voice cut through my own inner madness. "Call them off. Abby . . ."

"Why? This is what we're supposed to do, isn't it?" The sharks spread out, flanking the now balled-up Maurice.

The incubus emerged from the shadows above me, his antlered form feral and terrifying. "This isn't you.

His hatred is flooding the Shadow Realm." He laid a clawed hand on my shoulder even as he gestured at Maurice, a glittering bubble of a shield encircling him. "I can feel it, Abby. Sorry it took me so long to find you . . ."

I glared at him. "What else are we supposed to do? We can't let him get away with this!"

"Call off the sharks. Ease down."

"But—"

"If you don't, I will . . . and it won't be pleasant." A flicker of regret crossed his face. "Don't make me do that. Please."

The truth of his words rang hollow in my ears. He'd do it. And I didn't want to be that person. I swallowed hard, pulling the nightmares back inside. Pulling them into me, my anger and angst weaving back into my psyche, where it belonged.

Maurice lay in a ball, his breath shallow, his arm stumps over his head. He wouldn't make it through the next five minutes, let alone long enough for us to figure out a way out of here.

Bryston sighed, his tail flicking in irritation. "We need his soul for the Tithe. He's no good to anyone dead." He stomped a hoof. "I'll have to take it."

No. No. No. No. My inner voice was screaming at the thought of having that man's essence inside the incubus.

Wondering if we had any other way.

Which we didn't.

He'd never done this before—not since I'd known him, anyway. The fear that it would change him forever remained written in every quick movement he made.

And in the end, Bryston knelt gently beside the rattling husk of a body. Maurice's chest rose and fell in a shallow slowness.

"Open the Door, Maurice," he coaxed. "Open the Door so we may leave."

The old man cracked an eye, his face wrinkled and worn. "Go fuck yourself, incubus. I should have killed you when I had the chance."

"Yes. You should have." Bryston bent lower, and the flush of lust fluttered at the base of my spine as a wash of heat filled the room, the intensity magnified by the succubus blood still coating the place. I bit down on my lower lip as I remained rooted to the spot, staring in fascinated horror.

The antlered head lowered until his dark lips nearly touched Maurice's mouth. The old man struggled feebly, but Bryston merely pressed one hand down on his chest and he stilled.

Regret filled the dark shadows of Ion's face, a shiver running over his ebony skin.

I wanted to turn away. Some memories were not worth keeping. But if he would do it, then I would bear witness.

The incubus spared one last haunted look at me before putting his mouth to the old man's and sucking in a deep breath.

Maurice shuddered once, his eyes cracking open at the end. But they weren't focused on anything, dead reflections in a stagnant pool of a life that had rotted away long ago. A life that ended in a broken hole surrounded by broken dreams.

Bryston's lifted his head, his mouth parted . . . and the spiderweb of Maurice's soul came with it. I'm not sure what I was expecting. A light, perhaps. Something out of that movie *Ghost*. But this was dark and runny and tinged a deep red.

The incubus looked distinctly uncomfortable, his sides heaving as though he wanted to gag. I placed a hand on his shoulder to steady him, my gaze cold as Maurice slipped away without a word.

Ion moved away from me abruptly, his whole body shivering. "Don't touch me, Abby."

"We've got to get out of here. Nobu will know what to do with . . . it." I hesitated on the last word, glancing down at the husk of Maurice's body. "Should we take him with us?"

Bryston's upper lip curled in a sneer. "Only if I have to. Grab the Key."

Having witnessed what I did, I'd forgotten all about our main objective. I knelt, gingerly picking up the amulet. The clasp was still tied behind his neck, but it slid apart with an easy click.

"Where's the Door? We'll need to take the sapling too." I shook my head at it. "There's something wrong with its . . . song. It needs sunlight and to get the hell out of here." I gave him a wan smile. "Like us."

Something that looked oddly like panic crossed his face. "I think we fucked up, Abby."

"How so? I'll just throw the Key on and it will be like old times. I'll open the Door and off we go, right?"

He shook his head. "But you're a Shadow Self, Abby. Your real body is out there."

I froze. "Well, that's a rather conveniently shitty loophole. But I'm not staying in here." I picked up the pot with the sapling and thrust it into his arms. "You take this. I don't think I have the power to pull it into the Dreaming and back to reality."

"No. You don't. Hell, I'm not sure you even can pull the Key with you."

"Figures." I put on the necklace, frowning when nothing happened. "Um. Shouldn't this be glowing? Doing something?"

Bryston chuckled grimly, tracing a clawed finger over the silver edge of the amulet. A scarce heartbeat later and he'd palmed it, snatching it from my neck.

"What the hell are you doing?" Panic lanced through my chest, the irrational fear of being left behind here in the dark gibbering like a mad thing in my mind.

"You're a Shadow, Abby. You can't use it."

"Then how the hell do we get out of here?" I glanced up at him. "You can, right? Just pop straight into the Dreaming and somehow pull me along?"

"This isn't a Dream. You were able to pull me here because the succubus blood allowed you to use your Dreaming powers . . . and because of the TouchStone bond. Without a way back, I'm stuck here as much as you."

I stared at him, horror filling me with a sick sense of dread. "Give me that." I tugged at the Key, ignoring the bemused look he shot me as I tied it around his neck.

"It won't work for me, Abby. The Key only works for mortals, you know that . . ." His words trailed away as the Key flared to life with an immediate blue glow. "This isn't possible."

"You're carrying the soul of the last bearer," I pointed out dryly. "I don't know if that technically counts as dead or not, but the point is, if it requires a mortal soul to be its anchor . . . well, you've got one now."

The incubus looked as though he was going to be sick as he strode over to the wall, clutching the necklace between tight fingers. "I won't leave you here."

"You won't have to." I swallowed hard. "You can open the Door to anywhere . . ."

"Doors don't open on the Dreaming," he said. "For very good reason. I can take you to the CrossRoads. Sonja can take you the rest of the way to your Dreaming Heart."

"Why can't you?"

His face grew grim. "I don't want what I have in me anywhere near your Heart. Trust me on that."

It wasn't a perfect solution, but at least I wouldn't be stuck here with a half-eaten corpse and the faded nightmares of a madman. "Guess that will have to do."

He nodded once. "I'll try to send you there, but Abby, whatever you do, don't move until I or Sonja come for you. If you step off the CrossRoads . . ."

"I know. I won't." I squeezed his hand, his fingers oddly cold and clammy as they met mine. "Let's do this before we run out of time."

He bent down, but didn't kiss me. His forehead pressed against mine. "I will find you," he murmured. "I swear it. Wait for me."

"Like I have a choice?"

He snorted and backed up, concentration screwing up his face. Immediately the far wall lit up with a silver glow, the edges of a Door coming to life.

"It was like a radio dial when I used it," I noted. "Ask it for a safe place to send me."

He frowned and I could feel the uncertainty thrumming down our TouchStone bond, echoed in the sickly EarthSong of the sapling he clutched to his chest. Had the tune changed at all? It seemed curious, but there was still an indifferent bent that had me cringing.

The Door crackled. "Go," he murmured. "I'll find you, love."

My face flushed at the endearment, but there wasn't any more time to waste. I didn't spare a backward glance, bolting through the silver gateway. I was more than ready to be out of this hellhole.

A few steps later and the familiar warmth of the CrossRoads washed over me, silver dust stirring at my feet. Behind me the Door vanished, the light fading away. I knew the Door itself was still there, but without the Key it would only take me to wherever it was originally supposed to go. Not back to Ion, certainly.

My only option was to sit here and wait. Which sucked.

"One of these days I'll actually think things through," I muttered.

And then pain lanced through me with a violent rush. I was being split in half, my heart shredded and pulled out of my lungs. A rush of black swept over me, the CrossRoads disappearing as I slipped into oblivion.

Twenty-one

Hands shook me awake, the jarring sense of being slammed into my own body an aching jolt, as though I'd face planted on the pavement of a New York City crosswalk.

"Wake up, Abby. Wake up!" Talivar? Yes, that was Talivar.

I blinked rapidly. The sudden onset of lethargy sweeping through my limbs indicated I'd had some sort of seizure.

It's been a while, my inner voice pointed out snidely. Undoubtedly I was due to wet my pants again soon.

I rolled to my side, the soft grass pressing into my cheek as I gagged noisily into my fist. The sting of bile coated my tongue as my eyes finally fluttered open enough for me to get my bearings.

But for a moment I wished I hadn't.

"What's going on?" I cringed at the slur in my words as I struggled to sit up. Talivar propped an arm beneath me, and held a wineskin to my lips. I grimaced at the sour taste, sipping it slow.

"You seized." He glanced over his shoulder. "But it's more than that. Something's happened. Some sort of earthquake? I don't know."

"Oh." My head swam with *that* particular implication. I'd never had a seizure while in the Dreaming before. I shuddered. "I feel like I've been dropped off a ten-story building."

"You're lucky you weren't killed!" Sonja snapped beside me, her fingers rolling over my face to pry my eyelids open further. Satisfied, she crouched over me, wings mantled to shield me from whatever was happening.

My arms shook as I pushed past her, my head spinning and dizzy. The ground spun helpfully below me, and I swallowed another round of nausea.

"This is the part where you all stop keeping secrets and tell me what's going on."

I gently shoved her wings out of the way, biting back a cry as I saw Brystion prone upon the ground, the sapling lying in a pile of dirt beside him.

"Move!" I rolled onto shaky legs, apologizing internally for ignoring the incubus as I scooped up the plant, quickly shoveling the soil into the pot. The EarthSong was dim, but grew louder as I touched it. The tone remained curious, with a slightly sordid flavor to it.

I clutched the pot to my chest, and looked up to see Sonja and Talivar staring at me. "It's the Tree. It's the last bit of Eildon Tree. Can't you hear it?"

Talivar had told me the Tree had sung to him as a child but it wasn't as loud anymore, so maybe he couldn't, but still. I glanced down at Ion, his dark hair spread out like a silken wave, the bells in his hair dangling from the tangled braid. I frowned. His limbs were twitching, his mouth open. At his neck, the Key winked in the remaining afternoon light, but it was a sickly thing, the blue a faded semblance of its former glory.

"What happened?" I stroked his cheek, tearing off a shred of my T-shirt to wipe his face. "Why he is like this?"

"He came through the Door and said he'd had to leave you behind . . . and then he passed out. He's been like this ever since." Sonja glared at me. "What the fuck happened in there? How can he be wearing the Key?"

Talivar blanched. "He's wearing the Key?"

"Know of any other glowing amulets lying about? He's got Maurice's soul . . . I think that's why he's able to wear it."

Sonja nodded in sudden understanding. "And you couldn't because you weren't really there."

"Bingo. But we have to get him to the Tree, to Melanie. The sapling is our only chance now. Come on—help me get him on a horse."

Before Talivar could respond, the ground shifted beneath us, echoed by a crack of thunder. The wind picked up with a howl, tearing at my clothes like the sobbing of the damned.

The dogs began turning around in rapid circles, baying madly. Everything around us was filled with the rearing of pitch-black horses and rolling eyes, and deadly hooves. I threw myself on top of Ion's prone form, the grass beneath my hands wilting into crisp piles of ash.

"What's happening?" My voice whisked away into the wailing of the wind. The hillside opened up with a rumble. Mud and rocks tumbled past me as I clung to Ion's form, my heels digging into the dirt. Sonja snatched my wrist, struggling to keep me from rolling into the newly formed sinkhole.

"The CrossRoads . . . breaking . . ." Talivar's words were eaten, muffled against the ringing of my ears. Beside me, Sonja's wings flared open for balance as she grasped her brother's arm. Together, we pulled his still-unconscious body up and over to sturdier ground, keeping a tight hold on the sapling.

Talivar had mounted his black stallion, fighting for control as it bucked against his touch. His mouth grimaced tight, his heels dropped low as he clung to its back like a burr. ". . . will . . . submit . . . to me."

Around us the other Hunters were doing no better with their own horses. Another crack and a rumble and this time the ground refused to stop shaking. The Door to Maurice's Shadow Realm flared to life, sparks bursting from it in a silver radiance before collapsing in on itself with a wail.

"We have to go, Abby!" Sonja shrieked, launching herself to her feet. The white mare I'd ridden on before was hobbled, yanking hard on its lead as it tried to get away. Sonja grabbed the halter and threw a piece of someone's torn cloak over the mare's eyes so she quieted.

"Help me get Ion on the horse. I can't carry him myself."

Somehow we managed to half pull, half push him onto the mare's back, his dark skin stark against the white.

"Hold on," I whispered to him, trying to squash the rising panic in my chest. "Don't lose it now," I muttered to myself, giving Sonja what I hoped was an encouraging smile. I picked up the plant, holding it close to me. Its song had dulled again.

Talivar continued to struggle with his own mount, his voice tight as the horse pranced in irritation. "Can you get up behind me? We cannot stay here."

"I thought I shouldn't ride with the Hunt?"

"I have no time for this," he snarled. "Get your ass up here and let's go. The CrossRoads are fading and we are out of time."

Sonja boosted me up behind the elf and handed me the sapling. I wedged it between me and Talivar, my hands wrapped about his waist. "What about Ion?"

"Give me the reins to the mare." He snapped his fingers at Sonja. Her eyes narrowed, but she did as he asked, watching impassively when he tied them to the pommel of his saddle. "Good enough."

The stallion half reared beneath us, forcing me to scramble quickly to keep from pitching onto the ground.

Sonja heaved a sigh as she mounted Ion's horse. "I'll make sure he doesn't fall off."

"Hold on, Abby," Talivar murmured, his knees squeezing the horse sharply. It snaked forward, but he pulled its head tight, the remainder of the Hunt wheeling behind us. I wrapped one arm about the elf's waist, pressing myself up against him as hard as I could while still keeping a death grip on the plant.

I tracked the white mare beside us, hoping Bryston wouldn't be jostled too much. I cringed at the way his jaw slackened. Between the antlers and his hooves, it felt as though we had hunted down some rare and precious animal, and were bringing in the kill for butchering.

I exhaled against the vision, trying to push it away. The Hunt moved forward in a wave of fiery breath and ebony manes. Talivar shouted something over his shoulder in elvish, pointing toward the Door that lit up like a beacon in the dimming of the day. As a whole, the host poured through the gateway and onto the CrossRoads.

Another wave of nausea swept over me and I pressed my cheek against the elf, trying not to vomit all down his cloak. His hand fumbled over the one at his waist to give it a tight squeeze, the heat of his skin leaching into mine.

And then there was no more time for thought. The road bucked and trembled as we thundered over the cobblestones. Silver floated about us like snowflakes made of ashes.

The hounds loped besides us with an eerie silence, pink tongues lolling. Or perhaps they barked and I could no longer hear anything except the sound of my own breath or the rush of blood in my ears as my heart beat a sharp staccato against my chest.

We galloped through a void of cold, the chill seeping into my skin and through my veins, and I finally understood what Talivar had meant. The Hunt moved on the outskirts of reality, perhaps . . . the lost souls searching for something they would never have again.

Again and again we came across offshoots of the CrossRoads that were vanished, the cobblestones slanting into nothingness. Doors shattered upon our approach and we veered away only to find ourselves dead-ending more often than not.

The hounds milled around the horses' legs as we stopped again and Talivar swore. "Enough of this shit."

. . . and time *blurred* . . .

. . . *the Hunt slipped in and out of the mortal world, shadows among shadows upon a moonless night as we straddled the very edges of the fabric of the existence* . . .

. . . *through a cornfield and over the hillsides of a hundred hapless farms, through the waking dreams of poets, the almost-seen shadows of what might have been or almost was or could never be, night terrors wrapped in magic* . . .

Over a bridge spanning the sea . . . *up the middle of Times Square, black riders on black horses, crows and ravens, and white dogs with bloodred ears.*

For a moment we wavered in the mortal world and I caught the eye of at least one hapless bystander, his mouth dropping open as we thundered past. "Frodo lives!" *I shouted, fighting against the burble of hysterical laughter in my chest.*

And then we winked out of his vision, nothing more than a forgotten dream and an odd story he'd tell in the bar that night . . .

"Oops," Talivar muttered. We veered back onto the CrossRoads, silver dust churning, but it was stronger here, the road far more stable than before. We had to be getting closer. For a moment I let myself hope we'd get there in time, that we'd save everyone and make peace between the Paths.

Until the ground opened up beneath us, the magic of the CrossRoads melting into the blackness like snow into pavement . . . only there was nothing there. I choked back a scream as we hurtled into the nothing, and then I was falling, falling . . .

The world ended with a whimper, the way I always suspected it would . . .

Twenty-two

I clawed my way out of the darkness, my head on fire. In the distance, there was the muffled sound of music, but it was as though I moved underwater, every note thick and muted. My eyes fluttered open, but I was rewarded only with more darkness. I lay there for another minute, my brain trying to collect its thoughts about whether I'd just died again.

Because surely I had.

On the other hand, I was pretty sure the stiffness in my wrist hadn't been there the last time I'd passed on, and after another moment I attempted to sit up, grunting at the twinge of pain in my arm.

Oh.

That's right. I was carrying a potted plant.

"Shit." I lurched to my feet, staring blindly, but I couldn't see a damn thing. "Hello? Anyone there?"

In the distance a soft light flared, the plant in my arms beginning to hum, leaves unfurling with a delicate silver glow. I peered around me, swallowing a scream as the light expanded.

Bodies littered the ground, elves and angels, daemons and mortals. Frantic, I whirled about, my breath rushing out with a whoosh as I saw Talivar getting to his feet. Beside him, Ion sprawled, still passed out, but a quick check showed that he was still breathing. And Sonja . . . there, also on the ground, but otherwise unharmed.

Of the Hunt there was no sign at all.

"What happened?" I stretched out a hand to the elf, pulling him up. "What's going on?"

He let out a small cry of disbelief as he took in the carnage, his finger outstretched to point to where the Tree had stood, its burned-out husk toppled over . . .

. . . where Melanie crouched, still playing to it, even though the sound her instrument was making hovered so weakly that it seemed scarcely more than a seesaw note over and over.

I staggered toward her, still holding the sapling.

"What happened?" My voice was a hollow whisper and the breath of the wind carried it away.

Melanie glanced up, her soot-covered face streaming with tears. "Everything." Beside her, Nobu curled in a ball, the feathers on his wings shredded down to the bones. "He was trying to protect me."

I knelt at his side, turning his face so I could see it. Blood, ashes, cuts.

"He's got a pulse, Mel."

"His wings . . . they're gone. And he won't wake up. None of them will."

I took a closer look in her lap and realized Phin drooped between her knees, his once-brilliant white fur nothing more than cloudy ash. "It's like what happened before. When the Queen shut down the Cross-Roads . . . only far, far worse."

That had been a small group—only the OtherFolk

of Portsmyth had been directly affected. But this . . .

"The Tree cracked and fell over," Melanie said numbly. "And then, I don't know. It was like an explosion. I was knocked down, but Nobu threw himself on top of me . . ." She let out a half sob. "He was always so vain about those damn feathers."

I slumped and squeezed her hand. "He's alive. Let's make sure to keep him that way, okay?"

She blinked up at me. "How? The Tree is dead. It's not singing to me anymore." She let out a small gasp, turning to see the pot in my hand. ". . . but that one is."

I squatted beside her. "Maurice had it. It's the last surviving bit, but there's something wrong with it."

She nodded. "It's got an edge to it. Like it's angry."

"Well, it has every reason to be," I pointed out dryly. "Maurice was feeding it . . . his blood and his dreams and God only knows what else."

Her bow drew against the violin. "Where is the motherfucker now?"

"Dead. Or near enough." I pointed at Bryston, who still remained slumped on the white mare. "Ion has his soul." My lower lip began to tremble. "I don't know. It's just so fucked up."

She put her arm around me and the two of us sat there for a moment, two mortals caught up in a whirlwind of OtherFolk magic.

"We're pretty fucked, aren't we?" she said finally.

"Probably. Suppose we ought to do something about it, eh?"

"Yeah."

I glanced up to where Talivar was searching through his people laying upon the ground. "I cannot find Moira."

"She was here." Melanie pointed toward the closest edge of the ridge. "But I think her people may have spirited her away."

"You would accuse her of abandoning the field?" Talivar let out a disbelieving snort.

The sapling perked up at his outward display of hostility, the song changing into something eager. I laid my hand on Mel's shoulder, shaking my head at her, but she'd felt it too.

"Stop, Talivar. We're all under tension right now. We'll find everyone. Please."

Our gazes met but he looked away first, nodding at whatever he'd seen in my face.

He swallowed hard when he saw the wreckage of Nobu's wings and knelt beside me. "What do we do?"

"The Tree. We have to plant the sapling . . . but as to the rest of it?"

"Guess we'll start small, then." Talivar helped me to my feet and Melanie laid the violin carefully on the ground next to Nobu, placing Phin beside him.

Together, the three of us began hauling away the remainder of the old Tree. Chunks of bark sloughed off beneath the pressure of my hands, sap smearing like blood.

The branches were surprisingly light; whatever had made it so magical had truly fled. "I feel like we should bury it," I muttered. "Give it a proper send-off."

"A wake for the Eildon Tree?" Melanie arched a brow at me and even I had to admit it was a tad ridiculous, but somehow it seemed fitting, given what a mess everything was.

"We'll burn it," Talivar stated. "The wood alone could be used for some future dark purpose and we can't risk that. Perhaps we can place the ashes upon the soil of the new planting." He gazed sideways at me.

"Maybe the knowledge of what it was will seep in that way."

I shrugged. I was always a fan of osmosis.

We couldn't find a proper shovel, but I gently laid the sapling into the hole left by the Tree and somehow we managed to pack the dirt in around it, using a pair of abandoned shields to tamp it down. Talivar emptied the remainder of his wineskin on it.

"That's that, aye?"

I cocked my head at the sapling. Its song was oddly attentive. "I get the feeling it's waiting for something." I nudged Melanie. "Play for it. Something . . . kind. Something that tells it of the good in us."

"But there has to be a balance, Abby." She bit her lower lip. "I can tap into what's left of the Wild Magic . . . but if what you've said is true, it's only been exposed to Maurice's dreams. Even if I can undo that, it will be . . . I don't know. False?"

"Not to mention dreadfully unfair," came a smooth baritone.

Melanie nearly jumped out of her skin, her jaw dropping even as she snatched up her violin. "Y-you," she stuttered.

The owner of the voice slung a matching violin from his shoulder, the very twin to Mel's except for the golden gleam of the woodwork. Dressed in a fine wool suit that heralded from the turn of the nineteenth century, the stranger bore an air of smug anticipation. His fingers seemed abnormally long as they stroked the neck of his instrument. It hummed when he plucked absently at a string.

His eyes raked over Nobu's fallen form. "No one to save you now," he said gravely. "Would you challenge me again?"

"If I did I sure as hell wouldn't choose a song you'd actually written," Melanie muttered, stricken.

"The Devil's TouchStone, I take it?" I got to my feet, pushing my way in front of my friend to block his vision. Stupid, as always, but I wanted to give her a moment to compose herself. In the distance, I could hear the EarthSong of the Tree become a question.

The man smiled. "Merely a placeholder now, but the title still holds for the moment." He held up one of those elegantly fingered hands to halt my next words. "But I am not here for that." He glanced down at the sapling. "It needs more than the knowledge of mere mortals to make it whole. The Tree of Good and Evil, as they say, is about choices. One must know both sides of the story."

"To be *tempted* by it, you mean," Talivar said archly.

The violinist shrugged. "Hardly your concern, elf. My Master is not interested in your sort . . . save for that which is owed Him by your people." He eyed Melanie's violin, his hand outstretched. "May I?"

She hesitated and he chuckled. "I meant no offense, my dear. It's good to see you've taken such good care of it. Pity, though. Had you truly mastered it, you might have healed the Tree after all."

Her eyes narrowed. "What do you mean? I have mastered it. I know how to work the Wild Magic through it."

"Foolish child. This violin *is* the Wild Magic. It was made from Eildon Tree herself. Why do you think it holds the magic that it does? You've got the entire power of the CrossRoads at your fingertips and you've barely tapped its potential." He cocked a brow at her. "Our Master would be happy to show you how it works? No?"

"No." She withdrew a pace, cradling the instrument against her side.

He frowned at the sapling. "Well, then, the hard way it is. To be quite honest, it will take more than the two of us . . . ideally a representative from each of the Paths would be here."

"Well, you just wait here and I'll go searching for someone, shall I?" I muttered. "If you haven't noticed, nearly everyone here is passed out, so unless you plan to strap a harmonica to someone's snoring face, I'd say you're shit out of luck."

"Abby," Melanie hissed from behind me, finally moving forward to take her place in front of the Tree. Thrusting out her chin at the man, she scraped the bow down the strings. "No tricks and I'll play with you. At least get it started."

A twinkle appeared in his dark eyes as he tucked the violin beneath his chin. "Agreed. Caprice Twenty-four?"

Her brow rose. "A minor."

"Of course. *Together.*" He counted off a beat and the two of them started, the twin instruments singing to each other in near perfection. I knew the piece well enough; it was intended to be for a solo violin, maybe backed up with an orchestra, but these two played with such syncopated perfection I could barely tell there were two separate instruments at all. A hint of a genuine smile kicked up the corner of the man's mouth, growing broader as Melanie inclined her head toward him.

There was far more history here than I would ever know. She'd told me the gist of her story before, but I'd never thought I'd actually meet the man who'd beaten her . . . and condemned her and Nobu to an odd sort of half life. A moment later and I realized she was actually enjoying this . . . the musical give and take with someone who was her equal and then some.

I squatted down by the tree, trying to glean some semblance of its reaction. Its own song had died down as it listened, but there was an underlying current of interest and excitement.

I laid one hand upon the soil, the fingers of the other wending into the tender branches. Touching the old Tree I had seen the breadth of infinite possibilities all spiraling into an unending helix that I would never be able to decipher. I had no idea if this Tree would be the same, or if it had to learn as it went. Had the first sprung up and known what it was, or did it change over time?

The song wrapped up and the pair looked at me expectantly. "It's waiting. For something else. Keep playing, I guess. But . . . I don't know. Try to put more feeling into it."

The man looked rather offended at this, but Mel nodded.

"Less exercise . . . more life experience," I said.

Melanie gave me a wry smile and launched straight into "The Devil Went Down to Georgia," singing as she went.

"Apropos," the man murmured, joining in a moment later, but this time his music was less about showing off. More honest.

The sapling approved.

My gaze found the old Tree. A long time ago, I'd put a wish on it. An empty one. I'd tied a piece of cloth around one of its branches, the way so many other supplicants had . . . but I hadn't actually wished for anything.

Just in case, I'd said. And now it was too late to use it. But maybe not too late to make a new one.

I reached down to find the hem of my T-shirt, shredding off a scrap with a shaking hand. Talivar raised a brow and blinked, understanding flickering over his face. Abruptly, he pulled at his leather vest, tearing a strip of his tunic from beneath it.

I went first, knotting it on the lowest branch carefully, not even knowing what I was wishing for. I tried to focus less on what I wanted . . . and more on what I wanted for the newborn Tree.

Grow. Be strong. Store our dreams, our hopes, our fears . . .

A brush of skin against my hand and I saw Talivar bending, tying his own strip to a branch. He glanced at me sideways, the piercing blue of his eye filled with the memories of so much pain and loss.

"Give them to her," I murmured. "Let her guard them for you, nourish her with them."

When I finally walked away, he was tilting his forehead against the tiny tree, murmuring something in a hoarse whisper.

Melanie and the TouchStone were still playing; they'd finally tapped into the Wild Magic and it swirled about us all like a tangible force, calling the others to awaken. And that was it, I realized. The Tree needed the wishes of Dreamers to survive—good or evil, it didn't matter. It was hope that was required.

The first to come to was Phin, and I raised the little unicorn against me, his nose burrowing into the hair at the nape of my neck.

"I'm sorry," I murmured. "So very sorry."

He nipped me gently. "I'm too old for this bullshit. I'm officially retired."

"After one last thing," I agreed. I wasn't sure if a unicorn's Dreams would mean anything to the Tree . . . and he didn't have a piece of cloth to make a wish with, but . . .

He sighed as I told him what I needed him to do. "Cut off a tuft of my mane. It's not like it can get any more butchered than it is."

I nearly laughed at his mournful tone, but he really had been through more than enough. I sliced off a hank of the fine hair with a nearby dagger and tied it around a branch. Phineas reared up and touched the nub of his horn against it. For a moment he looked the part of the noble beast of legend and I could only imagine what sorts of regrets and hopes he harbored within that tiny body.

Aside from the ones involving booze and a drunken Pinkie Pie.

Talivar's hand on my shoulder brought me to myself. "The others . . . they're waiting for you." He pressed a quick kiss against my forehead. Somehow it felt like good-bye.

I peered over his shoulder and realized the others were finally starting to awaken.

Even Brystion.

I ran over to where he lay, placing a hand upon the incubus's cheek before helping him sit. Talivar caught him on the other side and gently held him upright. The incubus gagged and vomited noisily into the weeds, wiping at his mouth with the back of his hand.

He let out a pained groan and blinked up at me with an odd sort of incomprehension. "Abby?"

"Yes, I murmured to him, stroking his brow, my fingers lingering at the base of his antlers. "I'm okay."

He slumped. "I feel like shit."

I didn't doubt him. There wasn't even a hint of his normal sexual arrogance rolling off him, which meant he had to be hurting. "Things they don't teach you in Soul-Eating Skills 101?"

He smiled sourly at me before being lost to another coughing fit.

Talivar frowned. "I don't think he should make the sacrifice," he said quietly. "Not yet. Not now while he carries Maurice's soul within him."

"No. The Tree has already had too much of him as it is."

"He's got *what* inside him?" Nobu hissed from behind me. The daemon spared a glance at Melanie first, his face darkening when he saw her playing.

"Maurice. His soul. It was the only way," I added apologetically.

Nobu stared at Bryston, jabbing a thumb at the amulet around his neck. "What the *hell* is that?"

"The world's first daemonic KeyBearer, apparently. It's rather complicated."

"No shit. You realize that it's possible that Bryston is now the Tithe?" The daemon winced as his broken wings shifted.

"A trade for a trade, eh, Peacock?" Bryston let out a shuddering laugh, mirthless and terrible.

My heart plummeted into my belly. "Can't you guys, like, transfer it? One to the other?"

They turned to face me as one.

"No," Nobu said flatly. "We're not banks. It doesn't work that way. Bryston will have to deliver the soul himself." He tugged on the Key around the incubus' neck. "And way to fuck with the rules. This shouldn't even be allowed."

The moment was interrupted by the thundering of countless hooves thudding their way through the trees. Had the Hunt taken off again?

But, no. As they came into the clearing, I stiffened as I saw *her*, the Queen of Faerie, as she rode on a silver mare, her train flowing behind her in an otherworldly grace. A large assembly traveled behind her. My father strode at her side, playing his harp with newly healed fingers.

"Because this is what we need," I muttered. "Crazy lady on the scene."

Talivar flinched, but nodded, giving me a pained smile. "I'll handle this. King and all."

I slipped my hand into his. "Consort."

Blinking in surprise, he led me toward her entourage. I spared a backward glance at Brystion, but Nobu and Sonja appeared to have him well in hand. The incubus rolled his eyes at me, but I caught a faint amusement gleaming within.

United front and all that.

All around us, the wounded staggered to their feet, or attempted to sit up. The Queen made a curt nod with her head and a contingent of healers ran out onto the field and began setting up a rudimentary triage, as other elves went from body to body.

I exchanged a glance with Talivar. Such generosity was unexpected. I hated to think the woman might be scheming something even now with all the carnage, but I wouldn't put it past her either.

A moment later Moira trotted over on her own white mare, bridle bells jingling. Full circle. She met us halfway and dismounted to give her brother a hug before turning to me to do the same.

"Given the circumstances, I thought it prudent to

find Mother," she said, a quiet apology in her voice. "Aside from her . . . issues, there is much she knows. I was . . . unprepared for this."

"I think we all were," I said dryly.

"How long before we can expect the other Paths to show up to claim the bodies?" Talivar said it clinically, with a coolness that bespoke his experience on the battlefield. His sister's discomfort at the bloodshed before her shone on her face, but her brother had no such issues.

Yet another side to him that I'd only been half aware of.

I stared out at the field. The number of injured was staggering. I frowned, something Talivar had told me once niggling at the back of my mind. Laying my hand on his shoulder I frowned at him. "What about the pools?"

"The what?"

"You told me . . . before. When the Sidhe would have great battles in the past, everyone would bathe in some sacred spa or Jacuzzi or something . . . and it healed everyone? Seems like that might come in rather handy right about now, don't you think?"

His mouth pursed. "Technically they're not open to any but the Sidhe, and there are far fewer now than in the past, but given the circumstances, perhaps Mother would be amenable."

"Particularly if we tell her we can pay the Tithe," I muttered.

Moira sighed, craning her head over Talivar's shoulder. "You have him, then? Maurice?"

"In a manner of speaking." I edged around the subject. "Let's just say the Tithe will be paid and Maurice will no longer trouble us and leave it at that." There was a warning note in my voice to keep her from pressing further.

"All right. Let's see if we can't find a peaceable solution for all." She glanced up, a smile on her face as a contingent of angels approached, Robert breaking off to land beside us.

"Sparky. The powers that be have declared a moratorium on our usual . . . enmity." He pointed at a golden-haired angel holding a trumpet. "We were chosen to escort Gabriel to the Tree to add our Path's music to it."

I raised a brow. Goldilocks had a body of a bronze Adonis and a face of an . . . well, an angel. Honestly. The same sort of chiseled beauty the rest of them had, though the fact that he was dressed in street clothes threw me a bit.

"*The* Gabriel?" I asked. "And how did you even know about the music?"

"I get around." Gabriel shrugged, pointing to the sky. "Plus I've got friends in high places that know things."

I wasn't entirely sure what to say to this, so instead I nodded to where Melanie continued to play with her former enemy. "Over there with the others—I'll let you guys figure out what works best." My gaze fell on my father. "And . . . I think Thomas should be there too, don't you? He represents the Fae as well as any."

Bryston limped up behind me, his ears twitching as he laid a hand upon my shoulder. "I carry the Tithe. I should be with you when you present yourself."

Together we found our way to the front of the line.

The Queen dismounted, her long white dress fluttering like the soft feathers of a swan.

There was something different about her now. Less mad.

No less crafty, though.

Gravely she listed as Moira made her plea to open the Healing pools of old, so that everyone could have a chance to start over. My father gave me a tight smile, making his own way to the Tree with his harp.

I watched as the four musicians put their heads together for a few moments, a shake and nod of the head . . . and then they began to play. Whatever song it might have started off as was quickly picked up by the humming of the Tree, the EarthSong drumming out a deep echo within my chest.

"That's it," I whispered after a few minutes. "The tide's turned."

I glanced at the Queen, my tone respectful. "If it would please Your Majesty, each of those here should also gain a chance to leave a wish for the new Tree. She seems to be . . . strengthened by them."

"As you say." She snapped her fingers in her old impatient way, indicating this to be done. "We will gather up the wounded and take them within our borders, but only for a short while. Once this flag of truce has been lifted, all other Paths shall vacate Faerie lands unless they have needful business there."

It was the best any of us could hope for, and the relief written on Nobu's face was plain to see.

"No clipping of the wings yet, eh, Peacock?" Brystion snorted. "And here I thought sin-eaters had their own ways of healing."

Nobu glared. "Would you have me bathe in the blood of virgins?"

"Point taken. When do I get rid of this thing inside me?"

"That's what she said," I muttered, hiding a smile when Ion punched me lightly in the arm.

The Queen stared at him. "Am I to understand you harbor the traitor's soul within you, daemon?" Her eyes lit upon the Key. "How very interesting."

"Isn't it?" I glanced at Ion. "So what happens now? Please . . . you can't leave me again. Not like this."

"I have no choice, Abby. And where I go, you cannot follow." He laid a hand on my wrist. "If I can work something out, I will."

Nobu let out a grim chuckle. "Spoken like one who's never met Him. No. I will go with you. There are things you should be aware of. And temptation awaits even our kind."

"Always let a sin-eater be your guide . . ." I wavered on my feet, suddenly exhausted beyond measure. "How long will you be gone?"

"It could be minutes or months. He keeps His own schedule as *He* sees fit. It is not my place to question it."

The Queen cocked her head at me. "And you. What are your intentions? We ought to plan a true wedding if we are to make this union between you and my son . . . official." Her words were clipped as she considered the thought, her upper lip curling at me. "A King ought to have a Queen . . . and even if you're not my first choice, you are a known quantity."

I rolled my eyes as Talivar let out a groan. "How

flattering. But . . . no." I gave Talivar a regretful smile. "I will see out my year as his handfasted consort, but beyond that? I can't be what Faerie needs. I've got a life back home, and I want to live it."

Talivar's chin dropped, but I was right and we both knew it. "No. I will not ask that of you."

"Tradition dictates a year," the Queen groused, clearly not willing to let it go.

Her son shrugged. "And yet am I not a King in my own right? Perhaps it's time for a new tradition." He took my hand, his thumb rubbing over mine. "I release you."

"Witnessed," Phineas piped up from my ankles, giving a sense of finality to it all.

How many times had I said those words? The echo of my phrase to remove a TouchStone bond now seemed to mock me. It hurt far worse than I thought it should.

I chucked his cheek lightly. "I didn't say I would stop loving you. But I can't give any more. I can't." I exhaled sharply. "And Brystion and I are now permanently TouchStoned. It would be unfair . . . to everyone."

The Queen made a tired gesture at me. "Ridiculous. You're already committed to him. And after all that work I put into it, I'd expect a bit more courtesy."

My eyes narrowed. "What are you talking about?"

Talivar shook himself, shock flicking over his face. "It was a setup. All of it."

"The Tithe? But that was orchestrated between me and Nobu. The Queen didn't have anything to do with that."

"Not the Tithe. The handfasting." His voice grew

frosty. "Clever, Mother, to make me think it was my idea."

She gazed down at her nails with a sly smile. "Well, you needed a shove out the door. Now you've got a kingdom of your own, and Moira will have mine . . . when she is ready." She glanced up at me. "Never underestimate a mother's love for her children."

I went cold, searching my memories for that moment. Hadn't I said I wanted to leave? And hadn't she wanted me to stay? I'd thought the geas had been her trump card to keep me here . . . But what if it had only been her method to ensure I became a more permanent part of the family?

And we'd danced to her tune like puppets.

On one level, I admired her skillful plotting. After all, given the circumstances of Talivar's inability to rule the Seelie Court, it almost made sense. On the other, it was a super shitty thing to do and the sheer amount of pain it had put me and my friends through was beyond abominable.

I glanced over at Talivar, swallowing down my anger. "No offense, but I'm rather glad I'm no longer directly part of this family."

He let out a sad little laugh, even as the Queen rolled her eyes. "You don't really have a choice, you know. The handfasting is permanent now, regardless of your lovers or whatever little mortal thing you feel like doing."

I blinked at her, the sudden silence as loud as a thundering boom in my ears. "What are you saying? One year, that's what I was told—and that no longer applies."

"And you were told correctly," she snapped. "Mortals. Honestly."

I continued to stare at her blankly, frustration driving what little politeness I had left straight out the window. "You're nutters. Completely out of your damn gourd."

"And you, silly thing, are obviously pregnant."

Twenty-three

Two months later

For once, the Queen was actually correct. I was with child, as they call it. Not that I'd started showing yet, but a rather awful bout of morning sickness had begun to rear its ugly head within the last few weeks.

At pretty much any hour of the day.

The pregnancy test didn't show up positive for at least two weeks after she'd made her declaration. Quite easily the longest two weeks of my entire goddamned life.

But here I was.

Phineas kept a watchful eye on me, though he pretended not to notice when I dry heaved all over the kitchen floor one evening, the mere scent of whatever was in the fridge forcing me to my knees in gastric dismay.

Pregnant or not, I was still living in my shambles of an apartment, though with some extra help from Brandon and a few others, we soon had things back to normal.

Or at least as normal as things could be these days.

But tonight the Midnight Marketplace was in full swing, although it wasn't really a store anymore so much as a metaphysical coffee shop, with a side order of books and the occasional anime showing. Technically the place still belonged to Moira, but she wouldn't be coming back due to her new duties in Faerie, so I pretty much did what I wanted with it. The Pit still ran during the day, but I'd had it repainted and refurnished, and if the books we sold were still pretty much crap, at least the store itself no longer smelled like a cat had taken a piss in a rotting vegetable bin.

Charlie and I continued to exchange shifts there, but otherwise things were pretty much the same.

And quiet.

And somewhat sad.

My pregnancy had thrown an interesting kink in the gears, but babies did that. For the moment, I was taking my vitamins and trying to sleep. Though I visited the Dreaming most nights, there had been no sign of Ion.

Melanie glanced up at me from the corner stage, where she was playing an odd little version of Bon Iver's "Skinny Love." We'd changed, the last few months, the both of us—and even if things weren't quite the way she hoped, there was at least a brightness to her that hadn't been there in quite a while.

The catharsis of fighting inner daemons, perhaps.

I shifted in my chair, Talivar beside me on the floor, his head resting up on my knee. Absently, I stroked his hair, my fingers tangled in the haphazard locks. For a no-longer-handfasted couple, things were awkwardly . . . awkward.

I did love him. Not as much as he deserved, but if I carried his child, then Talivar had a right to be a part of its life. If it wasn't? Then I would deal with it when the time came. Though quite honestly, given the Faerie penchant for claiming children outside of wedlock, I had a suspicion Talivar would have acknowledged it as his either way.

At least, I assumed it was his . . .

Except for Brystion's short-lived mortality. Incubi were born of the Dreaming. They couldn't reproduce with a human woman, even for all the sex they partook in . . .

But then, Ion had been at least partially human the last time we'd had sex in the mortal world.

It wasn't exactly like I could run out and get a DNA test that would work on an OtherFolk child.

Still the question lingered. What if he never returned from Hell? Not even Nobu had reappeared to tell us anything and the weight of that hung heavy upon us all.

With a sigh, I got up and maneuvered around the jungle gym of seats and tables, all filled with mortals and OtherFolk alike, and made my way to the counter where Phin was holding court. A man in splint-mail armor shoved his way past me, his brow furrowed as he strode out the door muttering something about swooping. A curvy dwarven woman followed him, disgust written on her face.

Uh-oh.

"So. What was that all about?"

The unicorn snorted. "Who knows? They came in looking for cheese."

I blinked. "We sell cheese, Phin. The little cubes there. Goes with the wine?"

"Bah. Mr. Sword-Up-the-Ass wanted aged dragon cheese or something. We don't have that."

"Do dragons even produce a dairy product?" I frowned at the thought, trying to remember if I'd ever seen it on the inventory.

"Hell if I know." His face became sly. "I told the little lady if she rubbed my belly I'd make her a unicorn milk shake, though."

"But you aren't . . . oh." I shoved the vision his words produced into a box in the back of my mind and set it on fire. "Jesus, Phin. That's disgusting. You're lucky they didn't smite you on the spot."

"Bah. He was a virgin. I can't *stand* virgins. Whatever. We really should hire a bouncer, though. The standards here are slipping big-time."

"How could they fall any lower? Look who I've got working the register." I tweaked his beard.

"You could always put me in charge of the bar," he said hopefully.

"Because *that* would make things better." I leaned against the counter. "I think Tonia's doing just fine."

My latest foray into finding employees had resulted in hiring Katy's cousin. Both bartender and waitress, she'd taken to the work with an unbridled enthusiasm I could only envy.

"Mmmph. She likes pointy ears, I can tell you that much." He snorted in her direction, watching while she crouched by a golden-skinned elf, scratching his order on her notepad.

"Nothing wrong with that," I murmured, turning away as the elf captured her hand to kiss the palm.

"You didn't see the one she was chatting up earlier. I mean, come *on*. I can be as crude as the rest of them, but this?"

"Do tell."

"Eh. Glowy fellow. Had a shirt that said 'Fisting means I love you,' or some such. What else am I supposed to think?"

"I'd prefer not to know." I yawned. "Magical fisting elves or not, I'm heading upstairs. Try not to burn the place down, okay?"

"Sure thing, babe. I'll have Talivar close up."

I gave him a last pat before waving good night to my friends and slipping out the door. It felt weird not being fully in control of the place, but everyone agreed I needed rest more than I needed to be running a business, and I was more than happy to let the others take over for a bit.

Talivar had continued to spend his nights on my couch. I could only assume he'd left Kitsune in charge, but he waved me off every time I mentioned that he might want to go and check on his kingdom.

Not that I minded a little extra fussing, but after all we'd gone through, he should be able to reap some of the benefits. By all accounts, the Unseelie Court was beginning to flourish again. The lines of communication between it and the Seelie Court were still strained . . . but open—and the Tree continued to grow, strengthening the magic of the CrossRoads, to everyone's great relief.

The stairs creaked beneath me in their old familiar

way, but I hardly heard them, finding my way upstairs and into my living room with a heavy sigh.

Night seemed to be shorter and shorter these days, or maybe I was more tired than normal. I drifted from room to room, the fresh paint smell following in my wake. I steadfastly ignored the enchanted fridge and hurried into my bedroom, pulling off my jeans and slipping into a comfy pair of shorts that still fit well enough.

I tumbled into bed and flicked off the light, rubbing the small curve of my belly in an odd little ritual I'd started once the fact I was pregnant had really sunk in. I couldn't have said if I was saying hello or something else, but it was comforting.

I dozed off in the darkness, woken a few hours later by a shrill cry of anguish coming from the kitchen.

"Dammit, Anders! "

I started awake and then relaxed. "Phin . . ." I muttered.

Little shit had taken to playing computer games into the wee hours again, though not Warcraft this time. I'd let my monthly fee slip, so he had to resort to playing whatever else I had lying around.

I debated getting up, but decided it wasn't worth the effort. Particularly when I heard the soft snuffling whimper. Fucker was in his cups and I didn't want a hungover unicorn in my bed right now.

"Why'd you have to blow it up?" he mumbled sadly. "I would have bitten your ass. I would have bitten it so hard."

I rolled my eyes. If he needed to lose himself in a pixel romance for the moment, who was I to deny him that?

Assuming he shut up in the next ten seconds.

All was quiet after that and I slipped away again, curling beneath the blankets.

The Dreaming held an edge of quiet expectancy, the hum of Eildon Tree's EarthSong sifting beneath it. I wasn't sure why that was occurring either, but maybe it was a reward for my assistance. Or maybe my Dreams were restructuring themselves based on my experiences.

I would probably never really know.

My house at the Heart of my Dreaming stood tall now, the walls thick and sturdy and gleaming with fresh paint. The fireflies danced over an ocean of silver grass, golden lights winking in the distance.

A rattle at my gate sent me into a startled panic. Until I turned and saw Ion at the entrance.

My knees buckled as I raced toward him, flinging the doors to my Heart wide open and throwing myself into his arms.

He clung to me, whispering words I couldn't quite hear. But I didn't need to. I understood him just fine. His mouth found mine and a flurry of passion beat hard in my chest, but it was short-lived as he pulled away.

One hand pressed hard against my belly and he breathed in sharply. "It's true, then."

"You can tell?"

"There's the presence of another Dreamer here. She's sleeping too."

"She?"

"A daughter. Yes."

I bit down hard on my lower lip, this small fact slamming hard into my gut because now everything became more real than before. I tugged on his braid, the bells chiming out as I lifted his chin to me, inspecting his face.

"Are you okay? Did . . . he hurt you?"

His golden eyes became weary and amused all at once. "Let's leave that story for another night, shall we? There's something I need to show you."

Without another word, he took my hand and led me outside the gate to the rocky path. At his quiet gesture, the bubble of my Heart disappeared so that we were confronted with the infinite darkness of the Dreaming, the tiny Hearts winking in and out of existence with the rise and fall of the other Dreamers.

"There." He pointed to a light a short distance away. "Do you see it?"

"Yes . . . but . . ."

"It's mine," he said fiercely. "I don't know how . . . but I still have it. It's still there." He shook his head. "There's something else." He pointed again to the lights, aiming at a closer one, halfway between mine and his, although the pathway to it seemed much brighter as it connected to mine. "That's her, Abby."

"My . . . daughter's Dreaming Heart?" My head rocked with the knowledge. But more important was the thin strand of silver connecting it to Ion's Heart.

He nodded. "She belongs to you. For now. Eventually her Heart will break off on its own. Probably when she's born. You'll always have that connection with her, though."

He found my hand with his, pressing something cold into it. "I believe this also belongs to you," he said.

I glanced down to see the Key to the CrossRoads winking in my palm and my throat tightened.

"Someone should have it. Even if you don't wear

it . . . it should belong to someone like you, Abby." There was a hollowness to his voice, as though he wasn't quite sure what he was admitting, but it didn't matter.

"No," I murmured, kissing him softly. "It belongs to us."

Fantasy.
Temptation.
Adventure.

Visit PocketAfterDark.com, an all-new website just for Urban Fantasy and Romance Readers!

- Exclusive access to the hottest urban fantasy and romance titles!

- Read and share reviews on the latest books!

- Live chats with your favorite romance authors!

- Vote in online polls!

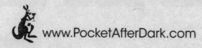

www.PocketAfterDark.com

26119

More bestselling
URBAN FANTASY
from Pocket Books!

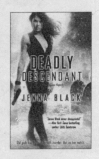

More Bestselling Urban Fantasy from Pocket Books!